GOD STORM

GOD STORM

COCO MA

BLACK STONE

PUBLISHING

Copyright © 2020 by Coco Ma
Published in 2020 by Blackstone Publishing
Cover and book design by Kathryn Galloway English
Illustrated map by Jimmy Ma

Printed in the United States of America

First edition: 2020
ISBN 978-1-982527-47-1
Young Adult Fiction / Fantasy / General

1 3 5 7 9 10 8 6 4 2

CIP data for this book is available
from the Library of Congress

Blackstone Publishing
31 Mistletoe Rd.
Ashland, OR 97520

www.BlackstonePublishing.com

To Miron,
The Orion to my Asterin, and the truest
and most honorable friend
I've ever had the privilege of having

NORD SEA

PRYDELL

ACADEMIA PRINCIPALIS

ERADORIS

ERADORE

ERMIR

GALANZIS

GALANZ

LETHOS

ICHAQAR

LETHIS

IGNATIA

SYR SEA

EYVINDR

WESTERWAY

VELCREST

VOLTERRA

XENITH

MOROVA

ZEMJA

MOROVIS

VOLTERIS

PROLOGUE

*D*own and down and down . . .

He couldn't remember the light. Here, the deepest of shadows gave way to a murk that seemed only a little less menacing, a little less sinister. The sky never lightened beyond a bruised purple before it darkened to an impenetrable, inky gloom.

To think that he had *reached* for that gaping blackness instead of fleeing far, far away and never looking back.

. . . and down and down and down and down . . .

How many days had passed? How many hours had dragged by since that fateful moment when his heart had told his body to move, to *move, you idiot*, to hurl himself without hesitation into that swirling, infinite void—

. . . and down and down and down and down and down . . .

The portal had devoured him, and he had begun to fall. Ribbons of shadow entangled him, strangled him, laughing and singing and whispering to him in tongues he couldn't understand.

He wouldn't stop falling. *Couldn't* stop falling. The shadows laughed and stole the screams right from his throat. He tried to keep track of the seconds, but he never made it past one thousand before losing count. He wondered when this would end, how it would end, if it would ever end at all—

The world flared white for the briefest second, and when he came to, the ground was moist against his bare face, filling his nostrils with the scent of rain and something he did not recognize.

Orion Galashiels pressed a kiss to the land and thanked the Immortals.

Then he rolled onto his back, closing his eyes as he sank into the wet ground, and breathed.

When he opened his eyes, he looked up into the dark heavens and thought them more beautiful than anything he had ever seen before.

With a smile, he lifted a hand toward the constellations scattered above as if to capture them.

The ground rumbled, low thunder in his ears. Orion had no chance to react when clods of dirt erupted skyward, slamming into his shoulder and arm, enclosing him in a death grip of mud and rocks before wrenching him down. He struggled to free himself as the ground began to *swallow* him. To bury him alive, one limb at a time.

Heart hammering, Orion let out a desperate cry. His fingers plunged through the roiling dirt, searching for his pocket and closing around his affinity stone. He held it aloft in triumph, but the moment he uncurled his fist, it crumbled to dust right before his eyes.

"No," he choked out. Dirt filled his mouth and nostrils, suffocating him. *No, no, no, no—*

In a burst of blinding light, his magic exploded from every pore of his body. The ground shied away from his radiance, relinquishing its hold upon him at last.

Blood roared in Orion's ears as he scrambled up the sides of the crater that had formed around him, clawing at straggly roots to haul himself out. Once clear, he ran for all hell's worth, his skin still pulsating with magic, certain that the ground would seize him once more if he so much as faltered for a second too long. Only when he couldn't bear the burning of his lungs did he finally slow—and thankfully, the ground didn't try to gobble him up.

Resisting the urge to vomit, Orion took in his surroundings. Trees of silver towered over him on all sides, glimmering with iridescent bark, their filigree leaves tinkling prettily in the breeze. Still panting for breath, he braced himself against a trunk but recoiled immediately. His hand came away slick, coated in an oily sap that reeked like hot tar. Upon closer inspection, he realized with horror that the sap was *moving*, churning and writhing in agitation along his palm, lapping at his fingers like tiny maggots.

Once again, his magic surged forth, this time with a scorching heat that sizzled the sap right off his skin and sent it skittering back up the tree trunk.

Orion stared up at the sliver of sky just visible overhead through the dense tangle of branches. Ragged exhales tore at his lungs as he tried to calm the fear coursing through his veins.

Everything was alive here. The rocks, the dirt . . . even his magic. It felt almost foreign in his body, as if he had suddenly sprouted a new limb. Here, his magic needed not bend to his beck and call. It refused to be summoned, controlled. Gone was his loyal hound, his most reliable tool—replaced with something primal. Wild.

Something powerful had always dwelled deep inside him, his skin, his blood, his soul. But now, it was *free*. Orion could run from the forests and the monsters within, but he couldn't run from himself.

And that was the most terrifying thought of all.

He still tried, though. He ran until his legs gave out, until he collapsed in an exhausted heap and hit his head on something sharp. White starbursts exploded across his vision. His groping fingers came away scarlet, and wherever the droplets fell, small red blossoms sprang forth.

As the world blurred beneath his half-closed lids, the shadows began to sing anew, their voices pouring over him in honeyed waves. There was no laughter this time, only a soothing, haunting melody filling his ears as the shadows wrapped him into their satiny midnight folds.

The ground shifted beneath him, and his consciousness faded as he heard the *fwip fwip* of something flapping.

He dreamt of flying, of being carried far away by great wings of darkness high above a city of daggers and blood.

So warm.

"Well, well . . ." a voice like syrup purred from above him, rich and full of sin. "What do we have here?"

Orion finally regained consciousness and let out a loud groan, his head pounding.

Whispers ghosted the air, fleeting and incomprehensible, but apparently the voice could understand them. There was a deep chuckle. "A present? How gracious of you all. And such a pretty one, too."

Orion cracked open his eyes at that, blinking blearily before squinting in the direction of the voice, gaze tracing up the sharp edges of a suit outlining muscled arms and broad shoulders. The top two buttons of a pristine white shirt had been carefully and carelessly undone, revealing a smooth collarbone flecked with tattoos. He drank in the delicious slope of a neck and a chiseled jaw before finally laying eyes on the face of the most beautiful man he had ever seen in his life.

The man's features could only have been carved by the hand of an Immortal. The blade-honed definition of his face was balanced by full brows and a supple pink mouth softer than chrysanthemum petals in full blossom. Coiffed hair the black of pitch gleamed beneath a jeweled circlet of silver ivy adorned with butterflies' wings.

"Tell me your name, pretty thing," coaxed the man, gloved fingers cupping Orion's jaw, gentler than a summer's breeze. His eyes were twin dark stars, luminous as the brightest constellation yet promising eternal night.

"O—" He coughed. "Orion." It occurred to him that he was reclining in the man's lap, his neck and the crook of his knees draped over velvet armrests. "Orion Galashiels."

The man's lips quirked. "How charming. And what are you doing in my kingdom, Orion?"

Orion's brow furrowed. Confusion cloaked his mind, his already hazy memory shrouded by a curtain of fog. He came up empty, his lungs aching as though deprived of air. He fumbled for his next words, and even then they felt stilted on his tongue. "I . . . I don't know. I can't remember."

"I must say," the man murmured, "you were quite fortunate to have ended up here with me . . . instead of in the hands of some other nasty beastie." He stroked a finger sensually from Orion's jaw up to his cheek. "You can thank my shadows for that."

Orion shuddered, unable to tear himself away from those dark eyes.

"Don't," he breathed. "Don't touch me." The man paused and withdrew his hand, something like perplexity flickering behind his expression.

A sense of conflict bubbled up within Orion. What right did he have to deny anything from a being of such beauty? He fought against himself. He wanted to quip, to break the tension, but he could summon neither the words nor the courage. In the end, all he said was, "Sorry."

"What for?" The man tilted his head, and the butterflies' wings crowning his brow fluttered. "Demanding respect is nothing to apologize for. Would you like to get up?"

Orion considered and then shook his head slowly. His legs might as well have turned to jelly.

"If you're certain." The man peered at him. "What lovely eyes you have . . ." Quicker than a heartbeat, those black eyes flashed the blue of glaciers, but quicker still they returned to normal. *A trick of the light?* "Like the northern seas of the Mortal Realm."

"Wait." *Mortal Realm?* Growing dread filled Orion's gut. "Where—where *am* I?"

The man's smile widened into a wolfish grin. "Why, you don't know?" He spread his arms wide, and when Orion turned to look, the air around them seemed to melt, shimmering like a mirage to reveal an obsidian city leagues below, with vicious spires for towers and arches of steel suspended midair, extending into oblivion farther than the eye could see. Rivers of scarlet and one of glowing envy-green cut across the land. Rising in the distance, Orion spotted a cluster of mountains pocked with waterfalls cascading gold.

From over the horizon, a swarm of birds approached. *No,* Orion thought to himself. With a start, he realized they weren't birds at all, but butterflies—thousands and thousands of black butterflies, rising over the city in a tidal wave of dark-tipped wings to block out the strange constellations above.

A gentle breeze weaved into Orion's hair, gentle and soothing. "You're in the depths of the Immortal Realm, little mortal," said the beautiful man.

Orion lost all words, all the air in his lungs. "Are . . . are you a god?" he asked hoarsely, still breathless.

The man leaned down. "I am no mere god, Orion Galashiels," he said with a soft, wicked smile. "I am King Eoin, Ruler of Darkness, and this is my home."

Orion's eyes widened and King Eoin lowered his voice to a velvet whisper.

"Welcome to the heart of the Shadow Kingdom."

CHAPTER ONE

The sun glared off Lux's gleaming ebony coat, almost blinding, but the wind stole the afternoon's warmth and kicked up the leaves strewn beneath the maple trees lining the avenue.

Asterin Faelenhart welcomed the wind's chill even as it nipped at her exposed neck and collarbone, every inch of her bare skin prickling. The hem of her skirt ruffled as they trotted, but the skirt itself didn't so much as stir. Half a dozen maids had helped her into the largest and most elaborate gown she had ever worn. A hundred folds of cream-of-gold taffeta supported by countless layers of crinoline spilled over Lux's haunches and teased the ground with her stallion's every proud stride. Sheer lace ran up her arms, and tiny ivory roses adorned the off-shoulder neckline. A fur-trimmed cloak billowed from her shoulders and she wore soft, supple leather gloves, but both accessories were more for style than protection from the cold.

Normally, she wouldn't have bothered with such formal attire—but this was her first official public appearance as Queen of Axaria, after all, and nothing could have made that more clear than the diamond tiara nesting atop her head, each icicle-like spire reflecting the sunlight in a thousand dazzling kaleidoscopic bursts.

"Make way for her Royal Majesty Asterin Faelenhart of Axaria and the Queen Mother!" Captain Eadric Covington called from his massive steed, Grey. The mighty pair led their party, while the other eight Elites surrounded them in diamond formation. Each member of Asterin's personal royal guard sat tall in their saddles, intimidating all who beheld them with the steel sheathed at their sides and their signature crimson-and-black cloaks snapping behind them in the wind.

Asterin waved to the onlookers crowding the avenue's pale-stoned sidewalks, as did the rider beside her—none other than Elyssa Calistavyn-Faelenhart. Her mother.

Her *real* mother.

For ten years, a different woman had masqueraded as Asterin's mother and the Queen of Axaria—Priscilla Montcroix. Using dark magic, Priscilla had cursed Elyssa from all memory and locked her deep beneath the palace in an enchanted dungeon that no one had known existed. But after exposing Priscilla's crimes and defeating her on Fairfest Eve, Asterin had discovered the dungeon with a little help from an ancient wolf god and reunited with the mother that she almost never realized she'd lost.

Now, Elyssa tucked her silken black braid over her shoulder and shot Asterin a sparkling grin. She rested one gentle hand on her steed's neck—a bay thoroughbred named Argo with a white star emblazoned across his forehead. "Something on your mind, my love?"

Giggling children squirmed out of their parents' grasps to frolic up and down the avenue's cobblestones. People cheered out Asterin's name in jubilance as they paraded past, calling her *all-wielder* and *the Immortals' Champion*. By now, tales of her omnifinity and victory against Priscilla had spread far and wide across the world, and Axarians knew such tales best of all.

"It's just . . . I still can't believe it," Asterin confessed, her fingers tightening on Lux's reins. "That you're here, beside me." If it hadn't been for Lord Conrye, the God of Ice and protector of her bloodline, the House of the Wolf, her mother would have been left to waste away in the darkness forever, destined to be forgotten.

Elyssa reached over to squeeze her hand in comfort, the corners of her eyes crinkling. The dungeon, while bewitched to provide ample survival necessities to its inhabitants, did nothing to halt aging—but her mother had fared far better than imaginable, and within a few weeks of sunshine and many, many hours spent catching up together, she looked as radiant as Asterin ever remembered.

Up ahead, the street bloomed into the entertainment district, one of the city's main quadrants. The entryway was marked by a gravity-defying canopy constructed of stone and woven iron cables that spiraled over a hexagonal plaza of white marble known as the Pavilion. The theaters, opera, and dance houses hugged the plaza, each building glorious in its own right. Elaborate stone friezes and carvings of creatures like winged sea serpents and two-headed wolves bedecked their cornices and towering colonnades. But it was the crown jewel of the Pavilion that they approached—the concert hall.

When they arrived, the Elites dismounted first. Eadric helped Asterin slide gracefully from the saddle while Silas and Jack lent Elyssa a hand. Laurel and Casper carried the train of Asterin's dress. With Gino's help, Nicole began passing the horses' reins to a dapper little quartet of stable hands, identical in uniform from the number of buttons fastened on their jackets right down to the angle of their woolen caps. Hayley and Alicia took up position by the doors to the concert hall, where they would remain for the duration of the performance.

"It's been so long since I last came here." Her mother sighed as they ascended the steps to the hall. "So much is just as I remember, and yet so much has changed."

When they reached the landing, Elyssa paused to hold Asterin at arm's length. Eadric and the Elites drifted back respectfully. Emerald eyes roved Asterin's face for a long minute before Elyssa pulled her into a tight embrace right there on the steps, her expression so full of love and warmth that it made Asterin's heart clench.

"I can't believe it either, you know," her mother whispered into her hair. "I must have dreamt these moments a million times. Only my determination to see those dreams come to light kept me sane through ten years of isolation. Sometimes I worry that I'm dreaming still." She pressed a gentle kiss to Asterin's brow. "I'm never going to lose you again. Never."

Asterin swallowed the lump in her throat. "Please don't worry. But come, we should go inside. Levain will be waiting."

"Is he still director?"

Asterin flashed a grin before donning her most queenly smile. "Definitely."

The ushers welcomed them into the grand lobby with a flurry of bows. Torches circled the space at varying intervals, casting a flickering ombré of shadow across the opalescent tiles. A stairway led upstairs to the balconies. Usually, the delicious cacophony of the orchestra warming up drifted through the ground-level doors, but tonight Asterin heard only the muffled chatter of the audience.

As promised, the music director of the concert hall waited for them at the foot of the stairs, his hands clasped in front of him. Even with his wild thicket of silver hair, he stood no taller than Asterin's shoulder, yet his presence could not have been more grandiose.

"Your Royal Majesty and Your Royal Grace. Captain Covington and Elites," Director Levain said with a deep bow. "An honor, as always, to have you with us." He eyed Asterin's dress, a merry twinkle in his eyes. "I take it Your Majesty and company shall be using the royal box this evening?"

Asterin hummed her affirmation. In the past few months, she had attended an increasing number of concerts. More often than not, she wore something plain and snuck into the performances along with the crowds—trying to blend in, just another audience member among thousands, rather than draw attention away from the actual performers by flaunting her status.

"Allow me to escort you upstairs," Levain said. Nicole and Gino jogged into the foyer just as the torches around them began flickering to signify the start of the concert. They took up position behind Elyssa. "The performance is set to begin in a minute or so, although I can of course notify the stage managers to hold—"

"We don't mind running," Asterin told him.

Levain grinned. "Then run we shall."

They ascended to the lower balcony, the accented *click-clack* of Asterin's stilettos echoing and Casper and Laurel still dogging after her with the train of her dress in hand. Eadric and Elyssa followed close behind, with Nicole and Gino at the rear, and soon they were hurrying through a set of heavy teakwood doors. Ushers held back rich plum drapes and shepherded them to the royal box. Levain tipped his chin in farewell just as the audience burst into applause and the performer emerged onstage.

In the darkness, almost no one had noticed the appearance of the Queen of Axaria.

Asterin blindly felt for her seat and watched in awe as a young girl strode toward the piano. The girl bowed center stage, her sleek red dress shimmering like fiery embers in the golden glow of the mammoth chandelier overhead. As one, Asterin and the pianist settled into their respective seats.

The pianist's hands rose to the keyboard.

Asterin leaned over the balcony rails in anticipation.

"Don't fall," whispered Eadric.

The pianist struck the first chord, a spark in the silence, like a match striking flame. Asterin inhaled sharply as the girl's fingers darted to the bottom end of the keyboard, notes chasing higher and higher in a tumultuous blur. On and on the passages went, until a soaring melody emerged from the maelstrom, its beauty stealing the air from her lungs.

I can't be Queen of Axaria, she'd told Quinlan an eternity ago.

He had reached forward to cup her jaw, tilting her face up to his. *You can be whatever the hell you want*, he had whispered, eyes blazing with indigo wildfire, his smoke-and-mountain air scent washing over her. *And I promise that if you so desire, I will stay by your side through all of it.*

The climax of the piece reverberated through the hall, burning with want, tearing itself apart, yearning for something unattainable.

Then the music began winding down—no, unraveling. Just barely holding together at the seams . . . until out of the dust emerged the melody once more.

One harmony at a time, the tatters began to mend. Some hole deep inside Asterin had yawned open, naked and aching, but the music soothed it. Healed it. The hairs on the nape of her neck stood on end as the melody warbled a final cry, utterly spent and dwindling to ash . . .

And then nothing.

Asterin leapt to her feet, clapping furiously, her throat tight and her eyes wet as the pianist bowed and walked offstage. Thunderous applause followed her back on moments later. The girl flashed a dazzling smile to her audience and raised her eyes, one hand over her heart as she met Asterin's gaze. The look seemed to set off a chain reaction, and Asterin felt herself stiffen ever so slightly as every neck in the hall swiveled to scrutinize the royal box.

She returned the pianist's gesture with her brightest smile, and though she could do without the stares, they were only to be expected—besides, as long as she could hold all her broken pieces together beneath the public's notice, those stares of admiration could only ever work in her favor.

Even so, Asterin loosed the faintest sigh of relief when the pianist's fingers fluttered over the keys and the crowd's attention returned to the stage.

The opening harmonies shuddered up her spine, hollow and bleak.

At that moment, a shadow slunk out of the glossy piano lid, which had been propped fully open.

Asterin glanced over at Eadric, but the captain's eyes were closed in rapture. *My imagination?* she wondered, and tried to refocus on the performance.

The music told a story of desolation, of grief. Her magic welled up within her at the memory of blackened corpses piled high in a pit, pleading for release. She shoved her tingling fingers beneath her thighs.

And that was when she caught the shadow again, skimming the arches of the ribbed ceiling. The light of the massive crystal chandelier and spotlights overhead made it impossible for such a shadow to exist, let alone *move.* Her eyes narrowed as it coiled around the chandelier canopy, writhing like a dark eel.

It happened so quickly that she almost missed it. A tiny glint of metal fell from the rafters and bounced off the piano, silent beneath the waves of music. The pianist played on, blissfully unaware and wrapped up in her song.

"*Eadric,*" Asterin hissed, elbowing him. He startled to attention, blinking at her in the dark. She jerked her chin at the chandelier and then below, where more silver pieces were now raining down upon the stage—enough that even some audience members were taking notice.

Asterin's heart stuttered when the chandelier emitted a sinister creak and veered violently to the left, chains and pendants clinking like the rattle of bones as screws continued to loosen and fall, *ping ping pinging* on the ground. People were rising from their seats, pointing upward and murmuring to one another, but as the pianist crescendoed into the coda of the piece, the sheer power of her playing drowned out their voices.

By the time Asterin finally had the sense to spring out of her seat, the chandelier was swaying in a drunken sailor's dance. She whipped back the curtains dividing the royal box from the other seats and sprinted for the gallery ring on the opposite side of the hall, directly above the stage. Eadric and her Elites were right at her heels.

The train of her dress caught on the corner of a seat. Eadric caught her wrist to keep her from nose-diving into the floor, and helped her yank the fabric until it ripped free.

Her magic thrummed beneath her skin, still electrified from the music, and when the piece drew to a close and the first scream from the audience pierced the air, she collided into the railing and flung her arms heavenward to unleash her power in one mighty blast.

Wind and ice roared forth, snagging the chandelier as it plummeted. Nicole, Casper, and Laurel seized the folds of her dress just in time to keep her from toppling off the balcony and earning herself a broken neck. Nearby audience members jumped out of their way, eyes wide with awe, but Asterin paid them no heed, focusing all her strength on safely lowering the hunk of metal—and Immortals be *damned*, it was heavy—to the ground. Shards of ice as tall as trees erupted from the ceiling to latch onto the metal, frosting over at the base. Wind pushed upward to lessen the weight. Slowly but surely, the chandelier descended like a final curtain, each flame hissing out one by one as her ice spread.

Audience members pulled out their affinity stones to combat the onslaught of darkness. Little orbs of light flickered to life all around her, submerging the concert hall in an eerie wash of color that danced along the walls like an aurora.

Once Asterin felt certain her ice would hold, she sighed, right arm still raised to keep the chandelier frozen in place. Silence greeted her.

Asterin signaled for the Elites to release her dress. Eadric made a faint choking noise when she swung over the railing without warning. She summoned a path of ice to deliver herself swiftly to the stage, where the trembling soloist was still seated at the piano, her arms shielding her head from the would-have-been death looming above her.

"You're safe now," Asterin murmured to the girl, reaching forward to squeeze her shoulder. "Everything is going to be just fine—"

A smear of darkness along the rafters blurred across Asterin's peripherals. With the speed and force of a meteoroid, it smashed through her reinforcements. She only had enough time to tackle the pianist aside before her ice blasted apart with an earth-shattering *bang* and the chandelier plummeted to the stage.

CHAPTER TWO

Clink. Clink tap. Tap tap. Clink.

Luna worked the claw against stone, gently striking it with the mallet. For her, nothing could beat the satisfaction of chipping away *just* the right amount, *just* the way she wanted it to. She glanced at the clay model beside her, making mental calculations and comparisons, before sighing and letting her arms fall to her sides. She sprayed some water onto the clay to keep it from cracking, and then onto her own face, relishing the coolness. Autumn might have been around the corner, but the sun blazed hotter than a furnace through the glass ceiling. While the natural light filtering down into her workshop certainly helped with the visual aspects of sculpting, the heat dried out the clay before she could blink.

Stretching her arms over her head, she took a few steps back to survey her work. The clay model depicted a man's head from the neck upward, his mouth agape and his brow twisted in a mixture of agony and torment. The stone matched the basic shape and contours of the clay man's face, but she had yet to carve the suffering into his features. She couldn't decide whether she was dreading it or looking forward to it. Maybe it was a bit of both.

Footsteps in the hall. They stopped at her door.

"Come in," she called before the knock even sounded.

The door cracked open and her father peered in. "Ah, busy, I see. Would you like me to return later?"

"It's all right," said Luna. "I have training with Adrianna in a few minutes." She rubbed the dust from her eyes, belatedly realizing her hands were no better.

King Jakob shut the door behind him and strode toward her, one hand behind his back. "Hm. I've got just the thing to help with the dust." He drew the hand forth in offering. "Goggles."

She stood frozen with reverence as he deftly unfolded them and slid them onto the bridge of her nose. They were a little unwieldy, but she would get used to them. "Th-thank you, Your Majesty."

"Of course," said her father gruffly. He gestured at her cheek. "You . . . you have something over there." She wiped her face, but he shook his head. "You've made it worse." Hesitantly, he raised a hand. "May I?"

She bit her lip and nodded.

Gently, he brushed his fingers across her cheek. His brow crinkled. "It's spreading." She laughed, but he persisted, giving Luna the perfect opportunity to study him up close.

Her father didn't strike her as particularly handsome—at least, in her view. Priscilla had apparently seen otherwise, perhaps in the broad set of his shoulders or the sheer bulk of his frame. He had a rather prominent nose and tanned, weathered skin from a recent half-decade at sea. His eyes were a clear and steely blue, the same shade Luna's eyes had once been, and his face was lined with stern wrinkles. Silver now peppered his sand-gold hair, but his smiles, rare as they were, always brought a mischievous, youthful glint to his eyes.

Whereas Luna had always considered herself a natural at coaxing people to open up, her father was awkward with her at best. But perhaps, more than anything, the fault lay in the nature of their relationship—after all, he was the King of Ibreseos, and she was . . . an accident.

Together, they exited her workshop, their footsteps tracking dust into the hallway. Her father nodded in acknowledgment to the six guards waiting outside—two for her, and the rest for the king.

"Has Ibreseos been to your liking so far?" her father asked as they strolled down the corridor. The walls were constructed of thick slabs of cold gray stone. In fact, the entire stronghold was hewn from the same stone, sprawling over three squat hills and likely double the size of the palace of Axaria. Here, the turrets rose short and thick, lacking the splendid elegance of the Axarian palace with its graceful parapets and silver-spun arches.

"Very much, Father," Luna replied.

Jakob's face tightened, and she could see his discomfort written all over it. She ignored the twinge in her chest, the reminder that she had been unwanted, might *still* be unwanted. She'd vowed to herself that she wouldn't take it to heart.

But to her surprise, he swallowed and put a hand on her shoulder. "I'm glad. The stronghold can be intimidating."

She snorted at that. *Intimidating* was a severe understatement. The Axarian palace might have had the Wall—but here, the only way into the castle was via the colossal drawbridge connecting its entrance to the rest of the capital. Barbaric steel spikes lined the pit below, glinting like black fangs after dusk. The drawbridge was opened twice a day at preordained times, depending on the day of the week or if a guest was to be expected, and only King Jakob had the authority to command the bridge to be lowered otherwise. Civilians and nobles alike waited across the pit all day to enter the stronghold, but even then they sometimes still had to answer to a multitude of security inspections, and *even then* some got turned away after hours of waiting. No one ever protested, however—all the guards had to do was point at the pit and the trespasser would sullenly return to the safety of the city.

"By the way," King Jakob added absentmindedly as they turned a corner, "I've assigned you three personal bodyguards. A royal entourage, if it pleases you. They're extraordinarily competent, but above all they should keep you in good company. Adrianna pointed out to me that you seem rather . . . *lonely*."

Luna's face warmed. He made it sound like a weakness. "Not exactly. It's just . . ." She trailed off, her throat tight.

"I understand," her father said, although she didn't think he did. "In any case, they're returning from Nyälkastle, in the north." It took her a moment to pinpoint the city in her head. She was slowly but surely familiarizing herself with her father's kingdom. "I expect that they'll arrive within the day, but I have some other errands I need them to run in the west, so you can make their acquaintance at the end of the week."

They drew to a halt in front of the chamber where Adrianna awaited.

"Well." Her father shifted and gestured toward the door awkwardly. "Enjoy."

Luna watched him leave, chewing her lip. *The King of Ibreseos*, she thought to herself. *Skittish as a horse toward* me, *of all people.* But then again, she wasn't just anyone anymore. Illegitimate or not, she was his daughter.

A king's daughter.

Luna smiled to herself as she nodded at her guards to open the door.

And Princess Luna Evovich of Ibreseos sounded pretty damn good to her.

Sometimes, Luna just really wanted to strangle her aunt.

Rivulets of sweat cut down her neck as she struggled to wrestle her illusion-affinity under obedience. Two hours in, and her legs were already wobbling. The hearth roared at her back. The stifling heat had forced her to strip down to her undershirt because she was too daunted to complain. On a day like this, she failed at *best*. At worst, she would be rewarded with throbbing migraines for the rest of the afternoon.

"Control it," Adrianna barked at her for the hundredth time as one of three disgruntled white doves flickered into visibility before them. Somehow, her aunt was surviving beneath her royal Ibresean long coat, a flamboyant purple affair of finespun wool and silk worn by all the nobles and highest-ranking officials in the court, complete with gold embellishments running from collar to cuff and an intimidating swoop of a tail at the back. "As its master, your magic is your ally. Yield, and it will one day ruin you."

"Thank you for the reminder," Luna snarled through clenched teeth, squinting hard at the floor-to-ceiling bookshelves lining the opposite wall as if will alone would help drive the dove out of sight. Not a speck of dust graced the books' surfaces, but their pages were yellow with age and disuse. The titles ranged from *The Legends of the Immortals* to *101 Needle-point Techniques for the Stitching Enthusiast.* "Auntie," she couldn't resist adding.

The younger sister of Priscilla Montcroix and now fiancée of King Jakob of Ibreseos let out a snort and drummed her manicured fingernails atop one of the many gilded cages filled with cooing doves beneath the window. The bronze waves of her hair gleamed like burnished copper in the noon light streaming through the glass. She kept her dusky blue eyes pinned on the shelves, tracking Luna's progress. "I find it hilarious that you seem to be under the impression that calling me *auntie* bothers me, Princess Luna."

"Well—"

"Save your snark for teatime," her mentor cut in. "Or if you finally manage to succeed."

The comment stung, but Adrianna was right. Even now, after so much tireless training, a telltale, glassy, marbled texture gave away the doves' locations. Of course, Luna could cheat if she really wanted to. It would be too easy—rather than trying to conceal each flapping dove individually, she could just conjure a facade of the bookshelf in *front* of them and hide them entirely. But that wasn't the point of the exercise. Adrianna had taken charge of helping Luna hone her relatively new powers, and no way in hell was she going to squander it in laziness.

All of this had started a few days after Luna had arrived in Ibreseos, during their first dinner together in King Jakob's private dining hall. Rather than dining in Mess Hall with the "rabble," as the king coined his court, her father preferred the company of a few select guests. On that particular night, "a few" meant a mere two: his fiancée and his bastard daughter.

It took four courses for Luna to finally blurt out the desire that had been plaguing her ever since Fairfest Eve—since her own mother had tried to kill her. Since Asterin had failed to save her. Worse still, since Luna had failed to save *herself.*

"A mentor?" her father had repeated, his knife pausing midslice. "For magic?"

"What a charming idea," Adrianna had murmured, her eyes sparkling.

Back then, Luna hadn't yet seen her aunt's other persona, the one she employed to whip Luna's magic into shape. She also wouldn't have recognized Adrianna as Priscilla's sister even if the two had stood side by side. *Especially* if the two had stood side by side. Not just in appearance, but demeanor— Priscilla could sit for hours on end like a statue, but Adrianna could never seem to keep still for more than a second. Her fingers tapped perpetually, and Luna remembered asking if she played the piano. Adrianna laughed heartily and commented that she didn't have a musical bone in her body. But Luna disagreed. There was something about her aunt that filled the air with sound and color and life, just like music, as if nothing thrilled her more than simply existing, dancing from moment to moment with insatiable vigor. Priscilla, in comparison . . . seemed too tame, too bloodless. Too *highborn.*

At the time, little had Luna suspected that her *auntie* had also spent years tutoring magic at an elite institution of some sort . . . and that she would volunteer for the job of mentoring Luna herself.

"You're slipping! *Focus!*"

Luna gritted her teeth and wrenched herself back into the present. Two doves had reappeared fully, glaring at her with their beady little black eyes. Her vision doubled. "Immortals," she gasped. Frustration coursed through her veins, beating and battering her from the inside out, until she wished she could rip out of her own skin and shed it to become someone new. Someone better.

"Do not yield," Adrianna murmured, her silken voice soothing the pressure in Luna's head. "One more minute. Get those doves out of sight."

Luna's knuckles strained white around her two affinity stones. Every muscle quivered, but she forced in a deep lungful of sweltering, stale air and squeezed her eyes shut. Rather than try to match the doves by sight to the bookshelf behind, she reached out with her magic and *felt* for them—

There.

She traced the contours of their plump little bodies in her mind, and then enveloped them in illusion like a second skin, magic clinging to every last feather.

Be gone, she thought.

When she opened her eyes, a smile rose to her face. The birds had vanished completely.

"I did it," Luna breathed. A bubble of triumphant laughter escaped her lips.

To her surprise, however, Adrianna frowned. "Release."

The coil of tension in her core eased. She loosed a sigh, ribs aching, and let her posture relax. Her magic followed, unwinding from the doves. *The doves.*

She blinked in disbelief and approached them slowly, one hand pressed to her mouth in horror. Her knees gave out and she crashed to the floor. Gingerly, she picked up the body of the bird closest to her. Its tiny snowy head had flopped to the side, eyes gone glassy, and its wrinkled pink feet dangled in the air.

Dead. All three of them.

"What happened?" Luna demanded, tears rising to her eyes. She choked back a sob and placed the dove back on the ground.

Adrianna walked to her and squeezed her shoulder. "You might have wrapped your illusions around them a tad too tightly, sweetheart."

Luna cursed herself. "How much longer until I can control my powers?" Adrianna didn't even deign to answer. Luna braced herself on clenched fists, rocking back and forth slightly to soothe her agony—at both the blood on her hands and her own incompetence. Sweat and hot tears mingled as they dripped down her face, plopping onto the floor in fat droplets. Only in a whisper did she dare ask, "What if they had been people?"

Adrianna sighed. "Just be glad that they weren't." When Luna looked up, her aunt's eyes had taken on a sharp, cobalt-edged glint, revealing just a hint of what truly lay beneath her matronly surface. She waved at the row of cages. The doves within flittered nervously, as if sensing their impending doom. "They were birds, and we have a lot more of them. You should take a rest first, though."

"No," growled Luna, startling even herself. Determination lit her veins like gunpowder set aflame. A phantom noose wrapped around her neck, the darkness set in, and there was Asterin, bleeding and exhausted and *helpless*, standing in the middle of it all as Priscilla fired her shadow arrows—

You chose Quinlan.

"No," Luna said again. She dragged herself onto her feet, trembling, and wiped the sweat from her eyes. *Fight, Luna.* "I don't need any rest." She could rest when she was dead. Today and tomorrow and however many days after, she would push her boundaries further than ever before, and then she would keep pushing still.

For herself, she refused to break.

"Good girl." Not a flicker of surprise graced her aunt's expression— only the ghost of a smile. "Let's see how many more doves you'll kill before bedtime."

CHAPTER THREE

The chandelier fell like a winged behemoth losing flight. Utterly silent—until it smashed through the piano in a deafening explosion of crystal. The strings severed in a chorus of unholy, ear-splitting *twangs*. Iron candelabra arms skewered the leather bench where the pianist had been sitting less than a heartbeat before. Screams tore through the air as chunks of ice and shrapnel rained down from above, but the wicked shards ricocheted off the shields cast by the Elites on the first balcony. Eadric and Nicole raised their affinity stones and summoned howling gales to blow aside shrapnel as best they could, and once the debris settled, all the shields extinguished and everyone let out a collective sigh of relief.

Asterin lay tangled with the pianist on the edge of the stage, sheltering the girl's body with her own. She left her magic humming just beneath her fingertips, and gingerly removed herself before helping the pianist shakily to her feet.

"Your Royal M-Majesty," she stammered, unable to tear her eyes away from the piano's mangled carcass. The people not fleeing the hall began mounting the stage to gather around them, staring in wonder at Asterin and whispering to one another. Those sitting on the balconies flocked close to the railings to peer over the edge.

"I'm so sorry your performance was cut short," Asterin told the girl, her voice soft. "You played beautifully."

The pianist startled everyone with a laugh. "It was either that or my life." She smoothed out her fiery ruby gown and sank to one knee in the traditional Axarian salute, her right hand clasping her shoulder across her chest. "I will never be able to repay this debt."

You healed a part of my soul, Asterin wanted to say. *If anything, it is I who owe you.* But she couldn't, not with everyone watching them. Instead, she placed one hand on the pianist's head and said, "Rise. Your art is payment tenfold."

Someone near the back of the crowd began clapping. Soon, everyone joined in, their cheers and whistles a dull roar in Asterin's ears.

At that moment they heard a *crash* from backstage and the stage door burst open to reveal a panting and extremely disheveled Director Levain. A dazed kind of horror dawned across his features as he slowly took in the destruction. His throat bobbed, and then he lunged forward to throw himself at Asterin's feet, a choked sob escaping his lips.

"Your Majesty, Immortals have mercy, thank you. Forgive me."

The applause died, shifting into leery mutters, and Asterin caught the word *sabotage* muttered numerous times.

I will have absolutely none of this, Asterin thought to herself. She grabbed him by the shoulders and heaved him onto his feet. For his stature, he was surprisingly unwieldy. "Director. *Director.*"

Finally, Levain looked up, devastation written into every line on his face.

She spoke with authority. She spoke so that her voice rang, and she let the acoustics do the rest. "What happened was unfortunate, but completely out of your control. Most importantly, no one was hurt."

Levain gaped. "Y-Your Majesty . . ."

The doors at the end of the hall swung open, and Alicia dashed up the aisle, followed by an usher struggling to keep up. The youngest Elite leapt nimbly onto the stage and hurried to Asterin's side. The usher took the stairs and bowed hastily to Asterin before turning to Levain. He held a hand to his mouth and began whispering furiously into the director's ear.

Alicia kept her own voice hushed. "There's been another incident, Your Majesty."

"Of what sort?" Asterin demanded.

Levain had paled considerably by the time the usher withdrew. He rubbed the bridge of his nose and exhaled. "It seems that there has been some sort of explosion at one of the theater cafés," he replied. "The plumbing, apparently."

Asterin's mind returned to that smudge of darkness slithering out of the piano and up the walls. Priscilla's horrible, lipless grin flashed through her mind, and suddenly she found herself back in the palace, helpless as the woman—the monster—summoned two serpentine shadows, two nooses. One for Quinlan. One for Luna.

I will end you, Priscilla had said. *Or better yet . . . I will* break *you.*

And then Priscilla had gifted their lives to her and forced her to choose.

"Your Majesty?" whispered Alicia. "Are you all right?"

Asterin shuddered and yanked herself back into the present. She glanced up to the ceiling, but nothing lurked there now, despite the absence of the chandelier's light. No oily stains of gloom to suggest anything out of the ordinary. Within minutes, the shadow had disappeared completely . . . only to wreak havoc elsewhere.

She heard the crackle of ice and looked up to find Casper trying to forge a rough version of the path she had conjured earlier from the lower balcony. The chandelier had severed the one she had made, but the Elite persisted until he and the others could slide down it. They strode across the stage toward her.

Belatedly, Asterin's attention snapped to the royal box, her eyes searching for her unguarded mother. The tension in her shoulders loosened—three other Elites had already taken up position at Elyssa's side.

She turned to Levain. "My Elites and I are going to get to the bottom of this," she promised him. Quietly, she added, "I fear darker forces may be at work here."

Levain frowned. "Darker forces?"

Eadric came to her right side, understanding sparking in his eyes. "Forbidden magic."

Asterin nodded. "I saw some sort of shadow come out of the piano right before the chandelier fell. I don't know where it came from or how it got here, but we're certainly not just going to let it run rampant, are we?"

Levain gave her a look of bewilderment and eventually shook his head.

Time to get out of this dress, she thought to herself. "So," she said, turning to survey her Elites with a grim little smile on her face. "Who's ready for a hunt?"

CHAPTER FOUR

King Eoin called his home the Shadow Palace.

"How big is this place?" Orion asked, turning in a circle as they walked down an endless corridor of silver tiles. The floor glimmered like liquid mercury beneath his feet, and wherever he stepped, it rippled outward, mimicking the shallows of a lake. The only light came from Orion himself, his skin glowing like torch flame even through his clothes, and the stars behind Eoin's eyes.

"As vast and wonderful as my imagination allows," the god answered, not bothering to temper his pride. "Just as the Shadow Kingdom is a part of me, the palace is my *hjerta*—my heart—born from will and wishes. Here, I'll show you. Close your eyes."

"Why?"

"Don't you want it to be a surprise?"

Orion obliged him. There was a *pop*. When he opened his eyes, a doorway had materialized to his left, its surface adorned with etchings of birds midflight. He looked to the god with a question in his eyes.

"Go ahead," Eoin encouraged.

Orion tugged at the handle, but the door didn't budge.

"Try pushing," said Eoin.

With a pink tinge rising in his cheeks, Orion gave the door a push and it swung open.

Orion gasped in awe as they emerged into a cavernous chamber with a ceiling open to the stars. The room was furnished with ornate rugs and metallic golden ivy that snaked along the walls, along with glimmering bronze candelabras dripping with jewels that set the room softly aglow. Dozens of windows of every shape and size opened the walls like paintings, each revealing a different impossible view of the Immortal Realm. There, through a diamond-shaped window, were the mountains he had spotted earlier, though they were much closer now. The panes were positioned so close to a waterfall that droplets of gold actually splattered upon them. An elliptical window next to the diamond one showed an orchard filled with fruits he could not name being plucked by creatures with foldable, knobby stilts for legs. And there, through a hexagon, he marveled at the Shadow Palace itself, and when he waved he could see a tiny glowing figure in a hexagonal window waving back.

"This is incredible," Orion breathed, rushing from window to window, utterly mesmerized and eager for each new wonder to reveal itself to him. He suddenly whirled on Eoin, the light from his body blazing so brightly that he almost blinded himself. "You're *extraordinary*."

Eoin raised a hand to shield his eyes, but Orion still caught his bewildered expression. "The windows won't actually lead you to any of these places, so please don't go around trying to open any of them."

"Can they, though?" Orion asked.

Eoin shrugged. "Maybe. I've never had any reason to try, since I can just—"

At that moment, Orion's stomach interrupted with a loud grumble. He flushed. When was the last time he had eaten?

"Poor thing, you must be famished," the god murmured. A table so long it verged on ludicrous unfolded before them, spanning the entire breadth of one wall. Perhaps a hundred people could have fit comfortably around it, and the amount of glistening dishes that sprung from its surface could have fed just as many. Steaming platters covered every inch of the table like something from a splendid dream: sizzling steaks and tender cheese pies, smoke-glazed vegetables stuffed with rice, grilled salmon with lemon and herbs, poached eggs in creamy tomato sauce, spiced lamb stew, and just about every other dish Orion could possibly imagine.

Two lonesome chairs appeared at each end, and Eoin pulled out the nearest one for Orion. As soon as he sat down, the entire room literally whirled around him with Eoin as the only anchor, so that after the table had rotated, the god needn't walk to his seat at all.

Eoin lowered himself and raised his glass of amber liquid in toast. "May this realm never eclipse you, Orion Galashiels."

Orion lifted his own glass, filled with something pink and bubbly, and took a sip. It tasted of fresh summer peaches. Four butterflies flitted over to him, carrying a satin napkin between them. They draped it across his lap. "Why are we sitting so far apart?"

Eoin shrugged. "Wish me closer, and so it shall be."

Orion frowned, and without much effort at all, the middle of the table suddenly sucked inward, like a taut rubber band snapping back into shape. He yelped as baskets of rosemary bread and tureens of pumpkin soup launched into the air.

The butterflies that had delivered Orion's napkin darted upward. Their wings and slender little bodies turned *inside out*, swelling and transforming into gaping maws with vicious pearly white teeth. They consumed the food—tableware and all—in a gulp so voracious that it caused them to flip inward once more, teeth nowhere in sight.

Orion stared slack-jawed as they fluttered back over to Eoin to rest delicately upon his shoulders.

Eoin raised an eyebrow. "Well, they have to eat *somehow*," he said, as if this were the most reasonable fact in history—and who was Orion to think otherwise? "It's either this or they go and infest the nectar arboretums. And *that* never ends well."

"Nectar?" asked Orion, sampling a bit of sausage and immediately forking an entire half of it into his mouth. He restrained a groan. The food here didn't just look beautiful—it tasted beautiful, too.

Eoin laughed at his bliss. "Yes. Nectar. The fare of the Immortals. A few spoonfuls are enough to revive us from exhaustion beyond your scope. Currently, I'm drinking nectar wine. I would offer you some, but it would turn your bones to ash."

"How very considerate of you," said Orion. He suddenly noticed

Eoin wasn't eating—no plate, no silverware. "So . . . you live off nectar?"

"Yes. Though I do allow myself to indulge in these sorts of things on occasion." The god swirled a finger in the air and a rib cutlet levitated toward him. It sliced itself midair and floated into his mouth. As he chewed, he propped his hand beneath his chin and gazed into his wine glass with a quiet solemnity. "Mostly to keep myself sane. I have forced myself to learn how to savor the finer things in this life . . . especially if I don't deserve them."

"But . . . why wouldn't you deserve them?"

Eoin looked up, blinking, as if he couldn't fathom the question. Then understanding flickered across his handsome face. "Ah. I forget that few mortals living today have read the *Legends of the Immortals.*"

"I have," said Orion in surprise, though he couldn't remember when or where. "Are they true?"

"Indeed," Eoin replied. "Soraya penned them, in fact, centuries ago. She is the eldest of my shadowlings. Perhaps you'll meet her one day. But if you *have* read the legends, Orion, then you'll know that as the God of Shadow, my existence serves no pleasant purpose."

"But you saved me," Orion argued. "Or your shadows did, at least. Besides, no other Immortal could handle such enormous responsibility, so you stepped forward to shoulder the burden. Surely you aren't a complete wretch. That counts for something, doesn't it?"

A soft, secretive smile bloomed on Eoin's lips, the subtle curl of chrysanthemum petals turning toward the sunshine. "If *you* say so, Orion Galashiels, then I suppose it does."

CHAPTER FIVE

"One absynthe," said the bartender gruffly, setting down the glass with a *clank*. The emerald-green liquid sloshed around, giving off its own ominous glow like a strange deep-sea creature that had never seen the light of day. "That totals to . . . eighteen."

Harry dragged the drink toward him with his elbows perched on the countertop, and took a lazy sip. "Cheers." Then he rotated on the stool and leaned back against the countertop's edge, his half-lidded eyes sweeping the underlit bar. Sickly sweet smoke from cigars and ember spirits wafted to the ceilings, swirling around the black lights in a haze of purple and gray. A small crowd had gathered around the pool table, and Harry watched as a gorgeous, serpentine *seishi* arched down with a cue stick, ocean-green hair slipping across one shoulder as they lined up their shot. There was a *crack*, like all the knuckle bones in a hand shattering all at once. The seishi blushed as a web of fractures spread across the cue ball. They glanced up and caught Harry's eye, smiling prettily, but he only lifted his glass to the mystical being before turning back around.

The bartender slung their towel over their shoulder. "You need to pay up," they grumbled as Harry raised the glass to his lips once more. "Absynthe doesn't come cheap, you know."

Harry inhaled long and deep, savoring the hellish burn that raced down his throat. He blinked back tears and reached into his pocket, blindly pulling out a handful of gold notes. He plucked two from his palm and tossed them into the air. "Here."

A black tongue shot out of the bartender's mouth, twisting over itself to catch both coins just before they hit the counter. The tongue darted back into the mouth, coins and all. The bartender bit down hard on the gold and let out a low laugh. "So what, you're the real deal, eh?"

Harry drained the glass, slammed it back down, and prodded it away. "Another, please."

The bartender raised a bushy eyebrow. They looked like any mortal, but that tongue could asphyxiate a human faster than the tightest choke hold. "You sure about that? That's some strong stuff, you know."

Harry forced himself to inhale patiently. His fingers curled around the pendant hanging from his neck. It heated at his touch, as if to comfort him.

He wanted to throw it into the Jade River.

"Another, I said."

"A'ight, a'ight, coming right up. Immortals be good." The bartender began preparing his drink with a gravelly chuckle. "I've seen beasts thrice your size pass out after a dozen of these. It's the strongest stuff on both sides o' the river, after all."

Of course I know that, Harry sulked to himself. *That's why I'm drinking it, damn it all.* His body flushed out toxins too quickly for most liquors to have any effect on him.

And tonight he was drinking to get drunk.

One hundred days had passed since he had begun searching for Orion. One hundred days since he had delivered Rose and a comatose Quinlan back to Eradore. One hundred days since he had summoned a portal to the Immortal Realm, without even hesitating to catch his breath. That had been his first mistake—not only had he shadow traveled halfway around the world three times in a row, but he'd torn a rift between the two realms. That first moment back in the Immortal Realm, when he'd hit the ground of his front yard in Dusk District, his legs had folded like wheat stalks and he'd face-planted directly into the grass.

Luckily for him, Soraya had been watering her lawn next door. His anygné neighbor dropped her garden hose and rushed to his side before dragging his ass into her house. He lay gasping on her fluffy rug, unable to summon even a thank-you to his lips. She pinched his chin with one manicured hand and force-fed him nectar out of a jar with the other, scolding him all the while, the delicate silver bracelets on her wrists jingling melodiously.

"Mark my words, Harry," she said, shoving another spoonful of nectar down his throat. Her wayward shoulder-length bob bounced when she shook her head, the raven-black strands glinting lavender at the tips when the lantern light hit her just right. "You're going to break yourself in half one day."

Harry only moaned around the spoon and swallowed. Sweet, golden *bliss*. A tingling buzz spread through his veins as the nectar revived him, healed him, warmed him to the core. He always forgot how *good* it was—sadly, it turned to ash when brought to the Mortal Realm.

Once he had regained some semblance of strength, he wobbled toward the window. He breathed in the comforting aroma of cinnamon and spiced ginger, a scent that had always clung to Soraya despite the absence of either in her home. Just another stubborn remnant of the eldest anygné's past, perhaps. Harry wondered fleetingly what remnants he brought with him from the Mortal Realm whenever he returned home—if this *was* home, though he still didn't quite know.

He ran his hand along the smooth varnish of Soraya's furniture as he strode toward the window, his fingertips hopping from one pale-wooded surface to the next. He always marveled at her eye for aesthetics. This century, she had transformed her home into a rustic wonderland, from the exposed stone walls and trestle tables to the tiny faerie lanterns skirting the oak beams that crisscrossed the ceiling.

In comparison, his home looked like an abandoned, dreary cave.

Peering out the living room windows into the indigo horizon, Harry asked, "How long was I away?"

Soraya joined him, cupping a steaming mug of nectar tea. She blew at the steam and wrapped her worn shawl tighter around herself with her free hand, the shimmering fabric woven with intricate whorls of feathers—her only memento of a life abandoned millennia before. The light in her eyes was teasing when she spoke. "Shall I give it to you in mortal days?"

"It wasn't *that* long," Harry groused.

Her face sombered. "Maybe not in mortal days."

Harry pursed his lips, still waiting.

Eventually, she took a long sip before answering. "Two thousand six hundred and twenty-five."

Harry's eyes widened. "That's not possible. It couldn't have been more than a year!"

She clicked her tongue. "I've been around far longer than you could ever comprehend, little shadowling. I'm never wrong." She pointed at the heavens, at two little specks of red. "The stars refuse to lie. There is mine, and there is yours." A third speck twinkled a few constellations away. "There is Lady Killian's." Her finger traced an arc through the sky. For each day he and Killian spent away from the Immortal Realm, their stars inched their way westward. When they departed the Mortal Realm, their stars vanished from the west and reappeared in the east to begin the journey anew. "This time, yours made it all the way past the third prong of Lord Tidus's trident."

Harry followed Soraya's gaze outside, where beyond Dusk District's four perfect emerald sprawls of grass lay the Jade River, and just past it, on the other side of the misted banks, rose the city of Rêvé—four times the size of Axaria, but still small by Immortal Realm standards. Its jewel-hewn dwellings glittered in fiery, psychedelic polychrome, almost too dazzling to look at. A few of Rêvé's younger inhabitants were playing in the shallows, dunking each other's scaled faces into the river no one could ever drown in.

"It won't be much longer, then," said Harry softly. "Until the next eclipse."

Soraya sighed. "And not much longer until the fourth house will finally have an occupant."

Centuries had passed since Dusk District had last expected a new inhabitant, and nearly two mortal decades since the fourth house had appeared on their street. A new house marked the birth of a new future shadowling. And though Harry didn't dare mention it, he had a sinking feeling that he knew exactly who it was meant for.

Soraya turned away from the window and raised a hand to brush a stray curl behind his ear. "I'm worried for you, Harry. You and Killian both.

Our worlds are changing. There are darker, worse things than nightmares, and they are getting ready to crawl out into the light. You must take care."

Dread rose fast like bile in his throat. He thought of Orion. "Soraya, have you heard any rumors recently?"

She gave him a long, hard look, her ancient gaze clear as glass and undulled by time. "Of what sort?"

He chose his next words carefully. "Anything . . . peculiar."

Her eyes narrowed. "Care to be a little more specific?"

"Anything about a young mortal man."

"You opened the portal to the Pit when you first returned, didn't you?" she whispered. "I felt it. And then something else—or rather, *someone* else—followed you, like a hiccup. An accidental ripple across the wrinkle between the realms." Her brow knitted. "I'm sorry, Harry. I wish I could tell you otherwise, but it's been quiet on my end."

He inhaled, quelling a sudden flare of panic. *If* Soraya *of all demons hasn't heard anything . . .* no. No way would he lose faith before he had even begun his search. "Well, the Immortal Realm is huge. There's hope yet."

At that, Soraya smiled and reached out to ruffle his hair. "There's always hope, sweetheart." She set down her mug and reached behind her neck to unclasp the precious pendant that she had worn for as long as Harry could remember. A single black diamond hung from the chain Eoin had gifted her when she retired from his service. And not just any diamond—her nebula diamond. She coiled the chain into a spiral before taking Harry's hand and pressing it into his open palm. "Take this. It will amplify your powers."

"I can't take this from you," said Harry immediately, staring at it in shock.

Soraya snorted. "Well, I'm not giving you a choice. I have a feeling that you'll need it." Her eyes twinkled. "To reject it would be a most unforgivable offense."

"Won't Eoin notice?" he asked.

She shook her head. "So long as you don't wave it in front of his face."

Even then Harry hesitated, but at her wink he finally obliged and fastened it behind his neck. "How, exactly, will this amplify my powers?"

"Who am I to say?" she mused. "All of our powers differ so vastly. Perhaps it will help you with fatigue from shadow jumping."

And how could he turn down an offer like *that*? Harry grabbed her hands and pressed his brow to her knuckles. "A million thanks, Soraya." With a sigh of dread, he released her. "I suppose I ought to go and find Eoin now to tell him that I'm long overdue for a vacation."

"Nonsense," she said, ushering him toward the front door. "You have no time to lose. I will speak to him on your behalf."

An enormous weight slid from his shoulders. "I owe you, Soraya."

She waved him away. "Just water my grass sometime, sweetheart."

Harry yanked the door open before the anygné could even finish her sentence. He leapt off the porch and shifted midair, shedding human skin for silken fur, a whole new world of sensation, and of course, *wings*. With a few mighty flaps, he shot into the sky, a great hulking beast that instilled fear into the hearts of every being that happened to glance up as his shadow devoured them from above.

From that moment onward, he had practically ransacked every city, forest, cave, town, pub, inn, and prison without rest, hunting for leads, no matter how minuscule. Soraya crossed paths with him once to deliver the message that Eoin had granted him an astonishingly generous one hundred days to rest. Of course, Eoin's so-called generosity was always a curse in disguise. Although Harry had never taken a day off before, the Ruler of Darkness would probably add a few decades to his indenture in exchange for the borrowed time. These one hundred days would cost Harry dearly— but he was willing to pay any price if it meant finding Orion.

He searched Rêve first, and then flew to Glassfall, with its crystalline towers that climbed farther than the eye could see, then to Llyrio, a city full of hoarders and hunters of wares from every corner of the Immortal Realm. Next came Vathalin, where he had to plug his ears with molten wax to prevent the Vathe's hypnotizing chants from siphoning his soul away. He even dared to search Oentheo—the home of the Council of Immortals, the city where the nine gods and goddesses played kings and queens in Highcourt Hall. The city where neither he, nor Eoin, nor any of his subjects would ever be welcome.

Harry snuck in anyway.

At the end of the first week, he paid a visit to Saint's Market, where he forked over a century's pay for the most powerful tracking stone he could get his hands on.

The stone led him to a forest of silver sterling trees. A patch of frost coated the bark of one tree, unmelted and perfectly intact. Mortal magic.

And more importantly, *ice* magic.

After combing the area for days, Harry spied a cluster of wilting blood blossoms and picked up a scent. *Orion's* scent. Riding on the sheer elation of his discovery, Harry scoured thousands of miles worth of nearby land, and yet, somehow . . . all other traces of Orion had completely vanished.

He chose to spend his last ten days in Harangirr, a terrifyingly immense desert metropolis of blue sand. The tracking stone proved useless after it had led him to the blood blossoms, and Harangirr was his last true hope. Because while cities like Harangirr and Glassfall and Rêvé were already impossibly huge, there was one place, one *underworld* that utterly dwarfed them all.

The Pit.

It was the eternal, inescapable grave Harry had thrown Priscilla into. The infernal hellscape *real* monsters called home. And with the exception of Eoin and his shadowlings, no living creature entered the Pit and ever returned—dead or alive.

Orion couldn't have ended up there. He just *couldn't* have.

Yet with every street Harry prowled, every building he broke into, desperately seeking out Orion's scent . . .

The more it seemed like Orion might truly be gone forever.

And now, Harry's hundred days had ticked down to zero.

The bar spun around him as Harry flagged down the bartender for his twentieth shot of absynthe. Each inhale ripped through his throat, ragged as a knife wound. But he still kept drinking until he slipped into murky oblivion. Vaguely, he noted that the seishi had won their game. They grinned a full mouth of pointy piranha teeth at him. He could only stare back.

Harry hadn't just let himself down. He had let Asterin down, too. He had promised her that he would find Orion.

Orion, his Orion, lost and alone and likely dead by now.

He finished his thirty-something glass and rubbed his face, too numb to even feel his own touch. The bar lights had faded to fuzzy neon blotches.

"Pardon me," Harry slurred to the bartender. He winced at the nause-ating pressure building at the back of his skull and fished out a few more gold notes, too wasted to bother counting them out, and slid them across the counter.

The bartender snapped the coins up only all too happily. They didn't count them either.

"Could you—" Harry hiccuped. Three iridescent bubbles floated out of his mouth. "Could you please summon a *sleijh* for me?"

The bartender chuckled. "Sure, son. Where to?"

"The Shadow Palace," he managed to murmur just as his eyelids drooped shut and his body sagged onto the counter. He inhaled a sharp whiff of the poor creature's terror, but by the time Harry thought to offer some words of comfort—not that he really had any—the absynthe had already dragged him deep down under.

CHAPTER SIX

Rose bolted through the secret tapestry connecting Fourth Wing to Ninth Wing and skidded to a halt in front of a tall blue door, her affinity stone in hand. White smoke seeped from the cracks in nebulous swirls. She leapt back with a yelp when a tendril licked at her shirtsleeve and corroded it to dust. A high, keening whistle pierced the air, and the fog sulked back underneath the door.

She cast a shield around herself, lest her skin disintegrate too.

Then she raised one leg high in the air and kicked the door down with a mighty *bang.*

"*Avon and Avris Saville,*" Rose thundered. "What did I say about the *bloody* experiments?"

The twins' heads snapped up at exactly the same time, golden eyes wide and blinking innocently. A greenish tinge pulsed along their skin, protecting them from burns and whatever toxic soup they were concocting today. They had thrown the windows along the cobalt walls open and shoved what little furniture there was into the corner haphazardly: a few stools, a shelf, and some tables . . . though most of it was unrecognizable from the traumas of their past stunts.

Unsurprisingly, Avris piped up first. She pointed gleefully at the white smoke pouring out of a large metal tub, her auburn ponytail bouncing. "Look, Rose! We finally figured it out!" Sweetly, she proclaimed, "Sentient acid fog!"

A few vapory tendrils poked out of the tub to send Rose a merry wave.

Rose pinched the bridge of her nose. It was all she could do to keep from hurling the tub out the window. Of all the hobbies her younger siblings could have picked, why did they need to choose creating substances of mass destruction? "Wonderful. What did I tell both of you, again?"

The pair of eleven-year-olds continued blinking at her, obviously a bit put out that their older sister hadn't immediately showered heaps of praise upon their ingenuity.

"Proper containment," Avon finally grumbled beneath Rose's flat stare.

"Correct. Is *that*—" Rose threw a finger at the smoke still gushing forth from the tub, "proper containment?"

The twins exchanged a look and then shook their little heads.

"We're sorry, Rose," they chimed together, all lovely smiles and angelic charm.

Rose let out a derisive snort. "Uh-huh. Clean this up."

Avon made a noise that sounded as though Rose had committed some tremendous injustice. "Now?"

"Yes, *now*."

"But we just got started!" Avris whined in disbelief.

Avon nodded emphatically. "And we cleaned up the mess from yesterday."

Rose refrained from shuddering. She did *not* want to remember the mess from yesterday. "Don't make me repeat myself. What would happen if your fog breaches the palace and someone breathes it in?"

Avris pumped her fist in the air. "Their lungs decay!" she cheered.

Rose inhaled deeply through her nostrils and harnessed every ounce of willpower to rein in her exasperation. "Yes, Avris. Which means they'll *die*."

The twins pouted.

Rose crossed her arms over her chest. "I'm going to count to three," she threatened. "One . . ."

The twins glanced back and forth between her and one another, trying to call her bluff.

"*Two* . . ." Rose pinned them with her most scorching glare. "*Thrrrr*—"

Avris flapped her arms. "Okay, okay, stop!" she exclaimed. With a great sigh of reluctance, she raised her affinity stone. The smoke began to spiral, funneling into a tornado. It moaned sadly and grew denser. The twins let out a squeal of delight when it dispersed briefly, fat droplets splattering onto the table with a sinister *hiss*.

Avon grabbed a quill and scribbled notes into a little leather-bound journal. "Maybe the extra dust particles—"

Avris pinched him. "Are you dumb? It's not water vapor condensing around the particles."

"Ouch!" Avon reached over and pinched her back. "Don't call me dumb!"

"Sorry." Avris snickered. "Dummy."

"*Rooose!*" Avon wailed. "Avris is bullying me!"

Rose walked over and seized her siblings by the earlobes. "Stop bickering or I'll ground you both. Work together," she added, raising her voice over their petulant protests, "and work hard. That's how you'll achieve greatness." Then she gave their auburn locks a last ruffle and headed for the stairs, leaving them to their scheming.

For their tenth birthday, Mother had gifted the twins this wing of the palace to perform experiments of their wildest dreams. Regrettably, the *wildest* experiments hadn't occurred until after Queen Lillian had died, but at this point Rose no longer had the heart to restrict the wing.

At least the Academia will keep them busy, she thought, fingers skimming the banister as she descended the stairwell to Fifth Wing. The Academia Principalis, next door to the palace, resumed session in just a few days, and Rose had made sure to enroll the twins in the most demanding classes the institution offered. Not to torment them, of course—she wasn't *that* horrible of a sister. In truth, she feared that any classes short of deathly challenging would bore them.

And bored twins were *dangerous* twins.

So lost in her thoughts, Rose almost crashed right into a man bustling up the stairs.

"Your Majesty!" Doctor Ilroy exclaimed, his medical bag clutched in his hand. He bowed. "My apologies, I wasn't watching where I was going."

She bowed back. "Nor was I . . . And what a coincidence—I was just about to come find you. How's the patient?"

The doctor had never been one to sugarcoat the truth, no matter how harsh. "Barely any progress, Your Majesty," he said, rubbing the dark-gray stubble on his chin, "but progress is still progress. So much time has passed that it's equally possible that he could wake up tomorrow or next year."

Rose swallowed and gave him a firm nod. "But no bad news?"

A muscle in the doctor's jaw twitched. He sighed and glanced around. "Perhaps it would be best if we spoke in a more . . . private location."

The rising steam fogged Rose's face as she cupped her tea close to her chest. She let Doctor Ilroy's words wash over her, the near-scalding heat of the tea seeping through the porcelain and prickling her palms, tethering her to reality.

"So you mean to say," she said, the sound of her own voice jolting her out of her stupor. "That even when—"

"If," the doctor corrected bluntly.

"*When* he wakes up," Rose insisted, glaring daggers at nothing in particular to keep the tears at bay, "that . . . that the dark magic might still be trapped inside him?"

Doctor Ilroy swiped his spectacles off his face in one deft movement and polished them on the hem of his coat. "Yes. In my experience— well, experience might not be quite the right word . . ." He held the lenses up to the light for inspection and blew away a remaining speck of dust before putting them back on. "From what little I've read and learned about the tenth element," he went on, "it always leaves some sort of a trace. A stain."

"A stain," echoed Rose.

"How that stain will affect him, I have no idea," Ilroy admitted. "My best guess is that the longer he remains in his current state, the more lasting damage he will sustain when he awakens. The dark magic could give him nightmares at best, or, at worst, rot his organs from the inside out."

Rose choked out a strangled laugh. "Has anyone ever mentioned that you can be rather direct?"

The doctor shrugged. "I'll be the first to admit that the prince's condition is grim, Your Majesty. Hope for the best, but expect the worst, is what I always say." He forced a smile. "I don't believe in softening the truth unless there is absolutely nothing left to be done."

Her fingers tightened in a death grip around the teacup. "In that case," she murmured, "I hope you remain your brutal self forever." Still feeling slightly lightheaded, she placed the cup aside and stood. "Excuse me, Doctor. I must pay a visit to my cousin."

"Your Majesty," Ilroy called out as she made her way to the door. She paused, glancing over her shoulder. His eyes were as hard as stone, but Rose found solace in them—in their brutality. "Remember to give him time."

Once she reached the medical wing, she strode to the end of the hall and slid open the door to the Saffron Room. She had to squint against the blinding radiance of the cheerful yellow walls and buttercup curtains, thrown aside to allow in the flood of brilliant afternoon sunshine. Sunbeams warmed her skin as she picked her way past the windows and empty cots toward the hidden door at the end of the room.

She murmured to the door as if to a lover. "*Ovrire fera Orozalia Saville.*" It rolled aside. After she stepped through, it rolled back into place behind her with a gentle *snick*.

Dustmotes danced in the shafts of golden light streaming through the galaxy of glass stars and crescent moons fanning the cupola above. While the constellations overhead were none Rose knew of, her mother had once told her that they actually belonged to the skies of another realm, one where the sun never shone and night reigned evermore.

Trapped in slumber, beneath the stars amid dove-gray silk and velvet, lay the Prince of Eradore.

Rose took a seat in the worn armchair beside the bed and gazed at her cousin. "Hello, Quinlan," she whispered.

His chest rose and fell in shallow breaths. Dark locks of hair were strewn across the pillow, overgrown from too many weeks without a trim. His lips were so pale, like peony petals leached of color. Directly beneath the sunlight shimmering from above, his skin seemed almost translucent. Ethereal.

The thought had no sooner crossed her mind than she spotted the thin trickle of drool drying on his cheek. She snickered to herself and pulled out a handkerchief from her pocket to rub it away. "Just wait until I tell Asterin that you drool in your sleep." She scooted forward in the armchair until she could prop her elbows on the edge of his bed. "Guess what? The twins finally made a breakthrough with the fog today. I'm almost scared to think of what their little conniving brains will come up with next. One alone is capable of unfathomable destruction, but the two of them together?" A half-hearted chuckle escaped her. "If they ever went head-to-head with an Immortal, I might put my money against the Immortal."

She cleared her throat and pulled a letter from the folds of her cloak. "Also, you'll be pleased to hear that Asterin's weekly letter arrived today." While opening it, she paused to shoot a nasty glare at her cousin. "You'd better wake up soon. Otherwise the Queen of Axaria will throw a fit. Do you really want that to happen?"

Rose could have sworn Quinlan's breathing hitched, just slightly.

Hope poured into her chest. Her body leaned forward of its own accord, her eyes roving his face for a sign, *any* sign, that he could actually hear her, that he was fighting. Louder, her tone more teasing than before, she asked, "What will you do if she comes to visit me and you're still lazing about in bed? Think of all the awful things she'll say to you, and you won't even be able to defend yourself."

Quinlan's index finger twitched.

Remember to give him time, Doctor Ilroy's voice reminded her.

Heart hammering, Rose scanned the length of the letter.

And then she began to read.

Of course, Asterin's words were originally meant for her, but Rose hoped they might spur along Quinlan's recovery. It had been at Taeron's suggestion—her other cousin, Quinlan's older brother—that she began bringing them with her, to read aloud to him.

For the entirety of the letter, she forbade herself from sparing Quinlan even the tiniest glance. Instead, she focused on the letter itself, on the deft strokes of midnight unfurling across ivory parchment, calming herself by running her fingers along the edges.

". . . and send all of my love to everyone except for Quinlan, until he wakes up," she finished a few minutes later. "The bastard. Yours truly, Asterin." She couldn't help but grin at the last line and finally allowed herself to look up. "She misses you, you know. Though I bet she misses me more."

The tiniest crinkle creased Quinlan's brow.

Rose wanted to scream. *Wake up, you bloody fool. You can do it, I know you can.* But she didn't. She knew her cousin—knew how stupidly stubborn he was, how he valued his pride and his ability to soldier on without anyone else's help. If she really wanted him to wake up, she would have to let him stand this battle on his own. And yet . . .

"PS," she added, a little softer. "Despite the fact that I want nothing more than to wring his neck, tell him that I love him."

Rose bit her lip and folded the letter before tucking it beside Quinlan's pillow. Throat tight, she brushed aside the hair from his forehead. Then she stood, turned on her heel, and fled the room.

All but collapsing against the hidden door as it closed behind her, she slid to the glossy lemon floor and stared at the ceiling. The color scheme was meant to cheer up patients and visitors, but Rose doubted all the yellow in the world could ease her pain. Chest heaving, she closed her eyes and sent a prayer up to the Immortals, pleading for whatever mercy they could spare.

She might have spent the rest of the day like that, her face buried in the crook of her arm, until a shadow crossed over her. She glanced up and swallowed, trying for a watery smile. "Cousin."

"Your Majesty," said Taeron Holloway, crouching in front of her. His violet eyes mimicked the indigo hues of his younger brother, shining brightly behind his horn-rimmed tortoiseshell glasses. He had a thick leather-bound volume tucked beneath his arm, bookmarked about three-quarters of the way through with a wooden spoon. His dark hair, once identical to Quinlan's, had grown more wild than Rose had ever seen—even longer than Quinlan's current length. As if noticing her gaze, he swept it away, but it only tumbled back again as soon as he let go.

"Shouldn't you be using that spoon to eat?" Rose quipped, forcing lightness in an effort to disguise the strain in her voice from unshed tears. "The Immortals know you need to. Eat more, I mean."

Taeron made a vague noise of affirmation and nudged his glasses farther up his tall nose. "Actually, I ate dinner already."

She raised an eyebrow. The dinner bell hadn't even rung yet. "Today?"

The corner of his mouth quirked. "You caught me."

Rose sighed. "Taeron."

He held up the book in defense. "Kidding. I thought I would join you for supper. I'll eat then. Promise."

Taeron straightened and stepped beside her to lean against the wall. He crossed his arms over his chest, the book dangling from his fingers. Rose looked up at him. From this angle, she could almost mistake the older Holloway for his brother, but the relaxed elegance of Taeron's posture gave it away. Quinlan always stood with a coiled tension in his muscles, as if he were prepared to strike at any given moment.

Rose caught her cousin's eyes lingering on the door at her back. "He's doing fine."

Taeron's fingers drummed along the book cover, expression unreadable. "And that's why you're sitting up here nonetheless, burdening yourself with a pain that we all share?"

That's not it, she wanted to say.

Though Taeron shared the most blood with Quinlan, everything from his timid gaze to the book he now clutched like a lifeline reminded her that the two were far less like brothers than they appeared on the outside. Quinlan lived for what Taeron shied away from, no matter the suffering, the struggle, the cost.

"Sorry," she murmured at last. "You're right."

Taeron held out a hand to her, his cheeks dimpling with a lovely smile. "I usually am." His face scrunched up as soon as the words left his mouth. "That sounded horribly egotistical. Apologies."

At that, Rose laughed fondly and let him pull her to her feet. "At least you recognize it."

Her cousin's face was pensive as they ambled out of the Saffron Room, his arm slung around her shoulders. "You know, I never understood what it was that kept my brother going when we were younger," he said. "Every single time Father shoved him down, he always just got up again.

Determination, drive, pigheadedness . . . whatever you want to call it, he had it." He squeezed her shoulder with sudden, uncharacteristic intensity, but even now his gaze only smoldered like coals when Quinlan's would have been blazing with indigo wildfire. "He'll wake up, just you watch."

His earnestness melted her heart, but she still couldn't find it in herself to respond.

CHAPTER SEVEN

*A*sterin.

The name throbbed through him, each iteration thudding in time with the dull beat of his heart.

Asterin. Asterin. Asterin.

He could feel the darkness residing in his body, his every cell, a wicked poison coursing through his veins and trapping him beneath this hateful veil of shadows and fleeting hallucinations. A black fog chased him, taunted him. Phantoms sang and whispered their sins into his ears.

But that name, that steady voice murmuring at him. Cool fingertips brushing his forehead, soothing the dark heat raging through him.

He gritted his teeth and *fought.*

He kicked and hollered and thrashed like a rabid beast, clawing his way up toward the pinprick of light high above even as the shadows chuckled and clawed at him playfully, dragging him deeper into the darkness.

Tell him that I love him.

He let out a scream that shattered their hold on him, just for a moment. He didn't hesitate, clambering away and lunging for that light.

The shadows snarled at him in disdain, but he could see his goal now, and he wrenched himself away from them with everything he had.

And when he finally emerged, wrecked and ruined but victorious, Quinlan Holloway opened his eyes to the world and smiled.

CHAPTER EIGHT

J ack had a hawk.

Mere minutes after he whistled for it, a black smudge appeared over the horizon and descended upon them with terrifying fury. He offered it some meat from a pouch at his waist and it latched onto the elk hide gauntlet protecting his arm to scarf it down. Afterward, the Elite pulled out a shard of crystal from the chandelier. The hawk cocked its head and snapped it up into its beak before soaring back into the sky to circle the entertainment district.

Eadric wished he had a hawk. Or even better, a falcon. Because, sure, he descended from the House of the Falcon, but apparently he wasn't worthy enough to have one himself.

"Why does Jack get a hawk?" he complained to Asterin while they waited. Four Elites remained: Jack, Laurel, Casper, and Silas. The others had escorted Asterin's mother back to the palace while they investigated the café where the pipes had apparently burst. They found nothing, so the *thing*—which Asterin had begun calling Chaos—must have already moved on.

"Why does the Captain of Axaria whine like a toddler?" his queen mocked. At his outraged gape, she held up her hands. "I never said that I don't, either." She sighed and straightened the sleeves of her sleek obsidian bodysuit, which she'd made a habit of carrying around with her. Tailored to her every limb, it made for easy changes in dire situations just like this. The Queen of Eradore had sent it overseas as a gift. It was nearly identical to Rose's suit but for the color—black instead of blue. "Guess it's about time we grew up."

High above, Jack's hawk let out a shriek. They mounted their horses and galloped away from the Pavilion. The horseshoes clattered like low bells against the pavement of the streets, designed specially by earth wielders to protect the horses' hooves on hard surfaces.

The hawk acted as their star, guiding them northwestward. Carriages and hansom drivers veered out of their way as they barreled past, but the horses had hardly settled into their stride when Jack signaled ahead and they came to a halt before a dimly lit tavern. A wooden sign dangled above the door. The Smiling Imp, it read in flaking blue paint. From within came the muffled shattering of glass and boisterous shouting. There was an unwieldy *thump* followed by a *crash*, as if a table had caved in.

They swept the perimeter on foot, scanning for alternative entrances—a side door blocked by wooden crates, and a back door. Eadric peered into the windows as they walked, but the sun reflected too brightly against the panes to make out any of the dim interior.

Once they circled back to the front of the tavern, Eadric cleared his throat. "Queen Asterin and I will hang back. Silas, Laurel, you two enter through the back and scout first."

Asterin, who already had her hand on the door handle, narrowed her eyes. "Come again?"

"There is no reason for you to rush in headfirst," said Eadric. He signaled to the two Elites. "You have two minutes. Do not engage and return quickly."

"Yes, Captain!" they chorused before jogging off and disappearing around the corner.

"Eadric, if you think—"

"Your Majesty," he interrupted, forcing himself to meet Asterin's flat, unimpressed gaze. "You must use your Elites to the fullest extent in ensuring your safety. That is their purpose, as well as mine." Before she could reply, he added, "Do not forget the decision Priscilla forced you to make.

If any one of us had been there to back you up—Orion, Rose, the Elites, or myself—things could have gone very differently. For you, for Quinlan, for . . ." He swallowed the lump in his throat. "For Luna. For all of us."

Eadric wondered if he had overstepped when Asterin turned away without responding. However, she didn't argue either, so he took her silence for assent.

As they waited, Jack scrutinized the sky with his hands on his hips, tracking his hawk's every swoop. Casper twirled his knives, keeping his eyes fixed on the tavern's entrances.

At two minutes and exactly two seconds, the noise swelled, accompanied by raucous cheers and more crashing. Eadric exchanged a glance with Asterin. The queen nodded once.

"Casper, with us," he said. "Jack, with the horses. Send for backup."

Together, they charged the front door.

Utter pandemonium greeted them.

Eadric ducked as a bottle went sailing over his head and smashed through a window at the far end of the tavern, though the sound was completely muted by the shouts of drunken patrons. A table *had*, in fact, caved in. A horde of people had amassed around a hulking brute of a man, and a young girl wove through the crowd collecting bets.

The crowd let out a cheer as the brute lurched forward and swung a meaty fist at a significantly smaller figure clad in a crimson cloak.

"Wait," blurted Casper. "Is that—"

Eadric's mouth dropped open. "*Silas?*"

Lithe as a cougar, the Elite dodged beneath the man's fist. It crushed the face of a nearby spectator. Silas lashed a leg out and his opponent went down with a roar. But before he could rise, the Elite descended upon him with fists flying.

Eadric let out a growl and stormed toward the brawl with Asterin on his heels. He was going to *skin* the Elite for such flagrant disobedience. And *Silas*, of all people? "*Do not engage*, I said!"

"*Captain!*"

He spun around and found himself face-to-face with Laurel. Her bun had fallen apart and ale soaked her jacket front. An angry bruise had already begun to blossom across her cheek. "What is the meaning of this?" he demanded. "I expected far better from you—"

"Eadric," Asterin cut in, her tone sharper than steel. "Something's wrong. Look."

While Eadric had been distracted, Silas had wrapped his hands around his opponent's neck. The cheers crescendoed to a climax. Ice crackled from the Elite's palms, spreading across the man's shoulders and neck and steadily purpling face. A strange, animalistic glint shone in his dark-brown eyes.

Eadric's stomach curdled with dread when he noticed the oily black spores spreading along Silas's ice.

"I couldn't get him to snap out of it!" Laurel shouted over the din. "It's like something is possessing him!"

Casper coughed pointedly. "I'm not sure if saving that second man is at the top of anybody's priority list right now, but I think Silas is about to choke the life out of him."

Asterin touched Eadric's elbow, fixated on the rotting ice. "I don't want anyone getting anywhere near that ice. Remember that cage of lightning you used to capture Priscilla during the battle?"

Eadric nodded in understanding and rolled up his sleeves. To the Elites, he said, "Get the patrons out of here."

Drowning out his surroundings, he focused on his breathing, focused on every stale, alcohol-tainted breath entering his lungs and cooling the buzzing in his veins. Affinity stone in hand, he sought out the fringes of his magic, pulling at the threads until they drew taut. He waited for the pressure to build deep within his core—and then, eyes still closed, he set it free.

Power shuddered through him as a vicious wave of electricity exploded from his body. It split into orbs of lightning that jumped from place to place, too swift for the eye to quite catch, sparking and spitting like mini bonfires.

Silas faltered for the briefest second, glaring up at the new threat. One orb nipped at his hand and shocked his grip right off his now-unconscious opponent. Without wasting a heartbeat, Asterin lassoed the unconscious man's limbs with howling funnels of wind and hauled him out of harm's way before

Laurel and Casper rushed back into the now empty tavern to lug him outside.

Eadric kept his breath steady as he flicked his affinity stone upward. His magic yanked at him like an eager hound, begging for freedom, but his grip only tightened on its leash. *Obey*, he commanded in his mind. The orbs convulsed into long shafts and arced over Silas's head, enclosing him in forks of blinding white light.

Silas fell still, staring at them through the lightning prison with eyes blacker than jet and his expression utterly blank.

Eadric suppressed a shiver. He would have preferred some sort of resistance, or some snarling, at the very least. "What now?"

"We get that thing out of him," said Asterin quietly as she curled her fingers into a fist. Silas gagged, his hands going to his throat to claw at emptiness as the queen stole the oxygen from his lungs with her air affinity. After a brief struggle, his eyes rolled back and he slumped silently to the ground.

Eadric let his lightning fizzle out. Without a word, they dove for Silas, each grabbing an arm and a leg. While they manhandled him out of the tavern, Asterin conjured a stream of water. It gushed over Silas's body, snaking all the way down to his ankles and up his neck, covering his hands and face completely. Bright-blue frost bloomed from her fingertips and raced outward to forge tailor-made confinements.

An icy white puff of vapor curled from her lips. "We have to compensate the tavern owner for the damages," she said as they reached the door. She shoved it open with her hip. "As well as the café owner. And the poor sod that Silas beat the daylights out of, of course." Two high-stepping horses waited at the street curb, harnessed to one of the more subtle palace carriages, their tails flicking and their chestnut coats gleaming. The Elites had already cleared the area, so they didn't have to worry about eyes. "And we'll need to hire a team to restore the concert hall."

Jack's hawk awaited them from its perch atop a lamp affixed to the side of the carriage. Hayley was picking at a scab on her elbow in the driver's seat. As soon as she caught sight of them, she leapt down to open the carriage door, causing the hawk to flap away with an irate screech and land in her abandoned seat instead, its feathers puffed in indignation.

"I should help with that, too," Asterin rambled on. "The restoration, I mean. Can't do much about the piano, but—"

Two more Elites—Gino, followed by Nicole—hopped out of the carriage. They helped lay Silas onto the bench, propping him against the cushions. Eadric got in after Asterin, only half listening as they sat themselves on the opposite bench.

"—I'll speak with the royal accountant, surely we can allocate funds for the purchase of a new one. If we have to send Levain and some experts overseas for it, then so be it. The last one came from Galanz, didn't it? But—"

"Your Majesty," said Eadric.

"—Immortals, the paperwork! Ah—"

"*Asterin*," Eadric exclaimed. Her teeth clacked shut. He reached forward to place a hand on her shoulder. "Relax. Please. We'll work everything out eventually, but first we need to focus on getting Silas back to the palace safely and eradicating the Chaos possessing him."

She scrubbed her face with the heels of her palms. "Of course." When she lifted her head, her entire demeanor transformed. Her posture straightened. The anxiety creasing her brow smoothed. With sharp eyes, she counted the horses and the Elites at her disposal. "Hitch Silas's mare to the carriage," she commanded, her voice even and strong. "Eadric and Hayley will return with me via carriage to the palace. The rest of you, on horseback. Move swiftly, but *leisurely*. Understood? We still don't know exactly what we're dealing with, so the last thing we want to do is alarm the citizens or fire up even more rumors."

The Elites saluted as one and sped into action. Horses and riders switched, with Gino and Nicole mounting Asterin's and Eadric's horses. The others helped Hayley hitch the third horse to the front of the procession before they, too, swung onto their steeds. Hayley shooed Jack's hawk back to its lamp perch and climbed into the driver's seat.

Asterin pulled the carriage door shut and stuck her head out of the window. "Split up, everyone. Stagger departures." The carriage jerked to life. "Meet in Training Hall C!"

As they clattered off, Asterin drew the curtains shut and slumped against her seat. She gazed at Silas, brow furrowed. Each jostle of the carriage—and, consequently, Silas's body—caused her to wince.

Eadric reached forward to give the blue frost covering the Elite a curious prod, half expecting his finger to freeze to the surface, but it was only mildly cool to the touch. "What if he wakes up?"

Asterin leaned her head against the window and closed her eyes. "He won't," she mumbled, and that was that.

"Do you think the Chaos came from the Immortal Realm?" asked Eadric. "And how did it infiltrate Axaris?"

"There are consequences to traveling back and forth between the two realms," Asterin responded. "Some scholars have speculated that it even causes the lines separating one from the other to blur . . . which I suppose could make crossing over easier."

"But . . ." Eadric trailed off. Over three months before, Harry had summoned at least three portals within the span of a few days. First to banish Priscilla, then to return to the Mortal Realm, then once more to begin his search for Orion. "That happened months ago."

His queen shrugged. "Like I said, it's all speculation. Maybe there's some kind of breach somewhere. Maybe someone freed it and sent it here."

A terrifying thought. "Maybe it just *really* wanted to hear that pianist play," Eadric murmured.

That drew a surprised laugh from her, but just then the carriage glided to a halt.

Hayley's muffled voice came through the door. "All clear!"

"You take his legs," Asterin told Eadric while gripping him under his armpits. He nudged the door open, and together, they hauled ass for the palace entrance, all too aware of the stares likely pinned on them from the windows above.

A familiar whinny rang through the air, accompanied by the thundering of hooves. Lux rocketed through the Wall's main gate seconds later, with Gino clutching the reins for dear life. Asterin's stallion nearly threw him into a hedge, but the poor Elite eventually managed to slide out of the saddle in one piece.

They found Elyssa Faelenhart waiting for them atop the stairs to the palace foyer. Asterin's mother ran down to meet them midway. "Thank the Immortals." When she caught sight of Silas, the color drained from her face. "What happened?"

Asterin transferred Silas to Hayley and Gino. "Get him into the hall."

After the two Elites rushed off, Elyssa grabbed her daughter's hands, distraught. Her voice shook. "Asterin. You can't just chase after trouble like this."

"I'm fine, Mother," said Asterin. "Don't worry."

"Don't *worry*?" Elyssa repeated incredulously. She flung her arm in the direction that the Elites had carried Silas off to. "What if it had been you?"

Asterin examined the floor tiles as if they were the most interesting thing in the world. "It wasn't," she said in a small voice. Then, with blazing intensity, she looked up again. "However, it *was* one of my Elites. Now he's in danger, and I have to help him."

Elyssa's grip tightened until one of Asterin's knuckles cracked aloud in protest. "Danger? You're risking yourself *again*?"

"I would risk anything for my Elites, Mother," said Asterin.

"Something else happened while we were away," Elyssa admitted. "There came reports of some kind of tremor beneath the palace. Several guards went to investigate and found an old crypt bearing the sigil of the God of Shadow with a gigantic butterfly fountain in the middle. It had split down the middle and was flooding the chamber. The guards managed to stop the flooding, but beneath the fountain itself they found a hole with no bottom in sight . . . and dozens of claw marks on the floor emerging out of it. Perhaps . . ."

"Perhaps that's how the Chaos crawled into Axaris," Asterin finished, shaking herself free from Elyssa's grip. Eadric hastened after her as she marched toward the palace. She paused midstep and turned to her mother. "Order the crypt to be sealed off and warded," she called. "I need to attend to Silas."

Eadric hurried after her down the grand staircase to the concourse. "Are you sure about this? The crypt seems like a priority."

Asterin exhaled. "No. The damage is already done. My only worry is what *else* might have escaped from that hole. But we won't know until they choose to show themselves. My priority right now is Silas." They arrived at the doors to the training hall. She turned to him before they entered, though she wouldn't quite meet his gaze. "All we have to do is find a way to destroy the Chaos without accidentally killing him."

Eadric stared at her. "How?"

Asterin raised her chin high. It was a challenge. A war call. "No idea. But I guess we're about to find out."

CHAPTER NINE

Luna killed fifty-seven more doves.

She even stopped sculpting in order to train longer and harder with Adrianna. Her mentor forced her to train under all sorts of conditions, from extreme cold or heat to utter exhaustion. At the top of the stronghold's tallest tower. In the darkest, smelliest cellar she could find. From dawn until dusk she exercised her magic, twisting and bending it until *something* snapped. Some days, that something snapped *into place*.

Most days, unfortunately, that something snapped wings. And necks.

It appeared that her illusion-affinity had a violent streak.

At first, Luna buried every fallen dove in the courtyard near the little gazebo where Adrianna liked to have tea with courtiers on sunny afternoons. By the dozenth dead bird or so, however, her aunt convinced her to start giving them up to the kitchens.

And when the cooks served up dove pot pie at dinner, she swallowed down every last bite without the slightest remorse.

Or maybe she was just too tired for remorse.

Finally, Luna came up with the idea to combine the air affinity she had inherited from her father along with her illusion affinity by creating tiny pores in the layer of illusion to allow air through, thus preventing the birds' suffocation.

"You know," her aunt remarked as Luna stroked the head of her very first, very much alive dove and bit her lip until it bled to keep the tears at bay, "suffocating someone *and* concealing them at the same time could prove to be quite the handy little trick."

Luna balked. "Why in the world would I suffocate anyone?"

"Not just anyone," her mentor replied. "An attacker, a rival, an enemy in combat. If used under the right circumstances, it could turn the tide of battle. Change an entire outcome."

Luna thought of the fifty-seven white feathers hanging in her room. She sure as hell wouldn't be adding human bones to that collection. "No thank you," she said politely.

Adrianna tilted her head. "Luna—"

Fury swept through her. "Do not make me repeat myself," she spoke, cold ire lacing her voice. "I am no murderer." She stepped closer to her aunt, her fists trembling at her sides. "I am no fool, nor am I ignorant. I am no weapon to be forged by anyone's hand."

"But surely," Adrianna murmured gently, "if you had no choice, wouldn't you wish to eliminate an enemy to save a loved one?"

Luna stopped short. Hadn't she been prepared to take down her own mother to save Asterin?

"That's different," she denied after a too-long hesitation.

Her aunt only gave her a half smile. A knowing smile. "Of course, sweetheart."

And though Luna had achieved a milestone victory, she left the training session feeling as though she had lost her most important battle yet.

"Lovely weather, isn't it?" said Adrianna as she poured herself another cup of tea, sitting on the settee with one leg hooked over the other. Intertwining gold branches dotted with tiny silk flowers crept up her russet skirts, the fabric gathered at her waist to show off her slender figure. Few could pull off a brown dress, but with her sparkling eyes and full smile, Adrianna was nothing short of mesmerizing in the glow of the afternoon sun.

The juxtaposition from mentor to . . . *this* was jarring, to say the least.

Luna broke apart a lemon shortbread cookie and dipped it into her tea, gazing out of the gazebo and into the courtyard. Mist floated low in the air, cooling her skin, flush from the afternoon heat. Every now and then they could hear the *splish* of vibrant fish darting about the little stone pools that were scattered among the azalea bushes, along with the droning hiss of cicadas. She shielded her eyes as dazzling sun rays pierced the clouds above to shimmer in the air as rainbows. "Mm-hmm."

"I love it when the stones soak up the sunlight," her aunt went on. They watched a squirrel dart through the grass, its bushy brown-and-white wisp of a tail bobbing as it uprooted a flower in search of a nut. "The whole castle feels warm and cozy."

"Cozy," Luna echoed distantly. Nothing about the stronghold struck her as *cozy*, except for her chambers, with their handsome hardwood flooring and rich tapestries that looked so expensive she hadn't dared even examine them too closely. Most of the rooms she'd explored had but a single window, though her bedchamber had three—a luxury, if the others could serve as an example.

Adrianna leaned forward and placed a soft hand on Luna's cheek. She smelled of spice and sugar. "You seem tired, sweetheart. Am I working you too hard?"

For her aunt's sake, Luna smiled. "No, not at all. I'm fine. A little . . . homesick, I suppose." The word tasted bitter on her lips. Could she even consider Axaria to be *home* anymore?

"Haven't you thought of returning to Axaris?" Adrianna asked casually. "I'm sure Jakob would be happy to arrange an escort for you."

Luna squirmed in her chair. "I'm not sure if I want to."

Adrianna's eyebrows raised. "You don't miss Eadric?"

"I . . ." Luna stared into the bottom of her empty teacup, shrinking beneath her aunt's assessing gaze. "I did. I-I mean, I *do*." She cringed. "I've had a lot on my mind lately." Of course he crossed her mind, but it seemed that other things were taking precedence these days—training and strengthening her magic, namely. And . . . one memory of the captain often jostled past the others to the forefront of her mind. The day of Fairfest Eve, before all of them had infiltrated the palace. After Luna had reclaimed her suppressed powers, she had woven illusions to disguise her friends in order to pass beneath Priscilla's notice. Though the task had pushed her to the brink of exhaustion, Luna's work had been a resounding success—and yet, afterward, Eadric couldn't stand to even *look* at her. He'd always thought her a helpless lamb among wolves, and himself her fearless defender. Even in his letters, he wrote of protecting her, of sheltering her from whatever storms lie ahead. Once, such words might have made her swoon. Now they filled her with resentment. He wanted her to rely on his protection. But she was a dragon, not a lamb, and her belly was full of fire.

Footsteps shuffled through the grass, and a moment later two guards rounded a hedge and approached the gazebo. Luna recognized one as her own and the other as Adrianna's. They bowed deeply.

"Good afternoon, Your Grace," Adrianna's guard greeted.

"Ah," Adrianna said, sweeping some crumbs onto an empty plate. "That must be your cue." She gathered the tea set on a tray and rose from her seat after tidying the table. "Have you two been properly introduced? Luna, this is Milli. Milli, this is Princess Luna, my niece."

"A pleasure, Your Highness," said the guard, and Luna actually believed her.

"Nice to meet you," Luna replied as they all followed Adrianna back into the castle. "This is . . . er . . ." She glanced at her own guard. "Geoffrey?"

The guard's eye twitched. "Greg, actually," he responded curtly. A pause. "Your Highness."

Luna winced, ears flushing with heat. "That was my second guess."

Adrianna, still carrying the tea tray, watched the exchange with a rueful smile on her lips. "Oh, Luna. Try to get to know your actual guards a little better than that, hm? Firstly, for your own protection, but more importantly . . . while we may have been born royal, we are all human, and thus deserve to be treated with the same level of respect."

Luna's reply bubbled to her lips—*obviously*, she wanted to say, but ultimately wavered. The old Luna had prided herself in remembering the names of every cook, maid, servant, and palace guard she ever spoke with. Yet . . . this Luna had failed to pay attention to even the names of her *own* guards.

Immortals, what was happening to her?

"Anyway, good luck with the meeting!" Adrianna called as she ambled off with Milli. Her voice echoed off the stone walls. "And don't forget what I said!"

Luna glanced at Greg. *Well, this is awkward*, she thought. "In my defense, you *do* look a bit like a Geoffrey."

Greg stared at her. "Okay."

Luna practically sprinted for Throne Hall.

"I'll be fine from here," she told Greg when they arrived. "Thank you." He bowed and departed. She heard him muttering *Geoffrey* under his breath, and cringed.

Once his footsteps receded, Luna exhaled through pursed lips and looked up at the colossal double doors. In Axaria, Lord Conrye and his wolf form greeted visitors entering Throne Hall. Here reared a three-headed viper instead, its thick, scaly body coiled around the limbs of its mistress, Lady Ilma—the Goddess of Air. She stood over Luna in billowing robes of purple, her gaze frigid and her neck circled by a choker of a thousand fangs.

Luna set her shoulders back and grabbed the door handles square in the middle. With a majestic flourish, she hauled them open and entered.

"—for the last time," a man exclaimed, his voice heavy with exasperation. Ahead, three individuals of varying heights—one female and two males—had gathered at the foot of the dais. "It would take at least two hundred apple seeds to kill someone."

"But what if they were big apple seeds?" demanded the female, the shortest of the group.

The first speaker threw his hands into the air. "That doesn't make any sense!"

"She has a point," the tallest figure murmured as he examined his nails.

They were so preoccupied with their quarreling that they didn't even notice Luna approaching until she cleared her throat.

At once, they went silent and turned to her, their sharp eyes raking over her, calculating, assessing. Thick purple cloaks rested on their shoulders, shadowing the startlingly white uniforms beneath.

"Oh my," the female finally whispered. She strode toward Luna, light as air, her shiny high-heeled leather boots not sounding so much as a *click* against the gleaming marble tiles. Luna froze, averting her gaze, but two fingers pinched her chin and forced her eyes up. Her pulse quickened at the other girl's proximity, the touch setting her nerves abuzz. Tousled black curls and a bold fringe framed the girl's petite face. Luna drank in her dark brown complexion. The amber glow of her irises. Lips painted midnight black, curling up in impish amusement. "What a *sweetheart*."

Heat rushed to Luna's cheeks. "E-excuse me?" she stammered, any semblance of confidence ripped to tatters beneath that luminous gaze.

The first male voice she'd heard interrupted them. "Ignore her, Your Highness."

The windswept frost-white hair caught her attention first, and then the quicksilver eyes. Luna frowned. *Why does he look so familiar?* she wondered.

"I'm Kane," he went on. "Kane Callaghan. That's Lady Eirene Killian, and that's—"

Recognition jolted through her. Her eyes widened. "*Kane?* Like . . . Rose's Kane?"

Eirene threw her head back in an explosion of laughter, which earned her a death glare from Kane. She didn't seem to care in the least. "Oh," she hooted. "Immortals have mercy." After her laughter receded, she wiped her eyes and grinned. "Yes, Your Highness. *Rose's* Kane."

"Damn you, Killian," Kane growled.

It was all Luna could do to leap out of the way when Eirene pounced three feet into the air and landed upon Kane's back. She knuckled his hair into a disheveled disaster. While he hollered and tried to fight her off, she simply hooked her knees tighter around his waist and cackled louder than ever before.

A pang of nostalgia struck Luna. Somehow, they reminded her of Asterin and Orion, albeit a lot more . . . *savage.*

Luna turned to the last member of the trio. "All right, then." He looked young, she supposed, though the oldest of the three. A sleek tail of blond hair as pale as her own fell to his waist, brushing against the leather chest strap of the sword sheathed at his back. Its pommel rose over his broad shoulders. His face was set in what seemed to be permanent disdain, reminiscent enough to Eadric's scowl that it tugged at her heart.

He bowed to her, his gloved hands clasped in front of him. "Your Royal Highness." His voice seeped through the air like smoky incense, a deep, sultry tenor. "My name is Rivaille Valle. Please pardon the behavior of my . . . associates." His nose wrinkled slightly. "We're hirelings in King Jakob's employ."

"He pays me enough to kill, but not enough to behave!" Killian called out.

Rivaille merely sighed. "They don't usually—"

"Act like this?" Luna cut in with a timid smile.

The corner of his mouth twitched. "Quite the opposite, actually. Lady Killian is the personification of trouble."

"I can hear you, you know!" Eirene sprung off Kane's back and dropped to the floor in a nimble crouch. In a flash, she had pulled out two wickedly curved daggers with glowing blue hilts from the sheaths at her waist. She grinned when Luna nearly tripped over herself in her rush to back away. "How's this for trouble?"

Rivaille didn't so much as blink. "Lady Killian, please—"

A cruel *clang* vibrated through the hall as metal met metal. Luna's mouth parted at the enormous sword that had appeared in Rivaille's hands. She hadn't even seen him draw it. Had he really been so fast?

"This is most unnecessary," said Rivaille, his gaze bored.

"Does it look like I care?" said Eirene, her knives braced in a cross above her head. At his unimpressed stare, she sighed. "Fine." She seemed to withdraw, but at the last second, she kneed him in the crotch. *Hard.* Luna thought Rivaille was done for, but he only let out a quiet *oomph* and staggered back one step before grabbing Eirene's collar and hoisting her high into the air, leaving her to claw and kick and curse uselessly.

"Damn," Eirene said in resignation, her feet dangling. "I swore I had it that time."

Rivaille released her and tugged at his cuffs. "You've wrinkled my shirt."

Luna buried her face in her hands in disbelief. She wondered if she had been transported into some alternate reality. *I want to go home*, she thought, but then she remembered that this *was* her home now. And these . . . these ruffians were to be her new guards, her new friends.

This uncivilized behavior simply won't do, she meant to scold. It was something her mother might say, with her brow pinched and her chin tipped loftily. Instead, what came out was, "What in hell is *wrong* with you people?"

Their eyes snapped to her. At least they had the grace to look slightly contrite.

Adrianna's words suddenly echoed in her mind. *While we may have been born royal*, her aunt had said, *we are all human, and thus deserve to be treated with the same level of respect.*

Luna took a deep breath. "A-apologies. I didn't mean to sound so harsh. The three of you took me by surprise, that's all. I'm grateful for your service and look forward to getting to know each of you better."

"We must be a little different to your usual crowd," Kane said quietly.

"Yes," Luna murmured. "But perhaps that's not such a bad thing." She cocked her head, an idea popping up as she watched Rivaille and Eirene tuck away their weapons. "Actually . . ." *My crowd didn't let me do much fighting.* "I know my father hired you to guard me, but what would you say to teaching me a thing or two about combat? I'd hate to be defenseless if you had to leave me behind on another errand for the king."

Kane hesitated, but Eirene only shrugged. "Sounds like fun," she said. "But fighting—and fighting *well*—is no easy thing, Princess. So you can't complain when we work you too hard." Eirene shot her a devilish wink. "Deal?"

That brought a smile to Luna's face. "I would expect nothing less."

CHAPTER TEN

Between seven Elites, one captain, and one omnifinate, Asterin felt fairly confident that they could handle this.

Slight emphasis on *fairly.*

Silas lay frozen in a block of ice about a foot thick in every direction. The Elites encircled him in two tiers—Gino, Hayley, and Alicia took up the front line with their light affinities, and the others stood ready behind them.

Eadric finished his second jog around the training hall, double-checking that all the doors were bolted shut. The three training halls were located in the basement, so luckily they had no windows to worry about. "Good to go, Your Majesty!"

"Good," said Asterin. "Light-wielders, commence."

Hayley, Alicia, and Gino raised their affinity stones, their palms facing Silas. "*Volumnus,*" they shouted as one.

Beams of glaring light radiated from their stones toward the center of the room, brightening exponentially and filling every inch of the hall. Asterin squeezed her eyes shut, but even then it flooded her head, setting her vision aglow like the sun. And still—*still*, the world grew brighter, until she had to rub tears from her clenched lids.

"Move in!" she heard Hayley order, and the light finally began to recede.

Asterin pried her eyes open and blinked away the spots dancing across her vision. The rays folded in on themselves, enclosing Silas in a coffin of pure white light, only the faintest glimmer of his silhouette visible.

"There!" yelled Alicia just as Asterin caught a glimpse of darkness amid the light, writhing just beneath the surface of Silas's skin.

Chaos.

It shied away, trying to retreat—except that it had nowhere to go, no darkness to hide in.

Asterin leaned forward in horrified fascination as the Chaos spasmed, overflowing into the individual strands of Silas's hair, decaying blond to black. It muddied his irises and lips, as though trying frantically to break out of any orifice possible. Bile rose in her throat when it burst past his irises, running beneath his skin and down his cheeks in rivulets of dark pus.

Eadric raised his arm. "Laurel, Casper, now!"

While Casper melted a tiny opening through the ice, Laurel conjured a dome of rock directly above it. Ice and stone melded as one, all gaps sealed save for the single hole leading straight into the dome.

Just as they had planned, the Chaos surged through the opening, vacating Silas's body completely in favor of the shelter of Laurel's dome.

The dome shuddered. Fractures raced down the sides, but Laurel simply gritted her teeth and repaired the cracks as fast as they appeared. Nicole stepped forth to aid her, but it was only a matter of time before the dome collapsed.

Asterin cursed internally and braced herself. Frost crackled overhead. "Eadric!"

He nodded, clasping his affinity stone between his palms. "Release, Laurel!"

With a gasp, Laurel fell to her knees and let the dome disintegrate.

The Chaos exploded forth, under the guise of finally escaping—only to find itself trapped yet again. Except this time, Asterin had forged it a prison of crystalline ice instead of rock, and the light shone through as brightly as before.

Like clockwork, Nicole raised her windstone and summoned a mighty squall to shove Silas's block of ice to safety. Casper and Alicia placed their hands on the ice to thaw it with their fire affinities.

The air began to shake. Not the walls, or the ceiling, or even the floor.

She could see the *air* itself in ripples around her, first in long waves that soon shortened and vibrated through space.

"Eadric—"

"That's not me," he said uneasily.

It took her a moment to realize that the Chaos was emitting the strange ripples. As a precaution, she conjured an energy shield, but the ripples passed right through. One ghosted her shoulder. Pain splintered from her collarbone and spread down her arm. Bruises unfurled in swirling blotches of blue and purple beneath her skin. But the only way those ripples could be passing through her shield was . . .

"It's wielding pure energy," Asterin hollered just as a huge wave surged from the Chaos and crashed into an unknowing Eadric.

She swore she could hear the cracking of his bones.

Asterin dodged a ripple and sprinted for him, catching him just as he crumpled forward and lowering him gently to the ground.

"*Immortals*," he gasped, his voice wracked with agony.

"Look out!" Casper yelled, giving Asterin just enough time to duck beneath another ripple. The Elite brandished his affinity stone and attempted unsuccessfully to divert some of the ripples with his air-affinity. The other Elites retreated as far as possible, to where the waves waned and decayed into nothing.

"We have to come up with a new plan," Asterin informed Eadric, her heart hammering. By some miracle, the ice surrounding Chaos was still intact, but she knew it must be weakening. "You can't even move on your own."

"No," Eadric hissed. "We need to finish this, now. Look at it. It's unstable. Like it's struggling to hold itself together." He met her gaze, eyes bright with pain and resolve. "Just try and figure out a way to keep those waves away from me."

Asterin bit her lip. "Fine. But we can't do anything about the waves. The best we can do is heal on the go." She cupped her hands around her mouth. "I need my three strongest healers on Eadric! *Quickly!*"

The Elites helped Eadric sit upright, healing him all the while. "Here goes," he groaned, his features twisted in pain. "*Peneretrae.*"

A peculiar buzz crept through the air, intensifying until her skull rattled with it. A piercing whine drilled the air. Several Elites clapped their hands over their ears, but no one could tear their eyes away from the Chaos. It began to split, every division revealing Eadric's magic coursing and crackling within its being. One by one, like puddles of oil frying in a pan, each section vaporized.

Eadric swore through clenched teeth, every inch of his body so charged up with electricity that strands of Laurel's ponytail stuck to his skin. "Asterin, now!"

A *bang* like a cannon blast ripped through the air as Asterin cleaved the ice prison in half to expose the last of the Chaos. Static bit her skin, crackling outward. The Chaos exploded, globules of slick black sludge splattering in every direction. Before it had the chance to re-form, the light-wielding Elites devoured every last speck in blistering effulgence worthy of the sun.

Eadric's chest went rigid. He toppled forward, and it took the combined strength of three Elites plus Asterin to keep him from face-planting into the floor. They laid him out on the ground, wincing from the literal after-shocks of his magic.

The moment the coast was clear, the other Elites bundled Silas off to the infirmary.

Once they whisked him away, Asterin set to work on Eadric, running her hands along his body while muttering healing spells. She had just mended the last fractured rib when the main door opened and her mother slipped in.

Elyssa came to kneel beside her. She brushed Eadric's forehead, only to recoil with a yelp when he gave her a nasty shock. "Will he be all right?" she asked, rubbing her fingers together.

Asterin nodded and suddenly noticed the letter in her mother's lap. "What's that?"

Her mother handed it to her. "See for yourself."

Asterin took it, immediately zoning in on the Eradorian seal stamped on the envelope—a green serpent entwined around a winged trident. She ripped it open, only to realize that the message had been written on the inside of the envelope itself.

Two simple words.

He's awake.

It was a good thing that she was already on her knees. She read those two words again and again. Euphoric laughter bubbled from her lips, shaking her entire frame as she pressed the envelope into her chest like a piece of driftwood that had saved her from drowning at sea. Still laughing, she threw her arms around her mother. Elyssa smiled into her shoulder and hugged her tighter.

They parted when Eadric hacked out a few coughs. He squinted at Asterin and croaked, "What? What is it?"

She waved the envelope at him, all too aware of the enormous weight she had borne for months finally lifting from her shoulders. "Pack your bags. We've got a ship to catch."

His eyes widened. "You mean . . . ?"

"Yes." Asterin grinned at him. "To Eradore." *To Quinlan.* "To Eradore, at last."

CHAPTER ELEVEN

Harry woke with a start when the sleijh very ungraciously dumped his body onto the ground in front of the entrance to the Shadow Palace. Below loomed the mighty thousand-step staircase that led up to the doors to King Eoin's fortress, hewn from black quartz. In his disoriented state, he almost rolled right off the landing.

A ghoul guarding the entrance approached, eyeing him as he teetered onto his feet, its face an asymmetrical array of features adorned with shards of jewels implanted just beneath the surface of its gray skin.

"Identify yourself," the ghoul rasped, pointed teeth clicking together at the end of every syllable.

Harry held up one limp finger and promptly projectile vomited onto the ghoul's face. He wiped his mouth and squinted woozily. "So sorry about that."

The ghoul wiped a dozen gaunt fingers across its face and shot Harry a murderous glare. "Your blood would have worked perfectly well, anygné, but thank you for that. Have you an audience with His Kingship?"

Such insolence. He bared his teeth in answer, a guttural growl ripping low from his throat. As if he didn't know that the moment he disappeared into the palace, the ghoul would slime over to some underground market to sell Harry's words for more jewels. "None of your business and you know it."

The ghoul's chin quivered. "Very well. Apologies. I shall make His Kingship aware of your presence."

"No need." Harry turned on his heel with as much grace as he could muster, his legs only swaying a little. Or so he hoped. "S'not like he doesn't already know I'm here," he muttered once the ghoul was out of earshot.

Every time was a first time when Harry wandered into the Shadow Palace. New hallways appeared and old hallways shifted at the capricious whims of a bored god. Mysterious doorways and windows skirted along the walls in a masquerade dance to an ever-changing tune, and only the King of Immortals held the conductor's baton.

Today, Harry recognized the hallway he first entered. One of his favorites, in fact, and perhaps Eoin knew it. Miles and miles of velveteen, midnight carpet stretched out before him, a vast ocean that billowed around his feet as he trudged along it. *Welcome home*, it seemed to say. Harry glanced skyward, squinting through the mists until they parted to reveal the clusters of Mortal Realm constellations bejeweling the impossibly high ceiling above.

He closed his eyes and inhaled the scent of damp grass and pine needles. *Ah*, he thought to himself with a bitter smile. *Finally*. The true effects of the absynthe were kicking in. Within a heartbeat, he could feel the earth of the Aswiyre Forest cradling his body, and a sly breeze shivering across the clearing to tickle his hair.

"That one was named after me," said Orion, pointing at the night heavens.

"Really?" asked Harry, just to humor him, lying spread eagle at Orion's side with the cottage at their feet. The chirrup of night insects and the rustling of leaves filled the air, and if he strained, he could just make out Eadric's snores rolling out of the cottage's second-floor window.

Orion snickered. "Of course not. That is my sword he's holding, though. Orondite, I mean."

Harry stayed transfixed on the stars as their fingertips brushed yet again. "Looks like a shapeless blob to me."

"Me too, honestly," Orion whispered.

Harry turned his face to gaze at Orion, his voice full of mirth, and teased, "Actually, I can see the resemblance now." He burst into laughter when Orion's jaw dropped in outrage. "I'm kidding."

A grudging smile. "Hmph. I'll let you have that one."

Their conversation lulled with the wind and they simply basked in the tranquility of one another's company. Harry stole furtive glances at the Guardian, admiring the way the starlight bestowed an extra twinkle in his glacial-blue gaze, the pearlescent sheen it gave to his cheeks and goldspun locks.

He had wanted to lean over to look closer.

He had wanted to lean over and kiss him.

But the moment he finally gathered enough courage to prop himself onto his elbow, Orion sat up and said, "We should head in. Early start and all." He grinned at Harry. "Maybe tomorrow we'll finally slaughter that stupid demon."

"Haha," said Harry automatically, hating every single cell of his own pathetic being. Stupid demon, indeed. "Maybe."

Even now, he could still remember how flustered he had been when Orion bade him a good night. How badly he had wanted to reach out and touch, to claim. And how *scared*—to offer himself, to risk. To even . . . dare to feel.

The memory dissipated by the time Harry reached the end of the hallway, less substantial than the mists overhead. What he would have given for it to be real. To *make* it real.

But it was too late.

No matter how much he drank or how many times he dreamed, it wouldn't change the fact that Orion was gone and Harry could never get him back.

A strangled cry of rage clawed out of his throat. He pulled his fist back and punched the wall to his left. All he succeeded in doing was shattering his bones, but they would heal anyway, so he pulled back his other fist and took another punch. He broke himself on the wall again and again, healing indefinitely. His shoulders shook, half from fury and half in agony. Like a rock plunging into the sea, he slipped into the depths of self-loathing, the disgust. He struck with all his strength, until hairline fractures spread across the black stone.

"What in the world," came a velvety purr at his shoulder, lower than the rumble of thunder, "did that poor wall ever do to you?"

Harry whirled around and found himself a mere inch away from the face of the God of Shadow. He lowered his eyes immediately and sank to his knees. "My king."

Eoin caressed the wall and mended the cracks with no more than a wisp of a will. He placed a hand on Harry's head. "I never thought you capable of such mania, dearest."

Harry lifted his gaze just past his lashes. He allowed his eyes to darken, to fill with the desire to please, and licked his lips. "Apologies, my king."

"Hm," Eoin murmured with a feline smile Harry knew all too well. The king crouched down to his level and looked him in the—

His *eyes.*

Harry tried to hide his shock at the startlingly blue irises, as clear and bright as ice.

"I forgive you, of course," Eoin went on, unnoticing. "As always." His crown of butterflies glinted atop his head. Little thorn vines snaked through his onyx curls, hanging with glistening blackberries. The thorns grew and receded in time with the god's breaths, blooming with tiny white flowers every time he smiled. "How have you—"

"Eo?" interrupted a voice at their back.

Harry's blood froze.

That voice.

No, he thought numbly. *Not possible. Not possible.*

"Ah," said Eoin while Harry kept his head down. "There you are. Would you like to meet one of my shadowlings? Come closer now, don't be shy. On your feet, Harry."

Somehow, Harry found it within himself to rise, albeit stutteringly, and guide his body in a half rotation so he could stare right at . . .

At . . .

"Orion," Harry rasped, softer than a dying breath.

Eoin's brows rose in mild interest. "You know him?"

Harry ignored him. *Almighty Immortals,* he thought, his chest clench-ing. *It's really him.* He had *found* him—no, Orion had found *Harry*—right here, of all places, alive and perfectly whole. "Orion," he said again, reverent.

A hesitant pause, followed by a small, unsure smile. "That's me."

At once, a hurricane of thoughts descended upon Harry—what was he doing here? And with Eoin? Was he hurt? When had he arrived at the palace? Next came all of the words—the regret, the guilt, the devotion— that he had kept bottled deep inside of him, threatening to erupt right then and there, Eoin be damned.

Harry stepped forward without a care for courage, beyond terrified that this was some sort of trick, some sort of hallucination or phantom from the absynthe that would evaporate at an exhale the slightest too strong. Beyond terrified that he would lose his chance again. He took Orion's hands in his own.

Orion cocked his head to the side, a puzzled crinkle appearing between his brows. And then he asked Harry the simple question that destroyed everything. "But who are you?"

CHAPTER TWELVE

Luna paced outside King Jakob's chambers, wringing her hands.

Did I overstep?

He hadn't spoken to her in days. Adrianna assured her that he had a lot of work piling up, but it still felt like he might be avoiding her. She saw him briefly at the odd meal or two, but nothing more.

She paused in front of the door.

Knock, Luna, she told herself, glancing around the empty, guardless corridor. *Just knock. He might not even be inside.*

From afar came the sound of stomping, a hollow *clomp-click* of heeled boots.

"—foul bastard. I hope one day he chokes on the *shit* he spews out of his mouth. I hope—"

As the stomper approached, the stream of curses never faltering for even a breath, Luna's eyes widened. She darted to the other end of the corridor and ducked around the corner. *Killian?*

The hireling stormed around the corner and skidded to a halt before the king's chambers. She lifted her leg like a hound relieving itself and kicked the door thrice, the deafening *bangs* nearly startling Luna senseless. When the door didn't open immediately, Killian snorted and spun on her heel, heading back the way she came.

The doors swung inward, and King Jakob's deep voice boomed out. "Heel."

The girl spat yet another swear at the floor but obeyed. On her way, her eyes flicked beyond the king—to Luna's hiding spot.

Crap, Luna thought, jerking back, but Killian's step didn't waver, and the doors slammed shut a second later.

Despite every rational voice in her head urging her to leave, Luna's feet shuffled closer to the door. She swallowed. With painstaking caution, she braced her palms on the frigid stone and pressed her ear to its surface.

She had only been in her father's chambers once before. She remembered having to crane her neck just to drink in the high ceilings, submerged in gloom both from torchlight and the lack of windows. From her memory, she imagined Killian and her father in the barren sitting parlor, adorned with a chaise and a low table by the unlit fireplace.

Thwack.

Luna recoiled, her mind racing. Had her father struck the girl? Her eyes darted around the hallway, searching for another way in, one hand gingerly testing the door handle. The king had left it unlocked. She reached into her pocket for her illusionstone.

Thwack. Thwack.

"Are you quite done?" Jakob thundered.

Luna took a deep breath and cloaked herself into invisibility. Then she conjured a replica of the door to overlap with the real door, so that when she inched the actual door open, her illusion allowed it to appear as though it remained shut. After toeing off her slippers, she wedged one into the doorway to keep it propped ajar. Her stockinged feet were silent on the stone floor, but she strayed no farther than a foot from the entrance in case she needed to make a quick getaway.

King Jakob stood like an unmovable pillar in the center of the parlor with his back to Luna. Before him, Killian stood on the chaise, twirling one of her strange knives. Three more knives were embedded in the table between them.

The king exhaled through his nostrils. "Eirene—"

Killian hurled the blade. It buried hilt-deep into the table. *THWACK.* "Call me that again," she hissed with such venom that Luna took an involuntary step back, "and I'll aim my next dagger somewhere new. Somewhere *softer*, if you get my drift."

Luna clenched her fists. And to think that she had been worried about the *hireling's* well-being—

Her father didn't flinch. "Very well, anygné."

Shock rippled through Luna. She gaped first at Killian, and then her father. Her pulse raced as she stumbled backward, a thousand questions bombarding her mind.

The king went on. "How did your meeting with the princess—"

The hireling sniffed the air. "Did you lock the door?"

Jakob frowned. "No. Why?" He turned around to face Luna, his eyes searching the room.

Though he never quite found her invisible stare, it was enough. Luna backed away as quickly as she could, but in her haste to flee, she nearly tripped over the slipper she had left in the door. It skidded into the hallway with a soft *fwish*. Her father's brow furrowed. Just before the real door fully closed, she saw him striding toward her. She bent over to grab the slippers and ran for her life.

Jakob poked his head outside. "Who goes there?" the king called, but she had already reached the end of the corridor and flung herself around the corner, out of sight.

Her heart threatened to explode out of her chest as she threw her back against the stone wall, fingers scrabbling against the rough-hewn edges. She panted, open-mouthed and silent, still certain that Killian or her father were coming for her.

She thanked all of her stars when the door slammed shut once more.

When her breathing slowed, she chanced a peek around the corner. To her relief, the corridor lay empty.

She sighed and bent to put her slippers back on only to realize that she only clutched one. With dawning horror, she stole a glance around the corner, scanning the hallway outside the king's chambers for the missing slipper. The completely empty hallway which had brought her relief only moments before now filled her with dread.

The other slipper—the one she must have accidentally dropped in her haste to escape—had vanished.

Killian had wrested her knives out of the table and laid them in a neat little row by the time Jakob returned, a lone silk slipper hanging from his fingertips.

That brought a smile to her face.

Jakob glowered at her. "Why the sudden cheer?"

Killian shrugged. "Nothing. She's growing into her fate, that's all."

The air grew thick. One step at a time, he drew closer, looming overhead as if he meant to intimidate her. "What is that supposed to mean?"

Oh, she was enjoying this. "Nothing, I said!" She wiggled her eyebrows. "Yet."

Jakob's menacing expression made her want to laugh aloud. "What do you want, demon?"

She stroked her chin and hummed. "To start, a new room would be lovely."

"What's wrong with your current one?"

She thought of the cramped, windowless room he'd given her and resisted the urge to stab him. At least the God of Shadow had given her a mansion to call her own. "*Nothing*," she mocked with a sarcastic little smile.

He got the point. "It is done."

She wondered what else she could barter for, but her only other desire was a freedom that he could not grant, so she relented. "Your bastard daughter is shadow-kissed."

Oh, how she savored the way he froze.

"What do you mean, *shadow-kissed*?" To her growing delight, he paled. "Like . . . like *you*?"

At that, her lips stretched into a rabid grin. She snapped her teeth at him just to see his face pinch. "Yes, like *me*."

The King of Ibreseos fell silent. She watched in curiosity as he lumbered over to his single, pathetic chaise and sat down heavily, bracing his elbows on his knees. "How . . ." he began hoarsely. He cleared his throat. "How do you know?"

Killian examined her nails. "Shadow magic leaves a signature. Whether a person has wielded it herself or has been subjected to it, you can always find some remnant. Or rather, anygnés can. In our case, King Eoin's shadow sigil burns above their head." She pointed to the air above herself. "Sometimes it fades after a few years. Sometimes it doesn't fade at all."

Jakob rubbed his temple. "So what exactly does this mean?"

"It means that the wretched woman you fornicated with to produce Luna bargained for shadow magic in exchange for your poor daughter's eternal service." Killian could hardly contain her glee when she glimpsed the fury in the king's eyes. His next words, however, surprised her.

"I knew that already." His fists clenched and unclenched in his lap. "I meant . . . what does this mean for *her*?"

She raised an eyebrow. "Do you actually care?"

"Of course. She's my daughter."

She snorted. "Oh, yes, the one you didn't know existed until a few weeks ago. Silly me—"

"Silence, demon," the king commanded, and she felt her lips lock, the words in her throat evaporating. She tried to snarl, her tongue numb and useless in her mouth, but he had rendered her utterly mute. "I paid a price for your obedience. Far more than it was worth, it seems. Even so, no matter what way you wish to look at it, you are in my debt. I freed you from King Eoin."

And bound me in chains of your own, Killian thought bitterly. *Sold— no, loaned—by one monster to another.*

As if reading her thoughts, he sighed. "You may speak."

"Eoin will come for her on the day the darkness shrouds all light," she told him. "He will steal her away to a place you can never follow." She began resheathing her daggers one at a time, smiling to herself. "You'd better have your little tea parties with her while you still can. She won't be around for much longer. I'd guess a few weeks, at the most, but I'm not very good at telling time anymore."

Jakob swallowed. "How can I stop this?"

Her smile stretched until her face hurt. She stared down at him and whispered, "You *can't*," letting her magic carry her voice to ghost along his ears.

"Stop that," he ordered, and her magic dissolved in a heartbeat, snatched from her so quickly that it left her gasping. "Respect me, Eirene, and I will grant you more freedom than you could ever wish for."

Her final knife flew out of her hand and lodged in the chaise between Jakob's legs. His eyes widened at the wickedly serrated edge buried a mere inch from his crotch.

"Whoops," she said sweetly. "My hand slipped."

Slowly, the king met her eyes, his expression glacial. "You cannot harm me."

"No," Killian murmured. "I suppose not." She snapped her fingers and the dagger whizzed back into her palm, leaving only a deep gouge in the cushion. *Just an inch farther*, she lamented. At her command, the chaise coughed out dust and stuffing all over the king's lap.

His brow scrunched in disgust.

She sauntered toward the doors to his chambers to let herself out. At the last moment, she couldn't restrain herself and poked her head back in. She tilted her chin to the side, memorizing every detail—from the defeated slouch of his spine to the displeased curve of his mouth—and grinned. "But someone else always could."

With that, she slammed the door behind her and ambled away.

CHAPTER THIRTEEN

Asterin departed her chambers just as dawn slipped its rosy fingers through her curtains, trailing streaks of pink along her walls. The encounter with the Chaos had left her drained, and for the first time in weeks, she had managed a full night of sleep. Perhaps it had more to do with Rose's news, but either way, she strode out of the palace and toward the stables with a spring in her step.

The forthcoming journey to Prydell wouldn't be easy—with winter around the corner, they would have no choice but to travel mostly over land, which, compared to sailing through the Nord Sea, would likely triple the length of their trip. Temperatures in the north were dropping, and ice formed rapidly into what could become unnavigable floes.

Dressed in a thick, high-collared coat of midnight wool embroidered with silver thread and her cloak snug on her shoulders, Asterin let herself into Lux's stable and saddled her own steed while the stable hands readied the other horses. Her Iphovien stallion nuzzled her palm and huffed softly.

"Planning to leave without us?" called out a voice, and she turned to see Eadric heading into the stables with Casper, Nicole, and Gino in tow. They all wore fearsome black, their signature double-sided cloaks turned inside out to match. Somehow, Gino had slicked his hair taller than usual, Casper was flipping a switchblade in each hand with dazzling grace as he walked, and Nicole . . . well, Nicole hovered between them, a phantom breeze, silent and lethal as always.

Asterin snorted. "As if. You would have tracked me down and flayed me alive."

The captain gave her a firm nod, his onyx eyes glinting like syrup in the fiery light of the sunrise. "Damn right, I would."

They set off down the wide garden path leading to the Wall on horseback. A wave of nostalgia washed over Asterin—another journey not months after the last, and only she and Eadric remained from their former six. The realization made her stomach clench with sudden foreboding, but she shoved it down. Nothing short of the end of the world would keep her from Eradoris.

Her mother awaited her in front of the gate with an entourage of her own guards, all hand-picked by Eadric and hopefully more trustworthy than Priscilla's and Garringsford's rotten batch.

Asterin swung out of the saddle. "Sorry for waking you up so early."

Elyssa embraced her tightly. "I didn't sleep much, anyway." She glanced past Asterin's shoulder. "Are you sure three Elites is enough? Surely more would be safer."

Asterin shook her head. "We would just draw more attention on the roads."

"And is it really wise to camp near the road instead of an inn?"

"An inn would be a waste of time," Asterin told her gently. "Plus, last time we were attacked *at* an inn. We'll rotate shifts, keep alert. Stop worrying, we'll be just fine."

"But—"

"Mother," Asterin cut off, voice firm.

Elyssa's chin dropped. "I'm sorry. I know it's not my place." She raised her gaze. "I just . . . I can't bear to lose you again."

Asterin gave her another hug, realizing with a start that she actually stood a few inches taller than her mother. Somehow, she hadn't noticed until now. "You won't," she murmured, kissing her cheek. "However, I will be gone for three weeks. And in case something comes up . . ." She knelt down and reached up to grasp her mother's hands, much to Elyssa's confusion. "In my absence, please act in my stead. I trust you to make any decisions in the best interests of the kingdom, and as such, I declare you as Queen Regent of Axaria."

"Asterin—" breathed Elyssa, her eyes wide.

Asterin smiled wryly. "This is non-negotiable." She had left her kingdom in the wrong hands once before, and she refused to make the same mistake again. "I know I can trust you." At the doubt still lingering in her mother's expression, she sighed. "Please. For . . . for Quinlan."

At that, her mother's jaw set. She nodded firmly. "For Quinlan." They embraced once more, and then Asterin mounted Lux and kicked him into a gallop, not allowing herself a backward glance until they made it well past the Wall and down the mountain. Only then did she look up, but already the figures standing beneath the gate had diminished to indistinguishable specks.

They took the southwest road. Though it was slightly crowded from Axaris-bound merchants freshly docked from Eyvindr and Prydell, the morning was still young enough for them to make decent time.

As if sensing her urgency, Lux pressed on, ever swiftly, forcing the others to keep up. Fields of rust-and-gold wheat shimmered past, rustling alongside treetops darkening with the ripening of autumn. Every now and then they flew by steel ponds as still as glass, tinged silver from the sky's reflection above. Daylight bled into the thick cotton-clumped clouds before finally piercing through, thrusting spears of cold white light upon them. Like an awakening, the air tasted sharper, sweeter. Asterin let out a slow, hot exhale, wetting lips chapped from the wind, and leaned lower in the saddle. She savored the heat coursing through her veins despite the air's chill, and spurred Lux even faster, her stallion responding with a burst of speed that left the others in the dust.

Even when the clouds blackened and swelled with rain, Asterin still resisted finding a place to set up camp. Only when the drizzle became a violent deluge, sheets of water slamming into their faces, did she finally surrender. At her signal, the five of them cut into the pine forest at their right, slowing to a walk and blinking the rain out of their eyes.

Casper helped her dry off the horses and all of their clothes with his fire affinity while Eadric draped tarps over dripping boughs. They ate a simple dinner of dried venison and cheese on bread. They fell asleep to the constant drum of the pelting rain and hit the road again before the sun came up.

Asterin pulled up next to Eadric and called out over the thunder of hooves. "At this rate, we'll reach Orielle just after tomorrow's sunrise!"

Eadric dipped his chin once. He threw two fingers into the air and whistled. His eyes flicked to her as the Elites pushed their steeds faster. "We'll get you to Eradore, Asterin. No matter what it takes, it will be done."

Asterin swallowed the sudden lump in her throat and nodded in thanks. Beside her, Argo let out a snort and drove past Lux to take the lead.

"Come on, then, Your Majesty!" Casper yelled above the wind from Argo's saddle. "You're falling behind!"

Asterin grinned and shouted back at him. "I'm just giving you a head start!" A moment later, Lux trumpeted a terrifying whinny and shot forward, overtaking Argo in a few easy strides. She let out a laugh at Casper's disbelieving gape.

Wait for me, Quinlan, she thought to herself as her kingdom flew by. *We're coming. No matter what it takes.*

CHAPTER FOURTEEN

P *link, ping-ping.*
   "A silver note?" Luna guessed, the blindfold rustling against her ears as she tilted her head.

"Good," Adrianna replied. Three days ago, Luna had walked into their daily training session and declared that she wanted to practice auditory production. Her mentor hadn't even blinked. "And this?"

The same sound, but pitched much lower, which meant . . .

"A gold note," said Luna, pushing off her blindfold. "Since it's heavier."

Adrianna began gathering a handful of coins off the table. Copper and bronze pieces, silver and gold notes. She held up a gold note. "Keep your objectives clear. Replicate the sound."

Luna squinted at the coin.

Plink, plonk-plonk.

Adrianna grinned. "Close enough. And the copper piece?"

A hollow sort of clanking, Luna reminded herself, and replicated. Before Adrianna could ask, she conjured an illusion of the coin—these days, it was easier than plucking a leaf off a tree. The coin fell from her fingers, catching the light, and clattered onto the table, accompanied by sounds she fabricated herself.

Adrianna sighed. "Not bad, sweetheart, but the timing is off." When

Luna tried again, her aunt clucked. "Don't forget that *you* control the actions of your illusions. You might not be able to foresee the movement or bounce or spin of a real coin, but your illusions exist to serve your intentions. So command them."

Luna let that message sink in. The next coin drop brought a smile to Adrianna's face.

A knock interrupted them.

"I'll get it," said Adrianna, stalking over to the door.

Luna picked up a bronze piece and let it roll off her fingertips. As it plummeted, she concealed it—and its sound—in a veil of illusion, so that when it supposedly hit the table, it may as well have vanished into thin air.

"Ah, Your Royal Majesty."

Luna spun around to find her father standing in the doorway.

Her breath stuttered when she caught sight of the familiar slipper he grasped in both hands.

"Please, Adrianna, if you would leave us for a moment." King Jakob gestured outside. "My daughter and I must have a little chat."

Her aunt's eyes flicked between the two of them, her expression unreadable. Luna pleaded silently for her father's fiancée to—well, she didn't know, exactly, but anything other than desert her and leave her trapped and guilty and alone with her father.

But in the end, Adrianna strode out of the room, rising onto her tiptoes to kiss Jakob's cheek on her way. She cast Luna a final, cryptic sidelong glance over her shoulder before disappearing from view.

The door clicked shut. Luna averted her gaze, looking anywhere and everywhere but at her father. Desperately, she wondered if she could somehow conjure a talking apparatus of herself or something equally ridiculous and escape—

"Lunarissa," said King Jakob quietly.

Luna's eyes snapped to him. "What?"

Gently, he placed the incriminating slipper on the table between them. "On one of my naval expeditions as a young man, I stayed for two fortnights on the island of Qris. There, I found a beautiful flower that bloomed only in shadow." She stood, frozen, as his fingers brushed her chin and tilted her face up, his azure eyes solemn. "It was called a *lunarissa*. Or, in the mortal tongue—"

"Moonflower," Luna breathed, remembering the nickname her foster siblings had once called her, long ago, before she had ended up in Axaria. Before she had met Asterin.

"Yes," said Jakob. "Priscilla was wrong when she said I didn't want to have a child. I just didn't want to have a child with *her*." Luna winced despite herself. He waved a hand through the air. "She was the spark to my fuse, and she made me brash and brazen—neither desirable traits for the ruler of a kingdom. Marrying her would have bound us in ways the throne would not allow."

Luna stared at him. "So . . ."

"All I mean is that . . ." Her father trailed off, rubbing the back of his neck. "I don't want you to feel unloved."

Her next exhale shuddered out of her lungs. *Unloved.* She summoned a smile. "I felt nothing of the sort, Father. But thank you for your sentiments."

"How much did you overhear?" the king questioned, tipping his chin at the slipper.

Luna wondered if it was worth denying ownership of the damned thing. But Adrianna had gifted them to her personally, so the lie would likely come back to bite her. Instead, she asked, "Why didn't you tell me that Lady Killian was a shadow demon? Doesn't that pose a risk to my safety?"

"She is under my absolute command," her father assured her. "So you have nothing to worry about."

Sure, Luna thought to herself, restraining an eye roll. *And mice needn't fear cats so long as they play friends.* "I thought only King Eoin could control anygnés."

Her father gave her a look of interest. "How did you know that?"

"I knew one," she replied. "We met him in the Aswiyre Forest."

Jakob stroked his chin. "Ah, yes . . . Harry. Adrianna mentioned him." He paused. "What about your other friends? Have you kept in contact with them?"

"My friends?" Of course, she'd previously mentioned Asterin to her father, though her name still felt raw passing Luna's lips. "I-I'd rather not talk about them." The letters from the Queen of Axaria had arrived by the dozen. She kept all of them in a box on her shelf. Unopened. Waiting. She had only replied to three of Eadric's letters, and all of a sudden she realized that she had no idea if Orion was even alive or not. *Let him be safe*, she prayed to the Immortals.

"Luna," her father said so sternly that her entire body stiffened. "What Queen Asterin did to you was unjust and—"

"*Unjust*," Luna spat, the anger bubbling up and boiling over so rapidly that she nearly choked. "She picked some *boy* she knew for a few months over me."

"And that is why I let Eadric save you."

Her brow crinkled. "What do you mean?"

"Love makes people irrational, Luna. Asterin never meant to hurt you, but she didn't love you for who you are—only *what* you were to her."

Her throat tightened at the sting of his words. *I was her best friend*, she wanted to say, but then she found the sense in her father's words. "I was there for her whenever she needed me," she mumbled. "Always."

Hesitantly, her father patted her head. "And this . . . boy? Quinlan? What was his relationship with her?"

"They'll marry someday, I'm sure." A bitter smile rose to her face. "Who knows? He might even try to propose the very next time he sees her."

Her father raised an eyebrow at that. "The Prince of Eradore and the Queen of Axaria?"

"And obviously she'll say yes," Luna went on, squinting at the floor as her vision blurred slightly. "It'll be so lovely. Of course it will be. They're perfect together."

The king squeezed her shoulder. Through her unshed tears, his face had smeared, twisting into something almost inhuman. "For what it's worth, I believe that Asterin failed her duty to you as queen—or princess, at the time. As her subject, she should have protected you with all of her ability. Not Prince Quinlan."

She glowered at him. "You're making me feel worse."

"And yet," he went on as if she hadn't spoken, "you would have done anything to protect her, without a care for yourself, or even Eadric Covington."

"*Still* making it worse."

He shook his head impatiently. "My point, daughter, is that you would make a much better queen than Asterin could ever be. And someday, you will." She whipped up to stare at him, shocked at his words and the staggering gravity they brought upon her future. Before she could even begin to scramble for a response, he asked, "What punishment should befall Queen Asterin for such a betrayal? Especially considering that, besides being responsible for her kingdom and its people, including you, she was also your dearest friend. So, tell me, daughter . . . what fate does she deserve?"

Struck speechless, Luna couldn't help but ponder his question. Of course she was bitter. And hurt. Yet . . . she could not bring herself to respond. But what was stopping her?

At her expression, her father sighed. "Would you like to know the reason I was so enraptured by the lunarissae on the island?"

She nodded slowly.

"There was a volcanic eruption a few decades ago," he told her. "It annihilated most of the wildlife, but against all odds, the lunarissae survived. They thrived, in fact, just as they always had, even without the light of the sun or the stars."

Luna glanced up, a small ember of warmth expanding in her chest.

"Your mother chose your name very wisely," her father said quietly. "I think it suits you perfectly."

She was the spark to my fuse, and she made me brash and brazen— neither desirable traits for the ruler of a kingdom.

New purpose blossomed within Luna. *I'm doing this for Asterin,* she promised herself. "Asterin and Quinlan deserve happiness," she said. Her father remained silent. "But . . ." Her heart hammered against her ribcage. *Am I really doing this?* "To be willing to sacrifice not just a friend but a subject of her own kingdom is unspeakable. Asterin would never have dreamed of such disloyalty before she met Quinlan," Luna insisted. "He changed her into someone new. Someone unsuitable for the throne. And

I would never want that for her. I . . . I almost think that they would both be better off alone. Without each other."

At that, King Jakob leaned forward and pressed a kiss to her brow. "I understand. Everything will be taken care of, daughter, have no fear."

Taken care of. Luna swallowed, mouth acrid, and forced a smile. "Thank you, Father," she said, without even knowing what exactly she was thanking him for.

Without another word, the king swept out of the room. He left the single slipper behind. A reminder? A threat? Or nothing at all?

Once the door closed behind him, she exhaled shakily, her strength leaving her so abruptly that she had to brace herself against the table to keep from collapsing. Only then did the horror sink in.

Immortals.

What had she done?

CHAPTER FIFTEEN

It had been three years since Asterin had last visited Orielle and the three mighty stone bridges spanning the jeweled waters of Horn Bay's bustling harborfront. The call of gulls and blaring ship horns resounded across the city, just audible over the crash of waves upon the crags of the twin cliffs that hugged the bay. Nestled in the bay itself were hundreds of vessels of all sizes, divided into ports by wide piers that towered above the water on stalky driftwood legs. From east to west of Horn's Bay lay Earl's Port, Dame's Port, and Knight's Port, named after the bridges that corralled them. The rest of the city sloped down along the twin cliffs, the redwood-shingled roofs clustering tighter and tighter as they grew closer to the sea.

With one hand shielding her eyes, Asterin watched from East Cliff as a sailing yacht with a mast at least twenty feet taller than Earl's Bridge stalled outside the port. Its captain, just a tiny smudge on the distant deck, signaled to the bright white lighthouse crowning the cliff. A moment passed and the very center of the bridge's arch began to fragment, glowing slashes of red light cutting swift across the stone in vertical strokes. One by one, each fragment slid upward like spikes on a beast's back. The sigil of Lady Siore, Goddess of Earth, flared as the yacht at last passed beneath the bridge, the masthead just ghosting the bridge's underside. Then, as quickly as they had risen, the fragments shifted back into their original place.

Nicole hummed as Lady Siore's sigil faded. "Neat."

"There's a team of wielders in each lighthouse overseeing the bridges," Asterin told the earth-wielding Elite. "My father once told me that centuries ago, during wartime, they would use the bridges to smash oncoming enemy ships to dust when they tried to pass beneath."

Nicole's smile widened. "*Neat.*"

Gino took a discrete step away from her and asked, "But how come enemy earth-wielders couldn't just counteract the bridges' shifting with their own magic?"

"The bridges are spelled against *all* magic," Asterin said. "Except for magic cast through the affinity stones embedded permanently in the lighthouses' walls. The only way to remove them would be to destroy the lighthouses or bridges entirely."

Casper's stomach growled deafeningly, halting the conversation. He gave it a mournful pat. "Apologies."

Eadric checked his pocket watch. "We've still got about eight hours until our ship is set to sail."

Asterin tapped her chin. "I guess we should find something to eat first, then," she said. "I know just the place."

Eadric grinned. "You mean that bakery you constantly rave about?"

"You read my mind."

They trotted along the multiple roads threading down the cliffs, each paved with stone tiles dyed in every shade of the rainbow to help differentiate one from another. With so many foreigners docking in Orielle every day, the simple system made for easy location of inns, shops, and other businesses. *And easy remembrance, too*, Asterin thought to herself as she led the others down the Ruby Road, where they eventually came to a halt in front of a charming little bakery with smoke puffing out of its stout chimneys. Already, Asterin couldn't help but salivate at the arrays of vibrant sweets and frosted cakes decking the display window. Sal's Bakery, the wooden sign hanging over the entrance read. They tied their horses up and headed inside. The bell tinkled above when she pushed the door open, the air drenched with the heavenly scent of baking banana loaves.

Casper inhaled lustily, his eyes fluttering shut. "I smell cinnamon rolls."

"This was my father's favorite bakery," said Asterin. "Sal used to work at the palace, actually, but then he quit to open his own shop here. My father said that after he left, the cake never tasted the same again." She leaned over the empty counter, peering around. "Sal? Hello?"

"They have chocolate croissants!" Gino exclaimed.

Eadric scoffed. "You mean chocolate *on* croissants."

Gino waved wildly. "No, Captain, I meant *chocolate* croissants! Come look!"

"That's preposterous." Eadric bustled toward Gino while Asterin weaved behind the counter, searching for any sign of the baker or the other workers. She squinted at a floury handprint on the floor and reached forward to push open the back door just as the front doorbell gave a loud tinkle and she heard Casper step out of the way.

"Pardon—*oh*."

At the silence that followed, Asterin frowned and looked over her shoulder. Hot wind gusted inside the shop, swinging the door back and forth. The bell continued to jangle on, almost menacingly, but the entry beneath remained unoccupied.

"Your Majesty?" Casper said, his voice strangely tight.

Asterin raised an eyebrow at the Elite. "Yes?"

He turned to face her.

Her breath stuttered as she lowered her eyes and caught sight of the long serrated blade jutting out of his stomach.

Their gazes met, his burning with pain and urgency.

"*Run.*"

CHAPTER SIXTEEN

"So . . ." Orion began, a little hesitantly, the frost-white silks draped diagonally across his bare chest fluttering with every rise and fall of breath. Harry watched, entranced, as Orion blew on his tea. The air around them fogged with rose-tinted steam, carrying the heady scent of sweet jasmine, honeysuckle, and a bit of illisantheum, a fragrant spice commonly found in the Shadow Kingdom. Eoin made a hobby of collecting loose-leaf variants from around the Immortal Realm. He kept them pressed in bricks and hanging from the ceiling of the tearoom in colorful nets. "You're quite the nectar fanatic, I see."

Harry blinked. "Pardon?"

Orion's lips twitched, and he gestured to Harry's cup. "Nectar."

Harry swore and jerked the little pitcher away, but it was already too late—he was so preoccupied with staring at Orion's face after spending so many nights just *dreaming* of it, his cup had long overflowed.

Eoin clucked and waved a hand. The King of Shadow wore his favorite ensemble—all black. A charcoal dress shirt unbuttoned at the collar and a waistcoat, paired with tight-fitting slacks. A stylish jacket hung from his broad shoulders. "Honestly, Harry. You're embarrassing me." There came a flutter of wings, and the three glittering black butterflies perched atop the god's crown fetched a satin napkin and mopped up the mess.

Harry pasted on a smile and bent a spoon in his fist beneath the table.

Keep it together, he ordered himself. *Or face the consequences.* "Apologies, my king."

Eoin's nostrils flared ever so slightly. He snapped a cookie in half and dipped it into his tea before holding it to Orion's lips, which parted obediently. The god's half-lidded gaze lingered on the pale column of Orion's throat as he swallowed.

Jealousy ripped through Harry. The tablecloth disintegrated to dust beneath his trembling fingers.

Eoin turned to him, that ancient gaze filled with a vicious darkness that Harry had prayed he'd never witness again.

The king dabbed at the corners of his mouth with a napkin and discarded it on the floor. "Orion, darling, I'll just be a moment," he said softly. "Come along, Harry. You seem like you have something to tell me."

The God of Shadow swept out of the tearoom and picked his way toward one of the glass arboretums scattered throughout the gardens, leaving Harry to stumble after him. Rows and rows of nectar flowers bloomed within, their opalescent petals glimmering like mother-of-pearl even without the sun's touch.

As soon as the door closed, Eoin seized Harry by the throat with one hand and shoved him against the wall. The king jerked him up into the air, his iron grip tightening around Harry's neck.

"*Holte*," Eoin snarled.

Time itself ceased to exist.

Actions that should have taken at least a moment, no matter how short, transpired instantaneously and infinitely, all at once. The nectar flowers bloomed and shriveled around them, their life cycle accelerating exponentially until they simply vanished, until *everything* vanished, until the only thing that kept Harry tethered to this realm was Eoin's bruising grip.

"We're in private now, Harry," the god whispered, enunciating each syllable so languidly, as if he were rolling a sweet around on his tongue. "You can tell me whatever is on your mind. I'll keep it a secret, I promise."

Unbridled terror coursed through Harry's veins even as he tamped it down. The threat of inexistence buzzed and reverberated along his every cell. He didn't bother struggling, didn't dare open his mouth for fear of the words that might spill out, knowing that the king could very well drop him into the wild white void. Perhaps the only way to kill him was to sever his wings with Eoin's sword, *Nöctklavan*, but was there any difference between dying and ceasing to be?

I won't speak, he thought desperately, his eyes darting between Eoin's face and the void.

The god's gaze swallowed him, almost disappointed. *"Zäär."*

The command rattled Harry's bones. His spine jolted ramrod straight as the god's power shuddered through him. His body began to shift to his demon form of its own accord, but it *hurt*. His claws shredded his skin, his skull throbbed from the force of his ears punching out of his scalp. His fangs pierced his tongue clean through when he tried to bite down on a scream as the air filled with the sound of his shoulder muscles tearing, the only warning before his wings exploded from his back and the agony folded him in two.

I won't tell him. I won't tell him. I won't tell him.

When it was finally over, Harry could only lie panting and limp in Eoin's arms. "Shall we go back and do that all over again?" the king purred. "Can you take it?"

No, Harry pleaded in his mind.

A second later, he was screaming again, his body betraying him at a single murmured spell.

Back in his human form, Harry curled into a ball, saliva dribbling down his chin and silvery blood weeping from cuts even as they closed, only to reopen moments later. Scraps of fabric fluttered to the floor, his tattered clothes ravaged by the force-shifting. With his skin exposed and crawling beneath the god's gaze, he let loose a shudder of disgust. At Eoin. At himself. His suffering seemed to appease the white void, subduing it to a soothed gray.

When Harry failed to speak yet again, Eoin traced a finger down his cheek with a crestfallen frown. "What is it, exactly, that you're so desperate to hide from your king? Hmm?"

Harry clenched his jaw. "N-not," he stammered out, his voice pathetically hoarse. His breath hitched when Eoin's hand brushed the ridges of his shoulder blades, where his wings grew. "Not hiding. Anything. My . . . *king*."

A chuckle rumbled forth deep from Eoin's chest. "King, master, god.

Call me any name you desire, little anygné. You are still mine." Those eyes had emptied of all light, revealing the hollow eternity beyond. "Orion must be wondering where we've gone off to by now. Shall I invite him over? Give him a little taste?"

The gray void recoiled when a snarl ripped from Harry's lips, blue ice and gold wrath crackling across his vision. "Don't." He shook, from pain and exhaustion and utter fury. "*Touch*."

As if his nerves had simply switched off, the pain stopped abruptly.

Eoin's silky whisper caressed his ear. "I see."

Harry blinked and the glass house slowly reformed, floating around him and slotting neatly back into place, piece by piece. Nectar flowers died in reverse, their petals winking at him like crushed jewels through the gloom. He lay on the floor with his head thrown to the side. It was all he could do to remind himself to breathe, to grit his teeth and ride out the excruciating ache in his bones. His eyes darted up past the glass to find the bruised sky stretching out above him, and a sudden, intense longing for the sunshine of the Mortal Realm nearly overwhelmed him.

The god straightened from his crouch, brushing away the smears of Harry's blood staining his jacket. It flecked off like peeling paint. "It's all right, darling, I understand now." His shoes clicked toward the exit, neat and crisp, but the door opened too early. Harry could only manage to tilt his chin sideways, just enough to catch a glimpse of Orion's reflection in the floor tiles.

"Eo?" Orion called. "Is everything alright?"

"Of course," came Eoin's easy reply. "Why wouldn't it be?"

Harry wanted to scream. He imagined the god slipping an arm around Orion's waist, resting a protective hand on his hip, snaking his slender fingers into those golden curls.

"Where did Harry go?"

"Oh, he's fine, he's just—"

Leather soles scuffed across the floor, dancing away from the god. "*Harry*? What are you doing down there?"

Before Harry knew what was happening, a pair of warm, strong arms wrapped around him, one hand sliding around his torso and the other bracing his lower back. Orion's scent washed over him, filling his chest with aching longing. He closed his eyes and breathed deep. And then exhaled, so he could breathe deeper still.

"Immortals, Eo, what in hell did you *do* to him?"

Harry could hear the pout in Eoin's words. "Nothing he couldn't handle."

That warm, comforting grip tightened. "Nothing he couldn't . . ." Orion scoffed angrily. "Are you out of your mind? Look at him!"

Harry's panic spiked when Eoin sauntered—no, *prowled* over, a ruthless glint in his eyes. Shadows pooled around the god's ankles like ocean fog, writhing up his legs and clinging to his every step. His shoe lifted out of the murk, his heel coming to rest on Harry's chest, right atop his heart.

Harry let out a sharp wheeze as Eoin put his weight forward, digging the heel into his ribs.

"Stop that," Orion scolded. "Or else."

And to Harry's shock, the king did.

"You're no fun," Eoin complained.

"Oh?" Orion cocked his head to the side, his brow furrowed. "Hold on . . . do you hear that?"

The god's brow rose in mystification as Harry, too, strained to catch anything unusual. Or, in fact, anything at all. "Hear what?"

"The sound of all the damns I give."

Eoin burst into laughter. Genuine laughter, unlike anything that Harry had ever heard him produce. It was almost . . . *human*. "Oh, Orion, you impudent wretch."

"Thank you," said Orion. He tipped his chin toward the exit. "Now, if you wouldn't mind, I'd like to have a word with Harry about inciting your tantrums."

The god threw a hand upon his heart in mock hurt. "Tantrums! How you wound me. But do as you wish." He slid his hands into his trouser pockets and ambled out the door—but not without throwing a last smirk over his shoulder. "Not too long, though . . . or I'll get awfully jealous."

They watched through the glass walls as the god disappeared around a hedge and out of sight.

Then Orion was scrambling to Harry's front, his fingers searching along what little clothed skin remained. "Are you hurt? Are you hurt?" he demanded twice, and then once more until Harry managed to shake his head. His immortal body had already healed itself, with no trace of violence to be found.

"I'm so sorry," Harry whispered, staring at the little crinkle between Orion's brows and the concern brimming in his ice-blue eyes.

Orion stopped short. "What for?"

"This is all my fault," Harry rasped. "You were stuck here, all on your own, and I couldn't find you. I promised I would find you, and so many days passed and I thought that you were gone, Orion, and—"

"Harry."

"—I said I'd be back, damnit!" Harry grabbed two fistfuls of silk and dragged Orion's face to his, their foreheads bashing together. Without releasing his hold, he closed his eyes to hide his anguish. "Why in hell couldn't you have just *listened* to me for once? Why did you follow me into the portal?" Harry gave him a haggard shake. Orion breathed a soft *ow* every time their foreheads knocked together. "Do you have any idea how *stupid* that was? You could have died!"

"Well, I didn't," Orion said weakly.

"Don't ever do that again," Harry whispered. *You nearly broke me. Asterin, too, and everyone else you left behind.* "Promise?"

"Harry . . ." Orion trailed off. He was smiling a little, but it was a stiff, stilted smile that made Harry's stomach clench. "I—I don't really know what you're talking about."

Harry cursed. He had been clinging onto the hope—a fool's hope, he saw now—that Orion's memory loss would wear off with time, or that mentioning the portal might spark *some* remembrance. "How much do you remember?" he asked instead, forcing down his frustration. Not frustration at Orion, of course, but at himself. This was and would always be his fault.

That half smile faltered slightly. "Not much. My name. That I fell and hit my head. How to charm handsome men."

A choked laugh escaped Harry. "Where would we be if you had forgotten that?"

Orion grinned in a way that brought down a deluge of nostalgia upon Harry, but even then . . . there was something missing, a sharp, reckless edge that the alleged fall—or rather, the landing—had dulled, like a blade reforged into something mellower, more pliant.

Harry swallowed. "So . . . I take it you don't remember Asterin, then?"

"No. Is she a friend?"

The blithe question punched the air out of Harry's lungs. He couldn't even begin to imagine Asterin's devastation. "Much more than a friend."

Orion reeled back. "A l-lover?"

He snorted at that. "Immortals, no."

"Your lover?" Orion tried, to which Harry began laughing so hard that he nearly choked. Orion glowered at him, though without any fire. "I'll take that as a no. Is it because she's . . . well, a she?"

Harry hesitated. "I told you this once, but I've been around for a while. Long enough to figure myself out. My heart cares not for the confines of a body. Immortal, mortal, male, female, both or neither . . . I am blind to all but my devotion."

"Ah." Orion seemed taken aback. "I just like men, I think."

Harry laughed again. "You said the exact same thing back then, too."

Orion bit his lip. "Were we ever . . . you know? Together?"

Harry's voice softened to something a little bittersweet. "We ran out of time before we could answer that question. But I've always liked you, Orion," he confessed, his gaze drifting over Orion's face. Tracing, lingering, memorizing. Their eyes met. *Dare to feel.* "Far too much for my own good."

Orion looked away, a rosy flush spreading across his face. "I'm sorry." It was the response Harry had dreaded most, and it must have shown in his expression, because Orion hurried to explain. "Eoin saved my life. Without him, I might have been lost forever." He sighed, running a hand down his neck. "It's just that . . . I'm not the person you knew anymore, Harry. And I don't think I'll ever be. I'm here with Eo now, and—"

"No," Harry blurted. The world blurred, a lake's mirror surface disturbed by a sudden and violent rainstorm. "You don't understand. You don't belong here. You have to leave."

Orion drew back with a frown. "Leave? Why in hell would I leave?"

"Eoin is a god. The Ruler of Darkness. He existed before time itself, Orion. The life of a mortal is less than nothing to him." To think that the hardest part of bringing Orion home wouldn't be *finding* him, but convincing him to *return* . . . somehow, that made it worse, because Orion didn't *know*, and he would never know until it was much too late. "Even if you spent your entire life rotting down here and never saw the light of day again . . ." Immortals, could he even remember the sun? "No matter how much you please him, all you will ever be to him is yesterday's souvenir."

Orion's expression closed off, unreadable save for the glacial fury blazing in his eyes. He shoved himself away from Harry and staggered to his feet. "Get away from me."

Harry cursed himself as Orion stormed for the door. "*Please.* I'm only telling you this because I—I experienced it firsthand." He bowed his head. "I was deceived. I was blinded. And I can't bear to let the same happen to you."

Orion halted in his tracks and glared over his shoulder. "What do you want?"

"For you to return to the Mortal Realm," he whispered. "To the people you love and who love you. To go home . . . to Axaria."

For the barest moment, Harry could have sworn he saw a flicker of doubt soothe the flame in Orion's eyes, *Axaria* passing briefly over his lips. But then he was turning away, shaking his head, nothing but a mixture of certainty and derision fueling his steps as he abandoned a broken Harry and his forsaken devotion on the floor.

"You're wrong, Harry. This *is* home."

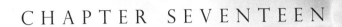

CHAPTER SEVENTEEN

"Go, go, *go!*" Eadric roared, vaulting over the counter and tackling Asterin to the floor. Another knife flew through the entranceway of Sal's Bakery, stopped less than an inch from Casper's chest by the air barrier that Nicole threw in front of him just in time. "Gino, Nicole, into the back room!"

"*No,*" Asterin hissed, fighting against Eadric's unyielding grip. "I'm not leaving Casper—" She let out a yelp as her feet swung off the floor and Eadric slung her over his shoulder like a sack of flour. "Put me down!"

Nicole cursed and shielded her face as the bakery's display window shattered, showering all three Elites in glass. The terrified screams of horses rang through the air. Silver-blue knives darted in the morning light like a school of fish, bouncing off Nicole's barriers. One managed to break through. It sank hilt-deep into Casper's shoulder and out the other side, piercing the nearby counter with a dull *thud*.

Nicole whirled desperately on Gino. "A little help here?"

"On it!" the Elite exclaimed.

A whimsical, melodious laugh drifted through the shattered window, raising the hairs on Asterin's neck. "Let *go* of me!" she snarled, writhing sideways and chomping down on Eadric's arm as he sprinted for the back room.

The captain swore but held fast. "Yeah, sorry, I was ready for that." He kicked down the door and barreled into the kitchen beyond. Asterin spotted Sal and a few other bakers sprawled across the tile in bloodied aprons, their starched hats strewn about like wayward leaves among the littered glass.

"Windows!" Asterin hollered in realization just as three glowing blue knives shot toward them. Eadric ducked just in time and the knives lodged into the wall, but to her disbelief, they shuddered and slid themselves out, hovering midair. "*Eadric*—"

Eadric only ran faster, dodging steel pots and pans hanging from hooks above and nearly causing her to bite off her own tongue. "You deal with them, damnit," he gritted out.

She hardly heard a word as the three knives whizzed straight for her face. Jets of ice exploded from her palms, knocking them off course. But like hounds locked on a scent, they surged at her again and again, relentless. Finally, she gathered her wits and blasted a huge jet of water upward. She froze the water immediately, trapping the psycho-blades within a huge slab of ice fixed to the ceiling.

Gino and Nicole skidded around the corner. Asterin just had enough time to yell, "Windows!" for Nicole to throw up an air barrier against another half-dozen knives. One blade rebounded into a baking pan rack. The rack teetered for a heartbeat before tipping over with a *crash*, raining unbaked croissants upon them. Asterin kept her eyes on the knives as they clattered to the ground, but to her great relief, they failed to so much as twitch.

Eadric released her at last. "Stay between us," he said. "Nicole, Gino, you take the wings and rear. I'll—"

"What about Casper?" Asterin demanded. "And the horses?"

The Elites shared a quick glance as they took up position. "Nicole managed to cut the horses loose," said Gino. "The rest doesn't matter. We need to get you out of here."

Asterin clenched her fists. "I'm not leaving without Casper."

Eadric whirled on her, fury scrawled across his features. "Yes, you *are*," he spat in a tone he had never before used with her. "And that is an order."

In her shock, she managed to blurt, "You can't order me."

Nicole's hand fluttered just shy of her arm. "Our duty is to protect you with our lives, Your Majesty. We're your Elites, and we will stop at nothing to keep you safe. So please—" The words continued to spill out, each a precious gem. "Help us honor our promise to you. Follow Captain Covington's orders. For—for Casper."

Asterin swallowed hard, thinking of Casper's blazing eyes and that horrible blade protruding from his body. Finally, she nodded. "But how do we get out? Whoever is after us obviously has eyes on the building and apparently an endless supply of knives. As soon as we step out . . ."

"Storage room," Gino suggested. "There must be one below us, to keep the supplies cool. Two of you are earth-wielders, and Your Majesty a powerful one at that. We'll tunnel our way out."

"Good thinking," said Eadric. He scanned the kitchen and pointed at Sal's body, sagging against the far wall, partly obstructed by the large brick oven in the center of the room. "There."

It took Asterin a moment to realize that Sal was actually sitting on a rectangular patch of iron, the crook of one knee draped over a handle. "So we just need to get past those windows again without getting stabbed."

They all stiffened as that sweet, horrible, musical laughter filled the air once more, drawing closer with each second, promising death. "Hurry," Eadric hissed.

"I've got this," Asterin said. She cast thick blocks of ice to replace the broken windows. "When I say go, everyone sprint for Sal. And . . . go!"

And then she dashed away in the opposite direction, toward the back exit.

"Asterin Faelenhart, what in *hell* do you think you're doing?" Eadric snarled, his arms already wrapped around Sal's beefy torso.

"Just get the hatch open. And that's an order." She frowned and peered at her makeshift windows. "My ice is still perfectly intact . . ." At that moment, she caught a glimpse of Grey rearing angrily outside and galloping up the road, a cloaked rider upon his back. "Someone just rode by on Grey!" *But who?* Two cloaked figures blurred past after Eadric's steed, and she just managed to detect a flash of white hair from beneath a hood.

"It must have worked, then," said Gino, relief palpable in his voice.

"What worked?"

"Hatch's open," Eadric barked.

"Fine," Asterin snapped, bracing herself for the splintering of ice and psycho-blades as she bolted for the door, but none came.

Eadric leaped down the ladder, whereupon her Elites practically shoved her down the stairs and into the captain's waiting arms. Just as Gino had predicted, the walls were covered with shelves of baking ingredients, and the air was cool and damp enough to raise gooseflesh along her skin. The hatch slammed shut above their heads, trapping them in darkness. Gino and Asterin summoned small spheres of light to combat it. Electricity crackled down Eadric's arms, casting his body in a bluish glow a little too reminiscent of the psycho-blades for Asterin's comfort.

"All right," she muttered, nudging aside bags of sugar. Her fingers found the wall that would lead them down to the harbor. The surface crumbled at her command to reveal the earth beyond. Nicole joined her to ensure that the sides of the growing hole remained stable.

Muffled footfalls sounded above them. They all froze.

"*What a mess. And a waste of croissants,*" a deep, unfamiliar voice rumbled above them.

Asterin cursed in her head. If the floor was thin enough to hear people talking, tunneling would surely disturb the ground above and reveal their location.

"*Hey, you,*" another voice grunted, laced with pain. "*I'm going to kick your ass.*"

Asterin's heart raced. "Casper," she hissed. "He's still alive." She was halfway to the ladder when she slammed face-first into an invisible wall. Wincing with one palm pressed into her bruised forehead, she stared dumbly at the affinity stone Nicole kept brandished in her direction. "What are you doing?"

"Keeping you safe," the Elite whispered.

A snort of disgust from above. "*Kick* my *ass? Are you unaware that I've got your wrists bound and you're leaking blood all over the floor?*"

"*Are you unaware that I'm about to burn you to a crisp?*"

"Nicole—" Asterin growled.

"*In your state? Somehow, I doubt that.*"

"No," Nicole bit out, her head shaking furiously. The air expanded, pushing Asterin backward, farther away from the hatch leading to Casper. "I won't let you."

"Well, surprise, you gloved bastard."

BOOM.

The explosion above decimated the sound of their shouts. It rocked the very earth, sending them all toppling over. Asterin barely had time to twist away as a shelf and the row of jars upon it crashed on the ground. Shards of glass sliced her face. Yet even disoriented, bleeding, and choking on scorched air, she began clawing her way toward the ladder. Then a pair of arms locked around her chest and dragged her away. She hissed and thrashed, until Eadric's face swam into view, his mouth moving in a repetitive stream of frantic words that reached her deafened ears only when the shrill ringing from the explosion finally abated.

"The tunnel, Asterin! The gods-damned tunnel! We need to get to safety!"

A sudden rage filled her. *This was supposed to be a simple trip to see Quinlan*, she thought, shoving away from Eadric and staggering forward.

"Your Majesty, please!" Gino exclaimed.

A feral roar clawed its way out of her throat as she stormed over to the unfinished hole in the wall. *Fine. I'll make a gods-damned tunnel.*

The rage in her head quieted into a lethal hush.

And after that, I'll find and hunt down every one of the sons of bitches responsible for this.

Then she planted her palms against the rugged, unforgiving earth and let her magic explode.

CHAPTER EIGHTEEN

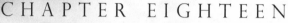

Queen Regent Elyssa Calistavyn-Faelenhart strode down the corridor toward Throne Hall, swathed in a long robe to cover the sleeping gown beneath. Restraining the urge to smack her cheeks a few times to better wake herself, she rounded the corner, where two more guards joined the four already flanking her.

"This should only take a minute, Queen Regent," Carlsby apologized.

"How often do these . . . life-or-death situations occur?" Elyssa asked.

Carlsby ran a hand down his neck sheepishly. "Not often, Your Grace. When they do, though, it's usually Captain Covington who deals with them. Since he's away, we were just going to keep the man in holding until morning, but, er . . ."

Elyssa stared at him. "But what?"

Carlsby flushed pink. "The intruder overpowered the guards at the Wall. And he surrendered only on the condition that he could have an immediate audience with Queen Asterin."

Elyssa hummed thoughtfully. "And has he been informed of my daughter's absence?"

"No, but since she named you Queen Regent—"

"I'm well aware, Carlsby," Elyssa interrupted. They arrived at the entrance to Throne Hall, and six more soldiers merged into her guard.

This seems like overkill, she couldn't help thinking. *But what do I know? It's been over a decade since I sat on the throne beside my Tristan.* She squared her shoulders and nodded at Carlsby, who reached for the door.

His hand faltered when muffled shouting broke out from within the hall. Immediately, he shielded Elyssa with his body. "Stay back, Your Grace. Until we know what is going on inside there . . ." He pointed at the guards. "You six take front—wait, Your Grace!"

With a scowl, Elyssa stormed past two guards. The doors, however, swung inward before she could push them open herself, and she nearly crashed face-first into another horror-stricken guard.

"Spread out! He's disappeared!" the guard exclaimed. Then he took her in and nearly tripped over himself. "Queen Regent, my most sincere apologies."

"What do you mean he's disappeared?" Elyssa demanded as two other guards skidded to a halt behind the first. Beyond the doorway, she observed more guards frantically searching Throne Hall. Were all of the guards truly so incompetent?

"He just vanished into thin air, Your Grace! Or, maybe not air—"

Elyssa whirled around as she felt a featherlight touch at her wrist. Before she could cry out, the touch hardened into a vice-like grip and the room around her dissolved into darkness. She gasped and struggled, her mind filled with an eternity of cold stone and endless shadow beneath the bowels of the palace, but in a heartbeat her back slammed into something solid and Asterin's chambers materialized around her.

"Who are you?" a deep tenor demanded above her.

Slowly, she lifted her eyes and met an utterly mystified chocolate-brown stare. She realized that the stranger had her pinned to the wall, so she punched him in the face and wrested herself free. From her pocket she whipped out her affinity stone and dug it into his chest. "Who are *you?*" she demanded right back. "And what in the Immortals was *that?*"

"Shadow jumping," the intruder replied, rubbing his jaw. "And I'm Harry. Asterin's . . . friend?"

Harry. Elyssa's hand fell in astonishment. So *this* was Harry, the shadow demon who had killed Priscilla. Before she knew it, she had seized him in a rib-crushing embrace. "*Thank you*," she breathed into his shoulder. "Thank you for protecting my daughter."

His arms dangled awkwardly at his sides. "Y-your daughter?" came the stammered response. He scanned her face. "I mean, I can tell, but you're actually . . ."

Elyssa released him. "Yes. I'm Elyssa Calistavyn-Faelenhart, Asterin's *real* mother. Priscilla had me locked up in the dungeon beneath the palace for about a decade."

Harry stared at her in shock. "But . . . how did you survive?"

"Well, the cells are enchanted with ancient magic to sustain—"

"No, no," Harry cut in. "I meant . . . well, I would've expected Priscilla to execute you, rather than keep you locked up for ten years." He bit his lip. "Sorry."

Elyssa shook her head. "No need to apologize. And she did give the order. But . . ."

Flint-gray eyes met hers in the darkness. Full of pain, of remorse. A pale, trembling hand, the gleam of scarlet-stained steel. The drip of blood from severed necks, the quiet sigh of silk and breath as she knelt on unforgiving stone. Waiting. Waiting . . .

". . . I was spared," she finished, swallowing the ache in her throat. She rubbed her knuckles and whispered, "We were both mothers, after all."

"Mothers?"

"Hm?" Elyssa blinked. "Oh, I'm afraid I was just lost in a memory. My apologies."

Harry smiled at her, timid but full of sincerity and warmth. "No need to apologize." His expression hardened slightly. "But the reason I came was to find Asterin. I need to speak with her urgently."

Elyssa's brow wrinkled. "She left Axaris yesterday, at dawn."

His eyes widened. "What? To go where?"

"Why? What happened?"

Harry went silent for a moment. "I—I found Orion."

Her hand flew to her mouth. "In the Immortal Realm?"

"Yes, and I need to get him out as soon as possible. So where is Asterin?"

"She should arrive in Orielle by noon, if she hasn't already," Elyssa replied. "Knowing her, she probably drove the horses into the ground, so it's quite likely. They'll be leaving from Dame's Port aboard the *Ocean Gypsy*."

Harry cursed under his breath. "I won't be able to shadow jump again for a few hours at least. What if they've left by the time I make it to the port? I won't be able to find them at sea."

Elyssa put a hand on his shoulder and gave it a soothing rub, smiling a little to herself when she felt the hard muscles beneath slowly unclench. She could practically see the overworked gears whirring in Harry's head, not to mention the exhaustion in his glassy-eyed frown. *Now here is a man that pushes himself past his brink on a regular basis*, she mused in her head, *only to keep pushing.* "Everything is going to be just fine, Harry. Even if Asterin has already arrived, the ship isn't due to depart until eve tonight."

Harry sagged. Elyssa watched in amusement as his eyelids drooped a little before snapping back open. "Thank the Immortals. I can make it, then."

"But first, you must rest," she told him. "Or you won't be much use to anyone at all."

"No, I'll be . . ." He accidentally cut himself off with a monstrous yawn. "Ah . . . on second thought, would you mind if I borrowed this floor for a few hours?"

"I *would* absolutely mind." Elyssa clasped his hands. "You will take my own chambers." She held up a finger when his mouth opened in protest. "I command it. No arguing."

Harry huffed out a throaty chuckle, shaking his head as he followed her out of Asterin's chambers. Every step swayed, and Elyssa almost worried that he would collapse right then and there in the middle of the corridor. Then, so low that Elyssa almost missed it, he mumbled out a drowsy, "I see where Asterin gets it from now."

Elyssa already knew that she wouldn't sleep a wink more that night, so she ushered Harry into her own bedchamber. Owing to his current state, it only took a little bit of bullying to coerce Harry into letting her tuck him in. He slept with his mouth slightly parted, drooling a little.

Unable to help herself, she smoothed a hand over his unruly curls, the same deep brown as his eyes. His breathing stalled for a moment. "Thank you, again, Harry," she murmured. "For defeating Priscilla. And protecting my Asterin."

As she turned to leave, he rolled onto his side and mumbled again. "I'll protect them all. Even if it kills me."

Better you than my Asterin, Harry, Elyssa thought to herself grimly as she let herself out into the hall. *Better you than her.*

CHAPTER NINETEEN

"Damnit, Killian!" Kane yelled as plumes of angry charcoal smoke swelled into the sky. A few streets away, bells rang and hooves thundered past, undoubtedly heading for the charred remains of Sal and his bakery. "Why couldn't you have just killed him right away? You missed, like, three times."

"You know I never miss," Killian shot back. "He was cute. I was just playing with him." She pouted. "And it's *your* fault we took off after the captain's horse. The rider illusion didn't even have any limbs!"

"Yeah, well, you only noticed that when the entire *body* started evaporating!"

"At least I noticed at all," she retorted. "Otherwise we would have actually chased it down, and that would have been a lot more embarrassing. And besides . . ." Her features shifted into her killing mask, her pupils dilating until they filled the whites of her eyes completely, save for a thin circle of amber in the center. Her canines tripled in length, sharper than knives. She traced her tongue down one languidly, her lips curling in fiendish delight when an unsettled Kane averted his gaze from the weight of her ancient, cruel stare. "They're just letting the game continue. And you know that toying with clever prey is my favorite pastime."

He shuddered. "Right. Well, we'd better find Rivaille. Make sure he didn't turn into a pile of ash or something like that."

"Try not to sound so eager," came a familiar drawl from behind them. Rivaille stalked over to them, his ponytail strewn with cinders and his normally pristine robes and gloves scorched black. "I'm right here."

Kane started. "How in hell—forget it. Gloved bastard."

Rivaille's lips spread into a full-on, pearly white grin. "Funny, one of the queen's Elites called me the exact same thing right before he blew himself up."

Kane bared his teeth. "Is that some kind of threat?"

Killian just rolled her eyes and took off down an alley dyed bright magenta. The wind moved in tandem with her as she glided along the cobblestones. "We're on a deadline here!" she called over her shoulder. "Get a move on!" Her own shadow took shape beneath her to soften her foot-falls, guiding her past shops just opening for business and spooked horses.

In no time, Rivaille caught up to her. His own steps never quite touched the ground, either. He flexed his left hand, lessening the horizontal pull of gravity that he had created for himself to match her pace. "Where to?"

"Downtown." She pushed herself harder, but he simply splayed his right hand and matched her for every step. "They're leaving via the harbor, so all we have to do is keep an eye on their ship."

Rivaille's eyebrows raised an almost unnoticeable millimeter. "And which ship would that be?"

"According to our mole, they'll be docking in Dame's Port, and only three ships leaving within the day share Eradore as their destination."

"How do we know that they're leaving today?"

"If your lover had been torn from you by sickness and had just opened their eyes for the first time in eight moons, how desperate would you be to see them?"

He simply looked at her.

"Right, I forgot, you wouldn't know," Killian muttered. "Anyway, you'd want to take the first boat possible."

"Well, then—"

"And before you ask which boat leaves earliest," she cut in, "they're all conveniently scheduled to leave at the same time." She frowned, glancing over her shoulder. Her shadow yanked her sideways, just barely saving her from a surprise encounter with a lamppost. "Immortals, Kane is *so* slow. Where is he?" She signaled to her fellow hireling and they veered around a brick wall to wait.

It took Killian a moment to notice that Rivaille was scowling at the ground. "What now?"

"I could have guessed, you know."

"What?"

His scowl deepened. "Just because I'm not interested in sexual intimacy doesn't mean I don't understand what it means to love."

"I never said that," Killian protested. She thought back. "Well, I didn't mean it. But I'm sorry that it came out that way. And besides, you know that of all people, I—"

Of course, that was the moment Kane finally chose to appear, panting like a cow in labor. "Damn . . . you . . . *both*!" he exclaimed, bending in half. "And . . . your *stupid* . . . magic!"

Killian smirked at him. "What took you so long?"

He straightened, his chest still heaving. "I found a trail. So I decided to follow it."

"A turtle's trail?" Rivaille deadpanned.

Kane flushed scarlet. "No!" he yelled over Killian's laughter. "A *queen's* trail. Some trees started shaking even though there wasn't any wind. At first, I thought it might be an earthquake, but it was too centralized. She must have escaped underground." He pointed farther down the cliff. "There's a grove over there, straight in their path and too thick to tunnel through. They'll have to diverge either left or right."

"Or both," Killian remarked.

Kane made a face. "How would you know?"

"I've been in this business for centuries." She tilted her chin. "And even if I'm wrong, we can just reconvene after the fact."

The white-haired hireling exhaled through his nose. "Fine. So what's our plan?"

"From what I've been told," said Killian, "the queen used to visit Orielle often with her king father. She must know the city's spread fairly well." She squinted down the twin cliffs at two identical squares of land, both covered in brightly colored rows of stacked boxes. "Shipping container yards on either side," she said, pointing them out to the others. "Perfect place to hide, and close enough to the harbor to make a break for it." She smiled. *The game continues.* "So we split up. Last one to the captain is a salted flounder."

"I hold first pick," Rivaille cut in. "It's me to both of you, one-nil."

Kane made a noise of protest. "You were the one who told us to go after the captain! Any of us could have killed that small fry."

"Yeah, and he basically fried himself," Killian said.

Rivaille shrugged. "Not my problem. I choose left."

"I'll take right, then," Kane said.

Killian grinned, glancing back and forth between them. "Ooh, goody. Who shall I choose to torment . . . ?"

Dread dawned on Kane's features. "No, wait, don't—"

She slung an arm around his shoulders, her shadow holding its stomach in mirth on the sidewalk. "Too late."

Kane let out a gloomy sigh and trudged along with her like a man bound for the gallows. "Damn everything."

She winked. "Brighten up, sweetheart. It's time for murder."

CHAPTER TWENTY

"White hair, white hair," Asterin muttered as an enormous clump of gnarled roots forced her to dig deeper yet again. "Who the hell has white hair?"

"What are you on about?" Eadric muttered, his back hunched. He glowered at the tunnel walls, crowding ever closer. "Also, are you certain that we won't be buried alive?"

"For the seventh time, yes." Asterin bit her lip, a revelation bubbling up inside of her—but then she lost it. She cursed. "One of our attackers," she explained aloud. "Young, with white hair. I swear that I've seen him before somewhere, but—"

Eadric paused. "Didn't that jerk who fought alongside Rose during the Fairfest battle have white hair?"

Asterin halted in her tracks. "Kane?"

"Yeah. She should have left him ages ago. She deserved way better. His skill in combat was decent, I suppose, but—"

She snapped her fingers. "The knives!"

Eadric frowned. "Do you think it was him up there?"

Asterin paused her excavation and began pacing, though it was more like walking in a circle since the space was so narrow. The earth they dug had to end up somewhere, so she'd been packing it back in behind them, sealing their pathway but also blocking off any pursuers. "But why in hell would he try to kill us?"

"Because he's a lying, selfish prick?"

Nicole snorted. "Damn, Captain."

Eadric threw his hands into the air. "It's true! He's a stone-cold bastard who broke Rose's heart multiple times—"

"And helped save lives at the battle," Asterin finished, brow furrowed. "It makes no sense."

"Sure it does. Think about it. He almost failed his exams at the Academia Principalis *twice*. That means he's either lazy or lacking in magical ability. It's unlikely that Rose would have risked her neck for a slacker, and on top of that I saw them fight together. If I'm remembering correctly, he barely even touched his magic, if at all. Maybe he's trying to find a way to become more powerful."

"If I may," Gino interjected cautiously, "No one could have possibly known about Your Majesty's impromptu trip to Eradore prior to two days past, since Your Majesty hadn't yet known herself." His light sphere bobbed at his shoulder, casting long planes of darkness across his face. "Unless Kane happened to already be in Orielle with, I suspect, two accomplices, and decided out of nowhere to kill you, he must have pursued us at ungodly speeds from elsewhere. And there's no reason why he couldn't have just attacked you back home in Axaris . . ."

Realization stabbed her. "So they *are* trying to keep me away from Quinlan."

"That's the other thing," Gino said. "If that *is* Kane's motivation, why not simply kill Prince Quinlan himself? Especially since Eradore is or was his domain? Kane managed to sneak past *our* guards during Fairfest ball, so why not Eradore's? And especially considering Prince Quinlan's vulnerable state . . ."

Asterin bit down on her cheek in frustration. "But that doesn't help us understand why he's trying to kill me."

"No, that's my point," Gino insisted. "Maybe he's not targeting *you*. Maybe he's working for someone. Someone who doesn't want you reuniting with Quinlan, and knows that the best way to keep you in

Axaria would be to eliminate your escorts instead . . . especially Captain Covington."

They all went deathly silent.

"Someone *who*, though?" Eadric demanded.

Gino shrugged, his hair flopping to the side. "Beats me. That's all I've got."

Asterin massaged circles into her temples. "Clearly, whether or not the assassin on our trail is actually Kane, they still need to finish the job," she said. "Meaning that they're probably hunting for us, right now."

Eadric jerked his chin at the massive tangle of roots obstructing their path. "So what do we do?"

"I hate to admit it," Asterin said slowly, "but these roots are basically impossible to penetrate without causing a noticeable earthquake. And we'll draw too much attention if we surface now." She scoured her memories for Orielle's layout.

"Perhaps something closer to the harbor?" Eadric suggested.

Asterin smacked her fist into her palm. "The Yards. We can't miss them since we'll know we're in the right place as soon as we hit concrete."

"Yards, plural?" asked Eadric. "How many are there?"

"Two. North and South, one on each end of the harbor." The captain's mouth tightened. Hastily, she added, "Don't worry, I'm not saying we should split up."

"No," said Eadric, his expression tightening. "If Gino's suspicions are correct, they're after me. So we *should* split up. The Elites will stay with you. We can meet up aboard the *Ocean Gypsy*. I'll go alone."

"That's a horrible idea," Asterin told him flatly. "And besides, how would you get there? You're not an earth wielder."

Evidently, the captain hadn't considered that. "Fine," he replied grudgingly. "Nicole, you're with me. We'll take South Yard."

Asterin folded her arms over her chest. "And then what?"

Eadric lowered his voice. "Asterin, I know this is a gamble. But I also think it's our best shot." He checked his pocket watch. "We've got four hours until our ship is due for departure. It's up to you."

Asterin lifted her chin, staring up at the earth surrounding them like the maw of some beast waiting to claim them at the slightest mistake. Desperately, she prayed that she wasn't about to make one. "Fine. But if you get yourself killed, I'll have you resurrected just so I can tell you *I told you so*. Neither of us wants that, so don't die. Understood?"

Eadric's mouth quirked up at the corners. He saluted. "Understood."

Gino had decided that he really did not like being underground. It wasn't claustrophobia or a fear of being buried alive or anything like that, and at first the cool damp air on his skin had even soothed him. But that was before he tripped over a root obscured in soggy brown murk and an earthworm fell onto his face.

They had parted ways with Captain Covington and Nicole awhile ago, agreeing to meet up at a tavern called *The Boar's Head* if their plan went awry.

Asterin forged ahead of him in tense silence, doing her best to tunnel onward without disturbing the earth above them.

Dirt covered them both from head to toe by the time they finally hit the promised concrete. The queen shot him a weary grin. "Jackpot." She steepled her fingers, her eyes slipping shut in focus. Clods of dirt directly overhead flew outward, tumbling down the sides of the new tunnel walls. The ground beneath their feet shuddered and began to rise as the queen redirected the excavated earth from above to boost them higher from below. With a deep breath, she brought her clenched fist above her head and the earth followed, thrusting them upward. Before they reached the surface, the final dirt layer above them gave way at her command, greeting them with a gust of gloriously fresh, sea-kissed air.

Gino shielded his eyes with a wince as blinding afternoon sunshine poured into their little ditch. "We made it!"

"See? Told you so," a voice above called smugly. "Like two hungry baby bunnies popping out of the ground to look for carrots."

Gino's heart jumped into overdrive as two hooded faces blocked out the azure sky overhead. Queen Asterin swore. He threw himself in front of her as they rose fully into North Yard, but it was too late—they were already exposed and surrounded.

"Shut up, Killian," a man said. Both strangers were clad head to toe in white, from their flowing robes to the simple garb beneath. A brutal blast of wind yanked the man's hood back to reveal a chaotic shock of hair so violently white that it almost made his robes look dull.

"Kane," Asterin whispered in horror. "It *is* you."

The other stranger—a young woman, slender and lithe, with tawny orange eyes glowing like a jungle cat's—let out a charmed laugh. She cocked one leather-clad hip to the side and tugged off her own hood to unveil a devilish smirk. "Kane, you never told me that you were so famous!"

"I'm not," Kane grumbled. Two wicked knives flashed into existence. "Well, two down, two to go. Shall I do the honors?"

Before Gino could grasp Kane's meaning, something sharp bit into his chest. He heard a little gasp behind him from Queen Asterin, and then a scream of rage.

Did they hurt her? he wondered dazedly.

But by the time Gino comprehended that the prettily engraved iron hilt swimming below him was, in fact, buried deep in his chest and he managed to think, *oh*, the crimson-stained world had already gone black.

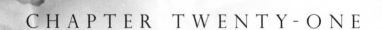

CHAPTER TWENTY-ONE

"I'd rather you just kill me," said Quinlan very matter-of-factly.

Rose glared at him. "For the last time, get out of bed."

The light streaming through the colored panes above them dappled his covers like a glassy meadow, hues of red and green swaying on a drunken breeze as the clouds shifted, far above and out of his reach. He had no desire to leave the warmth of his little sanctuary, even with the pillows long scantied of their puffiness beneath his neck and the air stale from his breath. Admittedly, he'd already counted the stars speckling the ceiling seven times over, but who wouldn't want to admire the streams of afternoon sunlight radiating through the stained-glass moons and flood of stars?

"Strange," Quinlan remarked. "I'm almost certain that Doctor Ilroy ordered me a week of bed rest." He narrowed his eyes on her with no little amount of suspicion. "You're usually a stickler for following doctors' orders. What's going on?"

Rose shrugged, all nonchalance. "Nothing. I just figured that . . . well, in the unlikely event that we happen to have guests over . . . you wouldn't want to be seen like this."

His eyes widened in sinking disbelief. "Rose."

She threw her hands up in defense. "Don't you '*Rose*' me. She's already on her way. And you and I both know that when the Queen of Axaria wants something, there's nothing in either realm that can stop her."

"No, I can't—just look at me, Rose, I'm a mess!" His chest constricted. A flock of clouds shepherded by the wind darkened the horizon. The meadow faded. "I told you not to send a damn letter."

Rose's glare grew hotter. "Yes, *after* I had already sent it. And you're usually a mess, anyway, so you needn't worry about that."

He grumbled several unsavory comments beneath his breath and rubbed his eyes—funny, he had done nothing but sleep for months and yet the exhaustion still dragged at him no matter how much he rested. He attempted to stare down his cousin, something which by now he should have accepted never *actually* worked. Defeated, he pushed the covers aside. "Fine. But you don't have to supervise me. I've been bedridden before, mind you."

She pursed her lips, thoroughly unconvinced. "For a week at most. Not months."

He flapped a dismissive hand in her direction. "Ah, what's the difference in a couple of extra weeks?" With a confident smirk, he swung his legs off the bed—and sure, he should have known something was off when the straightforward movement took significant effort, but perhaps his muscles were still . . . asleep. Or something. He cleared his throat to stall for time, suddenly noticing how much thinner his arms and legs looked beneath his robe. Scrawny, almost. "Just, ah, need to stretch a bit, that's all."

Rose raised a single, unimpressed eyebrow and crossed her arms over her chest. "Uh-huh."

"Getting out of bed? *Pffft*. Running a few miles? No problem for me. I am a strong, able-bodied young man." He inhaled, inspecting the floorboards at his feet. "Also, was the ground always this far away?"

His cousin exhaled in exasperation. "Let me grab you a cane."

"No, no! I'm fine!" He vaulted off of the mattress, throwing his hands skyward in triumph when his legs managed to sustain his weight. "See?" Then the ground began to shake. It took him far too long to realize that, in fact, *he* was shaking. Uncontrollably.

Rose dipped her chin at his legs. "You were saying?"

"They're just trembling with excitement," he informed her. "I'm fine. Truly."

In a heartbeat, her demeanor shifted entirely. "You know, I was *so* worried," Rose began, her voice dripping with sugary sweetness, "but thank the Immortals you've proven that you're fully recovered." Every instinct told Quinlan to flee when the Queen of Eradore took a step closer to him, but his legs refused to obey. Her hand floated to his shoulder. He cowered as it gave him a gentle squeeze. "*Truly.*"

He finally perceived his doom. "Wait—"

The hand tightened into an inescapable claw and bore down. Quinlan's foal legs buckled under the crushing weight. He crashed to the floor.

Rose loomed over him with a sympathetic smile. "Sorry, cousin dearest. But you just never learn your lesson."

There was a commotion from outside the door, and a moment later, the twins scampered in, chortling at Quinlan's pathetic state. Behind them followed Taeron, looking as genteel and dignified as he always did in a slim navy pinstripe waistcoat and blush-pink tie, the sleeves of his crisp white button-up rolled to his elbows. His horn-rimmed glasses were perched atop his head. As usual, he gripped a book loosely at his side, marked in place by what appeared to be a second, smaller book.

"Hello, brother," Quinlan said coolly from the floor.

"How's the view?" Taeron quipped, placing the book—*books*—on the bedside table and offering a hand.

Quinlan ignored both the hand and the genuine hurt that flickered in his brother's eyes as a result. "Fine. It's fine, I'm fine, everything is just fine."

The twins squatted beside his head and started poking his face. "Then why are you still lying on the floor like a dead fish, Quinnie?" asked Avon while Avris hid a giggle behind her hands. Her fingers were stained a suspicious neon yellow.

"Because fish are a staple commodity of Eradorian trade, little cub," Quinlan said, "and if they started flopping around on people's dinner plates, like so—" He demonstrated, much to the twins' delight, "—we would go bankrupt."

"Enough," Rose admonished. She hauled him upright and glanced at the twins. "Avon? Didn't you say you were going to bring a present for our smelly, dead, fishy-friend?"

The boy nodded, hopping onto his feet and bouncing on his toes. He produced a vial from his pocket. "It's supposed to help strengthen and repair your muscles, although it works best together with regular exercise."

Rose nodded. "Hence the cane. Walking is required."

Taeron coughed, fixing his stare onto Quinlan's forehead. "Actually, the cane will impede a smooth recovery, since you would be relying on one side at a time."

"So . . ." Rose tapped her chin. "Two canes?"

Quinlan glowered at his brother with enough poison to wither a forest. "Thanks, Taeron. You're the best."

With the help of Avon's mysterious concoction and a few hours of healing therapy with Doctor Ilroy twice per day, Quinlan soon managed stairs using only the banister. He could stumble around the palace without his crutches by the end of the week. After that, he allowed himself to tentatively ease back into his old training regiments—lessened in intensity, obviously, and by a frankly embarrassing amount, but progress was progress. Push-ups left him in a cold sweat, and he nearly decapitated himself doing chest presses. He woke up sore and went to bed sore, only to repeat the process again the next morning. It took a shockingly long time to regain his appetite, and every glimpse of his sunken cheeks and defeated gaze in any reflective surface made him cringe.

But nothing could have prepared him for the sight of his wounds—he had been avoiding it, turning away from the mirror every time he changed or bathed, shivering when his fingers accidentally brushed against the bumpy, upraised tissue while washing.

At last, one evening, fed up with his own cowardice, he eviscerated his dread and shucked off his long-sleeved shirt before a bath.

He stared. The blood rushed to his face, making him light-headed as a high-pitched ringing filled his ears.

Doctor Ilroy had predicted that the scar running from Quinlan's elbow to wrist would heal completely with time, but . . . his stomach was another story entirely. During the Fairfest battle, Rose had cauterized the puncture wound as a last resort to stop him from bleeding out. Ilroy had been forced to reopen the wound in order to siphon out the dark magic she had unintentionally trapped within—along with all of the rotting tissue, which had left a grotesque mass of scar tissue and puckered flesh, still red and tender to the touch.

In a society where any decent healer could mend cuts and bruises and burns without a trace, scars were hard to come by. Shadow magic was also hard to come by, Quinlan supposed, but the only thing that made the scar a little easier to swallow was that it belonged to him and not someone else. Like Asterin.

Asterin.

Quinlan sighed and slid to the floor, the tiles frigid against his flushed skin. He screwed the heels of his palms into his closed eyes. In that moment, back in Axaris, when Priscilla had held the lives of both him and Luna hostage and forced Asterin to choose between them, he hadn't even been conscious. If Asterin had chosen Luna, he would have never known better.

But she hadn't.

And he couldn't understand why.

Why had she chosen him?

Ever since Rose had relayed the tale to him, he couldn't stop thinking about Asterin's decision. He spun it in every imaginable way, but part of him still couldn't believe that Asterin had been willing to sacrifice Luna for *him.* Luna was Asterin's best friend, and he . . . he was just some smart-mouthed prince from a faraway land lucky enough to have caught her attention. The Queen of Axaria had crashed into his life like a meteorite—he had seen it all, right from the start, the attraction, the spark. He had *expected* her. Underestimated her. Braced himself for the collision, never guessing quite how much her impact would irrevocably change his world. It was the little things—the way she held herself, the way she fiddled with her hands when she paced, the way her eyes had sparkled after the first time they had kissed. And of course it was her strength, too. Her fierce loyalty, her bullheaded determination, and that stupid, irrational, unwavering bravery.

"Get it together, Quinlan," he whispered to himself. His reflection only gazed back disdainfully, like his face was privy to something his brain had failed to catch. "She still likes you. Why else would she rush over to visit?" He prodded at his stomach wound, nose scrunched in disgust. "Maybe she'll fall in love with some sea captain on the way to Eradore and forget about you." As absurd as it was, he suddenly found himself hating this faceless, imaginary sea captain, his stomach clenching so violently that he almost vomited all over the floor. He blamed it on Avon's potions.

Perhaps it was time for a nap.

"Up you get," he muttered to himself. His reflection's features twisted in discomfort. Twice more he attempted to rise, to push himself up onto his knees at the very least. With a grunt of frustration, he called upon his magic to help hoist himself onto his feet, a practice so natural and deeply ingrained in him that a swift gust of wind came to his aid without a second thought.

His magic had lain dormant during his coma for so long, restless, waiting—and now it sang through him, released like a pent-up sigh. Ilroy had advised him to devote all of his energy toward a full physical recovery before he even attempted any magic.

But I'm stronger now, he thought to himself. And Immortals, did it feel incredible to let go.

Like a giddy child, he rubbed his palms together. Red-gold embers sparked between his skin and jumped across the tile. He let them trail fire behind him, growing, spreading, fusing into a swelling inferno that devoured everything but burned nothing. The blaze seared down his throat as he breathed it in, deep, and extinguished with a snap of his fingers. He exhaled smoke through pursed lips and watched it drift to the ceiling, savoring the sudden sense of calm. His fire was as much a part of him as anything else could ever be, and it would never harm him, never hurt him.

Still high off the endorphins, Quinlan made his way out of his bathing chambers, shooting his reflection a mile-wide grin. Then, something registered in the back of his mind and he stuttered to a halt. He blinked a few times, reversing his steps, certain his eyes were fooling him, but then reality set in, and he gingerly approached the mirror.

He splayed his fingers across his abdomen in perplexity. No, there was no denying the stain marking the upper corner of the wound, an inky-black splotch crawling along his ribcage. Quinlan narrowed his eyes, desperately trying to recall its presence mere minutes before and coming up short.

That was when the pain hit.

It struck him like a dulled knife tearing clean through his body, only sharpening as he doubled over. He clutched at his abdomen helplessly, gasping for breath. Tears sprung forth, blurring his vision. Cursing, he staggered over to the side of the bathtub and slumped against it, heart hammering, blood roaring in his ears. He forced himself to breathe, *just breathe*, gulps of air, not enough, *not enough*, inhale, *exhale*—

Just when he thought the pain would never end, it finally subsided, swiftly dwindling to a throbbing ache. He raised his eyes to the mirror, expecting the blight, the infection, the *poison*, whatever in hell it was, to have spread—but, whether to his relief or disbelief, he couldn't decide, it remained unchanged.

He didn't bother wondering if using his magic had caused it. The only question was whether the *amount* of magic he used would affect how much or how quickly the poison spread, or how bad the pain would get. Because if a few measly fires resulted in this . . .

Something inside of him cracked.

Cruel.

He had no other word for it, for this newest horror. He was mere days into being awake for the first time in months, his eyes open at last and set firmly on the future. And yet his healing had led to something much worse. A bitter bark of laughter escaped his lips, and then another. Before he knew it, his whole body shook. Drunkenly, deliriously, he fell onto all fours, smacking his fist into the ground in time with his howls.

Life is such a bitch, Quinlan thought as his mirth bounced back at him from the tiles, cresting in a wave and finally crashing down upon him— drowning him, wrecking him, ripping him apart until his throat was raw and his body numb.

Eventually, sleep found him sprawled in a broken heap on the floor. It eddied around him, a lover's croon, a lulling wave pulling a shipless sea captain stranded on sirens' waters into its dark, merciful embrace.

CHAPTER TWENTY-TWO

Orion saw things in his dreams. Every time he drifted off, his head filled with vivid phantasms too striking and intricate to be anything but *real*. But every time he awoke, his dreams spilled through his fingers like water from the swiftest, iciest river, leaving him numb and aching the longer he tried to recapture them. He was cursed—all the answers he could ever ask for were *right there*, laying themselves down at his feet, but then he opened his eyes and he couldn't remember a single thing.

On just such an occasion, after a doze or a nap or whatever you wanted to call it since night and day in the Immortal Realm had the tendency to blend into each other, he resorted to staring at his star-speckled ceiling in frustration. How could he know that there even *was* a difference between day and night if not for his past? By now he had stitched together some semblance of a history for himself—he was mortal, that was certain, a fact that Eo made sure to hammer home daily.

"Never drink nectar," the god reminded him, sometimes multiple times a day. "Or leave the palace without an escort."

Or, "The Immortal Realm isn't just dangerous to mortals," the god would murmur against Orion's skin while trailing kisses down his bare neck and shoulder. "It is danger incarnate."

Still yet, "This is a dark, selfish, and cruel world. Only the palace can protect you when I'm gone."

So there he lay in a bed of demon feathers among blankets and pillows of silk and stitched lunarissa petals that sometimes glowed so brightly they jolted him out of his slumber, eternally confined to this lush, dark dream. Eo's butterfly minions saw to his every whim, bringing him platters of ripe fruit and sumptuous sweets that melted on his tongue and roasted winged delicacies that he had no name for. He frolicked in the gardens, keeping clear of the nectar arboretums, and waited for Eo to return from his godly duties.

It was a pitiful existence, and Orion knew it well enough, but he had no idea how he might break free from it. Or if he even wanted to. If Eoin disavowed him, turned him away from the palace and left him to his own devices in this realm, he had no doubt that countless horrors would swiftly and surely befall him. Though he couldn't remember a time before Eo, just the thought of foraging alone out there was enough for fear's ruthless talons to latch onto his heart and refuse to ever let go.

"Orion?"

Finally. He perked up. "In here!"

The God of Shadow sauntered into the room with his thumbs slung in the belt loops of his trousers. "Still lazing about?" Eoin quipped. He took in Orion with his midnight eyes, torturously slow and indulging.

At the beginning, Eoin had given him everything, and then stepped back. He put himself at Orion's side whenever his duties allowed him to. He brought him through the gardens. He plucked flowers, sang ballades, and teased him constantly, which Orion paid back in favor. Their repartee was a dance, a play of sharp wit. Every time they supped at the enchanted table, it shrank a few feet more, until it was forced to widen instead to accommodate their heavenly feasts.

Slowly, willingly, deliberately, Orion let his affections grow for the self-proclaimed King of the Immortals.

Now, Orion couldn't help but snort. "Says the man who spent *five* hours in the bath yesterday."

"*Four* hours in the bath," the god corrected before grousing, "and eight hours today in the Pit. The nine anarchies have gone missing and I have no idea *where*, the impertinent devils."

Orion's brow raised. "Anarchies?"

Eo held up his closed fists and ticked off his fingers one at a time. "Hostility. Prejudice. Ignorance. Conceit. Envy. Disgust. Cowardice. Greed . . . and Mercy."

Orion's nose wrinkled. "Mercy?"

"Indeed." The god exhaled through his nose and sat down on the bed. "It just so happens that mercy must be given in moderation. Something I learned the hard way." He sprawled out next to Orion, the demon feathers sighing beneath the added weight. "When I formed the Council of Immortals, each god and goddess brought with them a shadow beneath their feet—an anarchy. Those anarchies festered in secret, trapped by the semblance of civility we presented before one another. One day, Treachery broke free from Lady Reyva and the rest just burst forth like a pack of rabid wolves answering a howl. It would have been carnage, but I captured them all within the Pit." Eoin smiled grimly. "The Pit is *my* shadow."

Orion chewed his lip. The Pit, the true hell, the living grave of horrors too everlasting to ever die. "So where could the anarchies have escaped to?"

The god snorted. "Even the Immortals don't know. I can't sense them anywhere, not in this entire realm."

"What will they do?" Orion asked. "Set free as they are?"

"Wreak havoc, I'm sure," Eoin replied carelessly. "Sow the seeds of terror and distrust among all beasts and beings. Honestly, one on its own is more of a nuisance than anything—a horrid, grisly nuisance, but I would only worry if they decided to join forces. And that would be impossible, unless someone very, *very* powerful managed to wrangle them together." His fingertips meandered along Orion's abdomen, teasing as always. "I promise I would have noticed, though."

Orion shifted closer to him and reached up to brush his fingers along that exquisite jawline. Eoin allowed him to tilt his chin down as Orion arched his neck. Their mouths paused just shy of one another. The god tried to lean forward, but Orion kept them firmly apart.

"What now?" Eoin murmured, his lids shut and the warmth of his breath fanning along Orion's lips.

"How do I know that you won't think me a nuisance?" Orion whispered. "Or that once your new guest arrives, you won't just throw me into the Pit, too?"

Eo's eyes snapped open. "What? What are you talking about?"

No matter how much you please him, all you will ever be to him is yesterday's souvenir.

"I heard some ghouls whispering about some sort of eclipse," Orion admitted. "And that you were preparing to receive a guest when it arrives. Anyway," he added quickly, still unable to silence the echo of Harry's words. "You're the King of Immortals, and I'm just the mortal who hit my head on a rock."

He expected Eoin to laugh, but instead the god only stared at him.

"Is that all you think of yourself?" Eoin demanded. He ran his hands through his dark hair in agitation. "Orion, you are the only being who has ever seen me for myself. Truly."

Orion hesitated.

I experienced it firsthand. I was deceived. I was blinded.

And I can't bear to let the same happen to you.

Eoin seemed to sense his doubt and gripped his shoulders. "How can I prove my devotion to you?"

"Perhaps," Orion began, "if I should ever wish to leave the Immortal Realm—which I *don't*, currently, stop looking at me like that, thank you very much, but if I *should*, you could give me that option."

"I can do better than that," Eoin declared. "One departure and one wish, any wish, so long as it is within my power to grant it. Just say the word . . . though I pray you will not leave. Is there anything else you'd like?"

"I'd like to see the Mortal Realm." The words were out of his mouth before he had realized that the desire even possessed him. At Eoin's stricken expression, he added, "Not in person, necessarily. But perhaps through one of the windows?"

Eoin thought for a moment, and then pressed his palms together. When he drew them apart, a slender length of polished silver emerged from their center, widening and then tapering into an oval hand mirror with a filigree handle entwined with rose vines. "How about this?" As Orion felt its cool weight in his hands, the god added, "Just picture whatever it is you want to see. The north, the ocean, whatever you wish. As long as it exists in the Mortal Realm, the mirror will obey."

Orion clutched it to his chest. In itself, the mirror was a reminder of his curse—for he could not call upon what he truly wished to see most. That is, what he couldn't recall in the first place. All the same . . . His stomach fluttered at the gesture. "Thank you," he told Eoin with heartfelt gratitude.

"It's my pleasure."

Without looking into its surface just yet, Orion tucked the mirror under his pillow for safekeeping and crawled across the bed to kneel between Eoin's parted legs. He gazed up through his lashes and smirked when the simple act of licking his lips blew Eoin's pupils wide with lust.

Whoever he had once been . . . well, he certainly knew his way around a man's body. Even if the body in question belonged to a god.

"So, King of Immortals," Orion murmured as he tugged Eoin's tie with one hand and began undoing the buttons on his shirt with the other. "On the subject of proving devotion . . ." He pressed their hips flush together and leaned in close, speaking his next words right against the god's lips. "How about I show you mine?"

CHAPTER TWENTY-THREE

Eadric knew something was amiss from the moment he and Nicole punched out of the ground outside of South Yard. He couldn't quite put a finger on it, but something in him had flattened its ears, raised its haunches, and it wasn't from the pungent stink of fish and salt overwhelming his nostrils.

Then his eyes narrowed.

"Is it just me," he said to Nicole slowly, wincing as his voice rattled along the rainbow of crates stacked beyond, "or are those pebbles floating?"

Before the Elite could reply, a hulking man clad in a swirling white robe rounded a corner and strode toward them, his ice-blond ponytail swinging by his waist and the largest greatsword Eadric had ever seen in his life strapped to his back.

Eadric spun around and all but shoved Nicole back into the hole. "Retreat!"

A peculiar, weightless sensation enveloped him. Eadric's eyes widened as his toes left the ground and his body tipped forward like an unbalanced ocean buoy. Nicole flailed behind him, rising faster than a balloon. His fingers scrabbled at the sides of the tunnel they had emerged from, just barely managing to latch onto a handhold at the last second. He grappled for Nicole's ankle with his other hand a heartbeat before she slipped away.

"Air barrier," he gasped. Something hard bumped against his knee.

When he released Nicole, she floated upward for a moment and then bounced against the invisible dome she had conjured.

BANG!

A greatsword slammed into the barrier, startling an embarrassing yell out of both of them. An impassive, black diamond stare pinned them from above. Eadric only had two seconds to take in the man's vicious, clean-shaven face before the greatsword lifted into the air again, blinding sunlight glinting off the edge of the massive blade.

BANG!

The man drove the blade into the barrier hard enough for the impact to rattle Eadric's bones.

Beads of perspiration glistened across Nicole's brow. "Captain . . ."

Eadric gripped his affinity stone as the sword rose yet again. "On my signal, drop the barrier and roll." He zeroed in on those lightless black eyes, all the while watching the sword's falling arc from the corner of his eye.

The sky flashed white and Nicole hurled herself to the left, the blade cutting right through the air without the barrier's interference and missing Nicole's neck by an inch, cleaving through the earth down to the hilt. Eadric yanked at his lightning like a rope, wrapping it around the greatsword just as he and Nicole began floating out of the hole.

The man let out a pained grunt and fell to his knees as the electricity conducted through the blade and into his body. Gravity restored as Eadric let him fry.

Nicole landed neatly beside Eadric, and for a heartbeat, the two of them simply watched the man spasm at their feet.

Then they glanced at each other wordlessly and took off, sprinting farther into the grid of shipping containers, zig-zagging through aisles and past a lone crane, sticking close to the shadows in case any more nasty surprises awaited them up ahead—*although*, Eadric thought, *the more attention we draw, the safer Asterin and Gino will be.*

Once Eadric felt positive no one was tailing them—the yard appeared deserted—he motioned to Nicole and they took shelter in an unlocked shipping container. Neither of them had light affinities, so Eadric conjured lightning to his palm, raising his arm above his head as skittish bolts of electricity crackled down to his elbow, casting their surroundings in a ring of bluish-white.

Piles upon piles of crates swam out of the darkness, stacked in pyramids dangerously high. Eadric found a lone box in the corner and pried it open with the flat of his sword to reveal stacks of stationery—sheets of parchment, Vürstivale cards, envelopes, quills, ink, and more.

"I was kind of hoping for harpoons or something," he muttered. "Then maybe we could have shot the bastard down from afar." He scowled. "What kind of affinity was he wielding? Air?"

"Not quite," Nicole replied, examining the crate's contents over his shoulder. "Air-wielders influence the state of gaseous substances in focused areas only, increasing pressure or density, pulling the oxygen from your lungs, that sort of thing. It was closer to a wind affinity."

"But he wasn't riding on wind gusts or anything. You need to actually summon wind to wield it. He didn't do that. He was just . . . floating." Eadric shook his head. "This was something else. Something more."

Nicole paused. "Have you heard of the Asceae?"

"The Asceae clan?" said Eadric. From what he knew, while Eyvindré clan, like the Jikuli or the Rianmar, occupied territories spanning nearly half of the continent, the Asceae mostly kept to themselves along the Fatalian Passen—the deadly mountain range crisscrossing the shared border between Oprehvar and Cyeji.

Nicole nodded. "I heard a rumor that, as the distant offspring of earth-wielding Voltero lineage, they practice a special magical technique that allows them to manipulate gravity."

Eadric hummed thoughtfully and rifled through the crate. "*Gravity*, huh?" He fished out some parchment and began tearing it into strips. "Maybe we can use that to our advantage."

Nicole raised a questioning eyebrow.

Eadric pointed his index finger into the air and summoned a tiny bolt of lightning to the tip. He aimed it at the parchment strip. It scorched completely. "Lightning particles move too quickly to be affected by gravity, but only if he doesn't see me conjuring it, which takes at least a few seconds. Even if I managed to get a hit, we would need to trap him. Larger masses equal stronger gravitational pull, right? So if we could pin him underneath an object with a mass too large for him to affect its gravity . . ."

"What sort of object are we talking about?" Nicole asked.

Eadric cursed when he accidentally incinerated a third parchment strip. "A shipping container, maybe—except we wouldn't be able to lift that ourselves, either."

Nicole smirked. "Unless you're a wind-wielder." She squinted as he continued struggling with the parchment. "What are you even trying to do?"

"Light the damn thing," he growled. "Where's a fire-wielder when you need one?"

"Dead, for starters," Nicole said bluntly.

Eadric winced. "Right." He turned back to the crate for more parchment. "Maybe if you created some sort of air bubble around the edge of the strip to help it catch aflame . . ." He sniffed smoke and glanced up to find a triumphant Nicole holding a burning sheaf of parchment in her fist. His jaw dropped. "How did you—*have you been hiding a fire-affinity from us this whole time?*"

She snorted and tossed a small object into the air. "Nope." He caught it one-handed. "Sometimes, Captain, you just tend to overthink simple solutions."

Eadric scoffed and opened his fist. "Me, overthink things?" He glanced downward. "I have no idea what you're—"

It turned out to be a small bundle of matches.

They chose an intersection of four wide lanes that all ended in dead ends but for two. Eadric's job was simple—lead the Asceaen hireling as far away as possible until Nicole's signal.

He marked the crane's location in his mind, noting the containers in the vicinity by their vibrant logos—Westerling Shipping Services, Fine Fellow Faux Furs, Xenithur Overseas & Co. And then, armed with his sword, the matches, and pockets stuffed with parchment, he set off into the yard.

At the end of the lane to his left, Eadric crumpled up a piece of parchment and stuffed it into the corner of a shipping container between two slats of metal to keep it from blowing away. Then he struck a match and waited for the parchment to catch before hurrying off to his next target.

Moving in a calculated path, Eadric repeated the procedure again and again until he ran out of parchment. By now, the Asceaen must have either noticed the smoke or spotted some parchment detritus—unless Eadric had actually managed to fry the brute dead the first time around, which seemed unlikely since he hadn't had enough time to conjure up more than a small charge of electricity.

Sure enough, when he retraced his steps and peeked around the corner, he caught a glimpse of a white robe flapping around the far corner.

Slipping in and out of the shadows, Eadric trailed the hireling from a distance. Relief coursed through him as the man sniffed out the parchment trail like a well-trained hunting dog, leading Eadric through his own self-designed maze.

His pulse quickened as the hireling paused in front of the aisle that would lead him to Nicole, but thankfully he continued on a moment later.

Eadric took three steps out into the open when the man suddenly doubled back. Those malicious black eyes zeroed in on Eadric before he so much as had a chance to retreat. Between one heartbeat and the next, the shift in air pressure made his entire body sag. Even the most minuscule of movements took tremendous effort. Straining forward, Eadric managed to lift his left knee, followed by his foot. Gravity sucked him down like quicksand. As he let his foot fall, the hireling strolled toward him, both of his gloved hands still raised.

With two more steps and a final grunt of effort, Eadric made it around the corner, nearly crashing face-first into the ground when the weight suddenly lifted. *He can't affect what he can't see,* he realized.

Darting right, he sprinted past a block of crates and immediately took another right at the next junction, all too aware of Nicole's location straight ahead. Returning to where the Asceaen had first spotted him, Eadric veered left twice, cursing himself when the man materialized two rows ahead. Once more, gravity slammed into him with the force of a mountain. *Visual limit, visual limit,* he thought desperately, his eyes snagging on a shipping container door mere feet away. Fighting the crushing weight, he lifted his hand with a groan, his fingers just managing to close on the steel bar. He swung it open with all his strength and threw himself into the darkness.

Scrabbling blindly over wooden crates as the door clanked shut behind him, he found the opposite wall of the container and crouched down, his right hand clenching his skystone and his left crackling with white-hot electricity. He pressed his palm into the wall. "Come on, *come on*," he whispered as the metal began to liquefy, dripping to the floor and hardening.

The thump of heavy boots approached, mockingly loud—a predator taunting its prey. The door cracked open and Eadric didn't hesitate. He brought his right fist down, striking the container with a blast of lightning. The electricity conducted along the metal roof and into the door handle. Eadric dove through his makeshift hole even before he heard the bodily *thud* signaling his success, the still-searing edges of the hole singeing his shoulders.

"Hurry up, Nicole," he hissed beneath his breath, already running. No sooner were the words out of his mouth when the sea wind weaving through the yard picked up. As in, *truly* picked up. It shrieked past him, guiding his path and nearly tearing his cloak from his shoulders. He felt like a stray leaf caught in a hurricane. Down the aisles he stumbled, the trademark bear of Fine Fellow Faux Furs growling down at him.

Eadric scarcely had more than a moment to catch his breath before the hireling appeared at the other end of the aisle, trapping him between the concrete wall at Eadric's back and the man himself.

Befitting the grand splendor of an Immortal with his floating white robes unfurled like swans' wings, the hireling rose above the crates and glided closer. The violent wind did nothing to deter him. Like a master watchmaker, his fingers tinkered with gravity, adjusting it to his tastes.

Shit, Eadric thought. He raised his hands in surrender, thoroughly defeated and driven beyond exhaustion. While the hireling continued floating, it seemed as though Eadric's boots had taken root in the earth.

This time, he would not be able to escape. All he could do was await his demise.

Eadric watched the hireling descend, white robes rustling back into place. He couldn't help but gulp as the man reached across his back and unsheathed his greatsword in a single, effortless movement, drawing out the silvery *shiiink* of steel. Now that Eadric could get a proper eyeful of the blade's full length—an obscene four feet from hilt to tip—his own sheathed sword felt about as useful as a large knitting needle.

"Wait," Eadric blurted. The Asceaen halted in front of him and raised an eyebrow. With his gossamer hair, brutal build, and fearsomely cold gaze, he even *looked* like an Immortal. "I have traveling papers sanctioned and signed by the Queen of Axaria."

That gaze didn't waver. "No papers can save you from death."

Eadric thrust a hand into his jacket and practically shook a rumpled stack of parchment in the hireling's face. "Please, just take a look, Mister . . . ?"

His lips quirked into a shark's smile. "Rivaille."

Rivaille straightened the papers and read the two words that Eadric had scribbled earlier at the top in all capitals.

LOOK DOWN.

Confusion wrinkled the hireling's brow. He turned his gaze down, and in his distraction Eadric managed to charge up for a second and electrocute him. At such close range, it was enough of a shock for gravity to revert back to normal for about three seconds. But three seconds was all he needed to dash forward, *past* Rivaille, as fast and as far as he could, the buffeting winds giving him an extra shove forward.

As soon as Rivaille recovered, he thrust out his hands. Gravity mowed Eadric's entire body into the ground. But by then it was already too late because, of course, the instructions on the note were only meant to prevent Rivaille from looking *up*.

A large rectangular shadow swallowed the hireling as the shipping container Nicole had propelled off the concrete wall with a mighty blast of wind plummeted directly onto his head. His eyes widened, arms shooting up to brace it with his magic, but whatever his control of gravity, it couldn't withstand the container's weight. Metal smashed into the earth with a deafening *crash* . . . squashing Rivaille flat beneath it.

Silence fell.

And then, from atop the concrete wall, Nicole began to laugh.

Eadric had never heard the Elite emit such a sound. It was a stilted but loud *a-ha-ha-ha*, as if she had read it in a book syllable for syllable and adopted it as her own. He gaped at her. "*This* is funny to you?"

She nearly toppled over the lip of the wall, clutching her stomach. "Did you see his *face*?"

BOOM.

The explosion resounded across the bay. They whirled around to see a column of ice erupting into the sky like an off-course comet of blue frost.

"Asterin," Eadric said, his stomach sinking. Something had gone terribly, terribly wrong.

Nicole leapt off the wall, summoning a gale to cushion her landing, and together they raced for the quay bridging the two yards. "Weren't there supposed to be three hirelings in total?" the Elite called to him as they ran.

Dread coiled in Eadric's stomach. Only now did he realize that they had crossed paths with just one single hireling. And no magical knives had been involved.

If there were two more people like Rivaille hunting Asterin and Gino *with* said knives . . .

He ran faster.

CHAPTER TWENTY-FOUR

Killian liked Queen Asterin of Axaria very much.

After Kane killed Gino, he knocked the queen out and dragged her into a shipping container, whereupon he began tying her to a pile of crates lashed together. Unfortunately for him, the girl had awoken sooner than expected and kicked him in the crotch. Without hesitation, she froze him within a column of ice.

Killian nearly peed herself laughing at his petrified expression.

"Don't laugh," the queen snarled. "I'll ice you too."

A wave of frost surged toward Killian, but she merely clicked her tongue and dispelled it with a relaxed flick of her wrist. She wasn't an immortal shadow demon for nothing, after all. "Nice try."

Ah, but that was only meant to be a distraction—the queen had also summoned a razor shard of ice to slice through the ropes binding her to the crates. They thumped onto the floor in a heap. She stood victoriously, but another flick of Killian's wrist summoned a drove of shadows to shove her back down into the chair and yet another swarm to replace the rope.

With her affinity stone clutched behind her back, Asterin slashed through the shadows with blades—first of ice, then light. But the darkness simply parted around them and then fused back together.

"The nice thing about shadow," mused Killian, "is that it cannot be confined to any physical state. Or any physicality at all, now that I think about it." Her shadows leapt greedily from the gloom and wrenched the queen's affinity stone from her grasp. The stone decayed within seconds and disintegrated to dust.

"I'll kill you," Asterin snarled. "I'll kill you for what you did."

Killian glanced at Gino. He lay atop some boxes in the corner, staring up at the ceiling opposite icicle-Kane with glassy eyes. "Good luck with that."

The queen's expression blazed. "Rot in hell, you—"

Killian swirled a finger in the air, conjuring a black haze, and then jammed it into Asterin's mouth. A smile rose to her face as she watched the queen fight and jerk around in silence until her face flushed crimson. She approached the queen one step at a time. But instead of shrinking away when Killian leaned forward and braced her hands on the chair on either side of the queen, the rage in Asterin's eyes only flared hotter.

"Sorry, sweetheart," Killian murmured, gazing up through her lashes and batting them a few times for good measure. "All I meant was that you *can't* kill me. I'm no ordinary mortal, you see. Or mortal, at all, for that matter."

Realization flickered in those emerald eyes.

Killian leaned closer and lowered her voice as if to tell a secret. "Say, why don't we make a deal? You listen to what I have to say without interrupting, and I'll give you back your voice."

Asterin nodded slowly. But as soon as Killian waved the makeshift gag away, the girl spat in her face.

Killian only bent closer and wiped off her cheek on Asterin's own shoulder. "Rude."

"Why don't you just kill me already?" the queen growled.

"Kill you?" She smiled. "We don't want to kill you." Her gaze flicked over to Kane briefly. "Or at least, *I* don't."

"Then what is it you want from me?"

"A kiss, maybe," Killian teased. "I've always wanted a kiss from a queen."

Asterin's lip curled back. "Stop this farce."

Killian pouted but gave a reluctant sigh. "We came to kill your captain, that's all. In the meantime, we're keeping you here until your boat to Eradore leaves."

"Why?"

"Because that's what my employer told me to do."

"Who's your employer?"

"I'll tell you . . ." Killian tilted her head. "If you give me a kiss."

At that, Asterin's eyes narrowed. "Truly?"

Such inspiring conviction. Killian grinned, admiring those pretty greens. "Want to find out?"

Asterin lifted her chin haughtily. "Tell me first."

"Aw, that's no fun." She sat back on her haunches and yawned wide enough for her jaw to pop. "Face it, Your Majesty. You should have stayed home. Then none of this would've happened." Killian held up her fingers and began ticking them off. "Gino is dead, the cute fire boy from the bakery is dead, and so is that other girl and your captain. If not yet, then soon. Rivaille always gets the job done. Unlike you." She lowered her voice to a hush. "Poor thing. You're supposed to *protect* your people, aren't you? Instead . . . you got every single one of them killed."

The words hit something deep, if the slump of Asterin's shoulders and the grief lining her brow were anything to go by, like some acknowledgment of a fate foretold in times past.

"I know," Asterin whispered. Then, to Killian's surprise, the queen jerked forward, fighting against her bonds with her teeth bared, the fury in her eyes reignited. "But nothing—*nothing* you accomplish, short of setting all the ships in Horn's Bay ablaze, will keep me from getting to Eradore."

Killian snapped her fingers. "Now, *that* is a brilliant idea." She rose from her crouch and made for the door. "Fear not, Your Majesty, I'll take care of it immediately."

Asterin paled. "What? I didn't—I wasn't—come back here. You wouldn't." The chair legs began rattling as Asterin struggled, lashing out to no avail. "You *wouldn't.*"

Killian propped the door ajar with her foot and spared the girl a final pitying glance. "Be good while I'm gone." She jerked her chin at the body in the corner. "Or I'll have my shadows eat your poor Elite from the inside out."

"*Wait*—"

Killian gagged Asterin again before she could finish her sentence and

sent her a mocking little salute. "Bye-bye, Queen Asterin of Axaria. I've
got some boats to burn."

And then the door clanged shut.

Humming merrily herself, Killian stepped into the late afternoon
sunshine. Chains of shadow snaked from her palms, shackling the container's handles tight together. Sure, it probably wasn't in Kane's best interest
to be locked up with the Axarian she-wolf, but that wasn't *really* her problem. Besides, the girl couldn't use her magic without an affinity stone.

Stuffing her hands into her pockets, Killian turned her gaze forward
and strolled toward the harborfront. She matched her steps to the rhyth-
mic creak of swaying masts, the gentle lapping of water against the piers
and the snap of incoming boat sails caught in sea wind. A truly tanta-
lizing medley of brine and rust and mortal sweat filled her nostrils. Just
up ahead, a fishmonger hovered over a barrel rimmed with salt and ice,
hollering, "Fresh codders, fresh codders fer sale!"

Killian smiled at the fishmonger and slipped into the clamoring
crowds lining the docks. Someday, if she ever found a way to free herself
from Eoin—*permanently*, not whatever bullshit Jakob had negotiated her
out of—she would move to the coasts of some mortal kingdom and find a
nice little house with an ocean view. Maybe Morova, or Lethos. Not Volterra—she could never return to the place she had once called home, not
without remembering.

The Immortal Realm didn't have oceans. Just the Jade River, and
magic filled its beds in water's stead.

She had tried to drown herself in that river, once, after Eoin had
claimed her.

Two navy-tip winged gulls circled above, shrieking their misery. A
nearby docker leaned against a wooden post, eating a sandwich. He threw
a crust of bread to the ground. Killian watched the gulls nosedive and
fight over the single scrap. *Like two little rulers*, she thought with detached
amusement. *And one little throne.*

Farther up Knight's Quay, a trading vessel had dropped anchor. The
gangplank clapped onto the dock, and the crew disembarked in a jolly
mood, jostling one another on the way down with a round of back slaps and

boisterous laughter. A few feet away from Killian, a little girl squirmed out of her mother's arms and ran for the only clean-shaven man in the bunch.

When he spotted her running over, his face lit up like the sun. He snatched her off the ground to whirl her high in the air, much to her squealing delight, her ginger curls flying and the ocean breeze catching the hem of her buttercup-yellow dress.

Killian forced herself to look away. And then—*right there*, moored next to the trading vessel like it was meant to be, she spotted the *Ocean Gypsy*. She was a beautiful ship, with sleek curves as alluring as her name, gleaming decks, sails the hue of dark amethyst, and a hull that shone like gold in the water's reflection below.

Her eyes trailed along the pearlescent gunwales, the slender masts, the obedient little row of cannon ports. Cannons meant gunpowder—so all it would take was a single, well-aimed blast to blow the *Gypsy* out of the water, along with everyone on it. She could set off a chain reaction all the way down the quay if she wanted. Afterward, she could find the other two ships bound for Eradore and gift them the same fate.

But then what?

If she sabotaged today's ships, another fleet would arrive tomorrow anyway, and then another the day after that. Even in the face of disaster, the world would keep turning. And no way would Asterin give up so quickly.

Killian swallowed. *The lives of every person in the entire bay are at my mercy.* On a whim, she could bring down total annihilation upon the harbor. She glanced at the girl in the buttercup dress, at last reunited with her father after the Immortals knew how many weeks or months at sea. She thought about how easy it would be to break her bones, wondered how long it would take to drown the air from her lungs beneath the might of the ocean waves.

Mortals are so fragile, she thought to herself. *And yet, what I wouldn't give to be one of them.*

A deafening *boom* shook the earth, rocking the ships moored in the ports and sending sprays of foam onto the docks. Torn from her musings, her eyes jerked up to find a pillar of ice cleaving the sky to her right. The wicked white-blue barbs of wrath reminding her that perhaps some mortals were less fragile than others.

"How in hell?" Killian breathed as sailors emerged from belowdecks to point up in awe at the icy behemoth cresting North Bay. Without an affinity stone . . . it was impossible. Not that it mattered any longer. Her dawdling had cost her, and now it appeared that she had an angry adolescent queen to deal with.

Frantically, she glanced around. She had to do *something*. The *Ocean Gypsy* drew in her gaze once more, rising so gloriously against the backdrop of the Three Bridges beyond. For a moment, she fixated on the bridges— the gateway to the sea for every single ship in the harbor.

If she blocked off not just the *Gypsy*, but *all* the ships . . .

The moment she made her decision, the deed was already done. Shadows raced beneath Horn Bay's currents, staining the water in blossoms of black ink. Her shadows clambered up the foundations of Dame's Bridge first, and then Earl's Bridge, and finally Knight's Bridge, piling atop one another like starving ferals, desperate to ravage and ruin.

And she let them.

CHAPTER TWENTY-FIVE

The squealing of pigs shredded the air as Harry shadow jumped directly into a slop trough.

They assailed him with alarming fury, latching onto his ankles and trouser legs with their tiny demonic teeth. He fled for his life, past the bewildered stares of shopkeepers and passersby, his steps splattering slop and manure down the street with every disgusting *squelch*.

Centuries of shadow jumping and he was *still* shit at it. Quite literally.

As he turned a corner toward the harbor, his nose twitched. The scent of smoke tickled the air, along with something like . . . burnt toast.

He frowned. The scent grew stronger. *You have time*, he told himself, and let himself be guided along a magenta road for about ten blocks. The *Ocean Gypsy* wouldn't set sail until five in the evening, and the sun had just begun lowering from its midday peak around an hour ago. He took a shortcut through a small park and then swung left onto a bright-red road.

His eyes widened.

He stepped into the street to get a closer look, his head buzzing, and almost got run over by an oncoming hansom cab.

The driver shouted at him and shook her fist, but Harry didn't take any notice, instead completely occupied by the enormous pile of rubble on the other side of the road.

He shuffled toward the remains of what appeared to be a bakery, judging by the shattered decorations and display cases, not to mention the half-incinerated croissants strewn about the perimeter. The area had been roped off by constables, and several city guards were bent inquisitively over what must have once been a table or a counter. Someone had laid out a row of knives atop it—but not the kind for cooking.

In the end, it wasn't even the knives that tipped Harry off, though. Discarded by their owner, the hilts lacked their typical eerie blue glow, but the ghostlike signature of a familiar presence still clung to them like dark fumes . . .

"*Killian*," Harry whispered to no one.

Although the smoke from the fire masked any other hints of magic, her scent was unmistakable. What had she been doing here? And recently, too—dawn at the earliest, or maybe even just a few hours ago. Her signature was faint enough that Harry felt fairly sure that she hadn't actually wielded any magic . . . however, Killian was devastating enough on her own, with magic or without. Judging by the exceptional level of destruction, he didn't doubt she'd had a hand in this.

Dread spiked through him as he considered the possibilities. What were the chances that both Killian and Asterin were in the same city at the same time? Could it simply be a coincidence? Orielle *was* Axaria's largest port by far, the main hub connecting the entire kingdom to the rest of the world. Yet . . .

A whinny shrieked through the air, accompanied by the thunder of hooves. Harry whirled around as a familiar midnight stallion hurtled toward him. Passersby on the walkways screamed in terror and dove out of its way.

The stallion skidded across the cobblestones and halted before Harry, narrowly missing a wagon full of peaches.

Harry blinked in astonishment. "*Lux?*" he blurted. Not just Lux, but an Asterin-less Lux. The Iphovien stallion snorted at him, sides heaving from exertion. As he reached up to stroke Lux's velvety muzzle, a bay thoroughbred with a white star marking its forehead and a dappled gray beast that Harry immediately recognized as Eadric's horse came tearing around the corner to join Lux. They, too, were both riderless.

By now, the constables hovering by the remains of the bakery were casting him suspicious stares. Shopkeepers had stuck their heads out of their storefronts to yell at him, and Harry realized that the horses were clogging up the street traffic.

He tugged at Lux's reins, but the stallion wouldn't budge. "What's the matter with you?" Lux's nostrils flared, black ears pinned back. Even though Harry felt a little silly talking to a horse, he asked, "Where's Asterin? Will you take me to her?"

Lux huffed irately and pawed at the ground. Harry finally got the idea and mounted, clumsily—he had never needed a horse to travel, after all.

Before he could even settle into the saddle, though, Lux kicked into a gallop. Harry bit down on a yell. It was all he could do to ram his feet into the stirrups and not fly off Lux's back as Asterin's steed jostled his way down the street, cramming between carriages and cabs at breakneck speed. He jounced up and down in the saddle, teeth clacking, trying his best not to bite his own tongue off or piss himself in panic. Despite Harry's hysterical attempts to slow him down, Lux barreled down East Cliff toward the harborfront. The other two horses kept close at Lux's tail, and Harry wondered how long had they been running rampant around the city. It was a miracle that they hadn't been captured.

As if on cue, there came a shout. "There they are! *Halt!*"

Harry's gut clenched as a trio of mounted constables clattered into view at the end of the next street to form a barricade. Each officer clutched some sort of contraption made of a pole and some rope. *To lasso the horses*, Harry realized.

He tugged at Lux's reins in pleading. "Stop, you damned fiend!"

Lux might as well have been deaf for all the good the words did. Instead, he rocketed *faster* in a burst of godly speed.

Harry let out a quiet sob and vowed right then and there that he was never getting on a horse again for the rest of eternity.

Ahead, the constables' own horses danced nervously while Lux charged ever-faster toward them. Finally, the realization that the Iphovien stallion definitely wasn't slowing sank in and the constables cried out to break rank, throwing their poles over their shoulders in their haste to evade the maniacal horse.

Lux simply snorted at them.

Harry could hear the dissonant clanging of crisis bells following them down the cliff, but they grew fainter with each passing block—after all, no city nag could ever match the speed of a royal steed, much less an Iphovien stallion. A smile rose to Harry's face, but it vanished immediately when Lux swerved hard to the left and nearly decapitated him with a hand-painted shop sign. The stallion galloped into a side alley lined with traders selling jewelry and pottery and homemade candles on mats. They yelled out in horror as the brick walls flanking the street grew narrower and narrower, forcing Lux to trample over the mats, and Harry yelled right alongside them. He glanced over his shoulder and cringed at the shattered wares and thousands of beads they left scattered upon the stone in their wake.

"You didn't even have to go that way!" Harry hollered over the furious uproar behind them. He could have sworn Lux's answering whinny sounded like a gleeful laugh.

The road opened into a sweeping boulevard flanked by myrtle trees, their summer fuchsia blossoms succumbing to an ombré of vermillion-gold leaves. They passed beneath a massive wrought-iron gate spanning the width of the boulevard, "Harborfront" emblazoned across the top in burnished bronze. Directly ahead, the Loric Ocean stretched past the Three Bridges, farther than the eye could see, the crash of waves against the cliff crags on either side of the bay a constant white noise beneath the harborfront's clamor and the cries of gulls.

Eoin had sent Harry to Orielle enough times for him to remember the number of berths in each of the three ports, as well as the approximate groupings of ships based on their type and their destinations—so when Lux clattered into Dame's Port, Harry yanked the reins even before he located the elegant, proud-masted black ship docked beside a half-dozen foreign trading vessels.

But Lux ignored him and thundered right past the *Ocean Gypsy*.

"Damn you, Lux!" Harry moaned. "That's the ship Asterin is supposed to be on!"

Lux simply snorted and accelerated yet *again*, nearly trampling over a sailor holding a little girl wearing a yellow dress in his arms. The girl started crying, but Harry didn't even have time to shout an apology because at that moment, a fifty-foot tall spire of ice erupted at the other end of the bay with an ear-shattering *BOOM*.

Asterin.

"What in hell—" Harry began, but cut himself short when the scent of cinnamon and steel gushed over him. His breath stuttered—

And he shadow jumped.

About a minute later, he gasped and reappeared on Lux's back, completely disoriented and dazed. The stallion snorted and galloped on, unfaltering. Harry hadn't meant to shadow jump *at all*, but reflexes honed by centuries of danger and perhaps a little magical aid from the diamond pendant pulsing around his neck had forced his body to react faster than his mind. Sure enough, when he glanced over his shoulder and semi-shifted to enhance his vision, he caught sight of a white-robed figure far in the distance. The swinging hips, the square shoulders, the soft steps—he would have recognized that saunter anywhere.

Obviously, she hadn't detected his scent. He had no idea why his instincts screamed at him to avoid her in the first place—they were equals, sometimes allies. Borderline friends, when she pushed for it.

At that moment, however, all thoughts of Killian flew out of his head. Even Lux's gait faltered slightly.

A deep rumble sent ripples across the bay, causing the ships to bob up and down in a frenzy. Masts squealed, and sailors bellowed belowdecks. Then a darkness beneath the waves cast the blue of the ocean black.

A shoal of shadow fish.

They leapt out of the water and sank their teeth into the founda-tions of the bridges. Each piled atop the next in a rabid craze, spreading higher and higher until they stained the lengths of arches' pale stone black.

Dockers, fishermen, and sailors alike gaped in stupefaction at the spectacle, still oblivious to the sound only Harry's anygné ears managed to catch—the sound of their teeth scraping against the bridges, of splintering metal and crumbling stone.

All at once, the shadow fish finished their gnawing and flopped back

into the water with a colossal *sploosh* across the bay so mighty that the
ensuing waves overturned an entire schooner and some small boats.
Seawater frothed onto the docks.

A woman gripping a net in her weathered hands fell to her knees.
"The bridges are falling!"

"Rubbish," said the man beside her contemptuously. "The bridges
can't *fall*. The earth-wielders in the lighthouse will protect them."

They can try, Harry thought grimly. But no amount of earth-wielders
could withstand a shadow affinity, because only the power of the other
nine elements combined could ever hope to match that of the forbidden
tenth element.

And although he could no longer see Killian, Harry *knew*. There was
simply no other possibility. Worse still, Killian without magic was devastating. But *with* magic?

She was *cataclysmic*.

"What in hell are you doing, Eirene?" he muttered into Lux's mane.
What kind of coincidence was this, mere hours before the *Ocean Gypsy*
was scheduled for departure—

Coincidence?

Or . . . sabotage?

Harry didn't let himself wonder for long. Instead, he cursed under his
breath and urged Lux faster.

And for once, the damned horse listened.

CHAPTER TWENTY-SIX

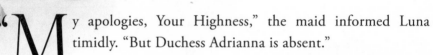

"My apologies, Your Highness," the maid informed Luna timidly. "But Duchess Adrianna is absent."

Luna resisted the urge to bash her head through a wall.

An hour. Today was the day, and she had wasted an entire *hour* pacing her chambers like a maniac, rehearsing everything she wished to confide in her aunt . . . only to discover that Adrianna had toddled off to Immortals-knew-where.

"When will she return?" Luna asked. Not that it mattered. Anytime but now would be too late.

The maid bowed her head. "I am uncertain. Her Grace often departs elsewhere for periods of time unbeknownst to anyone but herself and His Royal Majesty."

Luna's toes curled in her boots. "I see. Thank you."

The maid slipped back into Adrianna's quarters, leaving her to loiter awkwardly in the hallway with her guard, Greg. She wished her so-called personal entourage would return. It was a poor choice of title, really, since King Jakob kept sending them off on mysterious errands for days on end.

Usually, Luna would spend the day training her magic with Adrianna. In the evenings, so as not to arouse her father's suspicions, Kane had begun teaching her how to wield different knives and disarm opponents while Rivaille drilled her in swordplay. When the clock struck midnight, she would hurry to her chambers to find Killian leaning against the windows in wait, gilded by moonlight and wearing a secretive little smirk on her lips that she always seemed to save just for Luna.

For as long as Luna managed to stay on her feet—or rather, get back *onto* her feet—the anygné guided her through the basics of hand-to-hand combat. Again and again Eirene would strike her down, with such grace-ful ease, such *easy grace*, and then she would pull Luna right back up to teach her what had gone wrong and how to fix it. She would adjust Luna's stance herself, her fingers fluttering up and down Luna's arms, her torso, her calves. Every touch was so sure and steady, almost intimate, almost—

"—feeling all right?" asked Greg, his voice splashing into her like cold water. "Your Highness?"

Luna slapped both hands to her face, her cheeks embarrassingly hot beneath her palms. "*Fine*, Greg! Immortals."

"A-apologies," said Greg, his brow knitted in bewilderment. "I won't ask again."

"That's not what I meant," Luna exclaimed, even more flustered. She rubbed her temples. "It's—look, it's not you, it's me."

Greg's expression crumpled. "That's exactly what my wife said to me before she left me for another woman."

"Oh, Immortals." Luna covered her eyes. *I've made it worse.* "I'm so sorry to hear that, Greg."

"It's okay," Greg mumbled. "Honestly, they're a much better couple, anyway. If it makes her happy, it makes her happy. You know what I'm saying?" Luna began nodding, which Greg seemed to wrongly take as encouragement. "I just wish that—"

"I have to go," Luna blurted. "To . . . er . . . deal with . . . lady things."

Contrary to her expectations, Greg's eyes widened in concern. "Oh, no. Is everything all right? Do you need help with anything? I could—"

Who is this man? wondered Luna in disbelief. "No! Please, no. Thank you for your consideration, though. Goodbye!"

She hightailed it down the corridor, skidding around a corner toward her chambers and trying her best not to trip over her poofy skirts. Only once she dove into the safety of her private stone walls and slammed the door behind her did she finally take a second to pull herself together. Taking a deep breath, she closed her eyes and placed a hand on the frigid stone, waiting for it to shift beneath her touch before pulling away.

When her breathing evened out, she glanced at the pile of books on her bedside that she had filched from shelves all over the castle. *Legends of the Immortals*, astronomy charts. But she had memorized all of them, and so she stalked over to her full-length mirror instead. Staring herself dead in the eye, she began throwing punches, correcting her form as best she could while compensating for the gown she wore.

Punch. Block. Reset.

Repeat.

Day by day she grew slightly stronger, slightly faster. Every night she fell asleep, aching in muscles that she hadn't known existed. Every morning, she woke up and forced herself to do it all over again.

But no matter how many hours she trained, no matter how hard or smart or determined, she would never compare to Asterin.

Asterin would *always* surpass her by years of experience—not to mention in overall build. Without much thought, Luna had always maintained a slight, willowy physique. Now, even though she forced herself to eat four to five meals a day . . . she hardly put on any weight at all. Her body had become her enemy, and she hated herself for its betrayal. She increased her intake at meals, stuffed herself until she felt sick, and only stopped eating when she felt certain she would vomit from the next bite.

She knew it wasn't healthy, but she couldn't close her eyes without seeing Asterin's strength, her sheer brawn as she delivered a kick or swung her sword. Even Killian, with her rather underwhelming height, packed the muscle and ferocity of a tigress.

Sweat dripped into Luna's eyes. It stung like hell, but she only gritted her teeth. "What is *wrong* with you?" she snarled at herself in the mirror on the wall, her fists shaking as she held position.

You're too weak, berated the voice in her head.

"What do you want to be?" she hollered.

Strong, a new voice shouted back, bold and desperate and full of hope. *Strong, stronger, the strongest of them all.*

With a guttural scream, Luna drove her fist into the mirror. It shattered, a thousand broken pieces of her own reflection cascading to the floor. She panted heavily, rooted to the spot with her fist still upraised. Drops of bright scarlet dripped from her knuckles and spattered upon the mirror's remains. Unfortunately, the satisfaction of breaking it did little to dampen the pain.

The light in her chambers dimmed.

Her shoulders still heaving, Luna glanced up. The wicks of the torches lining her walls still burned just as bright as usual. Then her eyes fell upon the three windows in her bedchambers.

Through the glass panes, the midday azure horizon was bleeding out like a sunrise in reverse. Indigo blanketed the sky in a false tide of night . . . yet there, high in the distance, Luna spotted the sun, blocked by a speck of darkness.

Her veins buzzed with a strange sort of anticipation.

The eclipse.

It was finally here.

She whipped around as the air filled with the growing thunder of charging footsteps. They halted outside her chambers.

King Jakob's voice rang out. "Is my daughter in there?" he demanded.

"Sh-she should be!" exclaimed a man. It was poor Greg. He must have followed her back to her rooms.

"Luna!" her father shouted through the walls. "Open the door, this instant! Come to me, quickly!"

Luna ignored him and strode into her bedchamber. She straightened a few pillows on her bed and patted the jeweled belt at her waist, just above her skirts, double-checking for the sheath hidden within the tufts of periwinkle tulle.

"*Luna*! Guards! Break down that door! Protect the princess at all costs!"

The door quaked with the force of a dozen spells. Or at least, what the guards *thought* was the door.

"Morons!" her father yelled. "Get out of my way!"

Outside, the black speck that obstructed the sun began to writhe, to swell like ripening fruit, just to the point of bursting. Out slithered the shadows in her chambers, in the courtyard below, in the city beyond, from where they lurked beneath the underbellies of bridges and eavestroughs and even the outcast of torches flickering on hours too soon.

That lurking, slumbering darkness erupted into the sky . . . and surged toward the sun.

As each new shadow coalesced, the sky darkened a shade, then a shade more, until indigo deepened to black and black deepened to something . . . *darker.*

The feeble city lights snuffed out like candles in a blizzard, swallowed so wholly by the darkness that even stars ceased to exist. A silence too heavy to be natural enveloped the castle, and for a moment, Luna almost forgot how to breathe.

"Luna," King Jakob called through the walls, his voice taut with desperation. No—*desolation.* It almost caused her to hesitate, to turn toward the real door and let him in. "Run."

There was a laugh at her back. A splendid, rich laugh, fit to fill the entire sky.

Slowly, Luna turned around.

There was a figure reclining upon her windowsill as if it were the grandest of thrones. He wore a suit that seemed cut from the fabric of the dark heavens outside. He had passed through the windows like a slip of starlight, stealing away every ray of light from the rest of the world only to embody it within himself. With hypnotizing elegance, he rose from his throne and sketched a bow.

"Luna Evovich," murmured the God of Shadow, his voice a soft, deathly lullaby. Amusement adorned his expression. "You've been expecting me . . . haven't you?"

Luna smiled.

CHAPTER TWENTY-SEVEN

"Almost there," Eadric breathed to Nicole as he peered around the corner of the alleyway, the uneven wood slats of the Boar's Head digging into his back. Glass shards crunched beneath the heel of his boot when he adjusted his footing, and the stink of stale beer, tobacco smoke, and piss pervaded his nostrils with every breath.

When they'd arrived at North Yard, Asterin had been nowhere in sight. One of the shipping container doors had been ripped violently off its hinges, however, and when they peeked inside, they discovered an icicle-ized Kane. So the Boar's Head had been their next best bet.

Nicole braced her hand against the brick and recoiled, her palm glistening with some substance Eadric had absolutely no desire to identify. She wiped it off on her trousers with a grimace. "Nice part of town."

Located on the Rust Road along a small inlet where the tide washed up all the rubbish and the recesses of Horn's Bay, the Boar's Head would have been the last place anyone would look for a queen.

It had been years since Eadric had used the safe house last, but the dingy tavern hadn't changed one bit. With its sagging, woodworm-riddled roof, grime-caked windows, and crumbling facade, the shabby excuse for a structure truly did resemble a boar's head—at least, maybe after it had lain rotting in the mud for a couple of days.

At Eadric's signal, they crept toward the mouth of the alley. Just before they stepped out into the open, he threw an arm around Nicole. They slumped against one another and swayed toward the door, just two more stumbling drunkards searching for yet another keg to drown themselves in.

They staggered through the doors to the tavern. It took Eadric a few blinks to adjust his vision to the ghastly lighting. He waited for eyes to lift at newcomers, but all the patrons were so deep in their cups that he and Nicole might as well have been invisible.

Nicole knocked a mug of ale off a table as they squeezed between two stools on their way to the bar, spilling yellowish froth all over the floor. The woman slumped beside where it had teetered didn't so much as twitch.

The barkeeper eyed them as they approached, scratching at his stubble and slinging a filthy rag over his shoulder. "What'll it be?"

"Two absynthes," Eadric grunted. Every inhalation of the muggy, repugnant air made his stomach turn. He almost preferred the alley.

The barkeeper snorted. "You're in the wrong realm, pal."

"Then take us to the underside," he replied, sliding two silver notes across the counter.

The barkeeper smirked and the money vanished right before their eyes. "Come round the back, then."

Eadric and Nicole exchanged a glance before following the man into the storage room tucked behind the bar.

The man pulled out an affinity stone with the illusion sigil carved into the surface. "*Ovdekken.*"

A trapdoor shimmered into existence at their feet.

"There are tunnels leading to each of the ports from the main chamber," said the barkeeper. "Just follow the red markings. Your other two friends are already down there."

Relief rushed through Eadric like a river undammed. So Asterin and Gino had made it here safely.

Eadric wrested the trapdoor open and peered into the shady gloom below. "Slight problem," he said to the bartender, only to realize that he had already long departed. "The ladder is gone."

"How far is the ground?" asked Nicole.

"Well—oh, I don't remember," Eadric dithered. "Maybe fifteen, twenty feet, I guess, which doesn't *sound* like a lot, but—"

"Nice," said Nicole right before she crossed her arms over her chest in an X and hopped arrow-straight into the darkness.

"*Nicole Dwyer!*" Eadric exclaimed.

Boots slammed into stone, softened by a carrying wind. "It's fine, Captain!" her voice echoed up to him. "Come on!"

Eadric rolled his eyes, ready to jump after the Elite when he looked down into the darkness and a memory devoured his mind like flame held to parchment.

You've been sitting on your ass too long, Cap!

He remembered glancing up at Orion's voice. Remembered the lurch of his stomach as the toe of his boot snagged on something mere feet away from the edge of the roof . . . and the five-story drop below.

"I'll catch you!" Nicole yelled, but he barely heard her, because in his mind, he was losing his balance, his eyes wide and arms flailing. He tumbled off the roof, heart hammering in his throat, the street rushing up to meet him, Luna's scream ringing in his ears—

"Queen Asterin is waiting!"

Asterin. My queen, my duty.

The thought snapped him out of his daze. With his pulse still racing and his hands shaking, he lifted his left foot and forced himself to pitch his body into the oblivion.

Wind lashed upward at Nicole's command, slowing his fall to a feather's drift. His knees nearly buckled when his feet finally touched the blessed ground. "Th-thank you."

Nicole's hand gave his a reassuring brush. "Over there." A faint, keyhole-shaped pinprick of light glowed about ten feet or so away. Before they could move closer, however, there was a *click* and a *creeeak* that raised the hairs on Eadric's arms. Feeble golden light leaked across the cracked stone tiles.

Queen Asterin propped the door open with her hip. The tilt of her chin made it impossible to make out her expression in the gloom. "Thank the Immortals," she whispered, the tension deflating out of her shoulders.

Eadric's head spun from relief. "Asterin. Are you all right? Are you hurt?"

Asterin kept her face turned away. "I'm fine. Come inside."

They followed her into the main underground chamber. It resembled a small dining room, with a long oak table and chairs lining both sides. The walls seemed to tremble from the guttering flames of rusty candelabras shoved into the four corners of the room.

Eadric scanned the space and frowned. "Where's Gino?" When Asterin looked up, his breath hitched. Red rimmed her emerald eyes, still puffy from tears. "Immortals. What happened?"

Asterin's entire body locked up. "Gino's dead," she choked out.

Her words sucked the air from Eadric's lungs. "No. No—I don't understand. The barkeeper said there were two of you—"

At that moment, a black blur knocked Nicole sideways. Eadric caught sight of a smudge of shadow, and between one blink and the next, there stood Harry.

The anygné staggered forward, borne down with extra weight, hunching over it protectively. Eadric rushed to help him, but his steps stuttered when he realized what it was Harry held in his arms.

Gino's body.

Bluish-white frost tinged Gino's near-translucent skin, his veins a stark web of purple just beneath. Glazed brown eyes stared skyward, ghostly pale lips slightly parted. Frozen clumps of congealed blood ringed the knife embedded in the Elite's chest like an icy wreath of rubies.

Together, the four of them laid Gino across the table in solemn silence.

The despair struck first, like a punch to Eadric's gut. And then came the fury. "How did this happen?"

"Harry found me in North Yard," Asterin replied in a hoarse whisper, "before shadow jumping me here. Then he went back for Gino."

Eadric gripped the edge of the table hard enough for his nails to dig crescents into the wood. "But how did he get *stabbed*, for Immortals' sake—"

A tremor shook the queen's voice. "Kane," she said. "It was Kane."

Lightning scorched the table beneath his fingertips. He gritted his teeth and exhaled shakily. "I'm going to kill that bastard. I'm going to fry him."

"You'll do no such thing," Asterin snapped. "You know why they didn't lay a finger on me? Because they didn't need to. Because they're here to kill *you*, Eadric. Your death—*all* of your deaths—are meant to warn me away from Eradore."

"How can you be sure that their minds won't change? Or their employer's?"

Harry slammed his hands on the table and stood. "We're wasting time." He fiddled with the unfamiliar black pendant around his neck. "My jumping abilities have strengthened, but I don't know how much distance I have left in me. Eradore isn't exactly next door. I can only take two of you at most."

Asterin shook her head. "No. We're not splitting up again—"

"Your Majesty," said Nicole. "Shadow jumping is the only safety-guaranteed method of travel. You and Captain Covington need to get to the safety of Eradore. And besides . . ." The Elite scuffed the floor with her toe. "Someone should bring Gino home."

"Whatever you decide," Harry added quietly, "decide quickly. You'll find no sanctuary here. If Killian is still on the hunt, all of Axaria will be a deathtrap until she gets the job done."

"Gets the job done," Asterin repeated, disgust dripping from her tone. "She mentioned an employer. Someone who ordered her to assassinate Eadric and confine me to Axaria. Someone like . . ." The queen raised her gaze to meet Harry's dead on. "King Eoin?"

But the anygné simply waved her off. "Trust me, Eoin doesn't waste time with restraining orders. He only bestows death sentences upon targets. And no offense, but if Killian actually tried to kill you . . ."

"I'm sick of this," Eadric suddenly spat. "The lies, the doubt, the uncertainty . . . it's the Woman all over again." The faceless Woman, who had summoned Harry from the depths of the Immortal Realm, who had commanded the anygné to kill Asterin in the Aswiyre Forest . . . Back then, they'd pinned their suspicions on General Garringsford so easily, when the true villain had turned out to be Priscilla Montcroix all along.

Harry made a noise of frustration. "I wish I could tell you more. Eoin just doles us anygnés out to the highest bidder. We're forbidden from discussing who we're working for amongst ourselves."

"Kane and Killian will be waiting for my departure," Asterin muttered. She chewed her lip. "Nicole. You must pose as me." The Elite frowned. "It's the only way you'll make it out of Orielle alive," the queen went on. "We both have black hair and the same build. With your hood up, it will be difficult to tell the difference from afar." She took a deep breath. "Ride swiftly and stop for nothing. Bring Gino home."

Nicole took a knee in salute before Asterin, crossing one arm across her chest and clasping her shoulder. "Yes, Your Majesty."

"Gino's and Casper's families must be contacted upon your return as well," said Eadric, thinking of Casper's younger sister and mother and Gino's four siblings.

Nicole nodded. "May the Immortals guide you all safely to Eradore." She stood. "I need to find some rope."

"I'll help you get Gino upstairs," said Harry. The pair hefted Gino out of the room, leaving Asterin and Eadric to stew in strained silence until the anygné slipped back inside. He held out his hands. "Don't forget to hold your breath."

"Are you certain you can manage jumping two people at once?" Asterin asked.

"Most likely," Harry replied.

"Most likely?" Eadric squawked. "What do you mean, *most*—"

A *crash* from above cut him off. Angry shouting and a high-pitched cackle followed.

Harry's eyes widened. "Killian is here. We're out of time."

Boots slammed into the ground outside the door. The doorknob began to turn, but by then Harry had grabbed their hands and sucked them into an infinitely dark void.

CHAPTER TWENTY-EIGHT

"So the portal in the crypt just vanished?" Elyssa asked Carlsby as they passed Throne Hall on their way to the infirmary.

"Yes, Your Grace," the soldier replied. "All on its own. It appears that the fountain's enchantments combined with the guard's water affinity was the power source that triggered the portal in the first place. We're looking into possible methods to safely destroy or at least inhibit the fountain itself to prevent another incident, but it's a delicate situation. In the meantime, we've positioned a handful of our most powerful wielders of light, fire, and sky around the crypt just in case, as per one of the last orders Captain Covington gave us before he departed the city with Queen Asterin."

"Excellent," said Elyssa. "Keep this up, Carlsby, and I might have to promote you again."

The young soldier flushed and ducked his head to hide his pleasure. "Your Grace is too kind."

Elyssa had taken a liking to the bright-eyed boy, with his copper curls and refreshing energy. Although he had originally been drafted into Wall patrol, she had put in a request that he be promoted to her personal guard.

When they arrived at the infirmary doors, Elyssa spoke to the guard blocking the entrance. "We're here to see Silas Atherton."

Elyssa would never forget *that* night, just over a decade and a half ago, the second time she had ever seen the Elite—only a boy recruit at the time.

That night, when Tristan had shaken her awake, the oil lamps beside their bed burning low.

The guard stepped aside. "Your Grace and company may enter."

Handsome oak dividers separating the beds lined the room, decorated with carvings of prancing deer and leaping fish, and heavy curtains prevented them from seeing the beds' occupants.

Elyssa stepped into the infirmary and froze, her nostrils filling with the scent of disinfectant and the sickly sweetness of sleeping draughts. At the smell, the memory flooded her mind, too overwhelming for her to shove away.

That night, one look at the worry brimming in Tristan's eyes and the anxiety pulling at his brow had her scrambling out of bed.

"Hurry," her husband had said, but she was already nudging him toward the door. She grabbed the silk robe draped on the bedpost on her way, stuffing her feet into soft slippers. He was still fully dressed—he must have stayed up all night.

She followed him out of the king's chambers. They were adjoined to her own. She never slept in them. "The ambush?" she asked as he held the door for her. Outside, guards awaited to escort them.

Her husband nodded, and they simultaneously broke into a run toward the grand staircase, leaving the startled guards to catch up.

When they reached the infirmary, they found Theodore Galashiels standing alone in the corridor. The King's Royal Guardian clutched a little boy in his arms. He stroked the child's goldspun curls, staring blankly into the distance.

His son? Elyssa mouthed to Tristan. Theo had told many a legend of Orion, and his newborn daughter, Sophie, both of whom they had yet to meet.

Must be, Tristan mouthed back and they both hesitated on the same thought. Where was Isabelle, Theo's wife? And did she have baby Sophie with her?

"Head inside," her husband told her. Elyssa had her own duties to deal with. "I'll be there in a minute."

Elyssa cast one last look at Theo and his son before hurrying into the infirmary. The room was full of activity as healers rushed about to tend to the wounded.

A sea of faces turned to her the moment she stepped inside. Her heart lurched as she took in the blood-streaked uniforms, the expressions of grief and desolation.

Two squads of soldiers gathered around her and fell to one knee in salute.

"Rise," Elyssa commanded.

One soldier, dwarfed by those that surrounded him, struggled to get to his feet. Elyssa rushed over to help him, taking in the blanket swathed around his shoulders and the uniform that marked him as a recruit. Silas, she remembered vaguely. His mother had just retired from the Elites.

The boy kept his gaze glued to the floor as he whispered, "Thank you, Your Majesty." He shivered visibly and drew the blanket tighter around his body.

"Your Grace?" Carlsby said, snapping her out of the memory. "Are you quite all right?"

Elyssa realized that she was still standing in the middle of the aisle. Infirmary personnel busied themselves around her, checking notes or bringing medical kits to their patients. A few personnel bore a dark-green patch in the shape of a laurel wreath on their uniform sleeves, and the rest had a pair of white feathered wings crossed one over the other—wreaths for the healers, and wings for the doctors. The healers came and dealt with broken bones and gashes. The doctors dealt with issues that the mortal body couldn't necessarily repair on its own, even with the help of spells or potions: severed limbs, chronic illness, diseases—or poison, as had felled her beloved Tristan while she had lain alone and blind with nothing and no one but the voices in her head in the darkness far below his feet.

"Your Grace?" Carlsby asked again.

She wasn't going to beg, though she couldn't stop herself from crying. She made no noise but for her teardrops, an echo of the drip of blood from severed necks, the quiet sigh of silk and breath as she knelt on unforgiving stone. She bent her neck in invitation and waited. For mercy. For death.

But it never came.

Elyssa rubbed her temple. "Yes, I'm fine, Carlot—" She stopped herself just in time, righting her slip. The half-spoken name filled her with anguish. "*Carlsby.* I'm fine, yes, thank you."

A haunting little voice echoed in her head. *Are you, though?*

A nurse holding an empty vial emerged from the curtains a little ways ahead and caught sight of them blocking traffic. He had a green patch on his sleeve. "Can I help you?" he asked politely.

Elyssa stared at the vial and wondered what had been in it—if Priscilla had kept her poison in a vial just like that one. She realized that she had yet to reply only when Carlsby cleared his throat. She blinked and relaxed her shoulders. "We're looking for Silas. Silas Atherton."

The nurse raised an eyebrow. "Are you his mother?"

Carlsby nearly choked. "This, you fool," he managed, "is the mother of the Queen of Axaria, Her Royal Grace, Elyssa Calistavyn-Faelenhart."

"Oh," the nurse said, a little frown the only sign of his distress. "Apologies, Your Grace. I was unaware."

Elyssa waved him off. "Times have changed. I'll never forget the way the royal court used to bend forward, back, and inside-out just to carry out the whims of the king and queen, so this is quite . . . refreshing."

The nurse gave her a wry smile. "I'm sure that hasn't changed outside of the infirmary, Your Grace. With all due respect, we healers and doctors tend to prioritize the well-being of our patients above all else." He made a face. "The good ones among us, at least."

Elyssa returned with a warm smile. "I applaud you for such dedication. I must, however, insist that we visit poor Silas. I may not be his mother, but I've known him for many years and I've been quite anxious to check up on him."

"Very well," said the nurse. He gestured them forward and led them deeper into the infirmary. "I tended to him earlier. He's just woken up, so he's still a little out of sorts."

Eventually, they arrived in front of a set of curtains identical to all the rest, distinguished only by a sign suspended overhead that read S. A. Elyssa exchanged a parting nod with the nurse, and he hurried back off to work.

Carlsby held open the curtain for Elyssa.

As she passed him, she murmured, "You are certain you know what must be done?"

The boy averted his gaze and tipped his chin in a meek nod. "Yes, Your Grace."

This won't do. Her fingers found his wrist and gave a gentle squeeze. "John, dear, did your commander ever mention to you why I requested you to be promoted to my personal guard?"

Carlsby's attention snapped to her, his wide blue eyes soft with confusion. "No, Your Grace."

"I wanted you," Elyssa went on in her most tender tone, "because you seem like the kind of boy who has a kind heart but knows when to be stern. A good soldier who knows when to follow orders. And you're a good soldier, aren't you?"

As expected, Carlsby's chest puffed. "That I am, Your Grace."

"Above all else . . ." Elyssa's grip tightened ever so slightly. "I know I can trust you."

There was only one other soldier, one other *friend* she had trusted, but that had all ended years ago after that day. The day of the ambush, when three young recruits were killed.

When Priscilla arrived, she made an offer to bring those recruits back. One dark, false promise had been all it took for a friend to become a traitor.

Yet, somehow . . . when the time had come for that traitor to execute Elyssa, she had been spared.

She returned her attention to Carlsby and fixed him with her most earnest expression. "But . . . can you trust me?"

To his credit, the boy didn't even hesitate. "Of course, Your Grace."

Elyssa smiled sweetly and released him. "You have no idea how delighted I am to hear that." She swept past him, casting him a glance over her shoulder. "When the time comes, I know you'll do the right thing."

"Yes, Your Grace." Carlsby bounced after her like an overeager puppy.

There before them, propped up by a few lumpy pillows, lay the eldest soldier of the Elite Royal Guard. A silver wire fastened to the underside of his jaw connected him to a contraption hanging over the bed that displayed his heart rate via a pulsing orb of light. Elyssa's eyes lingered on his bedside table, where someone—another Elite, perhaps—had artfully arranged a collection of handwritten notes among the flower bouquets and a tin of biscuits. A trio of affinity stones rested at the edge of the table—ice, earth, and wind.

"Silas!" Elyssa exclaimed cheerfully.

At the sound of his name, the Elite's eyes fluttered open. Though his gaze didn't quite focus on her, he found it within himself to slump forward in a half bow. "Ah, Grace. Your Grace, I mean. Hullo."

"You poor thing," Elyssa murmured, hurrying over to his side and urging him back against the pillows. "Hush, now. You must be quite fuzzy in the head. That Chaos sure did a number on you, hmm?"

"Oh, I'm all right," Silas slurred. "The doctors want to keep me here awhile to monitor my condition, though."

Elyssa glanced at the pulsing orb. *Slow, steady.* "No permanent damage, correct?"

A goofy smile stretched across Silas's face and he shook his head slowly. "No, Your Grace, indubitably so."

Elyssa laughed. "What a relief to hear! You had me worried sick. Now . . ." She let her expression shift, her tone grow serious. "Silas, dear, your absolute duty is to serve and protect Queen Asterin, yes?"

The fog clouding Silas's eyes thinned. "Yes, Your Grace," he said, still slurring slightly but much more alert at the mention of the queen.

"Your purpose as an Elite is to ensure my daughter's safety."

"Of course."

"Yet you endangered her," Elyssa said. "Your careless actions could have cost the kingdom her life."

Silas went utterly still.

Elyssa exhaled, brushing her ebony hair over one shoulder, and took a seat on the edge of the bed. "Of course," she said, pursing her lips in remorse, "it wasn't your fault, not completely. But the truth is the truth, and the past cannot be undone even by all the regret in the world."

"Your Grace," Silas finally stammered out. "I . . . I beg your forgiveness—"

Elyssa patted his knee. "I imagine that Queen Asterin has never spoken such harsh words to any of you Elites. She is as gracious as she is good. Perhaps, I daresay, *too* gracious for her own good. Wouldn't you agree?" She reached over to the bedside table and tugged a stalk of bluebells from the largest flower bouquet. While admiring the delicate curl of their perfect little petals, she spotted a shriveled bud near the bottom of the stalk and plucked it off. She crumpled it between her fingers and discarded it on the floor. "Do you ever wonder if she does her Elites a disservice when she neglects to punish them for their faults?" she wondered aloud. "Their mistakes?"

"I—I don't know," said Silas. "But surely that is her decision, and hers solely."

Elyssa caught the subtext beneath his words. "My dear Silas, worry not. I can't promise you much, but I *can* promise you that I keep my daughter's best interests at heart. She is my light. She is my *everything*." Her voice quivered slightly and she paused to tuck the bluebell stem back into the bouquet. "Ten years I spent in isolation. Ten years, trapped in darkness." She shook her head, smiling ruefully. "Ten years, *hoping*. Imagining what could have been and what could still be. All for my daughter. So you must understand how I feel when my precious Asterin comes in harm's way. And I'm certain that, as her most devoted and longest-standing Elite, you must feel just as I do."

The crinkle in Silas's brow deepened. He opened his mouth to speak, but ended up answering with a firm nod.

Elyssa exhaled. "Good. My heart rests easier."

The tension began to unwind from the Elite's muscled frame.

He thinks that the worst is over, Elyssa thought. *That I merely mean to reprimand him.*

Elyssa stood from her seat on the bed and placed one hand atop Silas's head. With her other hand, she signaled to Carlsby. He sprang out of the corner and came to her elbow.

Silas's eyes darted between them. The pulsating orb displaying his heart rate picked up in pace. "Your Grace?"

"Silas, never forget that I hold you and your devotion to Queen Asterin in the highest esteem," Elyssa said as Carlsby pulled out his affinity stone. "I hope that you will one day see reason in my actions, and that you will spare me any animosity you might soon bear."

Silas's eyes flicked to his affinity stones on the bedside table, but they had already found a new home in Elyssa's pocket. To her dismay, he hadn't even noticed.

This is my daughter's most experienced Elite? she wondered to herself.

The stunned Elite tried to rise, but Carlsby froze his limbs to the bed in jagged blocks of ice. The boy then produced a pair of iron shackles from his belt, shooting a hesitant glance at Elyssa for approval.

She nodded, grateful that she had trusted the soldier to do the right thing.

And the right thing will always be to protect my Asterin.

Elyssa watched on with an apologetic smile as Carlsby clapped the shackles onto Silas's wrists.

"Silas Atherton," she declared. "In the name of the crown, you are hereby charged with treason and royal sabotage. As Queen Regent of Axaria, I declare you under arrest."

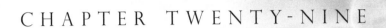

CHAPTER TWENTY-NINE

A storm is gathering, Luna thought when she first opened her eyes, holding hands with the God of Shadow, and found herself in a totally new world.

They stood on a high balcony overlooking a city of knives. The buildings pierced the horizon like bladepoints, glinting in a light that didn't truly exist. No sun or moon rose in the sky—the world below simply shone darker, wetter. The sun . . . somehow, instinctively, Luna knew that she could wait an eternity and it would never come. She could feel it on her skin, like a winter chill. She could feel something else, too—a strange, not-unpleasant energy that sent her every nerve tingling, the purr of electricity running up and down her spine.

Eoin released her and spread his arms wide, and it was only then that Luna realized his hand had actually felt warm and smooth and *human* in hers, not at all as she'd expected—though she had no idea why she'd expected otherwise in the first place.

His grin was blinding. "Welcome to my home! This is my favorite view. What do you think?" He pointed down at a patch of green situated along a winding river of scarlet. "See that lovely estate? That's the Dusk District. Killian's house is the one with the red roof and yours is just to the left—" A deep *boom* resounded across the city and far in the distance a column of oily black smoke billowed upward. Eoin frowned. "Oh, dear, there must have been another scuffle in the Pit."

The god narrowed his eyes, and a swarm of writhing darkness collected over the Pit. The sheer power of his magic rocked Luna sideways. It numbed her senses to all but its godly strength, engulfed her like the cold shock of pitching headfirst into a freezing ocean. High above, the darkness shrieked down, straight as an arrow, and plunged into the Pit.

Luna could hear the screaming all the way from over here.

Eoin clapped his hands together cheerfully. "Anyway! Shall we go inside?" Without waiting for a response, he spun on his heel and strode off.

What would it be like to be that powerful? To wield such potential for destruction?

Slightly dazed, Luna forced her gaze away from the sights below and followed the god, only to freeze again at the sight looming *above* her. Crystalline glass walls encrusted with huge chunks of raw gemstones rose infinitely skyward. From the right angle, the walls vanished, so that the gems appeared to float in midair. Beyond the walls lay a throne room, utterly barren save for a single, massive slab of glittering black stone.

Palms upraised, Eoin pushed open the balcony doors—no, not doors. Some sort of invisible barrier, surrounding the hall in every direction. It rippled beneath his touch and allowed him to pass through before congealing once more. Luna caught the already-fading outline of his figure in the barrier, an opalescent glimmer on the surface of a soap bubble.

Eoin beckoned to her.

Luna marched toward the barrier, her fingertips outstretched. She expected the touch of some cool, gel-like substance, but felt no difference between the barrier and the air around her. She only heard it—a little *pop!*—and then she emerged inside the hall.

Eoin cleared his throat. "Right, then," he said and reached into his inner jacket pocket to pull out a heavy charcoal envelope, sealed by wax stamped with a pair of butterfly wings. "Back to business."

She couldn't help but hesitate when he offered it to her, knowing its contents full well. But she steeled herself and accepted it, broke the seal, and slid out a crisp sheaf of equally charcoal parchment folded neatly into thirds. Line after line of flowing silver text flourished across the black expanse in sweeping cursive, each letter a work of art in its own right.

Eoin clasped his hands behind his back. "Please read this document over very carefully, my lady."

Luna arched an eyebrow. "As if I have any choice."

The god had the gall to look hurt. "You always have a choice."

The tiniest corner of Luna's mouth twitched upward. She already knew what choice he truly meant. As if in reminder, the sheath secured and hidden by the belt at her waist dug into her back. "I suppose so," she allowed, and then she began to read.

ANYGNÉ INDENTURE

THIS AGREEMENT is made this day of the eclipse between **EOIN**, God of Shadow, Ruler of Darkness, and King of the Immortals (hereinafter called "the King") and **LUNA EVOVICH** of Ibreseos (hereinafter referred to directly) in the Shadow Palace of the Immortal Realm.

WHEREAS, Priscilla Alessandra Montcroix has entered into contract promising her daughter shall choose one option as outlined below:

Option the First

1. Thou shalt be bound by thy word and immortal life to this Contract in both Mortal and Immortal Realms upon its formal signature until its formal termination, which shall transpire only under the willful decree of the King Himself.

2. Thou shalt obey the commands of the King above any and all others.

3. Thou shalt use any and all means to fulfill the aforementioned commands, within reason as defined by thine own judgment, under threat of corporal punishment should the King deem otherwise.

4. Thou shalt reside within the allocated living quarters bestowed by the King whenever thou dwell in the Immortal Realm.

5. Thou shalt never seek contact with any member of the Council of Immortals in any fashion or via any means unless under dire

circumstances imperiling the King, the Shadow Kingdom, or the Mortal Realm.

6. Thou shalt preserve secrecy between the King and thyself in all matters of Mortal Realm assignments, including but not limited to location, duration, employment, and purpose.

7. Thou shalt—

These went on for some time. Luna flipped through two more pages, her eyes carefully scanning each provision one by one until she spotted the section she had been hoping to find:

IN RETURN:

1. Thou shalt be granted temporal immortality.

2. Thou shalt be granted use of the full extent of the elemental power of shadow, equivalent to the might of the nine other affinities combined.

3. Thou shalt be granted an anygné form.

4. Thou shalt be granted unparalleled self-regenerative abilities in all but fatal wing laceration.

5. Thou shalt be granted wings impervious to all but the most formidable sword, *Nöctklavan*.

And finally, at the bottom of the last page, just above the line designated for her signature:

Option the Second

1. Immediate death.

It was so plain-spoken that she almost giggled. Twice more she read through the conditions of the first option, her head cocked in consideration as Eoin watched on with a smug expression. Most of the provisions were fairly reasonable, and as a whole certainly *more* reasonable than the second option. On top of that, the first option had perks and privileges galore. Minus the subtle threat of execution by getting her wings chopped off with Eoin's legendary sword.

She thought of Asterin and Quinlan and their omnifinance, powers they so often took for granted. For years, Luna had struggled to summon even a wisp of magic while Asterin had only to rein hers in.

Never would Luna forget those years before the curse suppressing both her true identity and her magic had been broken by the contralusio lake. Nor would she forget the days *following*. She hadn't needed private tutors or Academia Principalis professors. She had always been observant. Picked up things that Asterin missed. Watching her train with Quinlan back at Harry's cottage in the forest might not have taught her everything, but it had taught her enough.

So when the time had come to prove herself, to use her illusion magic to create disguises for Asterin and Rose and Quinlan and Orion to protect them from Priscilla, she had succeeded. When they'd had no one left to turn to, Luna had taken the helm and accomplished everything Asterin had asked of her. And more.

And *still* her best friend had not saved her.

As Eoin's shadowling, Luna would never need anyone to save her again.

Armed with shadow magic, a power equivalent to *omnifinance*, no mortal would ever look down upon her again.

Not even Asterin.

Luna let her gaze linger upon the second option of the contract. *Immediate death.*

She knew what she wanted.

Eoin sensed that she had made her decision and beamed his loveliest smile at her. "All we need is your signature on the bottom line." An exquisite quill of soft turquoise and emerald with an iridescent eye at the end materialized between his long fingers. A peacock feather.

Luna took it as a sign. She sent a prayer to Lord Pavon, the God of Illusion and the protector of the House of the Peacock. *Her* house—because regardless of which kingdom she lived in or that her father descended from the House of the Viper, her illusion affinity would always run strongest in her blood.

Eoin offered her the quill. "I really do look forward to working with you, Princess Luna. Although we've only just met—in person, at least—I sense that our souls bear a certain . . . camaraderie. A solidarity, if you will.

Don't mention it to the other anygnés though," he added with a wink, "or they might get awfully jealous."

Luna took a deep breath. And then, with unwavering confidence, she told the God of Shadow, Ruler of Darkness and King of the Immortals, "You've misunderstood. I choose Option the Second."

Eoin's smile froze on his face. He blinked at her in disbelief. "I beg your pardon?" he uttered. The quill slipped from his fingers and fluttered to the floor.

Luna's smile only grew. "I choose death."

CHAPTER THIRTY

"*Oh my stars.*"

It was the first thing Asterin heard when the daylight purged the darkness and the shadows around them dissolved. She staggered forward, pulling Harry and Eadric along with her, gasping in air to fill her oxygen-depleted lungs. Blinking to clear the spots from her vision, her eyes slowly adjusted to the brightly lit, unfamiliar surroundings rising around them.

A figure stood on the first landing of the staircase in front of them, her hair smoldering like fiery coals in the torchlight beneath the crown of sapphires atop her head.

Elation erupted in Asterin's chest. "*Rose!*"

Queen Orozalia Saville of Eradore flew down the stairs, her fingers racing along the mother-of-pearl banister, nearly tripping over her forest-green velvet gown on the way down. She leapt right off the last five steps and collided into Asterin's waiting arms, both young women cackling with maniacal laughter.

Asterin wiped her damp eyes. "Immortals, it's been an eternity. Sorry to surprise you with our early arrival."

Rose only hugged her tighter. "I couldn't be happier. Besides, I had your rooms prepared as soon as I received word that you were on your way." The Queen of Eradore gave her one more squeeze and held her from afar, that captivating golden gaze searching Asterin's face. "You look tired. Beautiful, but tired."

Asterin snorted at that. "And you just look beautiful. As usual."

"Wouldn't you know it." The Queen of Eradore kissed her cheek and relinquished their embrace to acknowledge the two men standing behind Asterin. "Harry! Lovely necklace. It suits you."

The anygné smiled wryly and closed his fingers around the glittering black pendant. "I don't think I would have been able to make it past your palace wards without it."

Rose gave him a confused look. "Oh, no. The Wardens alerted me that you were on your way. All I had to do was let you in." She let her gaze settle onto Eadric. "And hello to you as well, Captain Covington."

Eadric bowed deeply. "It's good to see you, Your Royal Majesty."

"Likewise . . . Eadric."

The captain's lips quirked. "Rose."

Rose's smile faded. "You're covered in mud. And . . . ash?" She scanned Asterin, too. Fortunately, Asterin had already removed the splatters of Gino's blood from her clothes, but somehow, perhaps from some lingering sadness in her expression, Rose knew. "Who?"

Asterin swallowed. "Gino and Casper," she murmured, voice going rough.

Sorrow welled in Rose's eyes. Although the Queen of Eradore had only stayed a few weeks in the Axarian palace, she had spent every moment of that time as an Elite, right alongside Gino and Casper and all of the others. "Almighty Immortals. I'm so sorry, Asterin. May their souls find rest in the afterlife. What happened?"

"Perhaps we could discuss it later," Asterin murmured. And Kane— they needed to discuss Kane. She didn't dare broach that subject now, not that she had the faintest idea of how to begin, anyway. *Ah, by the way, your ex-boyfriend went rogue, knifed Gino, and tried to murder us earlier today.* No, last she remembered, Rose couldn't even stand to hear his name uttered aloud. "I haven't quite processed it yet."

Rose squeezed her hand. "Of course. Whenever you see fit." After a solemn silence, the Eradorian nudged her. "Say . . . I imagine you'd like to see Quinnie."

Asterin's stomach clenched with—with what? Excitement? Dread? Longing? After everything that had happened in Orielle, she was finally here, right under the same roof as Quinlan . . . even if that roof happened to span leagues. "Immortals, yes. Do you have any fresh clothes I could borrow? We left our packs behind. And perhaps a bathtub . . . and a hairbrush . . ."

"Say no more." Rose slung an arm around her shoulders and led her toward the stairs. "Come along, boys," she added, beckoning for Harry and Eadric to follow them. As they ascended, Rose muttered out of the corner of her mouth. "Just for the record, you know that Quinlan wouldn't care about anything like that, right?"

Warmth kindled in Asterin's chest. "Thank you for the reassurance."

Rose leaned over to her to take a whiff. "Also for the record though, you do smell a bit."

Asterin elbowed her. Their laughter rang through the halls of Eradore, two queens and two friends reunited. It was almost enough to lessen the pain of today.

Quinlan lounged in his sitting parlor, drinking a cup of tea amid the plush cushions, a long-forgotten novel Taeron had recommended to him propped against his crossed legs. He stared out the windows on his left, lost in his own head.

It was agony, really—to know that there were only days left before he would see Asterin, without knowing *exactly* how many days it really was. Bad weather, sickness . . . so many factors could delay her arrival. His every waking minute seemed plagued by anticipation, and he could hardly focus on anything more than the simplest of tasks.

It was absurd. And yet he couldn't seem to help himself.

A coded knock at the door behind him snapped him back into the present. Hastily, he picked up the book and flipped to a random page. If he had been paying attention, he might have noticed that he was holding it upside-down. "Come in!" he called, keeping his eyes trained on the blur of words in front of him as the door opened and Rose's familiar gait crossed the floor.

"Hello, cousin dearest," she chirped. "I've brought you a surprise."

"Hm?" Quinlan lifted his teacup to his lips and took a sip while swiveling around to look.

Rose gestured toward the doorway, and a figure stepped into view.

Quinlan choked on his tea.

Really choked on his tea. He folded in half, descending into a violent hacking fit. Two pairs of fists pounded his back. He struggled to draw breath, every other inhalation hitching from the remnants of tea caught in his airway.

Finally, *finally*, he stopped coughing. In a daze, he set down his teacup and book. Slowly, he rose to his feet, his face burning with a mixture of embarrassment and—

No, it was just embarrassment now.

"Hey, asshole," said Asterin. And then she grinned at him, her emerald eyes twinkling, and nothing else in the world mattered.

Immortals, how he had missed her.

"Hellion," he breathed.

Her eyebrows quirked. "Oh, have I been promoted from lowly *brat?*"

Quinlan laughed, drunk on the mere sight of her, the black lace dress clinging to her body like a second skin. Her ebony locks flowed down her shoulders in silky waves, but the ends were damp, as if she had bathed but couldn't bother waiting long enough for them to dry.

"*Well*, then!" Rose interrupted. "I have some duties to attend to."

Neither of them responded, bewitched by the same spell, content to simply drink in one another's presence. Tension buzzed along Quinlan's nerves, setting his entire body aflame.

Rose inched toward the exit. "So . . . I'll be off." When they still didn't answer, she added, pointedly, "*Bye-ee!*"

"Shut the door behind you," replied Quinlan finally.

"Ugh," Rose muttered and escaped.

After the door closed, Quinlan let himself saunter over to Asterin, step by slow step. She watched his approach with sharp, steady eyes. He stopped only when they stood toe to toe, their faces mere inches apart. The challenge in her expression blazed bright.

"So," he began, lowering his voice to a rough whisper. Her shiver delighted him. He inhaled deeply through his nose, savoring the lingering fragrance of jasmine oil from her bath, and beneath it, something distinctly . . . *her.* "Did you miss me?"

She wound her arms around his neck. "Of course, you idiot."

Quinlan reached forward to cup her face with one hand, tangling the other in that sinfully silky hair. As their foreheads touched, her eyelids fluttered shut. He had to resist the urge to keep his eyes open, some small part of him afraid that she might slip through his fingers and vanish if he lost sight of her for even a moment.

But there she was, her body pressing into his, strong and solid and warm as their lips met at last.

The kiss was surprisingly chaste—yet his heart hammered in his throat just like it had the first time they had kissed, amid smoke and snow and a blazing forest that he did not let burn.

When they parted, Asterin exhaled in a shaky rush. "Don't ever do that again."

"What? Kiss you, you mean?" he joked, but he knew what she meant.

Her arms tightened around him. "I almost lost you, Quinlan."

"And I found myself for you." He kissed her again, chest aching. *Breathe.* "Because of you."

She huffed in fond disgust and threaded her fingers into his hair. "Sap."

"I won't deny it." He kissed the corner of her mouth, then buried his face into the crook of her neck, gently nibbling and licking up the column of her throat. When he nipped at the spot beneath her ear with a little more teeth than before, she let out a soft moan. He drew back to look at her, at the blush dusting her cheeks. With desire coursing through his veins, he rasped out, "Hell, Asterin."

She tugged him closer, her nails biting into his back. Their kisses grew frantic, messy, full of pent-up longing and hunger finally released. Her tongue swept along his bottom lip and he mirrored her. His hands roamed down her body to her hips. A low growl erupted from Quinlan's throat as she slotted one leg between his thighs. He yanked her toward the crushed velvet settee. They landed in a tangled heap, their lips locked together all the while. His knee banged into the edge of the coffee table, hard enough to bruise, but he was too preoccupied to do anything more than groan into Asterin's mouth as she scrambled atop him, her hands bracing the settee on either side of him. He latched onto her waist, gripping hard, and cussed aloud when one of her hands found its way southward. She had the nerve to break the kiss just to shoot him a smirk, her cheeks flushed and her lips as swollen and red as rosebuds.

With another growled curse, he flipped them over—or at least tried to. He hadn't actually regained full strength quite yet, and his arms gave in. They toppled sideways and he kicked a leg out, accidentally sending the teapot on the low table flying.

His magic surged from his core. A gust of wind carried the teapot into the air, so strong—*too* strong—that it sailed across the room and smashed to smithereens against the wall.

Asterin frowned at him, panting, her pupils dilated. "What was that for?"

"Sorry," said Quinlan. His heart pounded, but now for a totally different reason.

He knew what was coming.

After helping her back onto the settee, he tried for a smile and moved toward the entrance to his chambers. A whine began to build in his ears. "I—I'm just going to find a dustpan."

Asterin stared at him, eyes wide. He realized his mistake. "Did you say a . . . dustpan?" With a wave of her hand and a whispered, "*Reyunir*," the porcelain shards rose into the air and fused back together in the space of a heartbeat. "Quinlan . . . are you all right? Is something wrong?"

Yes, he thought. *Yes, there is.* "No," he said. "Of course not. Everything is fine. I just—" The ringing in his ears intensified tenfold. His fingers twitched against the door handle. *Shit, shit, shit.* "Stay right here. I'll be back in a few minutes."

And with that, he fled.

The telltale buzz at the back of his skull consumed him as he crammed his body into a tiny storage closet around the corner from his chambers and locked himself in. Staggering deeper into the shroud of darkness, Quinlan braced himself against shelves, braced himself for the pain like he did every time his magic slipped.

He was never ready.

CHAPTER THIRTY-ONE

L una knew she had chosen her fate correctly when she shocked the God of Shadow utterly and wholly speechless.

Immediate death.

Eoin's eyes narrowed on her grin. "You meant that as a jest, yes . . . ?"

"I meant what I said."

"You *are* aware that you're giving up immortality, a life of luxury, and power beyond your wildest dreams?" Eoin said, ticking each of them off on his fingers. At Luna's shrug, he threw his hands in the air in disbelief. "Are you suicidal?"

"I've seen what you've done with two of your shadowlings," said Luna. "I've seen the life you've given them, the way you've made them suffer."

Eoin scoffed in offense. "*Suffer?* I—"

"What an utter waste," she interrupted softly. Eoin fell silent. She began to circle him, one lazy stride at a time. She savored the intensity of his gaze, the way he instinctively turned his body along with her steps to track her every movement. "You've given your shadowlings so much. Immortality. A life of luxury. *Power*, beyond their wildest dreams."

Eoin's expression sharpened to a lethal glower. "What is your point?"

"My point *is*," Luna went on, praying that she wasn't prompting her own execution, "You've given them everything they could have asked for and more. You should own their absolute devotion, and yet you don't."

She paused in her walking. "Have you any idea of the loyalty of a hound who adores its master?"

"I don't keep dogs," Eoin replied with a cavalier smile that didn't quite reach his eyes. Eyes that, since the god had appeared in her chambers in the Mortal Realm, had now shifted in hue from green to teal.

"On the contrary." Luna spread her arms and threw her voice high. "You have the most powerful pets in both realms. So why keep them on such tight leashes?"

She forced herself to take a step closer to the god, and then another. And another.

It grew easier the closer she got.

With her heart pounding, she stared right up into Eoin's ethereal face. A face hewn from starlight and darkness. Beauty that only an Immortal could possess. "I think you and I are alike in even more ways than you believe." Luna lowered her voice to a whisper and let her expression fall open to display all of the secrets she kept locked inside. "We share the same desire . . . don't we?" The half smile had vanished from his face, and she could see *herself* reflected in those ancient eyes. When she spoke, she could see his pain, and knew it to be the same wound festering deep within her. "We just wish to be *wanted*."

Eoin didn't move.

Here was the gamble. Luna squinted slightly. "I can see through your enchantments." Surprise flickered in his eyes and relief rushed through her. "A mask that shifts depending on who looks upon it." It was similar to the charm Luna had cast on Rose for the Fairfest Ball to avoid Priscilla recognizing the Eradorian Queen as the Elite in disguise that had arrived in Axaris months prior. After all of that training with Adrianna, honing her senses to detect the presence of the slightest web of illusion in order to better wield it, she had spotted the charm the moment Eoin had material-ized on her window sill. "A mirage that appeals to the viewer's desires, takes on the traits of whomever they wish to see most."

Eoin's mouth tightened. "I—"

"I'm sure you're subtle about it," Luna mused. "You just pick up on the little things. Hair color. Height. Changes insignificant enough that it seems like you're merely switching up your style every now and then to keep your interminable existence . . . *fresh*." She tilted her head, leveling him with the most severe gaze she could muster. "How can you even keep track of yourself?"

Eoin exhaled in a rush and rocked back on his heels. "Enough. What do you want?"

Despite the question, Luna knew she hadn't won. Yet. "I want to negotiate."

Eoin snorted. "No."

Luna raised her hands in defense. "You don't even want to hear what I have to say? It's really not much, you know." Eoin regarded her warily. She dropped her gaze for a moment and then let it return to him. Clenched her jaw and pasted on a hollow smile. Meanwhile, her fingers inched behind her and found the dagger she had concealed underneath the belt of her dress back in the Mortal Realm. "Honestly, I don't care one way or another. The part of me that *did* care died when the rest of me was supposed to."

Swifter than the god could react, faster than even she thought herself capable, Luna whipped out the knife and drew it to her throat in one smooth sweep. "If you don't kill me," she informed him matter-of-factly, "I'll kill myself."

The god gasped in astonished delight. He was her audience, and this was her show. "You wouldn't."

"Don't underestimate me, God of Shadow." Luna pressed the blade deeper into her neck until it bit through. Bloodstains blossomed on the collar of her dress, wet against her skin. She didn't think he'd let her die. It would be a waste, really. She was far more useful to him alive. But maybe she was wrong. Maybe he wouldn't care. "Now, for the last time," she continued, her voice the smooth, flat pane of a frozen lake. She would not show him her fear. "Death or negotiation. What'll it be?"

After a long silence, Eoin let out a sigh. "You, Princess Luna Evovich," he announced, "are quite a piece of work. Fine." Then he snapped his fingers and an elegant table accompanied by a pair of matching leather wing-backed chairs materialized to their right. The peacock quill whizzed off the floor and the contract whisked out of her grasp. Both fluttered onto the table. "I have a feeling that this will be good, so I'll humor you."

Luna took a seat without his invitation, refusing to show even an inkling of her mind-numbing relief. She propped her elbow on the edge of the table and rested her chin on her hand. When he copied her, she shot him a feline smile.

He had meant the action as a taunt, but she would interpret it otherwise.

"Well?" said Eoin. "Let's hear your conditions."

Luna picked up the quill and crossed out the tenth clause: *Thou shalt reside within the allocated living quarters bestowed by the King whenever thou dwell in the Immortal Realm.*

Eoin arched one eyebrow. "Interesting."

Luna's smile widened. "Oh, I'm nowhere near done yet."

And then she began to haggle over her life with the God of Shadow.

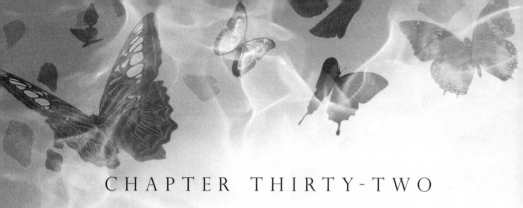

CHAPTER THIRTY-TWO

The pain exploded from Quinlan's abdomen, fifty fists and fifty knives rolled into one, driving into his stomach, knocking the oxygen from his lungs and folding him in half like a sapling. Hot tears seeped from his eyes, squeezed tightly shut to block out the garish bursts of color engulfing his vision. His lungs screamed for breath as he struggled to inhale, his body still convulsing from the aftershocks.

In the days leading up to Asterin's early arrival, his magic had already begun acting up. He had done everything he could to avoid letting it out, but it was like being forced to stand on one foot—eventually he couldn't help but lose his balance.

Before, when he was forced to repress his magic for situations requiring discretion, it had hummed beneath his skin, building in pressure with the passing of time. An itch needing a scratch—annoying, but bearable for at least a few weeks. But now . . . now, keeping it trapped inside him *burned*, like holding his hand directly over a fire from which he couldn't pull away. Worse, reminding himself that he couldn't use his magic somehow fanned that pyre. Every release felt as blissful as it had when he'd first awakened from his coma and summoned fire in his chambers, but the pain that followed each time broke him a little further.

And it was getting harder to piece himself back together.

Time ceased to exist as he crouched in the darkness, just floating on the cusp of consciousness. The pain continued to drill into him, digging its claws deeper and deeper still. He planted his clammy palms flat against the frigid closet floor.

It would be so easy to let himself surrender, to shut down, but he never allowed himself that mercy, terrified that he might never wake up again.

When the last of the pain ebbed away, Quinlan shuddered and collapsed to the floor, utterly exhausted. The absence of *hurt* felt like a divine blessing—and Immortals, did he savor it. Soon his breathing returned to normal. He grappled for a shelf and pulled himself to his feet. Even though he didn't check the mark, the *blight*, he knew it had probably crept up to his shoulders by now.

No one knew about the blight yet, and he wanted nothing more than to keep it that way. Using the same concealing charm Taeron had discovered years ago to cover up the scars Gavin Holloway had branded into his back, Quinlan had managed to keep all of it hidden so far. For secrecy, casting the charm had been a small price to pay, especially since he didn't have to recast it whenever the mark spread.

His greatest fear was that one day the pain would start and never end—which was why he had stolen a tiny tablet of poison from Avris and Avon's caches. He kept it tucked safe and sound in the locket he wore around his neck. Harvested from toxic shellfish and intensified with magic, the paralysis would cause his lungs to fail within minutes.

Rose would never forgive his death. Taeron would probably blame it on himself. And Asterin . . . Asterin had sacrificed so much to save him. Perhaps he was selfish to have prepared an out for himself, selfish to take his life after so many people had helped him, but it comforted him to know that the option existed.

Just in case.

Wiping away the drool that had dribbled down his chin, Quinlan took a moment to compose himself before pushing out of the closet on wobbly legs.

He was halfway back to his chambers when someone cleared their throat. Very loudly.

Nearly tripping over his own feet in his startlement, he swung around to face his very unimpressed older brother.

"Ah, Taeron!" Quinlan exclaimed with false cheer. "Didn't see you there."

Taeron's left eyebrow raised. "Obviously not. Rose told me Asterin just arrived. I would have thought you'd be with her. What were you doing in there?"

Quinlan resisted the urge to fidget beneath his brother's accusatory stare. "Grabbing something."

Taeron's eyes flicked pointedly to Quinlan's empty hands. "Air?" Without the slightest warning, his brother surged forward and latched onto the hem of Quinlan's shirt to yank it upward.

"What in hell?" he squawked, attempting to bat him away, but Taeron held fast, violet eyes scanning every inch of Quinlan's bare torso.

Taeron looked up. "You charmed away the scar entirely?"

Quinlan's heartbeat quickened, but he forced himself to meet his brother's gaze dead-on, knowing there was nothing to see but unmarred skin. "Of course. What if things with Asterin got . . . intense?"

Taeron's eyes narrowed and Quinlan's gut flipped. Finally, his brother shook his head, his usual good-natured smile returning. "Oh, Quinnie, I doubt she would care."

Then Taeron wrenched his arm back and Quinlan felt the chain around his neck snap off. He lunged forward, but his brother danced out of the way.

"Give it back," Quinlan snarled, but it was already too late. Years of brotherhood had taught Taeron to never hesitate, especially when Quinlan could so easily summon his magic to gain the upper hand.

"Never would have taken you for a romantic," said Taeron as he opened the locket. Then he found the capsule inside and his expression went absolutely blank.

Quinlan waited, shoulders tensing, despising the silence as it dragged on and on.

Without a word, Taeron snapped the locket shut and practically hurled it back at Quinlan's chest. His brother spun on his heel, fists clenched, and stormed off with nothing but a livid, "I'm going to the library."

Quinlan exhaled through pursed lips and watched his brother go. There was no question whether or not Taeron had pieced together enough clues to grasp the situation—his brother was probably the smartest person in the entire kingdom, after all.

Taeron was not an angry person. In fact, this was the angriest Quinlan had ever seen him, and the quiet fury that had ignited his brother's violet eyes left him feeling a little sick. But this wasn't the time to dwell on Taeron's feelings.

Quinlan's boots squealed against the floor tiles as he raced back to his chambers. How long had he abandoned Asterin? He had no idea, but suddenly the want for her—her touch, her warmth, her voice—threatened to overwhelm him. After smoothing his clothes and ruffling a hand through his hair, he knocked on the door. When he heard no response, he turned the knob gingerly and entered.

The first thing he noticed was that the sky outside his window had already faded to dusk, and that someone, presumably Asterin, had lit a few of the sitting-room lamps. They cast lengthening shadows across the oakwood floor like omens.

If the sun had set while he had been fighting through his episode, then . . . not just minutes had passed, as he had assumed—and as he had promised her—but *hours.*

Quinlan drifted around the sitting room, nudging into the other chambers, but they all stood just as empty. He called out her name, clinging to the slim hope that she had stayed. But it was pointless.

Asterin was long gone.

CHAPTER THIRTY-THREE

*D*rip. *Drip.*

The sound of water was to the Eradorian palace as waves were to the shore—constant, all-consuming. Splashing, crashing, trickling, lapping: the water had its own mystifying vocabulary, as intelligible as the chirping of crickets or the language of whales and wolves.

Asterin wandered the palace, marveling at the impossibly high ceilings, the little alcoves with walls bedecked in blue ivy entwined with tiger-orange honeysuckle trumpets. She passed chains of waterfalls suspended overhead, each spilling into another beneath it. Silvery mist shimmered low to the ground, and the occasional cool spray of water tickled her nose.

Why had Quinlan left so suddenly?

After so many months apart . . . Chills ran down the nape of her neck as she recalled the starvation in the way he'd touched her, his insatiability when they'd kissed. But between his loss of control with the teapot and the mention of the dustpan . . . she couldn't help but wonder if the battle in Axaris months ago had changed him in more ways than a few surface scars could reveal.

Up ahead lay a chamber with a blue floor. No—the floor was actually submerged in ten feet of water. At the other end of the chamber, two stone dragons with scaly, nubbed wings guarded a double door.

Asterin frowned, searching for a way across the water and finding none. Except swimming, of course.

No sooner had the thought occurred to her when the dragon on the left cracked its stone lids open, revealing two glowing blue gemstones for eyes. It unhinged its jaw and spoke in a rumbling voice as soft as moonlight on a lake. "Declare your intent."

Asterin considered her options. Finally, eyeing the water, she decided to go with the truth. "Exploring."

The dragon on the right opened eyes that glowed red. "A foreigner. Tell us your name, young one."

"Asterin Faelenhart."

"A Faelenhart," the left dragon said with an air of nostalgia. "It has been many a century since a Faelenhart walked these halls."

Asterin shifted, wondering who had been the last and if they now rested in the Faelenhart tomb back in Axaris. "What lies beyond those doors?"

"Find out for yourself, young wolf," said the right dragon.

Asterin threw out her arms for balance as the floor of the chamber quaked and bubbles gurgled to the surface of the water. Nine flat stone lotuses emerged to form a stepping bridge, a different affinity sigil carved into each one. Perhaps the stones acted in the same way the elemental wards at the Axarian palace did—for only the nine affinities combined could withstand the power of the tenth, if such a defense were ever needed . . . confirming her belief that something important did indeed lie beyond the doors.

Cautiously, she placed her foot on the first lotus. Lord Tidus's water sigil flared beneath her boot. The stone dipped slightly beneath her weight, but otherwise held steady. Nimbly, she advanced to the second stone, illuminating Lord Pavon's illusion sigil. Then came Lord Ulrik with his sigil of light, then Lady Fena with hers of fire. Asterin almost lost her balance on the fifth stone—glowing with the air sigil of Lady Ilma, the protector of the House of the Viper and Ibreseos. After taking a moment to collect herself, she hopped across the rest of the stones, each one lighting up as she touched them—the sky sigil of Lady Audra, the earth sigil of Lady

Siore, the wind sigil of Lady Reyva, and finally, the ice sigil belonging to her own house's deity, Lord Conrye.

In her haste to cross, her strides had shortened. The stones must have moved to accommodate her steps, because instead of spanning the entire chamber, they now ended only halfway across.

The right dragon made an odd clicking sound that Asterin took for laughter. "Guess you'll just have to swim the rest of the way."

Asterin rolled her eyes, about to summon her magic, when the left dragon tutted. "Don't tease her." The water gurgled again and the stones glided forward from behind her, zig-zagging into bridge formation once more and allowing her to cross the remaining distance at last.

Once she reached the other side, Asterin looked up at the two dragons in turn. "Thank you."

A *boom* rocked the chamber. Jets of water exploded from beneath the lotuses, rocketing them up to the ceiling. The jets ceased and the stones crashed back into the water with a colossal *sploosh* that soaked her from head to toe.

"What in *hell*?" screeched Asterin.

"That's what happens when you try to use your magic to cross," the left dragon explained. "Or lie to us."

She slicked her drenched hair back, spat a strand from her mouth, and shot her most withering glare at the dragons. "I didn't do either of those."

The right dragon made the clicking noise again. "Take it as a warning. We are Wardens, bewitched to sense deceit, malicious intent, and more."

"Here, young one," said the left dragon. There came a whooshing sound. Both dragons expelled a long stream of air from their mouths, so hot that the moisture steamed off her clothes—the dress Rose had loaned her, paired with an embroidered jacket that she had stolen from Quinlan's chambers.

"Thanks," Asterin mumbled the moment the last curl of steam dissipated from her sleeve. Then she lunged for the doors, praying for no more soggy surprises. The sound of clicking faded as the doors sealed behind her.

Finally safe, she looked up. Her jaw dropped.

"Immortals. That is a *lot* of books."

From afar came an angry *shhh!*

"Sorry," Asterin whispered, and drifted farther into the library on thick plum carpets so plush they swallowed up her slippers completely. The vaulted ceiling of the library soared toward the sky, taller than any throne hall she had ever seen and at least ten times more vast. From where she stood, she could just make out a central reading area crowned by a radiant sphere of glass hanging midair. Dozens of towering floor-to-ceiling shelves loomed down upon her, circling the reading area in concentric rings.

Asterin craned her neck and stared in awe at the stacks. Her mind simply could not wrap itself around the sheer magnitude of *books.*

"How strange," she whispered to herself, reaching out to run her fingers along the velvety spines of leather-bound volumes as she ambled toward the reading area. The scent of ink and parchment bled through the air. She swore she could hear the turning of pages, the soft mutters of self-debate, the muffled *skritch-skratch* of quill tips on parchment, but the reading area lay deserted, every chair and glossy table unoccupied. The tables, carved from warm walnut, ran as long as the ones in Mess Hall at the Axarian palace. Peculiar little orbs of light hovered over the backs of each chair; a handful pulsed green, but the majority pulsed red.

Perplexed, Asterin tried to tug out a chair lit with a red orb, but it didn't budge.

When she gave it a second tug, a girl wearing a smart blazer and tie materialized from thin air and twisted around in her seat to shoot Asterin a nasty glare.

Asterin slapped a hand to her mouth to stifle a startled scream.

"This seat is *kind* of taken," the girl said, sarcasm dripping from her tone. She sighed through her nostrils at Asterin's continued stupefaction.

A boy in the same uniform on the other side of the table appeared. From *thin air.* "Oh, play nice, Freya," he chided, and then fixed Asterin with a lopsided grin. "You must be new here." Before she could summon up a reply, he explained, "Any of the seats with red lights are taken. The library is cast with a concealing enchantment so students can study as comfortably as possible. You only see as many people as you want to see . . . so long as they're actually there. Good luck with your studies!"

With that, both students ducked their heads back down at the books in front of them and vanished.

Once Asterin finally recovered, she blinked, wondering just how many people were concealed by the enchantment. In response, phantom outlines around the room quivered to life. By her next blink, the reading area bustled with dozens and *dozens* of people. Students weaved between the tables with books piled high in their arms. A few professors in navy and maroon robes marked papers with quills dipped in pots of scarlet ink, and in the corner a pair of auburn-haired twins pored over a fortress of textbooks and jotted down notes with devious little grins on their faces.

"Immortals," Asterin breathed. Platforms she had originally mistaken for decorative fixtures zipped up and down the shelves with students crouched atop them for access to the higher shelves. An unmanned trolley glided past her, hovering a foot above the carpet, loaded with books that reshelved themselves.

The rest of the world had always seen Eradore as a place of incredible magic and mystery. Now, immersed in this world away from worlds, Asterin realized that the people here didn't just *use* magic, like in the other eight kingdoms. Here, magic was their way of life, as natural as breathing.

There was a tap on her shoulder. "Excuse me, dear." Asterin turned to find a young girl looking up at her. "You seem lost. May I assist you with anything?"

The usage of 'dear' threw Asterin off, since she would have pegged the girl's age close to thirteen. In the end, Asterin answered in the same way as she had to the dragons guarding the library's entrance. "Just exploring."

The girl smiled. "How delightful! This *is* a library, though, you know— surely half of the exploring must involve the books themselves? We have books on almost every subject imaginable here."

An idea formed in Asterin's head. Hesitating but a moment, she asked, "Do you have anything on shadow magic?"

"Of course!" the girl replied. "A general overview or anything specific?"

Asterin had been expecting a range of reactions—shock, disdain maybe . . . or at least a skeptical eyebrow raise at her interest in the forbidden element. But the girl only kept on smiling. Asterin lowered her voice to a bare whisper. "Erm . . . perhaps injuries caused by shadow magic?"

"My records show that there are thirteen texts relating to your inquiry," said the girl. "Four of them are overviews, five of them are anatomically specific texts, three of them examine cures and treatments, and the final one is a student dissertation."

"Your . . . records?" Asterin said, growing a little unnerved.

The girl nodded. "I'm one of the attendants tasked with aiding pupils from the Academia Principalis next door. Please, follow me."

At least that explained the hordes of students. Although Asterin had known that the school was nearby, in the inner city, she hadn't realized that it was *right* next to the palace. As the attendant led her away from the reading area and deeper into the rings of shelves, she asked, "Isn't that a security concern?"

"Students are forbidden from entering the palace, just as palace staff may not enter the Academia. The Wardens ensure it. However, most spaces that connect the school and the palace, such as this library, are shared."

"I see." Asterin skirted around a floating trolley, just as it, too, tried to skirt around her. It gave her an angry buzz before rattling away.

The girl laughed. "Oh, don't mind the trolleys. They'll avoid you themselves." She brought Asterin to a halt in the aisle of one of the outermost rings and gestured to a section of the bottom shelf. "Here are the materials we have. If they prove insufficient, do not hesitate to let any of the attendants know and we will attempt to obtain further materials from other institutions. Is there anything else I can assist you with?" When Asterin shook her head, the girl smiled. "Good luck with your studies!"

With that, she pivoted smoothly and disappeared around the corner.

Feeling a little self-conscious, Asterin peered around the stacks, but no students seemed to have ventured this far back. Squatting down to the section the girl had pointed out, Asterin traced her index finger along the titles. *Ten Traumas of the Tenth Element, A Beginner's Guide to Malignant Maladies, Dark Magic and Medicine: A History.* As promised, she found ten more texts relating to shadow affinities and various afflictions. Chewing her lip, she debated which books to pick out. Worried that she might miss some crucial tidbit of information simply due to her own poor judgment, she gathered up all thirteen books into her arms and rose to her feet. With the books balanced in a precarious pile tall enough to brush past her forehead, she began making her way back to the reading area.

Just as she had almost reached the end of the aisle, she heard someone storming toward her. She craned her neck around the books just in time to watch a man veer into her aisle, his eyes glued to the carpet as he muttered a furious stream of words under his breath.

Asterin's eyes widened. "Hey!"

The man's disturbed gaze snapped up to meet hers. Asterin tried to step out of his way, but it was too late, the books were too heavy, she was too slow—

The man collided into her. *Hard.* They both toppled to the ground, the books spilling from Asterin's arms. The books, luckily, must have been charmed with clumsy handlers in mind, and bobbed to a gentle rest above the ground.

Asterin and the man were not so fortunate.

Stars burst across Asterin's vision as her head smacked into a shelf ledge. Hands crashed into the ground on either side of her head, and when Asterin's vision cleared, she found herself looking right up into the face of . . . Quinlan.

No. Not Quinlan. *Almost* Quinlan, but . . . not.

Books floated in the air behind Not-Quinlan. Not-Quinlan, with his dark brows and rumpled locks a few inches too long, high cheekbones already coloring from embarrassment, and a jawline sharp enough to cut heartstrings. Thick lashes fluttered as bewildered violet eyes—*not indigo*, Asterin realized—searched her own face. A pair of handsome horn-rimmed glasses sat upon his tall nose. The fall had knocked them slightly askew.

Not-Quinlan's brow furrowed, his gaze still riveted on her.

"Are you Quinlan's brother?" Asterin blurted at the same moment that Not-Quinlan murmured, "You must be Queen Asterin."

He smiled at her, a warm, genuine thing that crinkled the corners of his eyes. The older brother Quinlan so envied spoke in a voice that was at once familiar but . . . *mellower.* "It is an honor to make your acquaintance, Your Majesty. I'm Taeron Holloway."

Asterin gave a breathy laugh, a little light-headed at their proximity. "The honor is mine." *No dimples,* she couldn't help but note.

Taeron gave a little start, as if abruptly remembering where they were. He scrambled onto his feet, the blush in his cheeks returning full force as he ran one hand along the back of his neck and offered the other to her. After helping her upright, he busied himself by plucking the floating books out of the air. His gaze flitted to her every now and then, never lingering for longer than a few seconds. "My most sincere apologies about that, Your Majesty." He hugged the books tightly to his chest like a shield. Or a teddy bear, depending on how you wanted to look at it. "As you might have noticed, I'm currently a bit of a mess."

Asterin reached for the books Taeron had missed. "Please, Asterin is just fine."

"Ah, of course. Just Asterin. I mean, Asterin. The *just* bit wasn't—oh, my." Taeron ducked his head sweetly, hiding his face behind the books. The tips of his ears glowed cherry red, the same way Quinlan's did whenever he got flustered, and Asterin couldn't help but find the similarity endearing.

She sent him a reassuring smile. "Not to worry."

"Oh," said Taeron as he inspected the spines of the shadow-affinity books. "May I ask why you need these?" When he saw her expression, he hastily added, "Out of intellectual curiosity, of course. Here, we embrace all thirst for knowledge."

Asterin recalled the unfaltering cheeriness of the library assistant that had aided her. "But surely . . . wouldn't a request for information on the forbidden element raise at least a few eyebrows? The library assistant I asked didn't even react in the slightest. It was practically inhuman."

Taeron frowned. "Library assistant? Do you mean the attendants?" His fingers brushed hers lightly and he gestured for her to follow him out of the aisle. He adjusted his hold on the books so that he could point at the stone sculptures lining the walls. "That's because they're not human at all. They're gargoyles. The Keepers of the Royal Library of Eradore, to be specific."

Asterin struggled to keep from gaping. Indeed, there was the cheerful girl, motionless, her marble hands clasped angelically at her front. Beside the girl perched a menacing griffin that, to Asterin's everlasting gratitude, had *not* come to her aid. "Is *everything* here enchanted?"

Taeron chuckled softly. "Honestly, I couldn't tell you. I should hope that the ceiling, at least, is normal." His grin turned disarmingly sly. "Actually, Asterin . . . coincidentally, I happen to be in rather urgent need of these books, too. Would you mind studying together?"

She returned the grin. "Of course not."

On their way back to the reading area, Asterin couldn't help but notice as everyone around them began to disappear until only Taeron remained at her side. *You only see as many people as you want to see.*

They might have spent the entire evening reading together—without any windows, it was impossible to tell time. The books were proving to be little help, but Asterin struggled on, choking down every sentence, knowing that she would find *something*. *Had* to find something. This was the Royal Library of Eradore, after all.

Beneath the sighs of turning pages, she could just make out the *drip drip* of water on parchment. It was unlike anything else she had heard while roaming the palace—and it was only when Taeron reached out to brush her cheek did she realize it was the sound of her own tears.

CHAPTER THIRTY-FOUR

"Well, then," Eoin said, pushing himself to his feet and holding out a hand. "Are we agreed?"

Luna rubbed her eyes and smothered a yawn. Hours of painstaking negotiating had crawled by. She was hungry, exhausted, and utterly spent. "We are agreed."

The idea of shaking on their deal with the God of Shadow still filled her with dread, but it was now or never. She gripped his hand as tight as she could, his broad palm enveloping her comparatively skeletal fingers. With a wolfish grin, he squeezed her hand tighter still and pumped once, twice, three times.

As soon as they parted, the peacock quill sailed through the air and into her hand. She stared at the bottom of her contract, where the empty line for her signature waited. Some invisible force pulled the tip of the quill closer to the parchment. She had shaken on the terms, and now there was no turning back.

Still, she made sure to take her sweet time. She stretched her limbs, allowed herself a few deep breaths. There was no inkwell to dip the quill in, but when she tested it on the side of the parchment, raven-black strokes unfurled from its tip.

"This quill would be great for calligraphy, don't you think?" Luna mused aloud.

Eoin shot her an unimpressed look. "Your stalling doesn't bother me, my lady. I've lived through your entire mortal existence an infinite number of times. For me, a decade is worth no more than a second."

Luna almost bought it, but then she caught sight of his hand, curled on the table. The most *minuscule* of twitches passed through his left pinky. *Doesn't bother you, hmm?* "You won't mind me savoring a few extra minutes of freedom, then," she told him with a snooty little smile, and began doodling cats in the margins.

Eoin slammed his palms against the table. "For hell's sake," he exclaimed. "Just sign the damned thing."

Luna grinned to herself and finally conceded, penning her full name—*Luna Evovich*—in a flourish of black.

Before she had even lifted her quill, Eoin practically snatched the contract away from her. He took a moment to compose himself and beamed at her, though his nostrils were slightly flared. "*Lovely*. Now, my lady, is when the fun truly begins."

The Ruler of Darkness made a surprisingly excellent tour guide.

"In the Shadow Kingdom, there are four main rivers—three of fire and one of pure magic," Eoin told her as they strolled along a path winding through the glade tucked behind the Shadow Palace. Soft blue moss and grassy stalks tipped with ghost blossoms bordered both sides of the path. Every now and then they passed elegant benches of varying sizes—some fit for a doll and some for giants. A hillside sloped down to their right, at first no more than a mild incline but rapidly descending into a thousand-foot vertical drop toothed with menacing black rocks.

Luna took care to always walk on Eoin's left side.

Unnoticing, he went on. "About a third of the beings living here are fire spirits who sustain themselves on magma, so the fire rivers are quite convenient for them. The Jade River, on the other hand, sustains no one. Yet it is the lifeblood of these lands."

"So . . . you can't drink from it?" asked Luna.

Eoin shook his head. "Or bathe. And with your fragile mortality, stepping into it would kill you. At least, until you've metamorphed."

Until you've metamorphed.

Luna still didn't know how to feel about metamorphing—the transformation that would bestow upon her both her new powers and her unique anygné form. Anticipation or trepidation? She couldn't tease the two apart, so she stopped trying. "So it can only kill mortals, you mean."

Eoin gave her a look of surprise. "On the contrary. Natural immortality differs from that of an Immortal or an anygné. There is, after all, a marked difference between living forever and never dying." Her expression must have been one of incredulity, for he elaborated. "The average immortal being may be born into a natural lifespan that stretches into eternity, but they are just as killable as mortals." The god made a face. "Some much less so than others, unfortunately."

"What sort of immortal beings are there?" Luna asked. Fire spirits, anygnés . . . how many wonders would she discover here?

Eoin waved a hand. "Oh, the list goes on and on. Every second a new horror emerges from the womb of its procreator." He paused. "I do mean womb metaphorically. I've seen births that tear skulls open, or—"

"That's quite enough, thank you," Luna exclaimed. She thrust her finger into the distance randomly. "What are those?"

"The mountains?" said Eoin. "I named them Verkove'h Aur. The Peaks of Gold."

"Named them," she echoed dazedly. "Yourself. Right. Almost forgot."

"You've heard the tales?" asked Eoin, cocking his head to the side.

Luna blinked. "*Legends of the Immortals?* Of course. Who hasn't?" Although she hadn't actually *read* the book herself until a few weeks ago when she had come across a copy of it on the shelves in the room Adrianna usually used to train her. It was a collection of stories, regaling the odysseys of every god and goddess. Their powers, their struggles, their triumphs. The origins of the Council of Immortals and the creation of the Shadow Kingdom were also included. The remembrance that Eoin had forged these lands himself from nothing but darkness and his own terrifying will . . .

"Anyway, there are over a thousand cities in the Shadow Kingdom,"

Eoin told her, "but this is Hjerte, the capital. In your tongue, it translates to heart."

Luna smirked. "How very original."

Eoin smirked back. "Well, it *was* . . . back when I created the word for this very purpose. It's not my fault that you mortals decided to pilfer my language."

She blinked at him, too stupid for speech.

He laughed at her expression. "Not that I mind, of course. But language had to come from *somewhere*, no?" he asked. "Everyone takes it for granted. Especially the Council, considering I spoon-fed every word to them." Eoin gazed beyond his city, expression growing solemn. "For nothing, I gave them everything. They gave me less than little in return. Perhaps I should have held back in the beginning. So as to let them realize the meaning of struggle in the absence of my aid. Perhaps then, they—"

"They might have realized your true value," Luna finished, speaking the words that resounded deep within her like a wolf call. *How strange*, she thought to herself, *to share the same hurt as the most powerful being in both realms.*

Heartache spared no one it seemed, not even the gods.

Luna swallowed past the tightness in her throat. "I know what it is, Your Majesty, to offer oneself wholly . . . only for it to not be enough." Her fists clenched and she found his gaze. "I'm sorry they wronged you."

He regarded her for a moment and then offered an elbow to her. "There is still much to see, my lady. We should carry on."

"We must," Luna agreed quietly, and slipped her hand through the crook of his arm.

They continued on in silence until they reached the abrupt, grass-tufted end of the path. Luna could imagine that there might have once been a bridge leading into the veil of fog rising before them, but it was as if a giant had trudged by and torn it free. The impenetrable fog concealed the full extent of the drop, and she was overcome with the vague sensation that perhaps there was no bottom at all.

Panic jolted through Luna as Eoin's hand clamped down on her shoulder and forced her closer to the edge of the cliff. He smiled when her foot scuffed the fringe of the path. She stared down into the dizzying white haze, her stomach seizing with a sickening lurch.

"Don't," she gasped suddenly. "Don't you dare!"

Confusion crossed Eoin's face, but his grip didn't loosen. "Pardon me?"

What kind of cruel, absurd game was this? Did she have to survive the fall in order to metamorph? Or else was Eoin executing her after all? She fixed him with her most scathing glare as her body trembled uncontrollably. "Do *not* push me off this cliff."

He stared at her, his mouth falling open in a mixture of astonishment and horror. Then he threw his head back and erupted into laughter, swaying dangerously close to the edge of the cliff. "*Push* you? Off a *cliff*?" he cried out between snorts of laughter. "After all those hours of torment you inflicted upon me during negotiations? I think not!"

Luna crossed her arms over her chest. "Hours? Didn't you say that an entire decade was worth no more than a second to you?"

Eoin's eyes glinted. "Ah, yes, but just like any old mortal, I must still endure the entirety of its passing." He slid two fingers into his mouth and let out a high, keening whistle. A moment later, the fog began to boil. A geyser of darkness erupted forth from below, scattering every last wisp of fog as a swarm of black butterflies a thousand strong rose at Eoin's summons.

Luna gasped as each butterfly seemed to meld into the next, their wings merging into the smooth contours of a sleigh with sleek runners, low rails, and a glossy midnight finish. Once fully formed, it hovered before them. Waiting.

"It's a sleijh," Eoin explained. "The main form of transportation in the Immortal Realm . . . other than wings, of course." He stepped onto the sleijh first and offered a hand to her. His eyes gleamed obsidian. "My lady."

With the slightest hesitation, she gathered her skirts in her left hand and placed her right in his before hopping onto the sleijh. It didn't so much as bob beneath the added weight.

"Tuck your toes into that little gap down there," Eoin instructed as they seated themselves on a satin bench softer than the most luxurious bed. She hurried to anchor her toes into the little nook below the dash, letting out a yelp when it parted like smoke and latched onto her slippers, reshaping and solidifying to fit snugly around her feet. Once she had settled in, Eoin slapped the side of the sleijh and called out, "Dusk District, please."

They shot into the sky. The force of the takeoff shoved her backward, and if not for the footholds, she might have tumbled right off the sleijh and into the void.

Eoin got to his feet, shielding one hand over his eyes and peering into the horizon. With a slight wobble in her knees, Luna cautiously rose, too.

The breath in her lungs exited in a single, soft *whoosh*.

The Shadow Kingdom unfurled below them like an impossible map, every lush, vibrant stroke of ink come to life. The wind tousled her hair and kissed her skin as she braced her hands on the railing and leaned out into nothingness to let out a whoop of joy. She waved at the tiny beings crawling along the jeweled streets far below, mere tiny specks of dust on a twinkling backdrop of psychedelic marvels. Buildings adorned with rubied roofs sprouted from beds of smoldering coals. Clusters of trees as white as clouds rolled past. The three red rivers wove around the Jade River in a hypnotizing web of flame, never quite meeting, always twisting away just shy of one another.

Eoin glanced at her. After a slight hesitation, he said, "You seemed to have been expecting me when I arrived upon your window, Luna."

She smiled. "I was."

That day outside King Jakob's chambers, when he had nearly caught her eavesdropping, she had fled out of sight and forgotten her slipper. Once he retreated into his chambers with the slipper and Luna had realized her mistake . . .

She had promptly continued eavesdropping.

Luna had already suspected her ties with the Shadow King for a while now. Ever since Harry had explained total eclipses and how Priscilla had gained her dark magic abilities, she had wondered. And so when Killian mentioned that the next eclipse was drawing close, Luna scrounged the castle for books. Books on the Immortals, books on astronomy. She found multiple charts dating future eclipses. Only one book had predicted the last eclipse correctly, so she memorized the date and read up on the Immortals in the meantime.

Eoin smiled back. "You are full of surprises, Luna Evovich."

With silent, lethal grace, the sleijh glided through the sky, a black swan cutting across a still winter ocean. They wound around towers with stairs climbing into the heavens, zoomed through puffy sheets of smoke that clung to the sleijh in trails of fuchsia. Another sleijh soared by a few feet below, full of creatures with silky beards and corkscrew horns twice taller than she. When Luna waved at them, their horns glowed and grew an extra inch.

The sleijh slipped into a descent as they approached a patch of green, every landmark sharpening and gradually enlarging to its true size. The runners skimmed the ground. The footholds warped, releasing Luna's toes.

When Eoin disembarked, the sleijh surged back into the air, as if it had forgotten that it was carrying a second passenger. Right before her eyes, the railings disintegrated beneath her fingertips, bursting back into a frenzy of wings. Then came the dash, the bench, even the runners, until Luna stood bewildered on the floor slats as they dispersed right beneath her. It happened so quickly that she didn't even have time to cry out when suddenly she was plummeting to the ground.

Ribbons of shadow arced up to meet her, entangling her limbs and easing her down. Eoin caught her in his arms as if she weighed no more than dandelion fluff.

"Apologies. I should have warned you," he said with a roguish smile. "I so rarely have guests. I forget they haven't learned the workings of what I consider mundane."

"Mundane," Luna echoed with a laugh, her skirts ruffling in the breeze. The high of her exhilaration still pumped through her veins. "You call *that* mundane?"

"As mundane as a mortal would call the setting of the sun," Eoin replied, lowering her onto her feet.

Luna thought for a moment before murmuring, "No. I don't think I'd ever call a sunset mundane."

"Ah." Eoin's smile sombered. "You shouldn't have said that. Now my heart will only yearn for it more."

"You can only travel to the Mortal Realm during a total eclipse . . ." Luna realized. "So you've never seen the sun at all, even when you do go there." Her brow knitted. "That's . . . that's so sad."

"Here is your house," Eoin said loudly, and thrust his hand out toward the mansion beside them. He pulled out a vial from his inner jacket pocket, filled with a viscous liquid that could have passed for molten-gold honey, and practically tossed it at her. "When you are ready to metamorph, drink this. Return to the palace once the transformation is complete. I have some business to attend to. Soraya, your new neighbor, is home." Luna glanced at the lit front-room windows of the house next door. "If you require any help, please knock on her door and she will be more than happy to assist you."

And with that, the God of Shadow threw his hand downward, blasted a hole into the ground, and jumped directly into it.

Luna gaped after him, but he had already vanished. Then she sighed and held up the vial.

"Well, then," she whispered to herself, uncorking it with shaking fingers. "Here goes absolutely everything."

She downed it in one go.

And when the vial shattered in her grip a moment later, the blood that dripped onto the ground no longer ran red.

CHAPTER THIRTY-FIVE

Quinlan stared at the Keeper, his stomach filled with dread. "What do you mean all of the books have been checked out?"

The gargoyle girl pursed her lips. "I'm very sorry, Prince Quinlan. Prince Taeron borrowed them yesterday."

Quinlan cursed his brother. The thought to research his condition hadn't even occurred to him until earlier today, when he'd spotted Avris and Avon arguing about a misplaced library book on the chemical compositions of archaic poisons. Taeron, on the other hand, must have seized the books right after their confrontation.

In a polite monotone, the Keeper inquired, "Would you like me to recall the books, Your Highness?"

"No," Quinlan said, a little too quickly. Forcing Taeron to return a book was as good as declaring war in his brother's eyes.

"If it helps," said the Keeper, "we do still have a selection of materials pertaining to shadow magic available. Would you like to take a look?"

Quinlan sighed and turned away. "Yes, but I know my way. Thank you."

Of course, both he and Rose had already pored over all of the texts in question cover to cover. The tenth element had captured Rose's interest years ago, and it had only intensified when dark, prophetic visions began plaguing her sleep—such as the vision of Quinlan's father impaling her own father, the King of Eradore.

To Rose's everlasting frustration, out of the hundreds of thousands of books in the Royal Library of Eradore, only a meager half-dozen shelves were dedicated to shadow magic. Though to be fair, Quinlan doubted most royal libraries boasted even a half-dozen texts on the subject in total.

Quinlan found a student leaning against a trolley in the aisle of his destination, flipping through a slim book with pages dipped in silver. He pressed his lips in a cordial smile, but she coldly ignored him. When he located the shadow magic section, he squatted down to examine the bottom few shelves. There was a large gap of missing books on the third shelf—most likely the ones that Taeron had already stolen.

After a moment, the student released an unhappy sigh and dropped her book back onto the trolley before stalking away. The trolley reshelved it on the second shelf right in front of Quinlan, slotting it between *A Brief History of Forbidden Magic, Volume I* and *Journal Entries of a True Shadow Wielder*, the latter of which was notoriously written by a man who could not wield magic at all.

Quinlan's eyes narrowed on the newly reshelved text. He couldn't remember ever seeing it before, let alone reading it. It was of extremely modest length, bound in fabric. Its spine lacked a title, only adorned with the gold outline of a tiny triangle. Had it been shelved mistakenly?

With his index finger, he tipped the book off the shelf and turned it over in his hands. The front cover was charcoal-black and just as rough. Equally as barren as the spine, it was once again titleless and marked solely by that gold triangle. Now certain that he had never seen the book before, he flipped it open to a random page.

"Excuse me, Your Highness," interrupted a voice at his shoulder.

Quinlan snapped the book shut and whirled around, keeping it hidden behind his back. Why did he feel so guilty? Like he'd been caught committing some sort of crime—by what, holding a book in a library? He blinked at the Keeper from earlier and gave her a smile with all of his teeth. "Hi!" he exclaimed, high enough that his voice cracked.

The gargoyle returned his smile with an equal amount of teeth, a terrifying image that seared itself into Quinlan's mind forevermore. "Queen Orozalia requests your presence in her chambers at once."

"Oh." He swallowed a sudden sense of foreboding. "Thank you." Unless she was pissed at him, Rose always met him in *his* chambers if she wanted to discuss something—meaning, of course, that she *was* probably pissed at him.

The Keeper bowed her head and turned to leave.

"Wait," Quinlan called, the book still tucked behind him. He almost asked to borrow it, but some instinct stopped him. Instead, he merely displayed it to the gargoyle. "Would you happen to know the title of this book?"

The Keeper's head tilted to the side with a gravelly scrape. "No. Where did you acquire it? You did not have it in your possession when you entered the library earlier."

So many lies came to his tongue, but in the end he went with, "Someone left it for me."

The last time he had tried fibbing to a Keeper had *not* ended well.

Apparently, his untruth was vague enough that it passed beneath the Keeper's radar. She frowned and opened her mouth to respond when Quinlan decided to cut her off.

"Well, never mind, I'd best be going! I would hate to keep Her Royal Majesty waiting!" Forcing another radiant smile, he swaddled the nameless book in his arms and made his escape out of the aisle. As he exited the library, he could feel the stares of the other Keepers sentried along the wall pinned on his back.

How the hell was he going to make it to Rose's chambers without getting caught with a stolen book? While he might have managed to fool the Keeper, the other palace guardians possessed much more complex thinking processes and would undoubtedly detect that something was amiss.

With his mind whirling with plans for how to make it past the Lotus Chamber without being drowned by Rufus and Rulus, he hightailed it into the watery room, only to find the two stone dragons snoring soundly overhead. The stepping stone bridge surged to the surface as soon as Quinlan stepped toward the water to allow him passage.

His suspicions skyrocketed.

After jogging through Seventh Wing, he took a shortcut to Fifth Wing through a storage closet. He couldn't believe his eyes. Whether they were statues or portraits or marble busts, every Warden he passed either had their eyes closed or their faces—or multiple faces—turned away from him.

"What in hell," Quinlan whispered to himself, clutching the nameless book tighter to his chest. He briefly entertained throwing it into a fireplace but quickly dismissed the thought. After all, he still didn't know what he might find inside . . . *like a cure*, said the little voice in his head, but he banished it.

He refused to hope. Recently, hoping had more often than not led him to crippling disappointment.

When he reached Fifth Wing and the great double doors that would lead him to Rose's chambers, the nine-headed serpent Warden carved into the doors swiveled toward Quinlan, fixating on him with their eighteen gold eyes. Apparently the influence of whatever or whoever that had caused the other palace Wardens to turn a blind eye to him didn't extend to the serpents.

"Hello, little prince," the middle serpent head greeted. *Vis*, for wisdom. Each of the nine heads represented a different trait—which, if the legends were to be believed, embodied the whole of Lord Tidus's personality.

"Hiding something?" the serpent head at Vis's right inquired in a smug tone. *Hras*, the serpent of audacity. *Khaz*, the serpent of wrath, hissed at Hras. A fourth serpent, *Mijya*—for mercy—flicked their tongue in disapproval at both of them. *Savir*, *Perstevo*, and *Armaré*, serpents of patience, perseverance, and adaptability, watched on in silence. Foresight, *Eloré*, seemed to be asleep as usual, though it was hard to tell since serpents didn't have eyelids.

"Yes, Hras," said Quinlan. "What are you going to do about it?"

If snakes could smirk, he was certain Hras would have. "Nothing, for once. Lord's orders."

Lord's orders? Quinlan thought to himself in a daze.

The eyes of ever-silent *Müse*, the ninth serpent head of mystery, flashed red. A moment later, the doors swung inward.

He bowed and crossed the threshold, all the while staring at the book in his hands.

"*Quinlan Maximillius Barnaby Holloway*," came a seething voice.

Quinlan all but stuffed the book into the back of his trousers as the

Queen of Eradore stormed into the main parlor with a half-eaten custard in her hand.

"Ah, hello cousin dearest, how are—*mrumph*."

Rose crammed the remaining custard into his mouth. "Shut up and eat, idiot." His cousin pinched him by the ear and dragged him into the tearoom, where he found the rest of his immediate family sprawled among the velvet floor cushions around a low teakwood table teetering with steaming platters of food, tea, and desserts. The twins were building a tower out of cookies. Taeron seemed to have dozed off, an empty cup of tea dangling precariously from his fingertips.

Along the wall were Rose's collection of maps, some yellow and cracking with age, some gleaming with metallic paint, some illustrating kingdoms or continents, and some the streets of a single city. In the center of it all was a world map, the largest in her collection. She had drawn all sorts of lines and squiggles across it, including a perfect triangle that nearly spanned the entire map and suddenly reminded Quinlan of the triangle on the nameless book still stuffed in his trousers.

"Taeron," Rose commanded. "Wake up." She prodded him in the stomach with her toe.

Taeron jerked awake. "Ngk."

The first thing Quinlan noticed was his brother's wrinkled shirt. He had never seen Taeron wear wrinkled clothes a single day in his life. "You look like crap," Quinlan told him bluntly.

"You too." Taeron picked himself up from his cushion on wobbly legs, looking slightly guilty but determined despite his disheveled state. He moved a plate of sandwiches on the floor and replaced them with a stack of books.

Shit, Quinlan thought when he caught sight of the topmost title. *Ten Traumas of the Tenth Element.* Everything clicked into place. "You snitched on me?" he spluttered.

Taeron folded his arms. "Of course I did."

The Queen of Eradore picked up a long loaf of bread from the spread of food on the table and whacked Quinlan hard across the head. "Quinlan Holloway, you atrocious, insolent, good-for-nothing half-wit." She accompanied each insult with a separate whack. Eventually the loaf ripped in two, but she just kept on clubbing him with what remained.

Avris and Avon observed the spectacle in wide-eyed silence. At some point their cookie tower had collapsed.

"Rose, please," Taeron finally piped up with a wince.

Anger swelled through Quinlan. "Go to hell, Taeron," he snarled, the brands on his back prickling as memories of his father washed over him. There was Taeron, lurking somewhere in the background, begging Gavin Holloway in a kitten's mewl to stop hurting, stop beating, *stop burning my little brother*. "It's your fault for telling Rose in the first place. You always try to help at the last second, especially when it's too late."

His brother flinched. "I—I know, I'm sorry, Quinlan. I just wanted to—"

Quinlan swallowed his resentment and looked away. "Save it." He sighed, the usual four words surfacing to his lips. "It's not your fault."

Everyone knew broken bones could heal at a spoken word. Gavin knew that most of all. That was why he had hired a healer to be at hand at all times and paid triple her fee for her silence—so he could break his youngest son again and again without a single worry.

Every time, after Gavin left the room, Taeron would be waiting outside the door with the healer and an apology on his lips.

And every time, Quinlan would say the same thing.

It's not your fault.

How many times had he uttered those four little words? How many times had he pushed them out of his throat after he had finished vomiting out his last meal, or fallen asleep on the floor because his aching body refused to rise?

In those days, all Quinlan had ever wanted was someone brave enough to protect him from his father's wrath.

He had so desperately wanted for Taeron to be that someone.

But Taeron could never find the courage or strength to stand between his younger brother and their father. The best he could ever do was clean up the aftermath.

"It's not your fault," Quinlan said again now, softly, because he loved his older brother. He really did.

Rose *harrumphed.* "Both of you are a real special kind of stupid, you know that?" She brandished what remained of the loaf of bread like a sword at the floor cushion between Taeron and the twins. "Sit, Quinnie."

Quinlan obeyed without hesitation and collapsed onto the cushion.

Rose reached over to the table and loaded two plates with steamed vegetables. She dumped the first plate into Taeron's lap and the second into Quinlan's.

Taeron wrinkled his nose.

"Taeron Holloway," Rose growled, "I swear to the Immortals that if you don't finish your food and lick every last morsel off your plate, I shall exile you from the library. Eternally."

Taeron actually gasped aloud. "You *wouldn't.*"

Rose simply jerked her chin at his plate with a glare that would have sent anyone sane running for the mountains. "Try me."

Taeron reluctantly stabbed his fork into a cauliflower.

They ate their vegetables in silence, with Rose watching over every bite with a gaze so cold and merciless that the late Queen Lillian would have been proud. The twins reconstructed their cookie tower until Avon sneezed and accidentally knocked it over. In retaliation, Avris crushed a cookie and shoved it down her twin's collar. Rose threatened to ground both of them—separately, of course.

Quinlan supposed it was about as domestic as their little family could ever get.

He finished his food at the same time as Taeron, washing the last of it down with some tea. He set down the empty cup. The dread from earlier had yet to leave his system, and it only worsened as everyone stared at him in expectant silence.

"What?" he finally demanded, wishing more than ever that he could sink into the floor and disappear.

"When did it first happen?" asked Rose.

Quinlan picked up his teacup again and fiddled with the ornate handle. "You're going to have to be a little more specific. My first kiss, for example? Several years ago. Next question." Hopefully she would reply with something vaguely sarcastic, and then he could dodge the question and—

Rose didn't even blink. "When did the residual shadow magic first attack your body?"

So much for sarcasm.

"You know," Quinlan began, examining his teacup. "Whoever made this really knew their craft. I mean, just look at the shape. It bears such a subtle elegance, it . . ."

Rose stood from her cushion and strode around the table. She wrenched the cup from his grasp and hurled it at the wall in an explosion of porcelain.

In the ensuing silence, no one dared to move. It was a new kind of silence, the kind that made Quinlan afraid of breathing at the wrong moment. He stared at his cousin, at her heaving shoulders and the dark fury blazing in her golden eyes.

"Fix it, Quinlan," said Rose.

His throat locked around his words. A strange noise escaped him.

Rose thrust her finger at the fragments littering the floor and yelled. "I said, *fix it!*"

"I *can't!*" Quinlan shouted. His hands shook uncontrollably. His vision blurred with tears.

The twins scrambled over to him. Avon stroked his hair while Avris lay her little auburn head on his chest, her ear pressed over his heart. He wondered what she could hear.

Rose muttered, "*Reyunir*," and the teacup remnants drifted into the air and mended themselves before drifting back onto the table, whole and unbroken once more.

How stupid, to be envious of a teacup.

Rose knelt before Quinlan and placed a gentle hand on his knee. The next time the queen spoke, her voice was soft. "I thought so."

Taeron, too, came to crouch at eye level before him. "I know it's hard for you to ask for help," he began. "I know you probably don't want our help. But we're your *family*, little brother. We love you more than anything, and we could never bear to lose you. So please. For the love of the Immortals, *please*, Quinlan. If you're hurting . . . let us help you heal."

Quinlan's grief streamed down his face. He cursed, trying to wipe the tears away, but for some reason they refused to abate. *Stop crying, for Immortals' sake*, he ordered himself as the shame and the guilt and the anguish crashed down upon him all at once, only making him cry harder. Avris wrapped her freckled arms around his neck and patted his back. Avon used his sleeves to dab at Quinlan's cheeks.

"Quinlan," said Taeron, despair lining the pinch of his brow, his glistening eyes. "I know that you don't want us to help—"

"No," Quinlan at last managed hoarsely. "You're wrong."

Rose sighed. "Cousin dearest, this really isn't the time to be stubborn—"

"I *do* want your help."

Rose went silent.

"I'm sorry I kept this a secret," Quinlan stammered. "I thought I could handle it on my own, but it turns out that I can't." He hiccuped. "I don't know what to do. I—I'm dying."

Taeron grabbed his hands. "No," he whispered fiercely. "We're going to get you through this, little brother." Taeron swallowed. "I . . . I know I couldn't always be there for you when Father was still alive, but I promise you that I won't rest until we find you a cure. I won't let you down, not again."

Quinlan maneuvered Avris and reached into his trousers pocket. "Here, Taeron." He pulled out the locket Taeron had ripped from his neck and tossed it to him—literally putting his fate into his brother's hands. And somehow, it felt . . . all right.

Rose craned her neck to peer at the locket clasped in Taeron's fist. "What was that?"

Hastily, Taeron tucked it away. "Nothing," he lied. Then he shot Quinlan a look of understanding. "From now on, little brother, no more hiding. You tell us everything. Promise?"

Quinlan closed his eyes and exhaled. "Promise."

CHAPTER THIRTY-SIX

Sixty-one . . . sixty-two . . .

Asterin pushed the air out of her lungs as she pulled herself up, her grip slipping slightly around the brass curtain rod. She released one hand at a time and wiped them on her trousers before resuming her chin-ups. In the corner, Eadric was doing push-ups, clapping his chest on every rep and grunting his counts under his breath. Exercising with him always forced her to push herself further, harder, and she craved the competition.

The chiffon curtains whisked around her, the same white as the lofty lace-spun clouds outside, carried by an invigorating sea breeze that cooled the sweat on her brow. Every time she dipped down from a rep, she watched the ocean toss and foam through the window. Seabirds with bright-orange hooked beaks and yellow Mohawks wheeled above the frothing cerulean expanse on speckled wings, their melodic warbles just as unfamiliar to her as their appearances. Every now and then, great blue fins crested above the waves, and sometimes she caught the massive shadow of a shy, elusive beast swimming far beneath the crystalline depths.

The Eradorian palace hovered on the coast of the Nord Sea atop a formation of metamorphic rock that glittered with ribs of obsidian and ivory in the sunlight. Freshwater springs deep beneath the earth welled up through the rock and cascaded into natural pools scattered in and around the palace, which only made perfect sense since the kingdom of Eradore was the domain of Lord Tidus, the God of Water.

"One hundred," Asterin hissed to herself, muscles straining. She liked to play a game with herself, where she set a goal, a number of reps she had to reach. Except, when she reached it, she added a few extra reps, and then when she finished *those*, she added a few more, pushing her boundaries a little further each time. Soon enough, she had reached one hundred and fifty.

Sounds less like a game than a masochistic streak, Orion used to say. Immortals, how she missed him.

A knock came at her door, causing Eadric to pause and glance up.

"I'll get it," said Asterin, dropping to the floor and rolling her shoulders as she approached the entrance to her guest chambers. They consisted of three separate rooms—her bedchamber, with its gradient blue walls inlaid with shells and mother-of-pearl, a spacious bathing chamber with nothing short of a pool for a bathtub, and a tearoom in place of a sitting parlor with padded floor cushions instead of chaises.

Asterin opened the door to find Quinlan holding a large box in his hands with a silk ribbon tied around it. "Oh," she said. *About time.* "It's you."

Quinlan bit his lip. "Yeah, it's me. Sorry."

Eadric picked himself up and stalked over to Asterin's side, bracing one arm against the door frame and leaning out. "Holloway."

"Captain." Quinlan took one glance at Eadric's glistening biceps and quickly averted his eyes elsewhere. "Is this a bad time?"

Eadric snorted and shouldered past Quinlan, though not without shooting him a final glower. "I won't do my queen the disservice of threatening you on her behalf, since she is more than capable of kicking your ass herself, but—"

"Thank you, Eadric," said Asterin, shooing the captain away. After he finally strode off, muttering unsavory things under his breath all the while, she turned back to Quinlan. "You were saying?"

"I'm sorry." He shuffled his feet. "For the other day."

"When you ran away from me, you mean?"

Quinlan winced. "Not *from* you. But . . . yes."

She tipped her chin at the box. "What's that?"

He wiggled his eyebrows. "Don't you want to let me inside and find out?"

Asterin scoffed. "Who do you take me for, to be so easily bribed?"

"It's cake."

That made her pause. "Fine, I guess you can come in."

He shot her a smile that she couldn't help but grudgingly return as they went over to the tearoom table. Quinlan placed the box in the center and then hurried outside again. Asterin briefly wondered if he was deserting her for the second time, but a moment later a tea cart came into view. Quinlan wheeled it through the door and steered it beside the table. While she watched on, he arranged the tea set before her. Then he passed her a plate painted with intricate gold swirls and a tiny fork surely meant for a doll.

"Bold of you to assume I would eat cake with a fork this small," she muttered as he poured out two cups of tea, the sweet, slightly citrusy aroma wafting up in curls of steam.

Quinlan raised his eyebrows. "Hmm? Ah, I thought you might say that, so I brought larger forks, too. As for the plate, we could just eat out of the box, if you'd like."

She grinned. "Well, only if you insist." Her fingers tapped the table. She leaned over the box like an impatient child waiting to open presents on Vürstivale. "Can I open it?"

Quinlan smiled so softly that her stomach flipped. "Of course."

Asterin tugged on one tail of the ribbon until it came loose and the flaps of the box fell open like a lotus flower. She gasped in delight at the blush-pink cake nestled within, heaped with fresh strawberries and raspberry meringues with white chocolate drizzling down the edges. Real fuchsia roses and cherry blossoms dotted the buttercream-frosted sides, their satiny petals dusted with flakes of edible gold.

"It's almost too pretty to eat, don't you think—" Quinlan began, but Asterin had already stabbed her fork right down the center.

She stiffened. Silently, their eyes met. And then they both burst into hysterical laughter.

He took his own fork and spaded the cake, reaching forward and offering it to her lips. "May I?"

For the sake of fairness, Asterin offered her forkful to him. They closed in and both let out twin exclamations of deliciousness. Tart berry jam and fresh whipped cream, soaked into three delicate layers of buttery sponge—a perfect balance of sweetness, exquisitely light. They maimed the cake bite by bite, laying the beautiful decorations to absolute ruin.

"So good," Asterin crowed as she licked the crumbs off the tines of her fork. She popped a leftover meringue into her mouth and scooted around the table to take Quinlan's face in her hands. She kissed him gently, savoring the hint of strawberries and sugar still lingering on his lips. "Thank you."

He rested his hands on her waist, his thumbs tracing soothing circles into her skin. "You know I didn't mean to abandon you so suddenly."

Asterin's eyes trailed over the anxious crease of his brow. "I know," she replied quietly and leaned forward to kiss his forehead. "I just wish you would've told me why you had to leave." She drew back to gaze at him. "So . . . why did you have to leave?"

Those indigo eyes averted. "I had to take care of something."

Frustration coupled with disbelief reared within her. She caught him by the wrists and removed his hands from her waist. With a deep sigh of resignation, she got to her feet. "Come back when you trust me enough to talk about this, all right?"

Quinlan stared up at her, stricken. "I—I do trust you."

"Clearly." Asterin folded her arms over her chest and waited. "Well? I'm all ears."

He didn't speak for a long minute, but she was fine with waiting. For months she had already waited. And for centuries, for him, she would keep waiting. At last, he spoke, with his head hanging down and his voice a rasp. "Why did you save me, Asterin?"

Her brow scrunched. "What?"

Quinlan's dark locks hid his expression as his chest convulsed with a rueful, bitter laugh. "Fairfest Eve. Priscilla. The battle. She made you choose. Between Luna . . . and me."

The silence squeezed Asterin by the neck, just like the nooses of shadow Priscilla had used to choke the life out of her best friend and the prince she had fallen for. She had been so powerless against the darkness, too cursedly weak to save both of them.

"Does there have to be a reason?" Asterin finally asked.

He seemed taken aback by that. "Well, there must have been at the time."

"I . . . I don't know." She shook her head. "I just let my heart choose for me."

"But why didn't your heart choose Luna? Why—"

"Stop asking me why!" Asterin exclaimed. "Why are *you* asking me these questions?" She stormed toward the door, and suddenly she was back in Axaris, a few days after the battle, when Luna came to tell her that she was leaving for Ibreseos—that she was leaving because she couldn't stand to even live in the same kingdom as Asterin.

What do you want me to tell you, Luna? she had shouted then. *What would you like me to say? That I regret protecting him?*

"I'm asking if you ever wished you had chosen differently," Quinlan whispered.

Time screeched to a halt. Shock crashed into Asterin like a tidal wave. "You mean, do I wish you were *dead*?" She strode back over to him and grabbed him by the collar. "Listen to me. I already lost Luna over my choice. Don't you dare play that card, too." Her voice broke. "Quinlan, I love you."

He blinked at her, his mouth opening and closing wordlessly.

"You told me you wouldn't leave me," she went on without waiting for a response. Desperation edged her voice. "You promised me that you would stay by my side, always. Don't do this to me. Don't push me away."

If anything, though, Quinlan just looked more wrecked than before. "Asterin . . ." He trailed off, clenching his jaw before turning his face away from her. "I'm so sorry."

She realized it wasn't an apology for her distress. It was because he had decided to keep her in the dark.

The ugly thing in her chest stabbed its claws through her heart. "Fine," she said, releasing him. *And to think that I'm supposed to be the stubborn one.* She spun on her heel, swiping a furious hand across her eyes to rid them of tears. "I have somewhere to be now, anyway." She cast him a final glance on her way out and saw his reluctant, silent inquisition. "If you change your mind about talking, I'll be in the library. With Taeron. Perhaps he'll prove to be more gracious company."

Shame filled her at the gratification she took in seeing the range of emotions flitting across Quinlan's face—shock, jealousy, resentment, doubt.

Before he could speak another word, however, she slammed the door behind her and fled, trying in vain to banish the memory of the destroyed cake still on the table and the taste of strawberries.

CHAPTER THIRTY-SEVEN

Once a day, Orion pulled out the hand mirror he kept hidden beneath his pillow and tried to convince it to reveal to him the secrets of the Mortal Realm. Sometimes, he even resorted to pleading with it aloud, but the best he could ever manage was summoning something ordinary, like a wooden chair or a wine glass. Any time he tried to picture a mortal, *any* mortal, the mirror just reflected his own face back at him.

He didn't confess his troubles to Eoin. The god had already done enough for him. No, Orion would find a way to recall some shred of his past on his own. The last thing that he wanted was to come off as desperate.

Orion gave the mirror a few shakes to see if it would help. It didn't. "Stupid thing," he grumbled to himself. Eventually, he let out a sigh of defeat and turned his gaze outside his favorite window—the view from Eoin's balcony of the Shadow Kingdom.

His eyes narrowed into the distance. There was a tiny black speck marring the horizon, growing with every second. From afar, he might have mistaken it for a person standing on a sleijh, but something wasn't quite right. He pressed his face to the glass, wishing he could see better. As if the window had heard him, the view zoomed onto the speck to give him a closer look.

A great winged creature with iridescent black feathers that shimmered teal in the starlight approached the palace. Its wings extended from its shoulders in armlike appendages, each feather edged by a knife's glint. As it drew nearer, Orion realized that some of the outermost feathers were, in fact, made up of actual knives. It had legs, too, in the form of lethal gold talons merging seamlessly with pale calves lean with muscle. A horned headdress of plumage crowned its brow, curving away from its face to reveal glowing red eyes as hard and bright as rubies.

As the creature soared ever closer, Orion watched, transfixed—first, in fascination, and then in alarm when it became clear that it meant to land *on the balcony*. He scrambled to an adjacent window, a front view of the palace, just in time to see the creature swoop down.

Wonder bloomed through Orion as the creature shook out its wings and the feathers receded from its arms, transferring onto its shoulders and back. The plumes surrounding its face bleached from dark to light, tapering into a cascade of silvery-blond hair. It wore nothing, but in place of clothes, every inch of its body was protected by obsidian-black chitin—an unbreakable suit of armor tailored to every limb, every muscle.

The creature arched its neck and turned its face toward the sky. When it blinked, irises of turquoise glittered in place of ruby.

And then it opened its mouth wide and began to scream with all its might.

Orion leapt back from the window. He couldn't hear exactly what the creature was yelling, but he could read *Eoin* from the shape of its moving lips. Some instinct made him bolt out of his room, made him sprint down the corridor toward the throne room.

Just as Orion skidded to a halt in the entryway, directly opposite him, the creature pushed through the magic barrier leading from the balcony into the hall.

When it glanced up, Orion stopped short. In the time it had taken him to arrive, the feathery creature had fully transformed into . . . a young woman.

The woman mirrored his stunned stare, her mouth parted in a perfect O. "Or-*Orion?*" She broke into a run. Too late he began backing away. She crashed into him, flinging her arms around his neck. "You're *alive!* I can't believe it! What are you doing here?"

He stood, rooted and unmoving, unable to summon a response. First Harry, and now . . . this.

"Orion?" At his silence, the stranger drew back with a frown to examine his face. "It *is* you, isn't it?"

"Yes?" He tried for a smile. "I'm sorry, do I know you?"

Anxiety flashed across the young woman's features. "Immortals, what happened to you? Did Eoin do this?" Her fingers snaked to his temples. "Hush, don't move," she murmured when he tried to shake her off. "I won't hurt you, I promise." She closed her eyes and inhaled deeply. When they opened, they had reverted to red.

A shudder passed through him—not because of her eyes, but from the strange energy radiating from her fingertips, traveling along his scalp and sending prickles down his spine.

"Ah," she murmured softly, still holding his face. She blinked again and her eyes glimmered turquoise once more. They were filled with pity. "Poor thing, you've lost your memories."

Orion's heart kicked into overdrive. "How can you tell?" he demanded. "Can you . . . can you give them back?"

"I don't know." Her mouth scrunched sideways in consideration. "I'm still figuring out my new abilities. I guess I could try. Where's Eoin?"

"He's not home yet," he replied. As usual, the King of Immortals had vanished long before Orion had awoken, the empty side of the bed long grown cold. The man had an entire kingdom to rule over, after all. Not to mention that the anarchies were still missing—eight of them, anyway. According to Eoin, the obliterated remains of Hostility had reappeared in the Pit. The Anarchies couldn't be killed, of course, but it would take at least a few decades for Hostility to regenerate fully.

The young woman's head tilted. "How do you know?"

"He always comes to see me first," Orion said. "We're . . . er . . . seeing each other."

"Oh." She struggled to smooth her expression into indifference. "I—I see." He could tell she was weighing her next words. "Before or after you lost your memories?"

The question made him uneasy. "After. Why?"

"No reason," she answered quickly. "Does he make you happy?"

It took him a few moments to gather a response. Eventually, he came up with, "He's very kind to me." Even he grimaced at his own words. Both of them knew it wasn't a proper response, but for whatever reason, the young woman smiled, as if the lack of affirmation pleased her.

Instead of further prodding him, however, she asked, "When will he return?"

He shuffled his feet. "I . . . I don't know. It depends. He never tells me." He cleared his throat. "He wouldn't be able to tell me, either, even if he wanted to. Which he does. Or, he would. If he could."

"Uh-huh," said the young woman. "Well, let me give this a shot. I've never really done this before, but I don't suppose we'll know until I try. Stay perfectly still, all right?"

Trepidation coursed through Orion's veins as her fingers locked onto his temples and pressed inward. Her words hadn't exactly given him a boost of confidence. "Wait—" he began, reaching upward to swat her away, but she possessed inhuman strength.

"Stop that, you craven," she scolded, stilling him into a compliance with nothing more than an unimpressed glower. "I'm just planting a few little seedlings. You'll thank me later."

"What seedlings?" The tingles running down his spine began anew, intensifying to a buzz that vibrated all the way down to his toes. "And I'm not craven. I just have a reasonable sense of self-preservation."

"Self-preservation, huh?" Her lips twitched into a smile tinged with melancholy. "Well, that's new. The Orion I knew would never hesitate to throw himself before the darkest monsters to defend the ones he loved. Now close your eyes for me."

He did everything within his power to keep them as wide as physically possible, but his lids still glided shut. He fought against the impenetrable swamp of blackness enclosing him, but in the end he had nothing to keep him afloat.

"That should do it," came a gentle voice. "You can open your eyes now."

Orion blinked a few times to clear the haze clouding his vision. He squinted at the empty hall, shaking off the last tendrils of his trance. He whipped around. *Where did she go?* His mind floundered, grappling with reality, struggling to catch up with the present as he scoured every corner of the hall for the demon who had landed on the balcony, who had transformed into a young woman, who had known who he was—

I'm just planting a few little seedlings, she had promised. *You'll thank me later.*

Except . . . she wasn't just any demon. Or any young woman.

The world ground to a jarring halt as a cold wind blew past him. It was like waking up from a dream already forgotten, until a single thought triggered another to emerge from the fog, until everything came together and *clicked*.

Orion stumbled forward and fell to his knees, staring past the balcony to the kingdom to which neither he nor the young woman belonged.

She had once been mortal, and now she was more.

She had once been mortal, and *he remembered her name.*

"*Luna*," he whispered reverently, and the dams broke free.

CHAPTER THIRTY-EIGHT

"What," King Jakob growled, "do you mean when you say that you *lost her*?"

Killian leaned against a pillar in Throne Hall and examined her nails, the picture of nonchalance when she was everything but.

Everything had gone to shit in Orielle, and Luna . . . Luna . . .

The eclipse had occurred sooner than Killian had told Jakob, sooner than even *she* had expected. They had been on the road back to Ibresis when it had cloaked the land in night. Eoin had come and gone, claiming the princess in one fell swoop.

It killed Killian to think of Luna at the King of Immortal's mercy, helpless and alone.

There was nothing you could have done, Killian tried to reassure herself, kicking up one foot against the pillar. *Absolutely nothing.* Of course, as soon as this was over, she planned to pay a visit to the Immortal Realm, but for now she had to face the harsh reality that Luna was simply out of reach.

If only Asterin hadn't escaped North Yard. If only the queen's ice hadn't rendered Kane useless even after it had melted. If only it hadn't left him drenched and half frozen and unable to do anything but curl into a ball on the floor and shiver violently.

Back in Orielle, he had tried to tell Killian something. She recounted the events in her head, trying to imagine what they could have done differently. She remembered how his teeth had chattered so fiercely that he couldn't even manage a single intelligible word. Killian's healing abilities were strictly bound to herself, and Kane, already magically weak, was certainly in no state to revive himself. She'd had no choice but to drag him into the sunshine to dry.

And then she'd run off to find Rivaille.

She had hoped to encounter the hireling locked in battle with the captain and the female Elite, but his targets were nowhere in sight, and Rivaille—

Well, she discovered Rivaille squashed like an insect beneath a massive shipping container.

Squashed, and most definitely dead.

By the time she returned to Kane, he had finally warmed up enough to speak. "I saw a man," he hissed, rubbing his palms up and down the sides of his arms. "He just . . . popped out of the shadows, looked around the container, saw me, and disappeared again. Melted right into the darkness."

Dread coursed through Killian. "What did he look like?"

"He was tall, with dark-brown hair and copper skin, and he—"

Killian cursed aloud. "*Harry*. What's he doing here?" The last she'd heard of her fellow anygné, he had been on leave. But if he had shadow jumped . . . then maybe she could track his signature. "Get up, Kane. We have a job to finish."

If Harry considered himself to be a lousy shadow jumper, Killian was absolute *trash*. The first time she had tried it, she had dismembered herself from the waist down. Even Eoin hadn't known what to do. So instead of shadow jumping, Killian and Kane settled for running, no severed body parts involved—because even though Killian could eventually heal from incapacitation, Kane most certainly could not.

In the end, though, it hadn't mattered. Killian managed to pinpoint Harry's location to a grimy tavern called the Boar's Head, but by the time they busted through the trapdoor and into the secret lair beneath, he had shadow jumped *again*, most likely taking Asterin with him. And this time, he had jumped far, far away—too remote for Killian to detect.

Her only consolation was that she could sense that Harry had only jumped once—meaning that the captain and the remaining Elite were either dead or still loose in Orielle, since he only had the ability to shadow travel with one other person at a time.

King Jakob pinched the bridge of his nose and exhaled. "Please tell me that the captain, at the very least, was taken care of."

Killian played with the hem of her sleeve. They had stuck around Orielle for a while before sulking back to Ibresis, trying—unsuccessfully—to catch any hints of the presence of either the captain or the Elite. "Maybe?"

The king practically leapt out of his throne. "*Maybe?*"

Kane cleared his throat. "Wherever he is, Your Majesty, we can assure you that he did not sail Orielle's waters."

King Jakob zeroed in on him. "How can you be certain?"

The hireling shifted his weight from side to side, keeping his gaze averted. "Well, Lady Killian took the liberty to bar all boats from departing Horn's Bay entirely."

King Jakob went dangerously still. In a slightly mocking voice, he asked, "And how, in the name of ever-loving hell, did *Lady Killian* manage *that?*"

Killian saved Kane the burden of answering. "I destroyed Horn's Bay. Or, rather, the Three Bridges. Completely. Unequivocally. No ships going in. No ships going out."

A moment of dead silence passed and King Jakob slowly sank back into his throne. So apparently the news hadn't reached Ibresis yet. For a long minute, no one moved a muscle, not even Killian.

When the king finally spoke, his voice had gone flat and calm as a dead sea. "So those ridiculous rumors were true." Killian almost wished he would go back to shouting. "What delusions prompted you to do such a thing?"

"Well, Your Majesty," Killian began slowly. "In your exact words, you ordered us to keep Queen Asterin from leaving Orielle's port."

King Jakob's index finger twitched against his armrest. "I *also* ordered you to assassinate the captain, did I not?"

How petty. "You know," Killian said, her tone icy, "you really ought to have gotten to know your precious daughter a little better before Eoin snatched her away for good."

The king's glare faltered slightly. "Pardon me?"

"Has it ever occurred to you that murdering your daughter's beloved might not be the *best* idea?" She threw a hand across her brow. "Stone cold, Your Majesty, even for you."

Jakob regarded her for a moment. "Her beloved? I . . . I was never made aware of this," he grudgingly replied, as if he couldn't be blamed. "However, if you really *did* destroy the Three Bridges—"

"Definitely did," Killian muttered.

"*Do not interrupt me!*" Jakob roared, deafening as thunder. "You *insolent* pest. Did it ever cross your mind that your actions could potentially cripple the entire continent's economy? You trapped hundreds of cargo ships inside *and* outside the bay. Trade will cease for months. I can't expect someone like *you* to understand the consequences of this catastrophe, but . . ." The king exhaled through gritted teeth and leveled Killian with an unforgiving iron stare. "I know what this is. I'm no fool, *Eirene*." A low growl rose in her throat at that name on his lips, but he went on, unnoticing, lowering his voice to a low, scornful murmur. "You count all of these little rebellions as victories against me, but they only prove how pathetic you are. How *worthless*."

Her fury transformed her. She lunged for the king, the shadows of the hall racing up to swathe her in a cocoon of darkness, and when she emerged in her demon form, snarling, she pinned the king down by the throat with claws like scythes. She could imagine what he saw—wiry limbs too long to be human, rippling with power beneath skin blacker than night. Millions of silver veins as thin as gossamer, webbing up her torso. Her white robes, hanging from her frame in tatters, shredded by the tiny jagged barbs covering her entire body. Seven-pronged ebony antlers extending from both sides of her head like cruel spears born from violence.

And of course, her killing mask.

"*Do I look worthless to you now?*" Killian hissed.

Jakob wheezed, his neck straining and the whites of his eyes bulging out. "Treason." Trickles of scarlet wept from where her claws pricked his soft mortal skin. "Get . . . *off* . . . *me*."

Killian spat curses as her claws began retracting one by one, against her every will. Her shoulders trembled with effort, muscles coiling tight with rage, but her body betrayed her and bent away from the king. She bared her fangs at him as her feet touched the floor, still struggling to free herself from his command—

"Stop," a voice rang out, capturing the cool authority that only Immortals had the time to master.

They all froze. From atop the dais, Killian turned slowly to find a figure standing at the other end of Throne Hall.

Kane gaped. He had retreated to the back of the hall to get as far away as possible from the danger. "Luna . . . ?"

Killian stared. *There's no way* . . . but there she was. The Princess of Ibreseos. In the flesh—or rather, from what Killian could tell, in her second skin.

King Jakob's eyes shone with wonder. "How is this possible?"

As Luna strode toward them, black fabric tumbled forth from empty air to wrap around her slight body, clothing her in a gown adorned with shattered crystals. Pure magic radiated from the newly forged anygné, a gravity that sucked everything around her inward. *Like a star*, Killian thought to herself numbly. *Or a dark sun among moons.* Luna reached up with both hands to smooth the loose tendrils of hair from her face. When her hands fell away, a crown of black diamonds and delicate filigree feathers glittered atop her head.

"Lady Killian," Luna greeted with an acknowledging nod. "Kane." Then she turned her gaze upon King Jakob. "Father."

"Luna, my dear," Jakob began with a tentative smile. He spread his arms wide and welcoming, all traces of hostility evaporating on the spot. "I'm so very glad that you're all right. How . . . how did you—how did you manage to escape back to the Mortal Realm?"

"King Eoin and I made a few negotiations," said Luna, and Killian could hardly believe her ears. "He allowed me to return on a few conditions."

Her father's brow furrowed. "Such as . . . ?"

Luna smiled. "Well, the first one was that I become Queen of Aspea."

"Qu-queen of *Aspea*?" Jakob spluttered. "You can't be serious."

"On the contrary," Luna replied, her affable tone at odds with her expression, her predatory stalk toward the throne. She ascended the dais and halted at Killian's side to look down at her father, the razored tips of her crown catching the light.

"Queen. Of the entire continent," Jakob said weakly.

"Four kingdoms," Luna agreed. "Two thrones to claim and two thrones to conquer. Cyeji and Axaria will be the hardest, of course, but Oprehvar . . . well, Mother *was* the Duchess of Oprehvar. Queen Belinda has yet to sire an heir and has no siblings. Should some unfortunate fate befall her and cut her reign short, Adrianna would be the first in line to rule . . . but I'm sure I could persuade my dear aunt to turn down such an onerous position. With no heir of her own, I would be the next choice." The princess brushed her fingers along her self-made crown. "And then, of course, there is the matter of Ibreseos."

The king paled. "Ah." Perspiration glistening along his hairline. Killian could see his pulse jumping at his throat, smell his fear dripping down his back.

She watched him suffer, and she did so with savage glee.

"As your only heir," said Luna, that sweet little smile playing on her lips, "you could very easily abdicate the throne to me."

"I couldn't . . . couldn't possibly—" Jakob began stammering. "Just think of my responsibilities as king! I can't simply *abandon* my duties, throw them all willy-nilly out the window." His voice grew frenzied. "You understand, Luna, don't you?"

Killian bit down hard on a grin when Luna's eyes widened with false innocence. "Oh!" the princess exclaimed. "I would never ask you to shirk such vital responsibilities! And certainly not rid yourself of them 'all willy-nilly,' as you so eloquently put it. In fact . . . I insist that you don't." Her smile turned serpentine. "I have other kingdoms to conquer in the meanwhile, after all."

Jakob seemed at a total loss for words.

Luna tilted her head angelically. "Well, Father?" she asked. "Will you make me Queen of Ibreseos?" Then, right before their eyes, a glorious pair of wings burst from her shoulder blades, engulfing Jakob and his throne in its monstrous shadow. "Or . . ." The sharp tang of the king's terror pierced the air, but his cowering only made Luna's smile widen. "Will I have to conquer *you*, too?"

CHAPTER THIRTY-NINE

Every time Orion closed his eyes, his head filled with vivid phantasms too striking and intricate to be anything but *real*. It was like experiencing everything he had forgotten in real time. And the last memory had been from the battle on Fairfest Eve.

"*Harry,*" he snarled.

"I'll be back," Harry swore. "But this I owe to all of you."

The anygné surged into the air on wings webbed and translucent, clutching one last dagger in his fist.

As the portal of darkness yawned open, Harry swooped down and grabbed Priscilla by the neck. She flailed pathetically, a final attempt to escape, gurgling and foaming at the mouth.

And just before the shadow portal swallowed them whole, Harry plunged the dagger into Priscilla's heart.

Orion shouted something hoarse and unintelligible and broken. He bolted forward. Something latched onto his wrist to yank him backward, but he wrenched himself free and lunged for the rapidly shrinking portal.

"Orion!" he heard someone scream, a voice he could not quite place, their fingertips brushing the fabric of his sleeve, so, so close—

He dove into the darkness headfirst. The shadows enveloped him, sucking him away, and then he began to fall. Ribbons of shadow entangled him, strangled him, laughing and singing and whispering to him in tongues he couldn't understand.

down and down and down and down and down . . .

Now he wouldn't stop falling. Couldn't stop falling. The shadows laughed and stole the screams right from his throat. He tried to keep track of the seconds, but he never made it past one thousand before losing count. He wondered when this would end, how it would end, if it would ever end at all—

The world flared white for the briefest second, and when he came to, the ground was moist against his bare face, filling his nostrils with the scent of rain and something he did not recognize.

Orion Galashiels pressed a kiss to the land and thanked the Immortals.

Then he rolled onto his back, closing his eyes as he sank into the wet ground, and breathed.

When he opened his eyes, he was standing in his room by the enchanted windows, his chest aching and his head spinning with vertigo. He staggered forward, bending over and bracing himself against the wall, forcing air into his lungs one breath at a time while he stared a hole into the floor.

Harry.

"Harry," he said aloud, a mess of feelings he couldn't even begin to untangle igniting in his veins and threatening to burn him up from the inside out.

I do like you, Orion. Those brown eyes on him, so warm, so adoring, and . . . something else, something heartbroken, so very, very heartbroken. *Far too much for my own good.*

It all made sense now—the way Harry had looked at him the first time they had run into one another, right here in the Shadow Palace. The way he had uttered Orion's name as if it was his salvation. The way his face had crumpled when he had realized that Orion didn't remember *his* name.

"Harry," Orion said again, to himself, to the empty room, to the entire palace. Like a prayer, like a mantra, like a promise. "Harry, Harry, Harry, Harry, Harry—"

He halted.

The mirror.

"Idiot," Orion berated himself. Summoning Harry had never even occurred to him.

Orion dashed for his bed, leaping into the air and bouncing upon it on all fours. He tossed the pillow over his shoulder and triumphantly grabbed the mirror beneath it, the engraved edges of the handle digging into his palm.

He glanced into the reflection and inhaled deeply. "Just picture whatever it is you want to see. That's all there is to it," he reassured himself.

His previous attempts at summoning a faceless person to mind usually resulted in the mirror surface presenting him with an impenetrable gray fog or a few meaningless images too obscure for him to properly distinguish. But now he knew exactly what—or rather, *whom*—he was looking for. And more importantly . . . why.

Orion tried to picture Harry from a single moment in time, but his mind bombarded him with a flurry of memories, a thousand strong—so instead of seizing a single one, he embraced them all as a collective remembrance of *Harry*.

The surface of the mirror rippled to life, and a second later a face filled the reflection.

"Immortals," Orion whispered to himself. It had worked.

Harry stood beside a window with a view of a churning ocean, the sky above crowded by charcoal clouds swelling with rain. The anygné's expression was haggard and lined with distress, but the euphoria of seeing him overpowered Orion's anxieties.

He couldn't help but marvel at every detail in the mirror—the elegant curlicues tracing the window frame, the muted daylight glinting off the crest of each wave. And Harry . . . the vividness of every little strand of hair, the outline of his jaw, his irises, gleaming russet gold when his face tilted at just the right angle to capture a sunbeam.

Heat rushed to Orion's cheeks as he stared into the mirror. Longing flooded his chest.

Harry seemed to have arrived at some decision, pressing his lips into a thin line and nodding to himself once before striding away. The mirror's view followed the anygné through an unfamiliar set of rooms, all connected by strange passages through closets and even a hidden portrait entrance.

Halfway through a chamber filled with cascading waterfalls, Harry paused midstride and turned around to wait for two figures to catch up to him.

Around the mirror handle, Orion's knuckles went white. He had never stood beneath a waterfall, but surely it felt like this—an onslaught, a deluge, an *assault* of memories.

His eyes had first settled on Eadric Covington—Eadric, how could he have forgotten *Eadric*—before sliding left, to . . . to . . .

Asterin. Asterin Faelenhart, Princess of Axaria.

A dark loathing twisted his stomach as he watched her, rancor bittering his tongue and blurring his vision. What was this hostility? Where had it come from? Then, somewhere, deep down, came a memory—himself at young Asterin's side, the two of them battling through thick and thin, every sparring session and meal shared, the first time she had defeated him, his overwhelming *pride*—

"My life is yours," Orion whispered aloud, as he once had in Harry's cottage to a fever-ridden Asterin. "I vowed to protect your life with mine, and I will never forsake that promise."

He banished everything but those memories and latched onto their warmth, their vibrancy. Then he set the mirror carefully onto the bed and buried his face in his hands.

Those feelings couldn't have belonged to him. But then . . . had they belonged to Luna, since she had been inside his head? *Make time later for worrying*, Orion ordered himself. He picked up the mirror again. For now, he had to figure out a way to communicate with the others. Though he couldn't be sure of much, especially himself, he did know one thing for certain.

He needed to return to the Mortal Realm.

Asterin had led Harry and Eadric to a new location—her chambers, most likely, although Orion still had no idea *where* those chambers were since it couldn't have been Axaris.

"Hey!" Orion exclaimed at the mirror, but she was as deaf to him as he was to their conversation. Still, it was worth a shot. "Asterin! Harry! Eadric! Can any of you hear me?"

The three of them kept their heads bowed together while Harry spoke, his hands gesturing rapidly in the air. Then the anygné said something that caused Asterin to grab him by the shoulders with shaking hands.

Eadric's expression grew grave as Harry continued speaking, but Asterin's eyes lit up with that fierce, familiar determination, and an inadvertent smile overtook Orion's face. Asterin cut Harry off, her mouth flying a mile a minute, even as Eadric shook his head and just kept on shaking it the longer she chattered on. It only made Orion smile harder.

His smile faded as he remembered his mission. How could he get their attention if they couldn't hear or see him? He drummed his fingers upon the mirror's surface. He even tried to flick a hairbrush off the vanity behind Asterin, though to no avail.

Then his eyes narrowed on the vanity itself.

As long as it exists in the Mortal Realm, the mirror will obey.

"Technically," Orion muttered to himself, "I *do* exist in the Mortal Realm. I'm there, right now. And if I were to look into a mirror, I would see myself."

His view through the mirror's surface lost focus on Harry and glided closer to the vanity. He took a deep breath and looked into its reflection, daring to hope.

A growl of frustration rose from his throat. There was nothing. In the vanity, he could still see Asterin and Harry and Eadric conversing behind him.

He was *so* close to them, and yet he had never been farther from them.

He felt so cold, so alone. Disappointment left him numb as he clutched the hand mirror tighter, completely oblivious to the frost creeping up the handle until the hand mirror's surface began to fog over.

His irritation evaporated when he realized that the vanity mirror, too, was clouding with frozen vapor.

Eadric noticed the fog first. His first instinct was to drag Asterin to safety while simultaneously drawing his affinity stone. Harry approached

the vanity cautiously and peered into it, unknowing that he was staring Orion dead in the eye. The anygné placed one hand onto its surface,
dissolving the fog, and Orion let out a gasp when a tiny matching handprint bloomed on the surface of the mirror in his hand.

Trembling, Orion raised his index finger to the hand mirror's surface
and traced out a message.

HELLO, he wrote, cringing every time he smudged a letter. *I
REMEMBER EVERYTHING. COME GET M—*

Orion cursed aloud. He had run out of space for the E. Hastily, he
refogged the mirror and added the E at the top left. Then, like an after-
thought:

IT'S ORION, BY THE WAY.

Harry said something and repeated it a few times, but Orion couldn't
catch it. Asterin raised her hand and his note faded back into the fog,
allowing the anygné to scribble his own message across the much larger
surface of the vanity mirror:

NO SHIT.

Orion burst out laughing.

And then:

WAIT FOR US BY THE PAVILION NEAR THE ARBORETUMS.

Harry hesitated a heartbeat before adding five more words that froze
the grin on Orion's face.

DO NOT TELL EOIN ANYTHING.

CHAPTER FORTY

"You stole a book," said Taeron in disbelief. "A *book*. From the Royal Library of Eradore."

"Hmm?" Quinlan lounged on the floor in his brother's tearoom, surrounded by a looming city of books. Like all of the towers crowding all of the other rooms, too, most were stacked so tall that they required charms to keep from toppling over. Taeron usually didn't keep company, but he had cleared just enough space to fit two cushions by what should have been a low table but instead had been replaced by a bookshelf turned onto its side to accommodate . . . even more books. "Oh, yeah."

Taeron pinched the bridge of his nose. "How did you evade the Keepers?"

Quinlan shrugged, his mind still half occupied by his fight with Asterin. "I mean, it wasn't stealing, exactly. It didn't belong to the library in the first place."

"Mm-hmm." Taeron held the book up to examine its exterior before letting it fall open to a random page in his hands. Hunger lit his eyes as he devoured the words, but whatever he read next caused him to falter.

"What is it?" Quinlan asked, craning his neck.

"Nothing," Taeron said quickly. He flipped through a few more pages and paused again, carefully unfolding a sheaf of parchment stitched partially into the binding—a map. The nine kingdoms sprawled across the parchment in gorgeous detail, each kingdom marked by a mini rendition of its palace and its name in flowing script . . . but something felt wrong.

Taeron frowned. "Hm. That's odd."

Quinlan squinted and finally realized what was off. The map only featured a few select cities—most of the major ones, and a handful of towns that he'd just heard of in passing, like Zemja and Belmora.

His brother pointed at a cluster of buildings near Axaris. "Aldville. Weren't you attacked there by a wyvern a few months ago?"

"Yeah." Quinlan reached out to angle the book for a better view.

"Wait!" his brother cried. "I saw something. When it hit the light."

It took a few tries, but they eventually found the right angle. Three lines of gold raced across the parchment and joined together to form the same triangle on the outside of the book, connecting three places: a mountain taller than all the rest called Hollenfér; a volcanic island in the Asvindr Ocean known as Qris; and Volteris, the capital of the largest kingdom in the world.

A buzzing filled Quinlan's ears.

"Say," Taeron mumbled. "Doesn't Rose have a map tacked up in her chambers with this same triangle?"

Quinlan's arm shot out when Taeron moved to turn the page, his fingers closing over his brother's hand and tugging it away. "Don't," he blurted.

Taeron arched one eyebrow in questioning. "What?"

"We should wait for Rose," Quinlan said. The Queen of Eradore had taken the twins out to the markets to purchase ingredients for antidotes that would hopefully help slow—if not halt—the rapid deterioration of his health. "Let her see it firsthand. She's been trying to crack this mystery for ages."

"What if it relates to a cure?" Taeron demanded. "We're running out of time as it is. Every minute that ticks by is a minute—"

"Closer to my death," Quinlan cut in. "Yes, yes, I know. But if it's *not* a cure and Rose finds out that we further investigated that triangle without her . . ."

Taeron pursed his lips. "Quinlan."

"Please?" he begged, not knowing quite why. Perhaps it had to do with the strange look that had darkened Taeron's face just a minute before.

"Fine." Casting the book an apologetic look, Taeron set it aside and folded his hands in his lap. "So . . . what now?"

In the silence, the hateful ache that had been plaguing Quinlan grew ever incessant. It was impossible not to think about Asterin. Her devastation, her blind faith in him. *Don't do this to me. Don't push me away.* Worst of all, her *hope.*

Quinlan's shoulders slouched. "I can't be who she wants me to be."

Taeron glanced up. "She?"

"Asterin, of course."

"What in hell are you on about?" said Taeron. "She's besotted with you."

Quinlan's face scrunched. "I know. Today she told me that she loved me. It was terrible."

Taeron stared at him like he had sprouted a horn in the center of his forehead. "I don't think I'm quite understanding you here, little brother. The girl you love . . . loves you back. This is terrible *how?*"

Quinlan tilted his head back and blew out a long, weary sigh into the air. "Because I promised her that I would never leave her. And to stay by her side. *Always.*"

"What a drag," Taeron deadpanned.

Quinlan's neck swiveled. "What? No, that's not what I meant." At his brother's expression, Quinlan threw his hands in the air. "Taeron, I'm *dying.* I can't always be there for her because I might be *dead by tomorrow.*"

His brother inhaled sharply. "I suppose you're right." He forced a smile. "I'm sure she took *that* news well."

That drew a laugh from Quinlan, bitter and bleak. "I can only imagine."

Taeron's eyes practically jumped out of his skull. "*What?* You haven't told her?"

"Obviously not!" Quinlan exclaimed. "Can you imagine how upset she would be? After everything I put her through . . ." He drew his knees to his chin, his throat burning. "Because of me, she lost her best friend. Because of me—"

"*Quinlan Holloway,*" Taeron thundered, his eyes blazing with such rage that Quinlan's mouth clamped shut. "What absolute *drivel.* After all the ordeals you two went through together, how could you possibly delude yourself into thinking that by hiding the truth, you're bestowing upon her some sort of *mercy*?" His brother surged onto his knees and grabbed Quinlan by the shoulders, his expression pained. "How could someone as clever as you be such an Immortal-forsaken idiot?"

Quinlan's voice died in his throat.

Taeron gave him a hard shake. "Asterin Faelenhart is the queen of an entire damn kingdom. She is strong, mature, and independent, and she has no need for your self-determined and extremely ill-advised benevolence. I thought she already knew because she was searching for books on the topic of shadow magic injuries, but now I can see that she is simply more astute than I gave her credit for. On top of that, she is more fierce than anyone we know—except for maybe Rose, but we're biased. What did you really think that being honest about your little ailment would do? Break her?"

Quinlan shoved Taeron's hands off his shoulders with a scowl. "Little ailment?" He knew Taeron was right, of course, but part of him couldn't forget Asterin's last words to him—*if you change your mind, I'll be in the library. With your brother, Taeron.*

"Oh, hell *no*," Taeron snapped, oblivious to his thoughts but obstinate nonetheless. His brother jabbed a finger into Quinlan's chest. "Don't you dare deflect my point. What are you afraid of? That she'll brush off your dying and move on without a second thought?"

That took him slightly aback. "N-no. Do you think she would?"

Taeron rolled his eyes like no person had ever rolled their eyes before. "Yes, the girl who chose to sacrifice her best friend's life for yours would also leave you to die without a backward glance—*of course she wouldn't.*" His brother sat back in exasperation. "The evolution of mortalkind truly accomplished an astonishing feat in producing a skull as thick as yours."

Quinlan shot him a scathing smile. "How sweet."

Taeron huffed. "You know I only mean it in the most loving, brotherly manner." His gaze drifted elsewhere, narrowing in thought. "What is it you like to say about mercy?"

Quinlan stared blankly at the empty space between them and

murmured, "That it is never a mercy to be at another's mercy. It only means you will suffer longer."

"Quite dreary if you ask me," said Taeron with a sigh, "but you always did have a penchant for melodrama." He reached out and gave Quinlan's hair a fond ruffle like he had when they were children. Quinlan batted him away. His brother's smile turned somber. "I think it would be best for you to go and sort things out with Asterin. As much as I hate to say this . . . you don't know how much time you have left. None of us do. We're going to do our very best to find you a cure, but . . ."

Quinlan finished the sentence so he wouldn't have to. "The blight could kill me at any time."

Taeron bit his lip. "Potentially. There isn't any way to know for certain when, and I doubt you'd want to leave your relationship with Asterin like this if something were to happen. So go to her, Quinlan. For the love of the Immortals, go to her."

Quinlan nodded, thoroughly chastised, and hauled himself to his feet. As he trudged out of his brother's chambers, he threw a last look over his shoulder. "Thank you," he said, albeit a little reluctantly. "For talking some sense into me."

Taeron waved him away, already reaching for one of his towers of books. "Isn't that what older brothers are supposed to be around for?"

Quinlan snorted at that, but he had no desire to stoke dead embers to life, not today. As he departed his brother's chambers, some impulse spurred him into a jog that quickened to a sprint the nearer he drew to Asterin's chambers. By the time he arrived, he had to rest for a moment to catch his breath. He could hear her conversing through the door, but too indistinctly to make out any words. Two other voices joined the discussion every now and then, though it was more of an argument—Eadric and Harry.

When Quinlan's breathing evened out, he rapped the door thrice. The arguing cut off. A moment later, the door cracked open and Asterin popped her head outside.

Her gaze landed on him. "Can't talk now," she said, and then immediately slammed the door in his face. A second later, she reopened it to add a hasty, "Sorry," before shutting it again.

Quinlan didn't know if he had the right to be offended in the light of his own pigheadedness, but he felt rather miffed nonetheless. He knocked thrice more. When there was no response, he continued knocking and didn't stop. He even changed up the rhythm to keep things creative.

Finally, Asterin whipped the door open. Quinlan took an involuntary step back at the lividity in her expression. "Would you *stop* that?"

Quinlan snuck his foot into the doorway. "We need to talk."

"Now is really not a good time," she replied. At his pitiful expression, she sighed through her nose. "Fine. I can give you two minutes."

He balked. "*Two minutes?*" How could he explain to her that he might be dead by tomorrow in two minutes? Other than literally saying *I might be dead by tomorrow*, of course. Which he was *not* going to do. He resorted to pleading. "It's . . . really important."

"Trust me," said Asterin. "Whatever it is, it can't possibly be more important than this."

It felt like a slap in the face, even if he deserved it. "But—"

"Asterin!" called Harry from farther inside her chambers. "We don't have much time left!"

"I'm coming!" she called back before turning to Quinlan. He could feel her attention slipping away like rain glissading down a window pane. "We can talk about it after I return, all right?" Without waiting for a response, she closed the door, but his foot kept it jammed open.

"After you return?" he echoed in bewilderment, his own voice muffled beneath the rush of blood in his ears. "Where are you going?"

"Asterin!" Harry yelled again. "Now!"

Asterin clenched her jaw and didn't bother answering his question. "Listen, Quinlan. I gave you multiple opportunities to talk and you dismissed me every single time. Now I have somewhere to be, so I would very much appreciate it if you would remove your damn foot from my door."

When he didn't budge, she threw her hands into the air in frustration. For a moment, he was foolish enough to think that she had given up, but then a gust of wind blasted him five feet clear of the doorway. He stumbled backward and fell right on his ass.

"Asterin, *wait*—" he shouted desperately, flinging one hand up toward her as she closed the door. A pillar of fire rushed toward the rapidly narrowing gap, but he was too slow, too late, and the flames snuffed out with a feeble *poof* against the surface in ashen tendrils of smoke.

His outstretched fingers curled around emptiness, crushing his hope to dust in his fist.

He cursed himself.

Much to his confusion, the world veered sideways. He collapsed onto the floor against his will, frigid stone pressing into his cheek.

It wasn't until the pain struck that he realized what he'd done.

CHAPTER FORTY-ONE

Portal travel was nothing like shadow travel.

They fell upward, or rose downward. With Harry's arm as her only anchor, Asterin couldn't really tell. Perhaps it was both, all at once. What would happen if she let go of him? She wasn't about to find out, of course, but it reminded her of peering over the edge of a balcony and contemplating what falling felt like.

Around them expanded an unhindered twilight oblivion, like a dizzying sky that hurt to look at, that required a glance at the ground to center oneself. Except here, there was no ground, no center, nothing to reassure them that this dark void wouldn't just swallow them right up—an anygné and two insignificant little mortal specks, spiraling into the unknown.

At least she could breathe, thank the Immortals.

"We won't have much time," Harry had told them before opening the portal back in the Mortal Realm. "Eoin will know the moment we arrive in the Shadow Kingdom. He might not know *why* we've come, however, which might buy us a few minutes, but our goal is to get to Orion as fast as possible, grab him, and get out. Clear?"

The world flashed blinding white and Asterin threw her arms in front of her face to shield her eyes. By the time she let her arms fall, they stood on a pavilion beneath a white diamond-lattice gazebo, surrounded by strange glass houses and exotic trees bearing phosphorescent fruit. Lucid flowers drooped from the eaves, crowned by translucent petals and thousands of jeweled stamen glittering with pollinia.

Asterin shuddered at the current racing along her bare skin.

Eadric sent her an alarmed glance. "Asterin? Are you all right?"

Her entire body tingled. Quivering, she released Harry's arm . . . and sneezed.

Magic exploded from her body, jagged whitecaps of ice surging across the pavilion and punching through the latticework with the sharp *crunch* of fracturing wood. The temperature plunged. Rain and hail and sleet pelted the gazebo from all directions. Swathes of wind and dazzling color swirled and swelled around them, shocks and starbursts of light crackling across the beamed ceiling like dynamite. Something tickled her legs. When Asterin looked down, tongues of blue fire licked up her body.

"What's happening?" Eadric roared.

"It's me," Asterin gasped. "It's my magic."

But she couldn't control any of it.

A river of darkness spilled into the air and corkscrewed around her before tightening. It wrapped her body into its folds, smothered her magic to nothing. The current within her quelled and everything fell silent.

When the darkness dispersed, liberating her, she collapsed to her hands and knees, her chest heaving with every ragged inhale.

Harry crouched at her side and gently coaxed her back onto her feet, shadows glissading from his fingers like liquid smoke. "You're okay, you're okay," he murmured. "Magic acts a little differently in this realm, but you're strong. Keep it on its leash and focus, Asterin. We're running out of time."

Still panting, she nodded. Harry approached the barricade of ice sealing them inside the gazebo and stretched out one arm. His shadows poured forth from his sleeve and smashed into the ice, demolishing a large enough hole for them to duck through and escape.

Asterin emerged and began scanning the garden. "So how do we find—*oh.*"

There was someone already waiting for them on the other side.

Her heart thundered in her ears.

"Oh," she whispered again, her feet carrying her forward one tentative step at a time. And then she was running, running faster than her still-wobbly legs could properly manage. She tripped and flew forward—

Right into Orion's arms.

"*Oh*," she sobbed. "Immortals." She buried her face into his shoulder, laughing and crying and holding onto her Guardian, never wanting to let go.

He hugged her back, fiercely, ferociously. "Hey, Princess." He rested his cheek atop her head and smiled into her hair.

She choked on a hysterical laugh. "Queen," she corrected between sobs. She pounded his back with both fists and then clung onto him again. "You *idiot*." Her attempt to stop crying only made her cry harder. "You absolute *idiot*."

Orion kissed her temple. "I'm so sorry."

She wiped her tears on his shoulder. "Why didn't you contact us sooner?"

He reached behind him to pull something out of his pocket and pressed it into her hand. "I couldn't. At least, not until I had this."

She took a peek over his shoulder with puffy eyes. "A mirror?"

He brushed a strand of hair from her damp cheeks and tucked it behind her ear. "An *enchanted* mirror."

Behind her, Eadric cleared his throat.

Reluctantly, Asterin unwound herself from Orion, her fingers aching from gripping him so tightly.

Orion grinned at Eadric. "Cap," he greeted. "How have you been? Fallen off any roofs recently?"

Eadric rolled his eyes and pulled him into a bear hug. "Just shut up, Galashiels."

Only after the two separated and Eadric had stepped away did Harry make his approach. Orion drifted forward, too, drawn by some invisible pull. They met halfway, stopping at the same moment, their toes just a few inches shy of touching.

Asterin watched the interaction in utter delight. Eadric crossed his arms over his chest with a little smirk on his lips.

"Well, hello there," Orion murmured.

Harry furrowed his brow. Quietly, he asked, "Is this a trick?"

Orion blew out a long breath and laughed. "I missed you, too." He reached up and brushed his thumb along Harry's jaw. His face softened, his voice achingly sincere. "Immortals, I missed you."

Harry had gone as still as a winter morning, simply staring into Orion's eyes.

Waiting, Asterin realized. Full of hope, and waiting.

Something unsaid passed between them and Orion bit his lip, misery creasing his features. He stepped back. Eadric's smirk vanished and Harry just looked . . . resigned.

"What? Why?" Asterin exclaimed in spite of herself. "What's wrong?"

Harry swallowed and averted his gaze. "He's with Eoin now."

"*For* now," Orion corrected. Then he shot the anygné an apologetic look. "But for now nonetheless."

The spell broke. Harry's demeanor shifted. He took a deep breath and began conjuring a portal, the muscles in his shoulders and neck gone rigid.

Asterin did her best not to gape at either of them in disbelief.

Orion was with Eoin. King Eoin. The *god*.

"How did *that* happen?" she demanded.

"There's no time for further discussion," Harry said sharply. "We've dawdled long enough. It's a miracle Eoin hasn't arrived yet." The portal yawned fully open, but instead of darkness, it led into a luminous expanse, like the shallows of a lake lit by the balmy rays of the afternoon sun. "After you, Asterin."

"Hell no. Orion goes through first."

Eadric let out a long-suffering sigh so forceful that his nostrils flared. He grabbed her by the elbow and began dragging her toward the portal. "Doesn't matter who goes first. We're not leaving anyone behind this—"

A mellifluous voice cut him off. "How impolite of you, Harry, to invite guests over without bothering to introduce them to me."

Before Asterin could understand what was happening, Eadric had yanked her into the portal entryway, the panic on his face making her heart jolt. She strained to catch a final glance of Harry and Orion—and another man, with his back turned to the portal, whose presence lured her inward like a collapsing star.

Only one other being she had ever met had shared that familiar gravity, that ancient power: Lord Conrye.

So not just another man, then . . . but a god.

By the time she came to the realization, her body had already submerged fully into the portal. Eadric kept her locked in his grip as they drifted away from the shrinking entryway, sinking deeper into the ether between realms.

Except . . .

Except they weren't *going anywhere.*

Asterin summoned her magic, perhaps to drive them in some direction. Nothing happened.

Eadric brandished his affinity stone and attempted the same, but the ether absorbed all of their attempts.

Asterin started kicking her legs to propel them toward—toward . . . where? Nowhere?

Maybe it was just as well that paddling proved no more effective than magic.

Eadric glanced at her, his face mirroring her horror.

They were stuck.

CHAPTER FORTY-TWO

Harry's stomach plunged as he turned to find the God of Shadow standing behind his shoulder, his eyes radiating cold ire and the crown on his brow absent of butterflies and sprouting wicked scarlet-tipped thorns in their stead.

"How impolite of you, Harry," the god drawled, "to invite guests over without bothering to introduce them to me."

"Eo!" Orion exclaimed, piping cheer into his voice. "You're back. You just missed—"

Eoin strode forward to cup Orion's jaw, keeping his frigid gaze locked on Harry all the while. Without breaking eye contact, he bent down to capture Orion's mouth in a bruising kiss, muffling the rest of his sentence.

With Orion distracted, the god waved one hand at the portal. Harry flinched as the entryway swirled shut . . . and trapped Asterin and Eadric within.

Eoin broke away to glance at the portal in faux surprise. "Oh, dear," he purred. "It appears that Harry's portal has gobbled up our guests." The god shot Harry a coy smile. "Well? What are you waiting for? Open it back up, little shadowling."

Harry swallowed the acrid taste rising from his throat. *As if you don't know.* "I can't."

Orion paled. "You can't?" He wrapped his hand around Eoin's tie and tugged. "They're my friends. They just came by to visit me. Can't you do something to help them?"

The god caressed his cheek. "Anything for you, my love."

Harry jerked his face away from the sight, utterly humiliated, biting down on his tongue hard to keep the expletives from spilling out.

Orion's shoulders sagged in relief. "Thank you, Eo."

"Don't thank me yet," Eoin replied grimly. "I can't control where your friends will end up since I'm not in the portal with them, but I promise to return them safe and sound to the Mortal Realm, at least." His eyelids fluttered shut as he began weaving his hands through the air in an elaborate dance.

It took every drop of effort in Harry's body to stifle a snarl. *Pigshit*, he thought to himself. Eoin could have reopened the portal with a mere thought. This was all for show. Yet Harry didn't dare rat him out to Orion for fear that the god would change his mind.

Eoin's eyes snapped open. "Two friends successfully delivered back to the Mortal Realm!" he declared, dusting his hands off. He shot Orion a wink. "You may now shower me with praise."

Harry nearly gagged, but Orion just laughed as if Eoin had said something very charming. "You were marvelous, as you always are. And your new look suits you very well."

New look? Harry swiveled back to examine Eoin in curiosity. From what he could tell, the god hadn't changed anything about his appearance in months.

Eoin's smirk evaporated.

Orion realized that he must have somehow slipped up. "Not that your old look didn't suit you. I just prefer the brown eyes."

It was absolutely and most definitely the wrong thing to say.

Around them, the shadows began to warp. They peeled off the ground like corpses rising under a curse. And then they advanced . . . toward Harry.

He scrambled backward, but the shadows enclosed him from all sides, suppressing him in a cage of darkness. They pried open his lips and slithered down his throat, his nose, blinding him, suffocating him—

"Eo!" he heard Orion holler. "Stop!"

The shadows parted around a single hand, stark white against the blackout. It latched onto his collar and yanked him halfway into the open.

The King of Immortals placed his lips next to Harry's ear. "*Iræs.*"

Harry gasped as something deep in his core splintered. Ruptured, like an organ cleaving in two, spewing gore and flooding his veins with freezing shock.

Eoin's fist flew at him, knocking into his jaw with enough force to snap his head backward. *Crack.* Orion's shouts blew out into a high-pitched ringing.

"I had no one," the god snarled. "For an eternity, I had *no one*, until I finally did." Eoin leaned close, hatred twisting his features into a grotesque caricature.

Harry knew pain. It was a crux that he had long ago learned to bear, an acquaintance that he tolerated in order to serve his king—his *owner.* He knew pain intimately, in ways that mortals could never dream of, could never *endure* because Eoin had enslaved his anygné body to eternally healing itself.

"*One* person to see me as I truly am," Eoin hissed, "and you *dare steal him away from me.*"

Crack. Spots burst across Harry's vision as the god struck him again. When his head lolled against his chest, Eoin simply yanked him higher so he had no choice but to stare down into that cruel, callous gaze through swollen eyes. By now, he should have blacked out—but the god kept him shackled to the cusp of consciousness. *Crack. Crack.*

Heal faster, Harry begged his body faintly as Eoin beat and battered him to a raw pulp with nothing but his fist.

Crack. The pain annihilated him. Blood streamed from his chin. Through his distorted view, he watched it spatter onto Eoin's pristine dress shoes—

And instead of silver, it was decidedly, mortally, *red.*

CHAPTER FORTY-THREE

"A million thanks for the meal, Mrs. Castille," Nicole murmured after she had drained the last dregs of her tea. With a deep sigh, she set down the cup with a delicate *clink* upon its painted saucer. "And the bleach, of course." She ran her fingers through her hair, the black lightened to an uneven blond. The strands crackled suspiciously, but there wasn't much else to do about it until she returned to Axaris. With Lux as her steed and the hirelings potentially still tailing her, the less she looked like the Queen of Axaria, the better.

Casper's mother wrung her hands anxiously, her red-rimmed eyes still puffy from bereaving. "Are you certain you'd rather not stay the night? Axaris is such a long journey to make on your own. It'll take you at least three full days of riding from Oprehvis."

Little Genevieve piped up. She had the same pale silk-gray eyes as her older brother. "Mama, Nicole is an Elite! She's not afraid of the dark." Those eyes turned on her, wide and innocuous. "Or monsters. Right?"

"Only sometimes," said Nicole.

"Not only that. There have been . . . whisperings." Mrs. Castille shifted uneasily, casting a glance at her daughter, and lowered her voice. "Of a malevolent spirit possessing the bodies of Oprehvans. Of officers killing one another for the medallions on their uniforms, of children murdering their parents for the last slice of cake."

Nicole frowned. Such unwarranted violence . . . it reminded her of the Chaos in Axaria. Perhaps . . . perhaps not only the Chaos had escaped the crypt? "I'll be careful, Mrs. Castille," she promised, pushing herself out of her seat.

"Wait," cried Genevieve. Nicole waited, but the girl suddenly shied beneath her gaze. "Um . . . my brother . . ." She bit her lip, her words failing her.

Nicole squatted, eye level with the girl. "Casper talked about you a lot, you know. He said you'd taken up wrestling."

Genevieve nodded. "I'm going to be strong like him when I grow up."

Nicole smiled. "Somehow, I have a feeling you'll be stronger."

Mrs. Castille came over to thread her fingers in her daughter's hair, full of motherly pride. "She wants to become an Elite like him, too."

Nicole's smile froze. Her voice died in her throat. Fortunately, Genevieve hugged her goodbye before the silence stretched on too long.

Mrs. Castille saw her to the door. "Safe travels."

"I'll be back soon," Nicole told her. "With Casper's death benefit." Although Mrs. Castille worked a steady job as a tutor, the money would still go a long way. It always did.

As Nicole stepped into the night, Mrs. Castille bowed her head, tears glistening in her eyes. "Nicole . . ."

She glanced over her shoulder. "Yes?"

"My son . . . tell me that his death wasn't wasted."

Nicole's throat ached. She thought of the queen, whisked away to a foreign kingdom halfway across the globe to visit her beloved. She thought of Gino and Casper and everything else they had almost lost. Eventually, she found it in herself to reply, "The death of an Elite is never wasted."

It rang hollow in her own ears, but Mrs. Castille only nodded in gratitude.

Outside the Castilles' cozy villa stood Lux, tethered to a picket and waiting patiently, his coat gleaming oil-black in the light of the stubby torches dotting the front garden. The stallion greeted Nicole with a whicker as she unhitched him and led him toward the road that would lead them back to Axaris. Soon they were racing the stars.

For days she had lain low on the outskirts of Orielle. After everything had gone to hell, she had been forced to flee the city and wait until reinforcements arrived. Unsurprisingly, it was *not* easy smuggling three horses and a body around.

Once Hayley and Laurel found her, they departed with two of the horses to deliver Gino's body to his family. Meanwhile, Nicole had to travel to Oprehvar to pay her respects to Mrs. Castille with nothing but kind words.

Through it all, she had refused to let her grief cloud her focus, or for exhaustion to hinder her purpose. She was an Elite, and she had been trained to soldier on. To sustain herself on strength and grit and determination alone. To serve the crown. To honor. To protect.

She had known Gino for three years, and Casper for five. Their absence gaped like a pit in her stomach. All of the Elites spent almost every day sharing a piece of their lives with one another, and any loss affected each and every one of them.

There was never a place for mourning on duty, but her work here was done. The road stretched ahead, and home was still a kingdom away.

So when the night bled past and even the moon mantled its witness in a veil of clouds, Nicole put her head down into Lux's mane and released the near-silent sob trapped in her chest. And then—and only then, with her hood pulled low and the shadows hiding her face, did she finally allow her heart to break.

At dawn the next day, she paid for cheap lodging in Aldville, already two-thirds of the way back to Axaris. No way could she have ridden as intensely on any other steed, but Lux trampled all of her expectations in the dust. Without anyone to hold him back, the Iphovien stallion hit speeds that blurred the ground into stillness. The legends about *the fastest horse in the world* made sense now. Supposedly, Lady Reyva, bringer and goddess of wind, rode in a chariot pulled by a team of winged Iphoviens. The strength from their wingbeats alone were said to be able to cause anything from devastating hurricanes to fluttering breezes that carried seedlings across lands far and wide.

By late afternoon they were back on the road, the bright fields of Axarian poppies waving them past and the Ljre River their shimmering aquamarine companion. Lux had no choice but to slow for the increased foot traffic clogging the roads near the capital, snorting and doing his best to weave around the more sluggish congregations. Eventually, Nicole resigned herself to the knowledge that they likely wouldn't arrive back to the capital until after dawn.

The shriek of a hawk pierced the air. Nicole glanced up to see its silhouette skimming the sun, its magnificent wings tapering to individual feathers that resembled slender fingers from below. It circled above her, the sleek plane of its body tilting to adjust to her course. She halted Lux on the side of the road and squinted at it, startling when it tucked in its wings and dove . . . at *her*. With every flap, it accelerated, and she scrambled to find something to protect herself with, but came up with nothing. Gritting her teeth, she turned sideways with her left arm outstretched without a glove to shield her flesh. It footed her, hooked talons tearing into her skin—but she was already distracted by the roll of parchment tied to its leg.

Her eyes widened. *This is Jack's hawk*, she realized. Fingers fumbling, she hurried to loosen the knot with her right hand. The hawk let out a shriek right beside her ear and she raised it away from her face reflexively, wincing—and immediately regretted the action when the hawk interpreted it as a cue to take off into the blue.

Nicole cursed silently. Lux snorted and shook his mane haughtily, as if to say *birdbrain*. She just didn't know if he was referring to the hawk or herself.

With a sigh, she transferred the note to her left hand and rummaged in her pocket with the other, pulling out her affinity stone to heal her cuts.

Her eyes narrowed in concentration. "*Haelein.*" Healing had never been her strong suit, so it would take at least a few minutes for her magic to mend the thankfully shallow gouges. In the meanwhile, she eased Lux into a walk and pulled the note open. Her heartbeat stuttered as she scanned its barely legible contents—scribbled, as if in extreme haste.

N—I hope this letter finds you swift and well, and I pray that you have not yet reached Axaris. Turn around. <u>Now</u>.

Ride to Cyeji, or Ibreseos, or Oprehvar. Go anywhere but home.

Elyssa Faelenhart has taken control of the Elites. After H and L returned with the news of C's and G's deaths, she placed us under lockdown in the palace.

We believe that she is planning to arrest us.

She claims that there is a mole within our ranks— someone who leaked QA's travel arrangements to the hirelings and endangered her life. She said a letter was found, signed with a symbol that looked like a crooked N.

She has sent out palace guards to patrol every road leading into the city and hunt you down. Step foot within Axaris, and you will be seized.

She knows that you were the only Elite to survive.

You are her primary suspect.

Silas has gone missing. If she gets her hands on you, she might make you disappear, too.

You must find a way to send word to QA before Elyssa decides to do more than simply detain us.

May the Immortals guide your path.

—J

Nicole reread the note twice through in disbelief, her mind whirling. She clenched her fists around the reins and stared at the horizon just as the outskirts of the capital rose into view.

Almost. *Almost* within reach. She was grief-stricken and worn down to the bone. All she wanted was her bed and the familiar walls of the barracks sheltering her head.

Go anywhere but home.

She could risk it. She could probably evade the guards long enough to reach the palace, break in, and free the others. But if she failed . . .

You are her primary suspect.

Nicole cussed loudly. Loud enough for the man pulling a hand-drawn cart in front of her to shoot her a glare over his shoulder—although his attention quickly snapped elsewhere upon glimpsing the wrath in her expression.

Her decision made, she wheeled Lux around and cut onto the opposite side of the road.

As she turned her back on Axaris, she closed her eyes.

How had everything gone so terribly wrong?

CHAPTER FORTY-FOUR

The first time she had visited the tomb, Elyssa had expected the air to taste of death.

Or at the very least, the sickly sweetness of decay, perhaps with a dash of rot.

Instead, the Faelenhart Tomb was all clean, bright marble made glossy from the harsh white light of enchanted torches. Every inhalation of the frigid air seared her throat and pricked tears into her eyes.

Those, too, quickly froze, before they even slipped off her cheeks.

She usually made the trip to the tomb every other day, but the last week had been rather . . . hectic. Yesterday had very nearly ended in disaster. Luckily, she'd managed to wrangle everything under control, and last night she'd slept without nightmares for the first time in years. She took it as a good omen, of sorts. So at the first light of dawn, Elyssa decided it was finally time to pay a visit to her husband.

With Carlsby and a half-dozen more escorts, she rode to the south residential district. By then, morning had conquered the horizon, revealing a sky blemished with slate-gray clouds. They swung onto a small, winding dirt path that led to a guarded gate. After Elyssa provided a password, they were asked to dismount before being waved onward through the sacred grove of birches ensconcing the tomb.

A veil of mist clung low to the grass, weaving around the great columns marking the tomb's entrance. No songbirds sang, no crickets chirped. All was silent but for their footsteps and the low moan of wind in the trees. The eerie peace was fitting, to say the least.

After all, this was the final place of rest.

Two wolves rested upon the thick slab of granite that marked the entrance to the tomb. One wolf howled while the other slept. Or perhaps it was dead, and the howling wolf was mourning.

Elyssa approached the wolves. Carlsby and the other guards drifted around the fringes of the tomb, but they would not—and could not—accompany her. The wolves' eyes opened. She spoke her name. A gust of arctic wind blasted her face as the granite slab ground backward. Already shivering, she drew her furs tighter around her shoulders and began her descent into the earth.

Within each tomb chamber rested a different Faelenhart. Their icy coffins glittered celestial blue, carved with snarling wolves and the faces of their most loyal and beloved.

When Elyssa had first seen the carving upon her husband's coffin, she had nearly smashed it to smithereens. Priscilla Montcroix's smug face taunted her even now, right above little Asterin's face. Her only consolation was Priscilla's own death. An excruciatingly painful death, Asterin had assured her.

Elyssa lowered herself onto her knees before Tristan's coffin, angling herself so that Priscilla's foul face flattened out of view.

There were two more people carved into the coffin. One was Theodore Galashiels, Tristan's Royal Guardian, and the other was Carlotta Garringsford, the General of Axaria.

"Apologies for my prolonged absence," Elyssa told her husband, her eyes lingering on Carlotta's face. "At least this time it was only a few days, rather than a few years."

Silence answered her. The jest had fallen short, anyway.

"You know, I never got to thank Carla," Elyssa murmured. She let her gloved fingers flutter onto the coffin, atop the general. "For sparing me. She executed everyone else under Priscilla's order without batting an eye. But when she got to me . . ."

Carlotta's flint-gray eyes met hers in the darkness. Her hands trembled around her scarlet-stained sword.

"Promise me one thing," Elyssa whispered. "Watch over Asterin for me."

"I'm not her mother," Carlotta rasped. "Why should I?"

"Because I won't get the chance to be."

Carlotta did not reply.

"When she comes of age, she will come into her full power," said Elyssa. "Just before she does, you must send her away from the palace. Keep her within the kingdom, but out of Priscilla's reach. That's all I ask."

And then Elyssa knelt on the unforgiving stone, refusing to beg even as tears streamed down her face. She thought of Asterin as she bent her neck in invitation and waited for death.

But it never came.

After a long moment, the general sank to the ground before her, breathing harshly, her blade slipping from her bloody grip with a clang. She shook her head, her voice full of pain, of remorse. "Priscilla will never know better."

Elyssa stared at Carlotta's face on the coffin for a long moment before looking away. "Then," she told the empty tomb, "without another word, she left."

It was the last time she had ever seen Carlotta. Or anybody else, for that matter. Until Asterin and Eadric had come to free her.

"I could never figure out if she meant it as a last act of mercy toward me," Elyssa spoke. "Perhaps it was her way of apologizing for that night. Or the complete opposite. I suppose I won't ever have the opportunity to ask anymore."

That night—the night they'd fought. After her sons were killed.

The memory that had engulfed Elyssa in the infirmary before she detained Silas came rushing forth once more. This time, there was no one but the dead to interrupt her.

The young recruit shivered in the middle of the infirmary, surrounded by troops. Beside him stood the General of Axaria. No amount of crimson fabric could disguise the blood soaking her sleeves.

"Carla," Elyssa exclaimed. For appearances' sake, she restrained herself from throwing her arms around the woman who had been her closest friend since the day she'd set foot in the Axarian palace. "What in the name of the Immortals happened?"

Carla pressed her thin lips together before speaking, those normally sharp flint-gray eyes a little muddy—from exhaustion or pain or both, Elyssa couldn't tell. "The hirelings happened. They ambushed the transportation convoy on its way to Axaris." She produced a tiny velvet satchel from her inner jacket pocket and held it out, the barest tremor passing through her hand. "But we managed to retrieve the goods."

Elyssa accepted the satchel without a word. She knew that in it rested an unassuming black stone pendant—unassuming, when in fact it was the legendary nebula diamond, said to possess the capability to multiply its wielder's power a hundredfold.

She forced herself to look Carla square in the eye. "At what cost?"

The general's expression cracked then, revealing anguish that Elyssa hadn't known her capable of. But only for the briefest second—no way in hell would Carlotta show weakness here, in front of all of these underlings. "There were over one hundred civilian casualties, and . . . three of the recruits were killed."

The floor beneath her tilted sideways. Elyssa pressed her fingers to her mouth. She felt sick. Over one hundred? And the three recruits . . . She turned to stare at the boy, the lone survivor of the four. Which meant—

Her sons.

"Oh, Carla," Elyssa choked out, tears welling in her eyes.

Carla jerked her face away, the muscles in her jaw twitching. "Alex was drowned," she said hoarsely. "Micah was stabbed to death. So was Joanne. We managed to rescue Silas." Beside her, the boy shivered again, his shoulders hunching inward like a shriveled leaf.

"Damn Tristan," Elyssa seethed. "Damn him."

Carla stilled.

"*You told him not to take the recruits,*" Elyssa hissed, well aware of all of the ears on them, but she couldn't stop the words spewing from her mouth. "*And I told him to take more soldiers.*"

The general blinked once. Then cold ire filled her eyes. "*So why didn't you make him listen? He is your king, and you are his queen. You have just as much authority over him as he does over you.*" Carla leaned close and lowered her voice to just a ghost of a whisper. "*You know very well that this is your fault as much as it is his.*"

Elyssa reeled back, stung by the accusation. "*Get out of my sight,*" she said softly, "*before you say anything else you might regret.*"

Garringsford's mouth twisted in disgust. She signaled to the soldiers behind her to file out. When the room finally emptied, she cast Elyssa a frigid sidelong glance. "*I only upset you because you know it's true. You would have done everything to stop Tristan if it had been Asterin in Micah's or Alex's stead. And if it had been—*"

Crack.

The general staggered back, cradling her mouth.

"*That is enough,*" Elyssa murmured. She rubbed her stinging knuckles. "*You would do well to remember your place. Titles be damned, we are both mothers. Don't think for one second that I wouldn't do unspeakable things to protect my daughter. I would die without hesitation for my Asterin an infinite amount of times over, and I know you would have for your sons, too.*"

Garringsford's jaw had already begun to swell. Her gray eyes met Elyssa's, dull and dark and lifeless. "*I didn't get that chance,*" she rasped. Blood stained her teeth, smearing them gruesomely scarlet as she spoke. She wiped her sleeve across her mouth and spat at Elyssa's feet. "*But I hope you do.*"

With that, the general spun on her heel, cloak flapping, and swept out of the doors.

Elyssa's legs had fallen asleep. She let out a weary sigh and shifted her position on the floor of the Faelenhart tomb. "Sometimes I wonder how many times I've replayed that memory over the last decade," she admitted.

"I couldn't stop thinking about how she lost her sons. All it took was a few moments for them to be gone forever, with no way to ever get them back. I promised myself that I would keep Asterin out of harm's way, and then suddenly I woke up and found myself trapped in the bowels of the palace." With a wince, she used the coffin to help haul herself to her feet and rubbed the circulation back into her legs. "I can't control what choices Asterin makes for herself. It wouldn't be fair to her, would it?"

A ghost of a breeze tickled her face.

Elyssa smiled. "All the same, I still have a duty to ensure her path stays clear of any possible danger. The Elites have proven their liability, time and time again. Their powers and abilities are greater than any other Axarian soldier, but if their alliances were to change . . . every day spent in Asterin's presence is an opportunity to sabotage her rule. And now, with a mole among their ranks . . . until I unearth who *N* or *Z* is, I refuse to trust a single one of them."

The *Z* could have been Hayley, whose last name was Zalis. However, she had surrendered freely along with the rest of the Elites yesterday, so at the very least Elyssa could keep an eye on her. The troublesome one was Nicole—who had not only accompanied Asterin to Orielle and gotten her fellow Elites killed, but additionally had fled when she should have already returned to the palace.

"I should send out a search warrant," Elyssa murmured to the tomb's cold walls. "Except Asterin might catch word. Obviously, she'd find out as soon as she returns home, but hopefully I'll have rooted out the traitor before then—upon which I'll more than happily release all of them."

Asterin wouldn't care about the potential repercussions of prematurely liberating her Elites. She would insist that they were all trustworthy. That the mere idea of betrayal was ridiculous. And if she spoke the word to release the Elites herself, Elyssa could do nothing but yield.

"I may only be Queen Regent," Elyssa told the tomb, knowing that all of the Faelenharts were listening, "but I'm still her mother. Sometimes my Asterin just doesn't know what is best for her. She's still so young. Someone betrayed her, and until I figure out *who*, no one is safe."

Asterin was fiercely loyal to her pack, as much of a descendant of the wolf god as her father had been, and that loyalty blinded her from the treachery of those she loved. And stubbornly blind she would stay, even as a further act to prove her loyalty, until it was much too late.

I didn't get that chance, Carla had said. *But I hope you do.*

If the queen refused to open her eyes, it was up to Elyssa to keep her from straying off the right path. She would guide and guard Asterin—with her own life, if need be.

It was time to go. Elyssa kissed the tips of her fingers and pressed them first to the crown of Tristan's coffin and then against little Asterin's icy forehead. It was her promise, the promise she made every time she visited the tomb—that Asterin would never rest here until Death arrived for her in its most natural form.

She'd ascended halfway up the stairs out of the tomb when the granite slab at the entrance groaned open to reveal a silhouette blocking out the sky. With his face swathed in shadows, it took her a moment to recognize Carlsby.

The young soldier bounced on the balls of his feet, fidgeting with a piece of parchment clutched in his hands. "Your Grace."

Elyssa leaned on the railing to catch her breath. "What is it?"

"A message from the palace," Carlsby replied. "A letter arrived from overseas. Immediate attention required."

"Immediate attention?" Elyssa repeated, raising one eyebrow. "Whatever for?"

Carlsby shrugged helplessly. "I wouldn't know, Your Grace. But it's not so much the nature of the letter itself that matters, I think . . . rather, it's the nature of the sender."

Elyssa's mind immediately jumped to Asterin. "From the queen, you mean? Is my daughter well?"

"The letter is meant for Queen Asterin, Your Grace. And yes, it's technically from the queen, though perhaps not the one Your Grace is thinking of."

"Rose Saville, then?"

"No, Your Grace. It's from Valeria Iyala . . . the Queen of Volterra."

CHAPTER FORTY-FIVE

E adric was a son of the Goddess of Sky. Lady Audra, the protector
of Cyeji and the House of the Falcon.

Yet when the portal spat him out thousands of feet above the
earth, in the middle of the Immortals-damned *sky*, his most potent affinity was utterly *useless*.

His body plunged through a damp blanket of clouds. The wind snapped
and growled at him like a feral hound. For a moment he was lost in a world
of thick gray haze, and then the clouds thinned and he emerged at last
to find the earth sprawling out in every direction. Below, a wide river cut
swiftly across rolling emerald slopes scattered with trees, rushing with white
froth silenced by the roar of the wind. A little farther north, blue-tiled roofs
surrounded a city shrouded in mist and enclosed by a circular wall.

Unless a storm cloud or a bolt of lightning could save a human from
splatting into a thousand scraps of flesh upon impact, he might as well
have chucked his affinity stone into the heavens and wished it to sprout
into a pair of wings.

He had his wind affinity, of course, but it was far weaker. And at this
speed, it would more likely cause turbulence than serve as any form of aid.

Eadric cursed, his heart slamming against his ribcage in panic. He had
never liked heights, and falling off that roof in Axaris had only augmented
his fear a hundredfold. Nothing could have made this worse—except,

where in *hell* was Asterin? The portal had torn them apart. He had no idea where she'd ended up—halfway around the globe, perhaps, but with her omnifinity she could easily harness a combination of the wind and the water and the earth and whatever damned else to catch her fall.

The hem of his shirt escaped from where it had been tucked into his trousers and flapped into his face. He clawed it down desperately, blindly, the fabric and the wind battering his ears, only for all of it to fly back up again as soon as he let go.

A voice that could only belong to Rose chided him in his mind. *Fighting your own shirt. What a way to squander your final moments.*

If Rose were here, he knew she would have come up with something clever. Eadric himself had always been resourceful—it was what had kept him alive up until now, and why Miss M had taken him under her wing. He could imagine his childhood mentor now, with her unsettlingly sharp cobalt eyes and silk gloves, the unyielding steel of her voice as she taught him how to use his magic to feel out the vibration and pitch of secrets spoken behind locked doors.

Think, damnit.

Gritting his teeth, he angled his body and finally managed to yank his shirt out of his face. With his affinity stone gripped in his fist hard enough to bruise, he conjured up a cloud. A tall, dense cloud—a *thunderhead*, stretching upward into the atmosphere and crackling with static at its heart. A cloud like this couldn't naturally form without warm air or water. But he descended from the House of the Falcon, and he would be damned if he let some chilly air get the better of him. The humidity increased with the building of vapor and he felt the shift in air pressure like the brush of a feather in the back of his mind. He rose higher as the wind picked up to a roar and the storm funneled into a column—a *tornado*—around him.

His brain told him he ought to be oxygen-deprived or even dead—but just like how Asterin's ice would never give her frostbite, and Quinlan's fire would never burn him, the tornado became a part of Eadric. It would not bring him harm.

And when he looked down, he had stopped falling.

"Immortals," he whispered to himself. Lightning flashed above him, illuminating the interior of the funnel in shocks of blue. He began to laugh. Maniacally.

Before he could bask in his glory for long, however, the tornado swerved and threw him violently sideways. He cursed and tried to rein it in, to compress it, but some other force out of his control had breathed the storm's embers into a raging blaze.

He shielded his face as debris from the ground below whipped into the air and sliced into his flesh like shrapnel. Sprays of crimson misted into the air, but the vortex quickly sucked them away. The rapid blood loss made him light-headed. He plunged right down the eye of the storm, the clouds near the ground dispersing, his hold on the tornado weakening.

A frightening *crackle* deafened even the loudest shrieks of the wind. Where water droplets whirled, they *froze*, crystallizing in a surge of ice so powerful that the tornado actually halted in its tracks.

He had nothing to cling onto, not a single wisp of magic to save him from dropping like a stone through the hollow shaft of ice.

A strangled cry clawed out of Eadric's throat.

As the frosted ground rushed up to claim him, a chunk of the ice at its base shattered.

Asterin barreled through, her expression fixed in a fierce snarl. She thrust her arms toward the sky. Toward *him*. As if . . . to catch him.

Then a gust of glacial wind knocked into his chest mere feet from impact. It buoyed him into the air before lowering him gently to the ground.

Eadric sank onto his knees upon the freezing earth, gasping for breath, his arms limp at his sides and his neck arched to the sky. Slowly, he lifted his stare to the twisted column of ice grasping for the heavens, hidden but for a perfect circle of cerulean.

Savage tempest, tempered to submission beneath Asterin's hand.

"Ah," Eadric managed.

Then he promptly blacked out.

CHAPTER FORTY-SIX

The impact of Luna's landing spasmed through her legs as she skidded along the stone rampart overlooking the spiked moat of the Ibresean stronghold. She folded her wings and combed back her windswept hair, her face scrunching as her fingers met tangle after tangle. With each step, she shifted back into human form, her iridescent plumage receding layer by layer and crystallizing into her second skin.

She loved flying under the cover of night, loved how the shadows blurred together and sharpened her already augmented senses, letting things usually invisible in the daylight bloom under the ethereal glimmer of the stars.

Kane and Killian leaned against the parapet, their silhouettes cloaked by the gloom. The white-haired hireling regarded Luna appraisingly as she approached. She ignored him. It was easy to recognize the glint that had recently manifested in his eyes. The way his gaze lingered on her when he thought she couldn't see.

As if she had time for *men* when she had kingdoms to conquer.

"Well?" Killian called out, shooting her a cheeky grin. "How does it feel to be an immortal shadow demon . . . Your Majesty?"

Luna inhaled the night air deep into her lungs and sighed in satisfaction. *Your Majesty.* Sweeter than syrup to her ears. She returned her fellow anygné's grin. "You would know."

It really hadn't taken much convincing for King Jakob to abdicate his title. Luna could tell that he had been hoping to stall her until Adrianna returned—perhaps thinking, *wishfully*, that her aunt could have persuaded her to reconsider. But nothing and no one but the might of all nine gods and goddesses could have deterred Luna from the mission that King Eoin had assigned her.

Even then, though, while signing the document that would officially pass his sovereign to Luna, King Jakob had faltered at the last moment. "My dear, must it be this way?" he murmured to her, his tone light, forcibly amiable. "There are other options. Together, we could—"

"I have no desire to conspire against the King of Immortals with you, Father," Luna interrupted. She leaned in close, smiling ruefully at the dismay that pinched his mouth. He looked like he had just bitten into a lime. "I must obey him, you see." Without quite touching his hand, she coaxed his quill back to the parchment. "For I have absolutely everything to lose, and absolutely everything to gain."

And just like that, without any fanfare at all, Luna ascended the dais in Throne Hall and crowned herself the Queen of Ibreseos.

"So," said Kane, drawing her attention back to the present. He kept his posture relaxed as he nothing short of *swaggered* over to her. "I was thinking that you might like to train with me later. In my rooms. Your Highness."

Luna struggled to keep a straight face at his boldness as she walked right past him and settled against the parapet at Killian's side. "Kindly, I'll pass."

Kane flushed at the casualness of her rejection, the arrogance he had oozed mere seconds before evaporating into the night air.

Killian stifled a snicker and pointed at his face. "You know, Kane, I've never quite noticed it before, but you bear a startling resemblance to a tomato."

Luna recoiled at the lethal flash of silver that sliced through the air toward Killian. On pure reflex, the anygné's hand shot up in front of her face, two clasped fingers halting one of Kane's knives an inch away from her left eye. A thin trickle of silver blood traced down her forearm. One flick of her wrist and the blade snapped into the air. She caught it smoothly by the hilt. The next time she spoke, the light didn't reach her eyes. "How uncalled for."

"As if you haven't already healed," Kane drawled back.

Killian cocked her arm. "Jealous?"

When she flung the knife back at him, Kane dodged it easily enough. Unfortunately, he definitely didn't expect it to loop over his head like a hornet and nip him in the ass.

Melodious laughter rang through the night as Kane spat curses at the anygné and her magic.

Luna shook her head. "Go to bed, Kane."

The hireling snatched the enchanted knife out of the air and stormed off.

Only after his footfalls faded did Luna speak again. "Sometimes I can't believe Rose *loved* him. Of all people . . ."

Killian raised her arms above her head and stretched. Luna's eyes darted to the slip of taut midriff revealed by the arch of her spine and blushed—first for looking, and then for being embarrassed about looking.

"I'll be the first to admit—*grudgingly*," said the anygné, "that Kane isn't always quite as shallow as he plays himself off to be." She released a sigh and lowered her arms. "It's all a ploy to get you to underestimate him. He knows the worth of his magic is very little. So he'll take whatever advantage he can get in a society that revolves around power by way of magic. Kane doesn't care for pride or honor, and he hates magic more than anything else." She flicked a piece of lint off her robe. "In fact, he wishes that it didn't exist at all."

The thought seemed inconceivable, but Luna remembered what limited power felt like, especially around wielders like Asterin and Eadric. And it made sense—she had never seen Kane use any magic, ever. Affinities could be trained, but everyone had a certain, definable capacity. Many were born with very little power, left with no other choice but to accept themselves as they were.

Magic, as it turned out, was a talent.

"Why did he attend the Academia Principalis, then?" Luna demanded. "Isn't it the most competitive school of magic in the world?"

"Kane's father used to be one of the professors at the Academia," Killian explained. "Until one day he tried to break up a duel between two first years and there was a horrible accident. He died. Kane was only twelve at the time."

Luna's eyes widened.

"The Academia offered Kane a place in the incoming class in reparation for his father's death, so long as he could keep up with his studies. But imagine . . ." Her mouth quirked to the side. "Being accepted to the best school in the world knowing that the only reason for it was because of the death of your father."

Luna bit her lip. "Couldn't he have stayed somewhere else?"

Killian shrugged. "No other living family members that I know of, so I don't think he *had* anywhere else to stay. The Academia offered him everything he could possibly need—a roof over his head, more meals than he could ever eat, the best educational facilities in the world—all without asking him to pay a single copper. So obviously he accepted."

The pieces were starting to fit together. "With hardly any magic to survive with," said Luna. Definite, spoken-word magic like a healing incantation was a skill and could be practiced, but raw elemental power . . . *indefinite* magic, shaped by the wielder's will and capabilities, was a born gift.

"He didn't need magic," Killian told her. "He survived by cheating. For the first few years, at least. No easy feat, by the way, from what I've heard." She sighed again. "That's always been his way of life. Stealing, taking advantage, lying. And he's damned good at it. Good enough that people never really find out *how* good."

Except for Rose, Luna thought.

Killian hunched over to prop her elbows on her knees. "But I imagine that the upper school exams eventually grew too difficult for him to rely on his . . . unorthodox means. Despite the fact that he probably excelled in non-magic areas. Like, say, knife wielding. As you may or may not have noticed, his aim is practically inhuman." She gestured vaguely toward her left eye, a reminder of their earlier skirmish. "Except it was just never enough."

Luna leaned back over the edge of the battlements and mulled over the new information. She had to brace her palms against the merlons to keep herself from toppling over. Even if she did fall, would it matter? Her broken bones would heal themselves in seconds. It suddenly occurred to her to try.

To simply let go.

Would she survive the fall in one piece? The thought kicked her heartbeat to a gallop. She closed her eyes, her fingers sliding along the stone. She let her body tip farther into the emptiness . . .

An iron vice gripped her wrist. Luna cracked one lid open to find Killian staring at her with a strange look in her eyes, almost fever bright.

"Hey," the anygné murmured. "What do you think you're doing?"

Luna glanced down at those slim bronze fingers enclosing her wrist, as stark against her skin as the first crocus of spring breaking through the snowfall. It was beautiful. "Immortality is funny, isn't it?"

Killian kept her amber gaze trained on her. "The novelty wears off rather quickly, love."

"What do you mean?" she asked. She felt intoxicated. On adrenaline. On euphoria. She had never noticed how, from a certain angle, the anygné's eyes glimmered with flecks of copper. How had she missed that?

It took Killian a moment to respond. "Most of the time, I avoid companionship. It gets rather lonely." She turned her gaze toward the horizon beyond the city of Ibresis. "Too often I forget that mortals have an expiration date." She still hadn't released her hold on Luna's wrist. "And a short one at that. Tortoises live longer, for hell's sake."

"Companions come and go, even for mortals," Luna reminded her. "Or has it been so long since you were a mortal that you've forgotten entirely?"

At that, Killian huffed out a breath. "I'll never forget my time as a mortal."

The nostalgia in her voice piqued Luna's curiosity. "How . . ." She wasn't sure how to phrase it. "How were you . . . claimed? By Eoin?"

"Hmm?" One eyebrow quirked. "Ah. I guess he just came to the Mortal Realm and then we left. Nothing interesting."

Luna scoffed. "I doubt that." She waited for Killian to elaborate. When the anygné remained silent, she nudged her. "What was it like? When you arrived in the Immortal Realm?"

Killian adjusted her sitting position, a crooked half smirk flitting across her lips. "It's a long story." Her eyes did not quite meet Luna's. There was such sorrow behind them, a faded melancholy blurred by the veil of time.

I avoid companionship.

A gentle brush of Luna's fingers along Killian's hand caught the anygné's attention. "I'm here forever now too, Eirene. So you can tell me every story you want, no matter how long. And once you've run out of stories to tell, we can go and make up an infinite more together."

Killian blinked at her, mouth agape. Then she ducked her head to hide her expression and mumbled, "You're really something else, you know that?"

Luna only gave her a sly smile. "Are you planning on letting go of me anytime soon?"

The grip on her wrist tightened slightly. "No, I think not." Mischief shone dark and wet in the anygné's eyes. "You're not falling. Yet." Before Luna could respond, Killian exhaled. "Fine, I'll tell you about my mortal life, but you tell me something about yours first."

"Like what?"

Killian stretched her legs out—the picture of nonchalance. "What was your deal with Covington?"

Luna's stomach churned a little at the thought of Eadric. Soon after she had stopped replying, his letters had ceased. And while she knew that she could likely restrike their correspondence, she'd kept putting it off until she forgot about it entirely. "We haven't spoken. Not since I left Axaris."

"Do you still love him?" Killian asked bluntly.

It surprised her that she didn't know the answer right away. "More than anyone before him," she finally admitted. "Except for Asterin." She blushed when Killian's head snapped up, realizing what it sounded like. "Ah, I meant—"

Killian dropped her eyes back to the ground. "No, no. I understand."

Does she? Luna wondered to herself. "Anyway, I must have loved him at some point. He courted me for years. But I guess I was . . . growing up. Even before I discovered my true identity. And after I became more independent, he couldn't reconcile with that. Especially after I became . . . this." She gestured at her face, the face that Priscilla had robbed from her—along with her magic—and that the enchanted lake in Aswiyre Forest had restored.

Eadric had fallen in love with a lovely, naive girl who had undergone a metamorphosis and emerged *changed*, with a new identity and even a new name.

"He couldn't stand it when I refused to stand aside and let him do the dirty work," Luna went on. "Or when I wanted to fight, even for myself. I resented that, and I still do. I can't make myself be with someone who won't let me grow. Is that . . ." She swallowed the tightness in her throat. "Is that all right?"

"Of course it is." Killian's quiet voice soothed the ache in her chest. "Thank the Immortals he can't see you now. His head would literally explode."

Luna snorted at that and prodded the anygné. "Well? Your turn. Tell me your story."

"I was wondering, actually," said Killian, "if you might like to see for yourself."

It took her a moment to comprehend. "You mean, with my shadow affinity?"

Killian shrugged. "I've found that shadow tends to enhance your most potent affinity in some way or another. Give it a try."

Luna scooted a little closer to the anygné and reached up to probe her temples, the skin warm beneath her fingertips. She watched, entranced, as Killian's eyelids fluttered shut, the dark fan of her lashes glimmering like liquid night. Their faces tipped closer, until Luna could have counted every single one of those lashes.

In her mind, Luna imagined herself standing on the edge of a cliff, like the one in the glade behind Eoin's palace. She took a deep breath, and then she dove straight into the abyss of Killian's memories.

The muffled shrieking of children's laughter filled her ears. Luna broke past the memory's surface and the world sharpened to startling clarity. Indistinguishable blotches of color disentangled themselves to form rolling hills of flaxen gold and spindly trees with wide, sparse boughs flush with fruit. The oppressive Voltero heat edged every half-hearted breeze, more like a bison's muggy exhale than a cool respite.

"I'm Ruler of the Rock!" Luna bellowed from atop a crop of boulders, her hands cocked on her hips and her chin tilted high. Her three older brothers and the stable master's son clambered onto the boulders, trying to reach her, but she was too fast, too sure-footed, pushing them off and sending them tumbling to their pretend deaths on the soft, hay-covered ground below. No one could ever beat her, and she soon grew bored. So she eventually relinquished her throne in favor of an ice-cold glass of black currant juice, kicking dust into the air as she ran for the family estate.

As she gulped down the sweet juice, the sky darkened like the cascade of night, only quickened tenfold. She set down her glass and rushed to the nearest window to see a black sun high and center in the sky. Just then, a knock echoed from the front entrance of the estate. People—servants, relatives, advisors, dwellers of their village—were constantly coming and going from the house, so the knock shouldn't have felt so out of the ordinary. Yet suddenly the air took on a chill, and the hunting hounds in the kennel downstairs began to howl.

Something drew her to the door, some inexplicable force reeling her in like a fish caught on a lure. In the foyer, she found her father, the mayor of Zemja, on his knees with his head bowed in submission and his hands clasped above him in prayer. Or pleading.

Before him stood a tall man in a star-speckled suit cut from a swathe of twilight. Luna's usual bluster shriveled when his eyes flitted to her. They were so dark. So ancient, so bottomless, pits of ink-drop black. He was so out of place among the bright yellow rugs and vibrant floor-to-ceiling tapestries woven only from the richest of threads, like a blight poisoning a blossom.

The strange man bent down to look her in the eye. In a soft voice that made her every hair raise, he said, "Hello, Lady Eirene. My name is Eoin. I'm here to take you to your new home."

"No," Luna blurted out. "Go away."

"Please," her father begged. "Please, have mercy. Return in a few years. She is too young."

Eoin shook his head. "Unfortunately, the next eclipse will not come to pass for over a hundred years." He held out a hand to Luna. "Come, little one."

She planted her feet. "I don't want to."

His head tilted. "Do you remember when that puma mauled your mother?"

How could she ever forget the infection that had spread across her mother's bloated flesh, the purplish veins snaking along her pregnant belly? "Yes."

"Do you remember when her heart stopped beating?"

"Yes."

"Yet she lives. She is upstairs, braiding summer zinnias into your baby sister's hair." Eoin pointed at her father. "He traded your life for hers."

"Liar." Luna spun to stare at her father, static filling her ears. "Right, Father?"

When her father's shoulders collapsed, the static went silent. "I'm sorry, Eirene. You must go with him. For your mother, for your sister, and for our family's honor . . . go with him."

An invisible force tugged her hand upward to clutch Eoin's. The tapestries and her father's face festered to darkness and the ground vanished beneath her feet.

Six-year-old mortal children did not belong in the Immortal Realm. She spent the first week crying inconsolably, and when Eoin finally managed to stuff a contract under her nose, she tore it into pieces while screaming her head off without reading a single word.

"How about this," Eoin growled. "If you accept your contract, I'll let you visit the Mortal Realm for one hour."

Luna stopped crying. "Two hours?"

Eoin frowned. "One hour and a half."

She shook her head, adamant. "*Two hours.*"

The god threw his hands into the air. "You win, child."

The outcome pleased her. Just like that, she thoughtlessly signed her life away in her chicken-scratch penmanship, a little zinnia doodled beside her name.

It was a struggle to control her new powers. Soraya, the oldest of the anygnés, supervised as much of her training as she could, but sometimes she disappeared from the Immortal Realm for months or even years at a time. Still too inexperienced and unreliable to take on an assignment,

Luna ended up stuck in the Immortal Realm—yet even as miserable as she was, and even with her heart constantly yearning for home, *nothing* compared to the first time Eoin punished her by making her force-shift.

Eoin's dark eyes filled her mind, accompanied by a single whispered word.

Zäär.

Luna screamed. She screamed and screamed and screamed. The pain tore her right out of Killian's memories. It burned through her every vein, crushed her bones in one blow, ripped her flesh to shreds. She recoiled, gasping for breath, her heart hammering and her nerves sobbing. Bile rose in her throat as she wrenched herself away from Killian and stumbled away.

"Did I hurt you?" Killian exclaimed, the panic clear in her voice.

Instead of responding, Luna simply leaned over the parapet and vomited into the moat below.

"Immortals." Killian scrambled over to her and held her hair back.

"I—I thought him kind," Luna whispered between heaves. "He . . . he was kind to me."

"The King of Immortals has no room for kindness in his heart," murmured Killian, rubbing circles between her shoulder blades, "because he does not have one."

Luna shook her head. "That's not true." When the anygné pursed her lips, she changed the subject. "How badly did you disobey him to deserve such punishment?"

Killian gave her a grim smile. "I didn't disobey him, exactly. Remember how you mentioned growing? He wanted me to grow, too. To emerge from my chrysalis as his weapon . . . but unlike you, I just wasn't ready."

Overhead, a fog passed over the moon. Instead of shrouding it, the moon bled through completely, luminescent white beams staining every last wisp.

Luna straightened and stepped onto a merlon, spreading her arms to embrace the night. The spikes in the moat jeered at her from below. A whirlwind of thoughts assailed her, but she wished to dwell on none. She did, however, have one declaration.

"You're wrong," she told Killian as she began shifting back into her demon form, feathers flourishing down her shoulders and breast and spine in a shudder of dark opalescence. "I'm not his weapon. The only weapon I've become is my own."

And then she stepped off the edge and plunged into the void.

CHAPTER FORTY-SEVEN

Eadric wasn't waking up.

Gritting her teeth, Asterin stood over him and blasted ice water directly into his face.

The captain jolted upward, coughing and spluttering. "Wh-what in hell?" he gasped, teeth chattering.

She grabbed him by the underarms and hauled him onto his feet. "No time for questions. We have to figure out a way to get back to the Immortal Realm."

The disorientation clouding Eadric's expression evaporated faster than mist in a desert. "Absolutely not. Not alone."

She shook her head. "We need to go back *now*. Orion and Harry might be in trouble."

Eadric threw his hands into the air. "Exactly! Asterin, that was the God of Shadow, for hell's sake! We can't take him on!" When she opened her mouth to retort, he grabbed her by the shoulders. "I want to rescue them, too. But—"

"Fine," she said. "We have to get back to the palace, then."

He blinked. "I didn't say—"

"You didn't have to," she muttered. Exhaling heavily, she wrapped her arms around herself. Even though her next words sent a pang of remorse through her, she gritted them out. "You're right. We can't risk running head-first into danger. Not with their lives on the line."

He considered her for a moment more before nodding. "Calling for reinforcements is the right choice. If what Harry said was true about the . . . nature of Orion's relationship with Eoin, we might not even have anything to worry about." He dusted himself off and exhaled shakily. "Also . . . thank you for saving me."

She merely nodded. It had only been thanks to sheer luck that Asterin had managed to spot him in time. The portal had jettisoned her about a league away from their current location. If she hadn't seen the tornado from afar, or if the portal had transported her any farther away . . . "Nice tornado, by the way."

"You mean until everything went to shit and I ripped all of the trees out of the ground?"

She offered her hand to him. "Don't be so hard on yourself."

He gave her a look of confusion but entwined their fingers nonetheless. "Er . . . why are we holding hands, again? It's not exactly helping my ego."

She only rolled her eyes. "I wasn't trying to comfort you." Wind howled at her summons. "Fortunately for us, the portal dropped us off right on the outskirts of Eradoris. We're flying back to the palace."

"Ah." The blood drained from Eadric's face. "Fortunate for us indeed."

"What's wrong?" she asked as his palm grew increasingly sweaty against hers.

He squeezed his eyes shut and exhaled. "Nothin'. All good. Ready to go whenever you are."

Something clicked in the back of her mind. *Heights.* "Ah." But they simply had no other choice. As the wind around them picked up and scooped them off the ground, she helpfully muttered, "Just . . . don't look down."

His grip crushed hers with every foot they climbed in altitude. "Not going to look at all, thank you very—*aughh!*" A gust knocked them side-ways, sending them tumbling, but Asterin managed to right them quickly enough.

"Arms over your head," she instructed in the calmest tone she could muster. "Keep your body straight and rigid, like an arrow."

"Like an arrow," he mumbled.

With their arms still extended high above their heads, Asterin twisted midair and pressed her back to Eadric's, hooking her ankles around his shins. He stiffened slightly, but she pressed onward. There was the river, sweeping westward across the land below. If they only flew alongside it, they would reach the capital.

Asterin narrowed her eyes at the low gray clouds flush with storm up ahead. She called the wind to swoop them lower, until they were skimming the treetops. Each gust spurred them faster, until the ground became an indistinguishable blur of greenery. She caught sight of their tangled bodies shadowing the landscape whenever the sun escaped the clouds, shooting across the land like a freakish, wingless bird.

Soon enough, houses began to cluster the riverbanks. They were grand houses, with sprawling courtyards and gardens and stables. Towering fir trees dominated the earth as they drew nearer to the inner city, obstructing their view of the more modest houses huddled beneath their great boughs.

Eadric let out a queasy groan that rumbled against her back. "Asterin?" he hollered over the wind.

"Yes?" she shouted back. They swerved beneath a V of flying ducks.

"How exactly are we planning on getting into the palace? What with the wards?"

As if she'd forgotten. Magical wards protected each of the nine castles and palaces. Usually, they were controlled by an entire team of wielders hailing from a diverse range of affinities, but for the palace of Eradore . . . "Remember when Harry shadow jumped us inside the Eradorian palace? Rose said that the Wardens somehow knew beforehand. So if they could sense Harry, they can't possibly miss us falling out of the sky."

Well, at least, she hoped.

In response, the captain merely groaned again.

A perfect ring of translucent quartz polished to a smooth shimmer marked their arrival to the inner city. Unlike the Wall surrounding the Axarian palace, the barricade itself wasn't impressive in size. Ten feet tall, perhaps, and manned by a handful of watchmen dressed in forest-green livery. But above the lip of the barricade extended a dome, an opalescent honeycomb of energy, separating the palace and Academia Principalis from the rest of the capital.

They soared above it. When the watchmen craned their necks to ogle at the sky, Asterin couldn't help but throw them a cheerful wave.

The mist from the waterfalls spilling out of the rock crevices beneath the Eradorian palace billowed upward to swirl around its towers in a hypnotizing dance. Whenever the mist caught the sunlight, the entire palace shone with a dazzling golden aura. Asterin had to squint past it to spot the wide, flat bridge on their right, connecting the palace to the Academia via the royal library.

She adjusted their course and aimed directly for the bridge. "Here goes nothing." From the corner of her vision, she managed to glimpse the subtle telltale glare of the wards shielding the palace. Like in Axaria, they were layered atop one another in a thick, glittering sheaf, about thirty strong.

"Could you do a countdown?" Eadric asked in a small voice. "Before we fall."

They hovered over the barricade and the wards and the earth below. "Of course," Asterin reassured him.

And then, without counting down at all, she freed them from the wind's grasp.

Eadric screamed. A proper, high-pitched scream usually reserved for small children throwing tantrums. "ASTERIN!"

"Counting would have made it worse!" Asterin argued as the barrier approached. She had never seen anyone force their way through a ward, but she doubted it would end well. Or that it was legal. Or that there would be a body left to prosecute in the first place.

Please let us in, she prayed to the Wardens. *Please don't fry us.* They hurtled toward the barrier, the wind tearing at their clothes, gaining speed the closer they drew. *Please, please, please . . .*

At the very last moment, a patch of the barrier flickered and cascaded inward, a tiny fissure for them to slip through unharmed. Her muscles tensed as the power of the wards crackled along her skin like an electric shock.

But they made it through in one piece.

Gritting her teeth, she called upon the wind to slow their fall.

Except she hadn't expected how *damn* heavy Eadric would be.

She scrambled to summon more wind. Except they were falling too quickly. It was all Asterin could do to brace Eadric upon her back and take the brunt of the impact herself.

They crashed onto the bridge.

Asterin's vision went white as pure pain splintered up both of her legs. Eadric let out a shout as her knees gave out completely, sending both of them sprawling to the ground. She lay on the bridge, her mouth agape and her chest stuttering to absolute stillness. Completely paralyzed, forgetting how to breathe. Terror seared through her veins. What had she done to herself?

Eadric scrambled over to her, his eyes wide with horror as he whipped out his affinity stone with shaking hands and frantically attempted to heal some of the damage. "What—what in *hell* were you thinking?" he yelled at her.

No way could she muster the strength to respond. The pain was so great she was far beyond tears. She struggled to inhale.

"Asterin!" hollered a voice. Boots thundered across the bridge toward them and a moment later Taeron and Rose were blocking out the sky above.

"Stay still, Immortals have mercy." Rose ordered. "You've butchered your legs. *Haelein*."

Asterin hissed angrily and clawed at the ground as Rose began mending her shattered body. The bones in her legs shifted, realigning into their proper positions beneath the Eradorian's touch. An eternity passed before the pain subsided to a dull throbbing, and a few moments later it had faded away completely.

Asterin shuddered with relief. "Thank you, Rose." If she hadn't showed up immediately . . . could one die from pain alone?

"Of course." Rose put her arm around Asterin's waist. "Come on, let's get you onto your feet."

"Is everything all right?" she asked, noticing the worry lining Taeron's brow. "Where's Quinlan?"

Taeron averted his gaze. "When was the last time you saw him?"

Asterin blinked at the offbeat question. "Earlier today . . . ?"

"Did he tell you anything?"

"Just that he wanted to talk," Asterin replied with a frown. "That he *really* wanted to talk, but I told him to wait because Harry had just told us about—" Remembrance jolted through her. "Oh, Immortals, oh—we have to go back to the Immortal Realm. We found Orion. We tried to bring him back." The words spilled out, accelerating, beginnings catching ends in an all-consuming cascade. "We entered through the portal but then Eoin showed up, and the portal started closing and we left him behind *again* and—"

"Whoa," Rose said, gripping the sides of Asterin's arms hard enough to bruise. "*Slow down.* You found Orion?"

Thankfully, Eadric stepped in. "Harry confessed to us that he knew of Orion's location. Except Orion suffered some brain trauma that resulted in severe memory loss, so he was originally hostile to the idea of returning to the Mortal Realm."

Asterin nodded frantically. "And I insisted that if I just *talked* to him, he would remember. Then, out of nowhere, he communicated with us through my vanity mirror. He told us to come and—"

"Vanity mirror?" Taeron interjected in disbelief.

Asterin's eyes widened. "The mirror! Immortals, the hand mirror!" She thrust her hand behind her to draw out the hand mirror she had almost unwittingly stuffed into her pocket during the madness of rescuing Orion. "It allowed him to contact us from the Immortal Realm. Eoin enchanted it for him."

"Eoin," Rose repeated. "As in—"

"Eoin, the God of Shadow, yes," Asterin finished impatiently, waving the hand mirror in front of their faces.

Taeron caught her wrist and took it from her, his expression knitted in deep thought. After a beat of silence, he asked, "Do you know if the mirror only allows for one-way communication? Between the Immortal Realm and the Mortal Realm, I mean. Or might it work the opposite way as well?"

"Maybe," said Eadric. "He didn't say."

The Eradorians exchanged a serious glance.

"What is it?" Asterin asked. "Were you hoping to try and contact someone?"

"We need to get to the Immortal Realm, too," said Rose. "We finally solved the mystery of my maps. The triangle symbolizes the Trinity of Gateways, as well as their locations on the map. The three gateways lead between the Mortal and Immortal Realms. Initially, we were going to sail to Qris. It's the nearest gateway to the Immortal Realm after Volteris and Artica, but it would still take a few days and we have no idea how to actually find the gate itself. It's a huge risk."

Now it was Asterin's turn to be befuddled. "Hold on. Immortal Realm? Why?"

Rose bit her lip. "It's Quinlan."

Asterin's heart lurched.

"A servant found him lying in front of your door, halfway through a seizure," Rose explained. "By the time we got to him, he wasn't moving."

The world didn't just tilt beneath Asterin—it felt like the earth was giving way under her feet, like the sky was toppling down. Eadric had to grab her by the arm to keep her from collapsing.

"The twins prepared an analgesic for him beforehand," Taeron went on. "More importantly, it also works to tranquilize and suspend all bodily functions. Quinlan only would have taken it if he thought the blight was approaching fatal, so . . ."

Asterin covered her mouth in horror, tears springing to her eyes. "He . . . he was trying to tell me that he was sick," she whispered. Only Eadric's arms kept her from keeling over.

"Not just sick," said Taeron grimly. "Dying."

The tears spilled down her cheeks. "And I—I turned him away . . ." She had known something was wrong. Of course she had. She'd even guessed that it had something to do with his injury—only, no idea of how seriously it was affecting him. "I turned him away even when he told me how important it was. When he *begged* me to talk."

Eadric rubbed her back. "Asterin—"

"I told him," she said, her voice tight with shame and rage at herself, "that whatever he needed to tell me—" She choked on her own words, a sob tearing through her chest, "—that whatever it was, it couldn't possibly be more important than finding Orion." She raked her hands down her face. "And I didn't even tell him that I was going to find Orion because I *didn't want him to come*."

Silence met her. A cruel, crippling silence that threatened to break her in half. She didn't dare look at the others' expressions. What were they seeing?

"Why didn't he just *tell* me?" Asterin clenched her fists and kneaded them into her eyes. She had never hated herself for anything, but at this moment, nothing and no one disgusted her more. "This is all my fault. I-I could have found a way to save him."

In the darkness of her closed lids, warm hands found hers and gently pulled them free. "No," Taeron murmured. The tender sorrow in his eyes drained the anger from her body. "It's not your fault. And nothing you could have done would have saved him. Only the God of Shadow can help him now."

She stiffened. "What do you mean?"

"Quinlan found a book in the royal library," Rose murmured. "Taeron read through the whole thing earlier. That's how we found out about the Trinity of Gateways. Artica, Qris, Volteris. Each of them lead directly to three different locations in the Immortal Realm."

Taeron nodded emphatically. "Besides that, I might have found a cure." Just as hope surged within Asterin, he grimaced and amended, "Well, not exactly a cure. A remedy, perhaps?" He took a deep breath before continuing. "Shadow magic has the ability to save people from the brink of death."

At what cost? Asterin couldn't help but wonder. But it was *something*, at least.

Rose pressed on. "Since we have the mirror, we need to try and contact Harry to open a portal for us to bring Quinlan through . . . cure or not."

Asterin held out her hand for Taeron to return the mirror to her. Praying that it didn't need some unknown charm or spell to activate, she gazed into it and thought of Harry,

Relief poured through her when the surface rippled. Yet a moment later it darkened completely, obscuring whatever might have been on the other side from view.

"May I try?" said Rose. As the mirror passed between them, the surface reverted to its normal reflective state. The Eradorian closed her eyes, and then, for a second time, the mirror went dark.

Dread pooled low in Asterin's gut.

"If Harry can't open a portal for us . . ." Taeron murmured, anxiety lining his features, "then no one—"

"Wait," Asterin interjected. She cringed. "There is . . . there is one other anygné that I know."

And even though she suspected that conjuring the anygné in question was a terrible, terrible idea, what other choice did they have?

Show me Lady Killian, she commanded the mirror, part of her already regretting it.

Her heart climbed into her throat as its surface revealed an umber-skinned girl sitting on a stone wall, staring wistfully into the night sky beyond. Her legs swung back and forth, the toes of her high-heeled boots not quite touching the ground.

"It worked," Asterin breathed.

The anygné's gaze narrowed. She glanced skyward. "Who said that?"

Asterin nearly dropped the mirror in her shock. "You can hear me?"

"Obviously."

"Perhaps it's because she's in the Mortal Realm, too," Taeron suggested. "Intra-realm communication and whatnot."

Killian's brow knitted further. "Again, who's speaking, please?"

Asterin drew herself to her full height. "This is Queen Asterin of Axaria. I—"

"Oh," Killian drawled. "You." Apparently, she had no qualms about speaking to one of her past targets, or any concern for a disembodied voice speaking to her through thin air. "What do you want?"

Asterin took a deep breath. "A few things."

The anygné grinned at the stars. "What's in it for me?"

"Honor?" Asterin tried hopefully.

Killian nearly fell off the wall in laughter. "You'll have to try a tad bit harder than that, sweetheart. I'm intrigued, however, so do go on."

Frustration coursed through Asterin. "What could an all-powerful shadow demon possibly want from a mortal?"

At that, Killian snorted. "Oh, don't you worry your pretty head about that. I'm sure I'll think of something. How does a favor for a favor sound? I do enjoy calling those in at the most inconvenient of times."

Asterin hesitated. "Fair. In theory."

Killian grinned wolfishly. "So it's a deal?"

She sighed, heavy and full of reluctance. "Fine."

"Lovely." Killian hopped off the wall and sketched a bow. When she straightened, her pupils and a barely visible ring of amber had swallowed the whites of her eyes completely. The vicious little smile on the anygné's face filled Asterin with fear, but it was far too late to turn back now. "Well then, Your Majesty. Consider me very unhumbly at your service."

CHAPTER FORTY-EIGHT

"Who were you talking to earlier?" Luna asked Killian as they descended the stairwell leading from the battlements side by side. Their larger-than-life shadows flitted across the floor in a macabre game of hide-and-seek, passing in and out of sight between the glare of the torches embedded in the stone walls. With every other step, one shadow rose taller than the other, peeling apart, fusing together, until Luna couldn't tell whose belonged to whom.

Killian shrugged, her fingers caressing the railing. She had wiped her brow clean, but Luna caught the lingering scent of sweat. "Myself."

Luna pressed her lips together but chose not to prod any further. "I see."

They reached the bottom landing that connected the ramparts to the castle. Killian sauntered forward all but two steps before holding out a hand. They came to a standstill. The whisper of footsteps reached Luna's ears, too furtive to be heard from afar without her enhanced hearing.

A phantom's tiptoe.

Killian shot her a glance, and in unspoken agreement, they silently ducked back into the gloom of the stairwell. The other girl crouched low to the ground and peered around the edge of the wall, allowing Luna to lean over her and do the same. Breath held, they lay in wait for their mark to wander right into their path.

But about ten feet away from their hideout, the footsteps faltered.

"Who's there?" called out a voice.

Luna's brow furrowed. Before Killian could stop her, she slipped around the wall and crossed into the corridor to find a woman halted a few strides away. Silk gloves ran past her elbows, silver bracelets adorned her wrists and her features were hidden by a veil, but . . .

Luna squinted, taking in the purple Ibresean long coat hanging from her shoulders and the glossy waves of bronze hair. *"Aunt Adrianna?"*

Adrianna lifted her face to the light, her expression shifting into a grin. "Luna!"

She blinked, a little dumbfounded. "W-welcome back."

"Did you practice your magic while I was away?" her mentor asked sternly.

"I—of course," Luna replied. "Where were—"

"Hold that thought for later, will you?" Adrianna interrupted. "If I don't get out of these sweaty robes right this moment I may have a fit." She bustled past Luna, giving her shoulder a squeeze and throwing her a fond smile on the way. "It's late, sweetheart. You should get some rest."

Luna stood motionless as Adrianna strode around the corner and disappeared from view, the *click click* of her heels fading into silence.

Killian slinked out of the gloom. "Well, that was odd."

"Yes," Luna replied, staring after her mentor. "Very odd indeed. But I'm just glad she didn't seem to notice my . . . outfit," she added, gesturing at the second skin covering her entire body from neck to toe.

"Where do you think she went off to?"

Luna considered the question for a solid minute. Adrianna hadn't been carrying any baggage with her, which meant that she had either lost it somehow or that she hadn't needed any in the first place, even though she had left the castle for at least a fortnight. Both seemed equally unlikely. "No clue."

"She was right about it being late, though," said Killian. "It's nearing dawn. You should sleep."

Luna shook her head. "I need to eat something first."

"Eat?" Killian frowned. "Eat what? Mortal food?"

"Yes?"

The anygné gave her a quizzical look. "What in hell for? Normal food won't provide sustenance for you now that you've metamorphed."

Luna's steps stuttered. "What?" The panic frothed up into her chest before she even realized she had kept it repressed deep within her. This obsession had evolved into a ritual—a ritual she was obsessed with protecting. "But I *need* to eat at least five meals a day."

"*Five* meals? Whose idea—" She cut herself off when Luna buried her face in her hands. "Whoa. Breathe, Luna." Killian grabbed her hands and pried them free. Luna's nails dug into the anygné's skin, but Killian didn't so much as wince. Instead, her amber eyes shone with concern.

"Stop looking at me like that," Luna bit out. "I've got everything under control."

"No, you don't. You—" Killian hesitated, clenching her jaw. "I'm so sorry, Luna. I should have realized sooner. Listen. We're only supposed to consume nectar from the Immortal Realm. Mortal food will do absolutely nothing for us unless we're extremely low on energy." She rubbed her temples. "I wish I could be of more help, but I'd probably make things worse. You should talk to Soraya. She's really good with—"

"I don't need to talk to anyone," Luna muttered.

The anygné grasped her by the sides of her face. "Luna. I know I can't replace Asterin, and I'm not trying to. But can you trust me?"

To her surprise, she didn't hesitate. "Yes."

"Then have mercy on yourself. It's not just about your eating habits. Your mental image of yourself, your frame of mind in achieving your ambitions . . . they're severely affecting the way you live your life. And I know we told you that you would have to train hard, but you can't just work yourself past the brink. You might be immortal now, but there are other ways for you to fall and break yourself. I'm too selfish to watch you do that. So for my sake, talk to someone."

"I am," Luna rebuked weakly. "I'm talking to you."

At that, Killian snorted. "I'm not good enough."

The irony, Luna thought to herself. "That's not—*ow*."

Killian released her abruptly. "Did I hurt you?"

She shook her head and winced. Absently, she pressed her fingers to the hard plates of chitin on her forearm. They came away stained with silver. "What in hell?" she breathed, staring at the blood seeping through her second skin. She shed it partway to reveal the soft mortal flesh beneath.

The soft, *marked* flesh.

Exquisite whorls of cursive flowed from her elbow to the underside of her wrist, carved into her skin by an invisible blade, her own blood serving as its stolen inkwell.

Hello, my little shadowling.

Luna clenched her teeth at the sting as each beautiful letter unfurled stroke by languid stroke. "Eoin." Who else, if not him? Her regenerative abilities were already working to mend the gashes from the previous letters, until each letter vanished without a trace—leaving her skin a smooth, blank slate once again for the god to engrave his pretty words.

I have a task for you.

Luna turned to Killian, her voice hushed. "Do you think he can hear me?"

The anygné shrugged. "Try saying something rude."

"You say something rude," Luna retorted. Nettlestings blossomed down her arm. "Oh, he's not done yet."

There is a convict—

"Eat maggots!" Killian exclaimed.

—who will soon be on the loose.

Luna winced again even as she snickered.

The convict is Harry.

Killian drew in a sharp inhale. Luna stared at the message in a mixture of dread and confusion, a tumult of questions reeling through her mind. There must have been some kind of mistake. Or perhaps it was a sick joke. Or a test?

Eoin scrawled on. *Harry was my second shadowling, and the oldest, excluding Soraya. Killian can guide you to him if you haven't had the chance to make the pleasure of his acquaintance . . .* He stabbed out the ellipses, punctuating the three dots with particular aggression. *Yet.*

"Ow." Luna whispered, blinking back tears. "What should I do?"

"Obey," Killian answered simply. Grimly. "Or face the consequences."

She shuddered, remembering the echo of agony from the anygné's mortal memories. "But . . ." After everything she and Harry had been through together, between spending weeks in his cottage in the Aswiyre Forest to fighting alongside him during the battle on Fairfest Eve . . . Harry had believed in her when no one else had any faith in her at all.

Hunt Harry down, Eoin wrote into her skin. The order burned like poison in her veins. *Prove your worth and bring him to me. I've already done you the favor of incapacitating him, so it's nothing you can't handle. Understood?*

Luna inhaled shakily and closed her eyes.

The only weapon I've become is my own.

She was a lethal blade. Eoin could point her hand, could tell her where and when to strike, but at the end of it, the final blow was hers to wield and hers alone.

By the time she opened her eyes, she had slain the storm within her heart.

"Understood," she breathed into the silence.

Good.

They both startled when a further response spilled out across her flesh.

And tell Lady Killian to eat maggots, too.

CHAPTER FORTY-NINE

"*H*arry," Orion's voice hissed at him through the darkness. "Are you awake?"

Harry fought past the dull pounding in his head, blinking sluggishly. Though, pitch-black as it was, eyes open proved no different than eyes closed. An impenetrable barrier of twilight crowded down upon him from all directions, pressing, suffocating—

"Harry," Orion hissed again from somewhere to his left.

How long had he been out for? He meant to ask but his voice came out in a ghastly croak instead.

A sigh of relief, all the same. "Oh, thank the Immortals. I was terrified that Eoin had beaten you to death."

Death. What a concept. Foreign as a color that his eyes could not see.

"What—" Harry stopped to cough, flinching at the soreness of his body and then wincing at how sore flinching made him, too. It was a new kind of pain, one that he'd never known before because he healed too quickly. "Why does everything hurt?" he rasped, gagging at the overwhelming taste of iron coating the inside of his mouth. He squinted uselessly into the dark, trying to discern . . . anything, really. "Where am I?"

"Eoin forged a new chamber to hold us. I did my best to heal the worst of your injuries."

With a loud groan, Harry hauled himself upright. "You shouldn't be here, then."

"Worry about yourself," Orion shot back. "I tried to find the door again afterward, but I think he removed it, so we're trapped in here for now, anyway. Unless you can shadow jump? I don't know exactly what Eoin did to you, but—"

The memory collided into him. The shadows, parting around a single hand, stark white against the blackout. Latching onto his collar and yanking him halfway into the open. The King of Immortals, placing his lips next to Harry's ear and—

Iræs.

Harry gasped now just as he had before. "*Iræs,*" he whispered to himself, suddenly numb. "It must have been the spell."

"What?" said Orion.

"The spell of extraction." Harry pulled his bruised knees to his chest with a long sigh and clung onto them. "Extraction of power."

Silence. Then—"That's not possible."

Harry propped his chin on his knees. "It is if the God of Shadow is behind it. And if you possessed no power to begin with so that the powers he one day granted you were all you had."

"What . . . what do you mean?" Orion demanded.

"What does it sound like I mean?" Harry snapped, and immediately felt badly. "Sorry. I'm so sorry. I'm just furious with myself for getting us into this mess." He dabbed gently at his swollen face with the back of his hand. It came away sticky. From what, he had no idea. If the smell was anything to go by, a little bit of everything. Harry took a deep breath that rattled his chest before confessing. "I was a hollow."

"A hollow?" questioned Orion with a frown in his voice.

"A magic-less person in a world of magic," said Harry. "Almost rarer to come by than omnifinates, though far less alluring, which is probably why you've never heard of one. I didn't have a single affinity. Nor anyone on my father's side of the family. Not a single drop of power in my blood. My mother came from one of the most affluent families in Morova. They fell in love, but there was no chance in hell her parents would have allowed them to marry. Too late did my father realize that she was already with child. When her parents found out, they threatened to rip the baby from her stomach. My father grew desperate. He vowed to do anything to save his love and their child. Even make a deal with the God of Shadow."

"And that's how you became—"

"A demon," Harry finished.

A minute passed before Orion spoke again. "Do you remember what I told you when you revealed to all of us that you were an anygné? Back in the Aswiyre Forest?"

"If I remember correctly, *you* were the one who exposed me," Harry muttered.

"Semantics," Orion replied. Harry could practically hear him rolling his eyes.

He pondered for a moment. The memory was not a pleasant one— still fresh with Orion's rage at his betrayal and broken trust. "You called me a monster."

"Yes," Orion murmured. "Yes, I did. And when you tried to tell me otherwise, I told you that I didn't care about what you were, but what you had done. I still stand by that. Harry, it doesn't matter if you were a hollow, a demon, or now back to being a hollow. You are so much more than a label stamped onto your life by circumstances beyond your control. Now put that big, ancient brain of yours to good use and get us out of here."

Harry fell silent as the words ignited a stubborn resolve within his heart that Asterin would have been proud of. He began scouring every inch of his mind for a plan. Even if they managed to escape this chamber, how would he smuggle both Orion and himself back to the safety of the Mortal Realm? Without any powers, he certainly couldn't rely on creating a portal.

Which meant their only other choice was a gateway. He considered their options. Harangirr was closest. They could hop on a sleijh right from the palace steps. The only problem was the ghouls, who would alert Eoin as soon as they spotted Harry walking free.

Something brushed his bare chest, beneath the fabric of his shirt.

Soraya's pendant. It had its own pulse—steady as the lapping of waves upon a tranquil sea shore. The loose threads of his plan began to weave together.

"Orion," Harry said at last. "I have an idea. Follow my voice and come to me."

He heard Orion shuffling around. "Keep talking, then."

"First we'll need to escape the palace . . ." Harry began outlining bits and pieces of his plan to Orion, the entire scheme growing clearer as he worked out the kinks aloud. Hope, if he dared called it that, kindled within him. Soon enough, a pair of searching hands grazed his chest.

"Ah," said Orion. "Found you."

"Stay right there," Harry murmured and reached behind his own neck. Orion complied. The heat of his palms seeped into Harry's skin.

He lifted Soraya's pendant over his head and transferred it onto Orion's neck, his knuckles brushing warm skin and soft locks of hair. "Here."

Orion blew out a shuddering breath. "What is it?"

"A nebula diamond," he answered. "It is the product of an anygné's powers."

Orion's fingers gave a slight tremble, right above Harry's heart. "You mean . . . extracted powers?"

"Yes. It acts as an affinity amplifier, which means it's wasted on me. This pendant belonged to Soraya—although, she gave up her powers *willingly*, after her contract with Eoin terminated." He smiled to himself wryly. "Eoin cannot detect its presence, so as long as you keep it hidden from view, he won't notice."

"It's so warm," Orion murmured, his fingertips curling around Harry's collar. He shifted an inch closer, and his scent, his nearness, struck Harry like a punch. Perhaps it was the loss of his enhanced senses, but all at once, he grew hyperaware of Orion's touch, the rift between them.

Or rather, the lack of it.

Harry's entire body locked up. "Orion—" he began, his voice rough. "*Please.*" He didn't even know what he was pleading for. For Orion to leave. For Orion to stay. He clenched his eyes shut, even though it didn't make a difference either way. He waited—waited for that inevitable step away, for the last fraying seams holding them together to finally tear apart.

Torturously slow, Orion's fingers crept upward, skimming Harry's shoulders before sliding behind his neck and tangling into his hair.

"Please what?" Orion whispered, his breath ghosting Harry's lips. "Tell me."

A shudder of pure, blind *want* ripped through him. Harry shook his head. *Stay. Leave. Stay.* His heart thrashed wildly against the inside of his ribcage, a tempest, a riot, a cannon firing out of control. "What about Eoin?" he managed to choke out, regretting it even before the words left his throat, and yet he knew he needed to ask.

"Eoin can go and fuck himself," Orion responded simply.

It was embarrassing, the relief that flooded through Harry. "But I thought you said—"

Orion scoffed. "After what I saw him do to you? The first time, in the arboretum, I wasn't sure. I couldn't base my judgment off a single incident. He had always treated me with respect. But showing kindness to some is no excuse for cruelty to others. It is not a trick to be pulled out of a hat as you please, or meant to be doled out like a party favor. And yet, even then . . ." Orion's voice softened to a whisper that sent a shiver of feverish heat along Harry's skin. "I just needed to remember that I was already yours."

Leave. Stay. Feral desire clashed horn to horn with every semblance of reason in Harry's head, both bellowing carnage no matter which rose triumphant.

In the end, Orion chose for him. His thumb brushed Harry's jaw, tracing beneath his chin and tilting his lips up to meet his. All of the thoughts clamoring through Harry's mind vaporized. His breath rushed out of his nose in a sigh of surrender. Of salvation. He couldn't quite figure out what to do with his hands as Orion's soft, devious mouth coaxed him pliant—but he wanted, *wanted so damn badly.* And so, with the slightest of hesitations, he wound his arms around Orion's waist and tugged him forward, close enough that he could feel the rapid rise and fall of Orion's chest pressed flush against his.

They kissed like the world was theirs.

They kissed like it was falling apart around them.

They kissed like they were dying.

Orion broke away to nip at the edge of Harry's lips, featherlight and fleeting, as teasing as the bliss of a summer breeze that only lingered long enough to serve a reminder to the unbearable heat in its absence.

Harry trembled. He grabbed Orion by the hair to drag him impatiently back to his mouth, and Orion—Immortals have mercy—let out a strangled moan that nearly brought Harry to his knees.

Let the darkness come, he thought to himself. *Let kingdoms fall.* For centuries he had subsisted on nectar and a relentless will to survive, but for Orion, he would give it all up. He would sacrifice his hollow, mortal heart without the slightest hesitation, even knowing that it would never heal.

Especially knowing that it would never heal.

Panting hard, they separated at last. Orion leaned his forehead against Harry's. "My life is yours," he whispered, accompanying it with a kiss that felt like a confession. "I vow to protect your life with mine, and I will never forsake—"

A crack of light spilled into the pitch gloom of the chamber, bright enough that they both jumped. Harry panicked and shoved Orion backward, hoping that the other could somehow conceal himself before Eoin walked in.

For a terrible minute, nothing happened. The crack didn't close or widen, just a beckoning sliver of naive, innocent hope no less than an arm's length away.

Warily, Harry inched toward the door, all too aware of his reinstated fragility. He felt too clunky in this body, as if he wore an ill-fitting suit of armor when the simple truth was that immortal blood no longer pulsed through his veins. Before, he could prowl upon a forest bed without so much as a leaf's crinkle or a twig's snap. How many centuries had he spent honing his abilities, his hunter instincts? His anygné powers may have come along as part of the deal, but he had worked hard to perfect every skill nonetheless.

Except . . . all of those skills belonged to a body that had perished at a single spoken word. And that frustrated him most of all. Plus, he was still sore as hell.

Peering out of the crack, he toed it open a hairsbreadth wider.

The corridor of midnight velvet—his favorite corridor, the one he had first come face-to-face with Orion in the Immortal Realm in—stretched out on either side of the newly materialized door. Completely empty. Not that it usually wasn't, but . . .

Harry inhaled deep and trapped the breath in his chest, his entire body tensing as he nudged the door fully open with his foot. The light from the corridor sent the edges of the chamber's darkness up in swirls, like disturbed dust motes in sunlight, but it could not purge the viscous murk.

Outside, the enchanted carpet billowed just as normal, swelling with waves pushed by invisible squalls. Harry craned his head as close to the doorway as he dared, trying to catch the slightest rustle of fabric, the snuffle of breath.

Nothing.

He poked his head out and glanced right and left to the end of the corridor, half certain that Eoin would appear in the space of a blink and kill him for real this time.

Heart pounding, he placed his foot on the carpet.

It rippled away from him.

When nothing else horrible happened, he stepped entirely out into the open and exhaled.

His eyes widened when the door gave a wobble and then lurched inward. He rammed his foot into the gap a second before it closed—meant to seal Orion within. The eruption of pain in his foot left him cursing, but with Orion's help, he eventually managed to force the door open again.

When the door finally gave way, Harry caught Orion by the wrist before he could escape into the corridor. "Wait."

"For what? We have to get out of here!"

"Eoin wouldn't just let us escape like this," Harry insisted. "It might be a trap."

"It's almost definitely a trap," Orion agreed. "But what other choice do we have? We can't just cower in the darkness and hope that Eoin forgets that he's holding you captive. Besides, maybe the door *was* the trap."

Harry swallowed the knot of apprehension lodged in his throat and nodded. Orion was right. They needed to act fast. Each precious second of freedom fell away like the cascade of sand in an hourglass, their chance of escaping slipping into the abyss with every moment wasted. "Fine."

"The closest way out will be from the balcony in Throne Hall," Orion whispered. "How fast can you whistle for a sleijh without Eoin noticing?"

"Not fast enough," Harry replied. "He'll sense us crossing the barrier as soon as we touch it."

"But either way—" Orion cut himself off, his eyes widening. "Wait. I have an idea. It might not work, but if it does . . . we could travel to any city in this realm with a single step."

"Without shadow jumping? How?"

"Soraya's pendant," Orion answered simply. Determination had written itself along the lines of his brow, burning cold and sharp in those glacial eyes. He slid his wrist out of Harry's slack grip and grabbed him by the hand. "Come on."

Together, they raced into the corridor, completely exposed. Harry felt stripped naked by fear and his own vulnerability, but there was Orion's hand in his, solid and reassuring. He guided Harry through the halls, somehow more familiar with the sprawl of the palace even after all of these centuries.

When they managed to reach Orion's room undiscovered, Harry's anxiety only grew. "This is too easy."

Orion huffed a laugh and pushed open the door. "Don't complain." He tugged Harry in after him, leading him to the great gallery of windows sweeping along the wall to their left. "Where are we headed, again?"

"Harangirr," Harry answered, blinking up at the dozens of scenes playing out just beyond the glass. There was the entrance to the Pit—or rather, the edge of the Pit, guarded by legions of Eoin's faceless ghoul puppets. And there, the silent golden cascades of Verkove'h Aur's waterfalls, and even Highcourt Hall in Oenthneo, the marble coliseum where the Council of Immortals gathered, with its towering silver-veined pillars and nightmarish, lifelike sculptures of the Immortals' sacred animals prowling the exterior. It seemed like almost every city in the Immortal Realm had found a place in the wall of windows.

Orion smiled. "Find it for me."

CHAPTER FIFTY

It didn't take long to locate the window to Harangirr—the aggressive blue desert city was impossible to miss, its blinding white monolith buildings jutting into the dusty sky. It was the brightest and hottest city in all of the Immortal Realm. Both its jagged buildings and citizens had been hardened by millennia of brutal storms that sometimes left half the city buried up to its crowns in peaks of cobalt sand.

"I still don't understand," said Harry, even after they had found the window. "How are you going to . . ."

Orion clasped the pendant in one hand. "You said this would amplify my magic."

Harry's stomach plummeted. "*That's* what you were counting on? You can't just—"

"Just trust me," Orion interrupted, taking a stand in front of the window. "My magic acts differently in this realm. It doesn't always listen to me, but I think I've figured out the pattern. It wants to *survive*. Whatever stands in its way be damned. And it sure as hell should know that I'm as good as dead if we stay here." His brow scrunched in concentration. "Eoin did most of the work, anyway. The windows show exactly what's happening in each of these places, so there must be some sort of magical connection already in place."

Harry finally realized the simple brilliance of Orion's plan. "So all you need to do is widen that connection. And by the time Eoin notices we've left the palace, we'll already be in Harangirr."

Orion nodded and braced his palms against the window pane. "Hopefully, yes."

Harry watched in astonishment as the glass began to pulse, vibrating from the sheer outpouring of Orion's magic. He couldn't sense the magic itself, but he could certainly feel the effects, buzzing through his bones like electricity. Orion gritted his teeth and shoved his palms outward, and the glass melted to sludge right before their eyes. A vicious wind howled into the room, carrying with it swirls of blue sand that stung their eyes.

"You first!" Orion shouted over the wind, holding a hand out for Harry to grab. "Hurry, before Eoin comes!"

The wind wailed, dragging Harry backward, but he finally managed to latch onto Orion. They helped each other through the window, wriggling and squirming through the opening until they tumbled headfirst into a scorching sand dune. The window swallowed itself with a *pop* and vanished.

Without daring to squander a single second, Harry raised his fingers to his mouth and whistled high. No more than a few moments later, the sand at their feet trembled and a swarm of butterflies of vivid lapis lazuli exploded forth in a geyser of wings. Orion gasped as their little bodies blurred and began to merge into the shape of a sleijh, complete with a hood to keep the sand out.

"Up we get," Harry said, snatching Orion by the waist and hauling him onto the sleijh even before it had fully solidified. "Isenynesi, please!"

With the desert storm battering the curved rails of the sleijh, they zipped into the sky, the sleijh's exterior camouflaging seamlessly with the blinding cobalt backdrop overhead.

Soon the sleijh dipped down to skim the sand, the dark-blue crests below them rising and falling like ocean waves. "Keep your eyes sharp on the dunes," said Harry. "The gateways conceal themselves to everyone except those privy to their true names." And the only beings who knew those names were Eoin, the Council of Immortals, and anygnés—since they always had to use them for travel when summoned to the Mortal Realm.

"There!" Orion exclaimed, waving down at the ground just up

ahead, where a whirlpool of sand writhed as if some beast were trapped beneath. It took Harry a moment to spot it properly—without the aid of his enhanced eyesight, he almost mistook it for another windblown sand dune. "Now what?"

"We jump," Harry replied, his heartbeat hammering against his throat. "It will open for us only if we jump." Ever faster, the gateway approached. Having arrived at their destination, the sleijh quivered beneath them and began to unravel into individual pairs of wings.

"We made it." Orion laughed and interlocked their fingers. "We actually made it."

A giddy grin crept across Harry's face. "Yes." There it was—*freedom*, lying no more than twenty feet below. "Against all odds."

"On three," Orion said. They coiled down in the scattering sleijh, bent their knees in preparation to leap for the gateway entrance. "One . . . two . . . *three!*"

Together, they vaulted off the sleijh into open air, clinging onto one another as they hurtled down toward the gateway.

We are going to make it, Harry thought to himself in amazement. After all of the hardship, all of the struggle and torment . . . somehow, by the grace of the Immortals, they were *actually going to make it.*

The sands below heaved in anticipation. Like the bottom half of an hourglass, they spiraled into a great, churning vortex. Harry squeezed his eyes shut and held Orion closer. He felt the brush of smiling lips against his own, fleeting and victorious—

A pained shout escaped him. The sharp sting of blades laced down his torso, piercing through his flesh. Claws tightened around him and jerked him to a halt mere *feet* away from the void of the gateway below. Orion dangled beneath him, clutching desperately onto his hand, his ice-blue eyes wide with shock as he stared past Harry's shoulder.

Harry craned his neck, trying to follow that gaze. His vision was already fading to black at the corners. He managed to glimpse an eyeful of feathers, but nothing more.

The claws dug deeper into Harry's sides. A glistening trail of crimson spilled down his arm, first running along his knuckles and then dripping onto Orion's, painting a line across the bare flesh to entwine their bodies in blood.

So close.

So fucking close.

Despair crashed down upon Harry like buildings toppled by an earthquake. Then, in the collapse, as hope disintegrated to dust around him, a precious realization—

Those claws only held onto *him.*

Meaning that Orion still had a chance.

Harry didn't let Orion's gaze find his. He didn't let Orion realize when he let go, when he forced his fingers, already slick with blood, to slip free.

Ice erupted from Orion's palm, surging up Harry's forearm and binding them together. Just hanging on.

"No," Harry choked out.

Orion shot him a sad, lopsided grin. "You think you can get rid of me that easily?" he quipped. Sand and blistering hot wind lashed at them, but his ice held strong.

"Go home," Harry begged. "Please."

Orion sighed in fond exasperation. "Idiot," he whispered. "Home is nowhere without you."

By then, it was too late. Wings pumped them higher into the sky and Harry could only watch on as the gateway fell away and freedom—wretched, wonderful freedom—escaped their clutches once more.

CHAPTER FIFTY-ONE

They brought nothing to the Immortal Realm save for the mysterious book tucked in Taeron's back pocket and Quinlan's freezing body.

They also carried a certain desperation that they disguised, poorly, to one another as feverish determination. *The most dangerous kind of desperation, then*, Asterin thought to herself. The kind that saw reason in the unreasonable and blinded all senses from sense.

Bearing Quinlan's dead weight between them, they staggered out of Killian's portal and into the Immortal Realm—Asterin working with Rose to carry Quinlan's upper half while Eadric lugged him by the legs and Taeron cradled his head.

Asterin's palms tingled. A gale of wind hurtled through their legs like a feral hound tearing off its leash, easing Quinlan's weight from their hands and propelling his body higher into the air. She swallowed her discomfort. Even though her magic was helping her, its ability to act without her consent in this realm unnerved her. How strange—to feel used, violated by her own magic.

Rose pointed upward. A thousand floating steps rose from the ground before them, leading to the entrance of the Shadow Palace. "There."

As soon as they ascended the first step, it levitated higher to match the height of the second step, then the third step and so on, creating a ripple

effect that allowed them to walk straight across the stairs like the flat platform of an ever-shifting bridge.

When they reached the final landing, they found the front doors flung
wide open in greeting. Not a soul stood guarding the inky murk that lay
beyond.

"So that's it?" asked Eadric. "We waltz right in? Just like that?"

As if in answer, a single black butterfly glided out of the gloom, skimming the air on paper-thin wings. Or perhaps it had been there all along,
anticipating their arrival.

Asterin took a deep breath. "Yes." She raised her arm, one finger
extended, and shivered when its tiny legs grazed her knuckle. A wisp of a
touch, barely there. "Just like that."

Then, together, they plunged into the maw of the Shadow Palace.

The moment they set foot inside, the doors swung shut and the corri-
dors flickered alight. The walls began to shift, the floor tiles began to roil,
everything deconstructing and reconstructing itself in the space of a few
seconds. It was like watching a thought process, ideas forming and devel-
oping or disintegrating on a whim. The outline of a door frame formed
halfway before crumbling to dust. In its place, slabs of stone and molten
metal assembled to create a new hallway bending leftward.

The butterfly resting on Asterin's finger quivered to life and darted
into the new hallway, leaving them no choice but to scramble after it.
Soon they were struggling to keep up, their surroundings blurring as they
broke into a run.

"How fast can butterflies normally fly?" Asterin exclaimed. She
glanced toward Quinlan and the wind pushing him upward—*only*
upward, not forward. Which could only mean . . . "Stop!" she shouted.
Her fists clenched as she wrestled her magic under control and summoned
a jolt of wind to sweep all of them off their feet and into the air. Even as
they remained stationary, the floor and walls continued to blur past.

Meanwhile, just up ahead, the butterfly continued to leisurely flit
about.

They had been running to nowhere.

"What in hell?" Eadric breathed.

A deep, pleasant laugh colored with amusement echoed through the corridor. The world around them halted still. "Apologies. I couldn't resist." The walls peeled away to reveal a room—an enormous bedchamber, connected by a gently spiraling staircase to a second floor. Glittering windows of all shapes and sizes encrusted the wall like a tapestry of jewels, each displaying a strange new curiosity within.

A man lounged on the edge of the bed by the wall, his black hair a wicked mess and his crown sitting crooked atop it. The God of Shadow had changed his appearance from the last time Asterin had—albeit briefly—glimpsed him. Now his hair was as black as hers, and his posture bore a slight air of . . . defeat.

Slowly, Asterin dispelled the wind buoying them aloft and the four of them sank back onto the floor.

"King Eoin," she greeted with a low bow. The others followed suit. "Thank you for seeing us at such short notice."

"Two mortal queens, two desperate princes . . ." Eoin trailed off. When his gaze fell upon Eadric, a languid smile curved his lips. "And you, whoever you mean to be." The captain stiffened but said nothing. "When my dear Killian told me you were coming, I must admit that I was curious. So, enlighten me. What have you brought for me today?"

Taeron, who had been oddly quiet until now, cut in before Asterin could answer. "We did not *bring* anything for you." His eyes simmered with heated resolve. "We're here to bargain. For my brother's return to full health."

Eoin quirked a single brow and tipped his chin at Quinlan, still bobbing in the air. "Is he part of the deal?"

Taeron seemed slightly taken aback. "Er, no? Just his health." The older Holloway lowered himself to one knee and offered his right palm up to the god. "I understand that the cost for acquiring the powers of shadow magic to bring a mortally wounded loved one back from the brink of death is half of my remaining life span and whatever I hold dearest."

Shock rippled through Asterin. She didn't know what she had been expecting, but it certainly hadn't been this.

"That is true," Eoin allowed.

"Taeron, you can't do this," said Rose. "If you return to the Mortal

Realm with dark magic running through your veins . . . by international decree, you would be executed. Even if we manage to keep it a secret—"

"It's the only way," Taeron insisted in a meaningful tone, a tone that said, *I read the mysterious book and you did not, thank you very much.*

Eoin sighed. "Now would probably be a good time to inform you that, given the nature of your brother's injury . . . you can't actually heal him. Even with shadow magic. None of you could. Regardless of your omnifinance," he added when Asterin opened her mouth to interject.

Her heart plummeted to her toes. "Why?"

"Shadow magic is a finicky thing," the god replied. "I, for one, can heal no one but myself, but some humans, aided by the power of shadow, have managed to undo fatal damage inflicted by mortal wounds."

"Exactly," Taeron agreed, though doubt tinged his voice.

Eoin shook his head. "You don't understand. Your brother's wound is beyond fatal. Beyond mortal. Something like drowning, or a sword through the chest, or even getting mauled by a puma . . . it might work. But not for this. No human infection rots his flesh—just a deep, festering darkness."

Taeron sank to his hands and knees. "Immortals."

"Why are you even telling us this?" Asterin demanded, an urgent, high-pitched whine filling her ears. "Why not just make the trade and leave us damned? Leave Quinlan—leave him to . . ." She couldn't even finish her sentence.

"Who do you take me for?" Eoin spread his arms. "I have a heart, too, you know. I have my own dreams. My own unfulfilled desires."

"Enlighten us," Rose said coldly.

Eoin hesitated and averted his gaze to the wall of windows. "The sun," he murmured, so softly that Asterin swore she had misheard. "My greatest wish is to see the sun."

"Seriously?" said Eadric, brows shooting up with incredulity. "That's it? The greatest wish of the most powerful being in both realms is to see the *sun*?"

"We seek what we cannot have, little mortal," Eoin snapped. He ran a hand along the back of his neck, almost self-consciously, and went quiet. His gaze lingered on the right side of the flower-petal bed. "And my other wish is one you cannot grant."

Rose bit her lip. "Is there truly no bargain to be made, Your Majesty?"

"There is," Eoin replied reluctantly. "One, and only one. I could revive Quinlan if I allowed my magic to flow through his being and fully inhabit his body . . . meaning, since my magic and myself are a single entity, if *I* inhabited his body."

The words sucked the air out of the room.

"A-absolutely not," Taeron stammered.

Eoin shrugged helplessly. "Apologies, then. Unfortunately, I have nothing else to offer. Such a transfer would usually be impossible, as my powers would decimate the body of an ordinary mortal." He reached for Quinlan and gently smoothed a stray lock from his forehead. "His omni-finance is his saving grace. But after this sedative wears off in a minute or so, he will be too far gone for any amount of magic to salvage."

Asterin's breath shuddered through her chest. It was the battle of Fair-fest Eve all over again, another life-or-death decision where the life on the line didn't belong to her. And once more, the time to decide had rapidly ticked down to the very last dregs.

Rose's fingers fluttered onto Taeron's back. "I think—"

Taeron slammed his fist into the ground, causing them all to startle. "*No!*" he shouted. "There is no thinking. This is unthinkable. Quinlan would *never* allow—"

"*You don't know that!*" the Queen of Eradore exploded. "Years. *Years*, Taeron, I have spent at Quinlan's side, when you could not. When you *would* not. A final stand of self-sacrifice does not exonerate a lifetime of cowering, not here, not now. As your queen—"

Betrayal flashed in Taeron's eyes. "As his brother—"

"As his *family*," Rose snarled, her voice breaking off in a sob, "I ask you to hear the God of Shadow out." Her shoulders heaved. "*Please.*"

Asterin's own words clambered up her throat, but she kept her mouth firmly shut. She wouldn't even have questioned the exchange. For her, a life was worth anything. Everything had a price, and whatever it was, she was willing to pay.

The problem was just that it was a price *she* couldn't pay.

Eoin held up both hands. "One moon. One moon, to see through his eyes. That's all I ask for." Solemnly, he placed one hand upon his heart and began his pledge. "I will eradicate all traces of Prince Quinlan's affliction fully and immediately upon this agreement. For my powers to flow through his veins so that I may heal him properly, I shall merge our existences. I will not take control of his mind, nor his body. And upon the setting of the sun on the final day, I will remove myself wholly from his person with no physical consequence, leaving him just as he currently is, except in a physical state liberated completely from pain and bodily harm."

Even Taeron looked surprised at the god's heartfelt earnestness. His eyes narrowed in skepticism, and Asterin couldn't blame him. It all sounded too good to be true. The terms were clear and thorough, and apparently, *impossibly* in their favor. "You won't harm him?"

"I, myself, will not. Not directly," Eoin replied. "By which I mean, if he gets into trouble and accidentally hurts *himself*, I cannot justifiably be held accountable."

"Fair," Taeron muttered, casting a pointed glare at his brother's floating body. He exhaled. "And how do we know that you will keep your word?"

"I may be the Ruler of Darkness," said Eoin with a wry half smile, "but I am an Immortal of honor . . . unlike most of the others. I have made my vows, and present them forth with naked honesty. Take them or leave them as they are."

"One moon?" asked Rose. She glanced first at Eadric, briefly, and then at Asterin, who nodded resolutely even as trepidation churned in her gut.

"One moon," the god promised. "No more, no—"

Quinlan spasmed.

Horror dawned upon Taeron's face. "The sedative—"

"Decide," Eoin urged as Eadric began cursing. "Before it's too late."

"I . . ." Taeron started, but then wavered. His face crumpled. "It can't be me, I can't condone—"

"Do it," Asterin and Rose commanded Eoin at the exact same moment. The two queens looked at each other, their expressions mirrored.

Rose stepped forward to offer her hand to the God of Shadow. "On your vows."

Eoin shook it once. "On my vows."

Without another word, he crooked one finger at Quinlan's body and dragged it toward him. It drifted down to rest upon the bed.

Quinlan had gone terrifyingly still. When Rose grabbed Asterin's hand in a crushing, nerve-wrought grip, she merely returned it. They watched, transfixed, as the god leaned down, his eyes slipping shut and—

Pressed his mouth to Quinlan's.

Asterin surged forward, shocked, struggling to free herself from Rose's grasp.

"Wait," said Rose. "*Look.*"

Asterin faltered when she realized that Eoin was . . . dissolving. A translucent sheen crept over his form like ghostly hoarfrost, until they could see right through him.

Quinlan gasped. In a single *whoosh*, he whisked Eoin through his parted lips. His eyes rolled beneath his lids. His spine arched like a bending bow. Before any of them could rush to his side, however, the rigidity snapped out of his body and he collapsed back onto the bed.

Lifeless.

Asterin cried out. Rose lunged for Quinlan, her fingers scrabbling for his wrist, searching desperately for a pulse. A second later, she released him only to begin pumping at his chest while counting feverishly underneath her breath.

The rest of them gathered around Quinlan and waited in horrible, cursed silence as Rose worked.

After a long while, the Queen of Eradore sagged onto the bed, her head hanging down. Tears dripped off the tip of her nose.

"Rose," Asterin said hoarsely when the girl said nothing. "*Rose.*"

"We were too late," Rose finally answered in a broken whisper. "He's gone."

CHAPTER FIFTY-TWO

Halfway to Harangirr, Luna couldn't take it anymore. Orion's misery permeated her nostrils, as inescapable as the stench of a wet mongrel abandoned in the rain. Misery, and the underlying fear that he was trying to hide from her.

Fear, she thought ruefully. *Of me.*

How coveted Priscilla had made fear seem, that power over others. How almighty. But now, with her talons tearing through Harry's torso and Orion barely clutching on, swinging over death like a stranded acrobat, the thought of striking fear into anyone's heart brought Luna nothing more than a queasy sort of discomfort.

The dunes and the darkening horizon around them blended to form a seamless stretch of perpetual cobalt. For reasons she couldn't fathom, the stars blinked out one by one. Below, she caught glimpses of a sleek shadow prowling the sands, stalking their path—Killian.

Harry had passed out ages ago from blood loss. Once in the air, she'd adjusted her grip on him so as not to puncture any critical organs, and allowed Orion to heal him enough to keep him alive.

I've already done you the favor of incapacitating him, Eoin had told her, *so it's nothing you can't handle.*

Not in a thousand years would she have guessed the degree to which the god had 'incapacitated' the anygné. She still couldn't believe it. Harry, the untouchable immortal demon, reduced to . . . this. In a way, it felt like a warning. Surely Eoin could have hunted the anygné down himself, but he had entrusted Luna with the task instead . . . *as if to show me firsthand how truly powerless I am against him*, she thought to herself grimly.

Orion's head jerked up in surprise when Luna angled her wings and swooped toward the sea of sand, the wind buffeting her feathers. The plumage around her face curved inward to shield her eyes. When they landed, she snapped her wings fully open, wide as sails, to encase the three of them within her makeshift shelter.

Killian would stay out of their way, hopefully choosing to lurk somewhere in the background instead.

Luna's features contorted in concentration as she semi-shifted, struggling to hold onto every aspect of her demon form except for her face and talons. As her mandibles recast themselves into a human jaw, her talons also retracted to release Harry, who planted headfirst into the sand.

Orion spat sand from his mouth and used his fist to shatter the ice cuff binding him to Harry in one strike. He brushed the shards away and immediately began running his hands over Harry's wounds, muttering *haelein* furiously beneath his breath. Only when he had knitted the last of the gashes back together did he finally turn his attention to Luna.

She had never seen his gaze so cold.

"Why?" he asked simply.

She winced as a bout of nausea from semi-shifting washed over her. "You're going to have to be a little more specific than that." She remembered Harry semi-shifting once back in Axaris, remaining in his human form but borrowing his enhanced senses from his demon counterpart. How had he made it look so easy?

"Why do you want to kill us?" Orion growled.

Luna stared at him. "I think there's been a slight misunderstanding."

The Guardian scoffed. "A slight misunderstanding? A *slight misunderstanding*? You abducted us *seconds* before we made it through Isenynesi Gateway. Then you nearly gouged Harry to death—"

"Wait," Luna tried.

Orion barreled on with his rant. "—and now you've flown us into the middle of a desert to execute us."

"What in hell are you on about?" Luna demanded. Her stomach lurched suddenly. Feathers popped back onto her cheeks. She tamped down the urge to dry heave. "Listen, I can't keep up this form for much longer. Point is, I'm not trying to kill you." Orion shot her an unimpressed look and she threw her hands in the air. "If I was, we wouldn't have landed here—we would be on our way back to the Shadow Palace right now." She jerked her chin at Harry. "What happened to him? Why is Eoin after him?"

"So Eoin *is* behind this," Orion murmured.

"Of course he's behind this," Luna snapped in irritation. "But how did he manage to . . . incapacitate Harry?"

"A spell," Orion replied. "Eoin stole away all of his powers with a single spell."

The world slowed. "He can . . ." she breathed, something akin to panic burrowing deep into her bones. "He can take them back?" When Orion nodded, her brow furrowed. "But . . . *why?*" And why Harry, but not Killian? What had gone wrong?

A long, guilty silence followed her question. "Because of me," Orion finally whispered. "It must have been because of me. Something I said, something that made him blame the recovery of my memories on Harry."

Luna swallowed. "What did you say?"

Befuddlement wrote itself across Orion's face as he recalled the catastrophe. "He changed his appearance," he began slowly. "I was just complimenting him on it, that's all. I still don't understand why that caused him to—"

Revelation clicked in Luna's mind. "Oh." Eoin's enchantment . . . *a mask that shifts depending on who looks upon it. A mirage that appeals to the viewer's desires, takes on the traits of whoever they wish to see most.* Her own words. "Oh no."

Which meant that Eoin had nearly destroyed one of his most loyal servants over the Immortals knew how many millennia because he was . . . *jealous.*

Luna eased back into her demon form, deciding to keep the newfound knowledge to herself since she saw no point in furthering Orion's misplaced guilt.

But *knowing* it changed everything.

Jealousy wasn't worth dying over.

To obey Eoin's commands and deliver Harry to the Shadow Palace would ensure his damnation. And yet . . . to disobey might damn *her*.

In the Aswiyre Forest, after the enchanted lake had stripped away the spells concealing her true identity and Asterin's suppressed memories, Orion had exposed Harry's secret to them all. That fateful day, he had knelt upon earth stained with his immortal blood and bore the burden of Asterin's mercy. He had said many things, many Luna couldn't quite remember, but she would never forget the confession that had convinced Asterin to forgive him for his lies.

For centuries, I have slaved beneath Eoin's hand. I have never found the courage to disobey him, but then I met all of you and witnessed your strength, day after day. You taught me what bravery was. You taught me how to care. Your kindness gives me hope that even though I am a demon, I can still be more.

Luna knew what she was.

A shadow demon.

A human girl.

A servant.

A queen.

And someone never to be underestimated.

She closed her eyes. When they opened, the world looked considerably blurrier. Orion stood a head taller than her and she had to shield away the sandstorm with a hand over her brow in place of feathers.

"We have to move fast," she told Orion.

It took him a solid five seconds to summon a response. "What?"

"Immortals, do I have to do everything around here?" she grumbled, bending down to hoist Harry out of the sand. She hefted his torso over her shoulder. Not as heavy as she'd expected—or maybe it was just that she'd gotten stronger.

Hell, of *course* she'd gotten stronger.

With her free hand, she whistled for a sleijh. It took her a few tries, but eventually the dune to their left trembled and out burst a swarm of wings in a cascade of blue. She trekked toward it.

Orion stumbled after her, just as confused as before. "What are you doing?"

The last of the butterflies settled into sleijh formation. Luna stepped up onto the platform and gingerly propped Harry against one side of the bench. "Get in, Orion."

He only hesitated a moment before clambering in after her. "Where are we going?"

"Home," Luna answered, shaking the sand from her hair. "Immortals, I hate sand." Every grain clung to her, dusting the space behind her ears and chin, filling every crevice like an infestation.

"You—you mean we're going back to Isenynesi?" Orion stammered.

"Obviously," said Luna, tucking her toes into the nook beneath the dash as the sleijh purred beneath them. It began climbing the incline of a particularly tall dune. When she glanced over her shoulder, she caught a pair of slightly puzzled amber eyes glowing behind them in the gloom. She prayed that Killian could keep up with the sleijh. "You know any other ways to get back to the Mortal Realm?"

"N-no, it's just—"

"Then hold on!" Luna interrupted as the sleijh shot forward in a ruthless burst of speed. It pitched itself right off the peak of the dune and into the sky, probably spurred on by the filthy obscenities Orion was yelling all the while.

Only once they had stopped ascending and found a comfortable cruising altitude did Orion turn to her and ask the very question weighing on Luna's mind, too. "If you betray Eoin . . . won't he punish you, too?"

Luna craned her neck over the edge of the sleijh, relieved to see a black blur darting across the dunes below, never quite touching the sand. She settled back into her seat. "Yes," she admitted softly. "Most likely." She paused. "Do you remember what Asterin used to do when she knew Priscilla might sniff out something she didn't want her finding out about?"

"Do it anyway?"

Luna rolled her eyes. "Well, yes. But other than that, she would always accomplish something more worthy of Priscilla's praise than her displeasure. Something exceptional enough to outweigh all of her misdoings. Like mastering a new affinity."

Orion arched an eyebrow. "You're going to win Eoin over by mastering a new affinity?"

Luna snorted. "No . . . something much, much better."

"Like?" he prompted.

A surreptitious smile graced her lips. "You'll see."

They glided toward Isenynesi Gateway in silence—at least, until Orion broke it again.

"Thank you, by the way," he said. "For deciding not to kill us." Before she could respond, his brow creased. "Hold on. Why didn't you just call a sleijh earlier? Or open a portal? Instead of carrying us across a whole damn desert yourself?"

"I needed the time to think about what I stand for. Who I stand beside. And who has stood beside me."

He fell into quiet contemplation, mulling over her words. After a minute, he glanced up at her. A crooked grin had risen to his face. "You really are the same Luna after all."

The comment irked her slightly, though she forced herself to take it as a compliment. But after everything that had happened, after all of the storms she had weathered and the ordeals she had overcome, it was laughable to think that she hadn't made it out the other end entirely unchanged. Untransformed.

Orion could think whatever he liked. In fact, the less he thought of her motives, the better. Other than smuggling Orion and Harry safely back to the Mortal Realm, where they would be far out of Eoin's reach given that the next total eclipse was centuries away, Luna had her own plans.

Plans for herself.

As if reading her mind, Orion turned to her again. "So, will you be coming with us? I think we'll sail from Volteris to Eradoris to meet up with the others."

And Asterin, went unsaid.

The sleijh began to slow.

"Thank you for the offer," said Luna. Up ahead, the sands of the gateway seethed. "But no. I've still got a job to do. I'm going home." Orion went very still, but Luna was too busy smiling to herself to notice. She gazed into the horizon, imagining those elegant turrets and pale rosy walls . . . and the fate awaiting her within. "Home, to Axaris."

CHAPTER FIFTY-THREE

The air in the Conservatory always smelled of dirt. Of mist, of leaves. Of earth.

Dazzling sunlight filtered through the arched glass panes high, *high* above, bathing the hundreds of rows of plant life in all its radiant glory. Iridescent dragonflies and other insects zipped past. Birds with wings so vibrant they seemed dipped in oil paint darted overhead. The Conservatory knew their songs like the sea knew the sound of gulls. All day, the birds warbled and trilled and shrieked at one another, calling and answering, a symphony of a thousand counterpoints.

Queen Valeria ambled down the aisles of the Conservatory with her teenage brother, Prince Viyo, at her side. The prince was as sullen as usual, dragging his feet along the gravel and kicking a round rock ahead of them every few strides.

Whap! The rock skittered ahead. *Crunch, crunch, crunch.* Viyo's sandals against the gravel. *Whap!*

Elsewhere, Valeria might have scolded him, but simply basking in the Conservatory's finely tuned ecosphere gave her the patience to tolerate his childish antics. Besides, no one was around to witness them, since at her own request the entire space was always empty of visitors and upkeepers in the morning.

She paused in front of a bright little cluster of plumeria flowers, their charming teardrop-shaped petals shaded fuchsia at the tips and then fading saffron toward their centers. A few buds had yet to blossom.

"Here, Viyo," she commanded.

Her brother made a face but complied, though not before jogging ahead to pick up the rock he had been kicking.

"Immortals," Valeria exclaimed. "That was your affinity stone?"

"*That was your affinity stone?*" Viyo parroted in a high-pitched voice and thrust his hand toward the buds. They bloomed as he inhaled, the petals unfolding gracefully.

Valeria inspected the blossoms and hummed in satisfaction. "You do realize that my voice is deeper than yours, small child?"

"That was your affinity stone?" Viyo repeated in the deepest tone he could muster, but his voice cracked on the last word. He flushed angrily when Valeria threw her head back with laughter. "I'm sixteen!"

Valeria smirked. "Still small, still a child." She raised her hand toward the next aisle, where a sequoia sapling poked out of an empty plot of dirt. Then she braced herself and *pulled*. Its tiny green sprigs exploded outward, chasing height faster than steam rising, its trunk swelling and its boughs bursting with needles. The taller it grew, the *faster* it grew, and in less than a minute, it had shot two hundred feet into the sky with a trunk twenty feet thick and cones that brushed the ceiling.

The Conservatory was a magical place, to say the least.

Viyo folded his arms across his chest. "You don't intimidate me," he informed her, very unconvincingly.

Valeria sighed. "You miss my point, small child. At the end of the day, even the tiniest of saplings can grow to be the mightiest of them all."

That drew a reluctant smile from him. "You're like a walking fairy tale, oh wise and *elderly* sister." And with that, he dropped his affinity stone back onto the ground and resumed kicking it around.

"Elderly?" Valeria demanded. "I am still in my mid-ish twenties! By the time you—"

SCREECH!

Viyo yelped and clapped his hands over his ears. The deafening *fwumph* of thousands of wingbeats exploded through the air. The birds scattered and surged up to the top of Valeria's sequoia, huddling together for safety upon its towering branches.

"Viyo! My chambers, now!" Valeria ordered, already shoving her little brother into a stumbling run.

"But my affinity stone—"

"*Now*, I said!"

Thankfully, the prince had the good sense to obey, sprinting for the exit closest to the royal wing. Valeria kept right on his heels, flying over the gravel. They passed the humongous statue of Lady Siore, the Goddess of Earth, with her kind, gentle face and her antler crown of branches and blossoms curving from her brow. Stone stags grazed upon the slopes of her palms and their horns clashed atop her shoulders.

The goddess's eyes, normally closed in serenity, were wide open.

Less than a moment before they made it through the doors, the earth shook. It *shook*, like thunder incarnate. They both tumbled forward, but Valeria managed to command the gravel to rise up and catch their fall.

As soon as they passed through the exit, the ground stilled beneath their feet even as the Conservatory continued to tremble.

"Go," Valeria told her brother, already turning back to the Conservatory. "I'll meet you there."

"What? Where are you going?" Viyo cried, but she merely glared at him over her shoulder until he ran away.

Valeria waited until the prince was safely out of range before she plunged back into the Conservatory. With her earthstone locked in her grip, she stretched her arms out. The gravel shuddered to life and carried her forth upon a never-ending wave. When the ground quaked too violently for her to keep her footing, she called upon vines to secure her balance and propel her forward.

The statue of Lady Siore loomed above her. Just the slightest trace of a fissure crept along the goddess's left shin—a shortcut to the gateway.

"*Ovrire fera Valeria Iyala*," Valeria roared above the rumbling of the earth. The stone groaned outward, a wound tearing open. She leapt through and slid down a descending spiral overgrown with slippery moss.

A cavern of stark white rock opened around the spiral. This was the entrance to a gateway connecting the two realms—right here, right beneath the Conservatory. She had only witnessed the gateway opening once—many, many years ago.

The walls shook and rained down dust from the force of the gateway's power. Valeria's eyes widened as the air began to churn and a white vortex formed in the exact center of the cavern above her head. She made it to the bottom of the spiral *just* in time to see three figures sail out of the vortex. Two young men, one blond and the other dark-haired, and a majestic, feathered demon with wings for arms.

Valeria's eyes narrowed.

She *knew* one of those young men.

The blond one. He was Axarian. She'd seen him most recently at the Fairfest Eve Ball. He was the Imperial Guardian of the Queen of Axaria, or something like that. Now, the Queen of Axaria was an entirely different dilemma all on her own—Valeria had already sent her *four* urgent letters without a single response—but . . . what in hell had her Guardian been up to in the Immortal Realm?

The winged demon snatched up the two men by their collars. A shadow danced along the walls, and in the mere moment that Valeria took to frown at it before returning her attention to the strange trio, they had already vanished into nothingness.

The gateway, too, swallowed itself in one self-destructive gulp, waiting for whoever would seek it out next.

Valeria glowered at the now-empty cavern.

What madness.

And then she began shouting for the Goddess of Earth at the top of her lungs.

CHAPTER FIFTY-FOUR

He's gone.

Asterin approached the bed one step at a time, her eyes fixed on Quinlan's bloodless face. But with the sluggish thud of her heart, everything in her went utterly numb. *Not possible. Not possible.* The words looped over and over again, in time with her pulse. Quinlan wasn't dead. She refused to believe it. He wasn't gone. No— in a moment, surely she would escape the shackles of this unspeakable nightmare and Quinlan would wake.

Perhaps Eoin had concocted the entire thing. Perhaps this was just another one of his horrible tricks.

She watched her own hand raise before her, fingers out-stretched. Felt nothing but *emptiness* beneath her fingertips as she brushed them along Quinlan's cold jaw.

Emptiness. An absence of magic . . . and an absence of life.

The agony came, all at once. It split her in half. She buried her face into the space between Quinlan's neck and shoulder and *screamed.*

Never had a scream so full of rage and grief torn from her throat. Never had she hurled her fist into the floor so hard that the *crack* of shattered bones drowned out her every thought.

After everything she had said to him. After everything they had done to get him back. After everything Eoin had promised.

"No," she gritted out, her voice scraped raw. "*No*," she said again, because she had nothing else to say.

It wasn't fair.

She was the Queen of Axaria.

The Immortals were not meant to be cruel to her.

Rose knelt at her side and took her hand, all gentle grace. Asterin hardly even registered the pain in her hand fading away as the Eradorian murmured a healing spell and pieced her knuckles back together. Rose was summer rain when Asterin had nothing left within her but the unforgiving wrath of a winter storm.

"What went wrong?" Eadric croaked.

Taeron wiped his eyes with the back of his hand. "Who knows? No one truly knows anything about the forbidden element, do they?" He held up the nameless book and threw it down in disgust. "It's forbidden for a reason."

"I guess even Eoin overestimated his own abilities," Eadric murmured. He glanced anxiously at Quinlan. "I—I wonder if he's somehow trapped inside now."

Well-deserved, Asterin thought nastily. She resisted the urge to touch Quinlan's face again. The furrow between his brows had yet to smooth. "He doesn't look like the dead," she whispered. "He doesn't look like he's resting." How cruel, that even now, he seemed to be caught midstruggle. She rose to her feet and let her hand drift above his abdomen, where the fatal wound had carved its mark into his flesh.

As soon as her hand neared his body, scorching heat singed her palm. She recoiled so quickly that she tripped over Taeron.

He caught her just in time. "What is it?"

She rubbed the angry red welt on her skin. It had been like holding her hand over a bonfire. Without responding, she approached Quinlan a second time and tugged his shirt up, careful not to singe herself again.

Her eyes widened.

The others crowded beside her in dazed disbelief.

Together, they watched the darkness infecting Quinlan's flesh and veins and arteries gradually recede, expunging inward, driven away by a power that could only be a certain god's doing.

To their bewilderment, a message inked itself onto the skin above Quinlan's heart in crimson. It vanished as quickly as it had appeared.

Insolent mortals. Have a little faith.

A hoarse laugh escaped Asterin's lips, a laugh that cut off abruptly when Quinlan's chest surged upward in a strangled gasp of air.

His eyes flew open and he shot upright, his face imbued with color and light and life—from the bright flush blossoming across his cheeks to the feverish shine of his indigo gaze. That gaze locked onto her.

"Asterin," said Quinlan, his voice rough from near ruination, but she knew she would have traded every sound in the world to hear it again. She grabbed his hand and nearly sobbed at the restored warmth of his palm against hers. He shoved himself off the bed and seized her, wrapping her in a furious embrace so tight that it robbed the breath from her chest. "Immortals. *Asterin.*"

"*Easy,*" she gasped. Apparently Eoin had revived him *past* full strength. Quinlan relented. Slightly. Enough for her to gulp down a few proper lungfuls of air, at least. She ran her fingers through his hair and buried her face into the crook of his neck.

"I'm so sorry, Asterin," he mumbled. "I'm so sorry. I shouldn't have— you didn't deserve—" He swore. "Immortals. I love you, Asterin. I can't believe I almost died without ever telling you."

Tears streamed down her face. She laughed, hysterically, and pressed a kiss to his forehead. "Damn you, Quinlan Holloway. I love you, too."

"Thank the Immortals." He kissed her hard on the mouth once before breaking away to throw his arms around Rose. "Sorry to you, as well."

His cousin pinched him by the ear and tugged. "For what?" she said. "Forcing us to watch you kiss someone or . . . you know, *dying?*"

He shot her a sheepish grin. "Both?" he tried.

Rose sighed. "I'll take it." She sent a quick wink Asterin's way over Quinlan's shoulder.

Once they separated, Quinlan turned to Eadric. "Thank you, Captain. For everything."

"I didn't do much," muttered Eadric. "I'm just grateful that you're alive."

"Shut *up,*" Quinlan growled. When Eadric's eyebrows rose, he flinched immediately and averted his gaze. "Sorry. Wasn't talking to you. Just . . . forget that I said that."

I will not take control of his mind, nor his body.

The hairs on the nape of Asterin's neck rose as a chilling thought occurred to her. When Eoin had laid out his terms for their deal, he had mentioned existing in Quinlan. With death as the only other alternative, it had seemed a lesser evil.

For one moon, the god had pledged that he would dwell within Quinlan and then leave forever. Except . . . no one had thought to ask him *where* he would be dwelling.

Asterin exchanged a glance with Taeron and saw in his expression that he had guessed much of the same. Obviously, Eoin hadn't opted to merely squeeze himself into a dusty little corner of Quinlan's mind and keep his mouth shut.

Before either of them could comment, however, Quinlan moved in front of his brother and opened his arms. He pretended not to notice when Taeron hesitated.

"I heard what you offered Eoin," said Quinlan softly. He drew away from the embrace. "I'm thankful he didn't accept."

Taeron's smile didn't quite reach his eyes. "I just wish we could have found a cure for you sooner, little brother."

The implication wasn't lost on Asterin, but she thought it best to avoid discussion. *For now.* No, right now, they had other pressing matters. Like—"How are we getting back to the Mortal Realm?"

Rose tilted her head at Quinlan. "If Eoin's power supposedly runs through your veins, Quinnie, does that mean you could open a portal back to Eradore for us?"

A wistful look crossed his face. "Actually, I might be able to shadow jump all of us to the Mortal Realm." He held out his hands to them. "I guess it wouldn't hurt to try."

Taeron didn't seem convinced. "Unless, of course, you muck it up and we get devoured by the infinite void between realms." But he joined hands with his brother anyway.

Quinlan smiled and beckoned for Asterin and Rose to grab ahold of his right hand while Eadric joined the left with Taeron. Once they had formed a neat line, he merely said, "Have a little faith."

Asterin shivered at the echo of Eoin's earlier message.

It was going to be a very long, very nightmarish month.

"Will you be able to shadow jump past the palace wards?" asked Rose. Asterin remembered Harry explaining that he had only managed it with the help of the nebula diamond augmenting his powers—a fact that, pointedly, neither she nor Rose chose to mention. "The Wardens might allow you access, but if they don't . . ."

"Trust me. I can handle it," Quinlan promised. "On the count of three, hold your breath. One, two—"

"Wait," said Eadric. "Right on three or after three?"

"I said *on*, didn't I?"

"Then why not just say *on three*?" Eadric demanded.

"It's a valid point," said Rose while Taeron nodded supportively.

Quinlan glared. "I am going to shadow dump the three of you into the ocean." He exhaled through his nostrils. "Fine. *On* three, then. Happy?"

"Quite," said Eadric. "Though I would have been happier if—"

"Immortals!" Asterin interrupted loudly. "One. Two." They all drew in deep inhales. "*Three.*"

The shadows around them shuddered to life. They surged upward, a wave encircling them from every direction. When they crashed down, they pushed and pulled at them like a capricious ocean current, a strong-willed tide with no destination in sight.

Asterin saw Quinlan beside her. He wore a crown of swirling darkness upon his head, and it stained the air black.

He closed his eyes and ripped them right through the divine fabric separating the two realms. They burst out on the other side and found themselves standing in the middle of the bridge connecting the Academia Principalis to the Eradorian palace.

As the ether clinging to their bodies dispersed, they released one another's hands. All except for Quinlan. Asterin couldn't help but smile to herself when it didn't seem like he would be letting go of hers anytime soon.

Rose grinned up at the palace and elbowed her cousin. "Not bad, Quinnie. Not bad at all."

They turned toward the Academia at the sound of small feet pattering across stone. Two children raced toward them, still in their school uniforms.

"Avris and Avon!" Rose exclaimed, crossing her arms over her chest. "What are you two doing out of class?"

Still holding Asterin's hand, Quinlan let out an *oomph* as the twins simultaneously pounced upon him. He somehow managed to bundle them into his arms. "Hello, little cubs."

"We missed you," said Avon, his words almost completely muffled.

Avris peeked up at him. "A Warden flew into our class and told us you were coming. Did our analgesic work okay?"

Quinlan tugged at her braids. "It worked perfectly, you clever little delinquent."

"Hey! I'm here, too!" Avon whined.

"Delin*quents*, sorry," Quinlan amended.

Avris let go of Quinlan and fiddled with the buttons of her blazer. "A letter came while all of you were away," she said quietly. She looked up at Asterin. "It was addressed to you, Your Majesty. From someone named Nicole."

Confusion struck Asterin first, and then worry. "Nicole? The Elite? *My* Nicole?"

Avris nodded. "The letter arrived from Cyejis."

"What?" said Eadric. He pushed closer with a frown. "That makes no sense. She should have long returned to Axaris. How in the name of the Immortals did she end up in *my* hometown?"

Avon scuffed the ground with his shoe. "Uhh, well . . ."

"You read the letter, didn't you?" said Rose with a disapproving eyebrow arch.

"Of course not," Avris exclaimed at the same time that Avon mumbled, "Maybe," to which Avris gave him a hard shove.

Asterin smiled at their antics. "It's all right, I'm not mad. Could you tell me what Nicole wrote, please?"

"You tell her," Avris hissed at her brother. "Since *you* said maybe."

Avon opened his mouth to retort, but then Rose put her hands on her hips and he surrendered. "Uhh . . . it was a pretty short letter, I guess," the boy began timidly. He ducked his head. "Nicole wrote that you must return to Axaris as soon as possible, Your Majesty. For urgent matters."

Foreboding settled in the pit of Asterin's stomach. "Such as?"

"It's your mother," Avon responded. "The Queen Regent. She's taken full control of the city and arrested all of your Elite guards. And . . ." The boy trailed off, looking desperately to his twin sister for help.

Avris took pity on him. Her expression had gone eerily grave. "And afterward, she executed one of them. His name was Silas."

CHAPTER FIFTY-FIVE

"Isn't it so good to be home?" Luna sang, throwing her arms to the sky. Her new black cloak fit snug and warm against her second skin, trailing all the way down to the cobblestoned ground below. She took a great, deep breath of chilly Axarian air and smiled at her travel companions.

They stood together at the bottom of the mountain. Overhead, the ornate iron gates loomed high, but the palace loomed higher. She could see the ripples of magic where the wards began, stretching all the way to the Wall.

Orion grinned wide as Harry blinked up at the mountain. They had linked arms. It was adorable. "Sure is." After realizing Luna would be heading directly to the capital, they had changed their minds about slogging all the way across the ocean to Eradoris. She didn't blame them.

"Will you be all right heading over to your father's house on your own?" she asked Orion. Theodore Galashiels lived in the west residential sector, bordering the outskirts of the trade and entertainment districts of Axaris. "I could have Killian escort you there."

Her fellow anygné was bent over by the gates, examining the ground with her hands in her pockets. She glanced their way at the mention of her name. "Killian what?"

"Don't worry about it!" Orion called back. "We'll be fine. And I won't be on my own, anyway." He nudged Harry. "I've got an anygné of my own. Thank you for offering, though."

"Send your father my dearest," said Luna with a soft smile. She hadn't seen Theo for nearly a year, since last Vürstivale—the winter holiday honoring the Immortals. Or, at least, all of the Immortals excluding Eoin.

"Will do." Orion leaned his head on Harry's shoulder. "It's about time I finally introduce my father to this one."

Harry blushed. "As kindly as Orion says he is, I'm quite terrified."

Luna's smile grew. "I'm sure he'll be very happy to meet you. Just don't forget that he was the King of Axaria's Royal Guardian for many, many decades and probably knows more than a thousand ways to kill you if you break his son's heart."

Harry scrunched his face, obviously offended. "I would never."

Orion laughed and entwined their fingers. "I, for one, am thoroughly convinced. Anyway, we'll be off. Good luck with . . . whatever it is you have to do."

She beamed and pulled them both into a hug. "Thank you. That means a lot to me."

After they all separated, Orion and Harry turned onto the street that would lead them to the west road, where they could hail a hansom. The Guardian sent her a last wave over his shoulder.

As Luna waved back cheerfully, Killian sauntered to her side. "So, what now?"

She pulled up her hood. "Time for a heist."

Side by side, they strolled toward the gates. Several mounted guards awaited their approach. Luna turned her face away. By the time they had almost reached the guards, she had painted the inner fabric of the cloak crimson and donned a brand new face.

And this time, it wasn't just an illusion.

"How do I look?" she whispered to Killian.

Killian's mouth dropped open. It turned out that dark magic had its perks, after all. "Damn. You sound like her, too?"

When the guards' eyes landed on Luna and widened in shock, her heart stuttered for the briefest moment.

Would they see through her guise?

Then, in a flurry, they broke rank and rushed to open the gates. As Luna and Killian entered, a pair of guards graciously offered them their steeds to ride up the mountain.

"Welcome home, Your Majesty," one of them said.

"Why, thank you," Luna replied, unable to hide her delight. The guard beamed back at her, completely ignorant, and saluted.

As Killian mounted her horse, she regarded the soldiers like a cat watching birds trapped in a gilded cage. Once the guards were safely out of earshot, she smirked at Luna. "Nicely done, my queen." Her amber eyes glinted garnet in the fiery glow of the setting sun. "So . . . what are we heisting, again?"

"Nothing much," said Luna, in Asterin's voice. "Just the throne of Axaria."

CHAPTER FIFTY-SIX

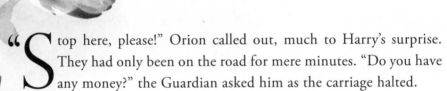

"Stop here, please!" Orion called out, much to Harry's surprise. They had only been on the road for mere minutes. "Do you have any money?" the Guardian asked him as the carriage halted.

Harry gave him a look. "And what if I didn't?"

Orion only sighed and made a grabbing motion with his fists. "Please?"

Harry snorted before rummaging through his pockets. Eventually, he fished out a gold coin and offered it through the roof hatch to the driver, seated behind them. "Thank you, sir."

The driver stared at the coin as Orion hopped out of the carriage and offered a hand to help Harry down. "This isn't Axarian currency."

"No, it's pure gold," Harry replied. "Promise!" Then he grabbed Orion's hand and they made a run for it.

They plunged into the trade district, past the upscale shops facing the main road. The din of the marketplace reached their ears, loudening with every stride. Only once they had crossed into the market squares did they slow to a walk.

"Don't look behind you," Orion whispered out of the corner of his mouth.

"Wha—*augh!*" Harry nearly tripped as Orion yanked him into an empty side alleyway.

"Do you have any more money?" the Guardian asked over-enthusiastically, his voice echoing against the brick caging them in on both sides. "We should buy my father a gift of some sort!"

"Oh," said Harry guiltily. "I hadn't thought of that." Mortal customs usually eluded his memory, but this one really should have occurred to him. He did still have a bit of gold left, but what sorts of things would constitute as a good gift? "Does your father have any hobbies?" he asked as they exited the alley and rounded the corner. Orion tugged him to a standstill. "Or maybe we could get him a bottle of wine? Is that too generic? I mean, first impressions and all—" He cut himself off abruptly when he realized Orion didn't appear to be listening. Instead, the Guardian was cautiously peering around the wall. "We're not actually going to meet your father, are we?"

"Sadly, no," Orion murmured, still squinting into the alley, which lay just as deserted as before. "I don't think Killian tailed us, but I didn't want to risk it." He let out a resigned sigh and slumped back against the brick. "I'm worried about Luna. She's changed."

Harry frowned. "So? Everyone has changed. What makes her forbidden from doing so?"

"Nothing, of course. That's not what I meant." Orion shifted uneasily. "I . . . I just have a bad feeling that she's about to do something stupid. That's why I thought we should follow her back to Axaris instead of going to Eradoris."

Harry arched an eyebrow, unimpressed. "Luna is many things. Stupid is certainly not one of them."

"I wasn't *calling* her stupid." Orion made some vague hand gestures, as if grasping for the right words. He ran a hand down his neck. "I don't know. She's my friend. She gave me my memories back, too. I care about her."

Eventually, Harry let out a sigh. He took Orion's hands in his own. "Whether we agree or agree to disagree on Luna," he began, "I trust you. And more importantly, I trust your instincts. So if you want to head back to the palace, or anywhere else, anywhere at all, I'll follow you." Gently, he pressed his lips to Orion's knuckles, never breaking his gaze. "To the end of the world, I'm yours."

CHAPTER FIFTY-SEVEN

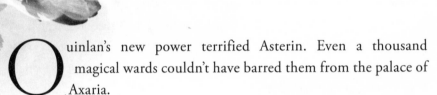

Quinlan's new power terrified Asterin. Even a thousand magical wards couldn't have barred them from the palace of Axaria.

The four of them—five, if you counted Eoin—emerged on the dais of Throne Hall, the stone circle of the Council of Immortals staring down at them from the ceiling. Taeron had chosen to stay behind in Eradoris with the twins.

Eadric collapsed onto the steps leading to the throne, the pallor of his face sickly. Rose sat down beside him and began rubbing his back. "No more shadow jumping," the captain mumbled.

Just beyond the throne stretched the floor-to-ceiling windows bordering an entire side of the hall. Outside, the sun was sinking toward the horizon, streaks of vermilion bleeding across the steadily darkening sky like smears of wet paint.

She glanced at Quinlan. The dwindling rays seeped through the glass, setting his face softly aglow. He stared at the sunset like he was seeing it for the first time. His eyes glimmered with firelight. His parted lips curled up at the edges—in reverence, in wonder.

Asterin stifled a shudder. "Are you sure Eoin isn't controlling you in any way?" she whispered, giving his hand a squeeze.

Quinlan never took his eyes off the sky. "He's not, but . . . but I can feel what he feels. And he feels . . ." He shook his head ruefully. "There's no word for it in the mortal tongue. It's indefinable. *Ineffable*."

Eadric broke the silence that followed. "We should find Elyssa."

Asterin's pulse picked up. How badly she wanted to forget about her mother and what she'd allegedly done.

She's taken full control of the city and arrested all of your Elite guards. And after that, she executed one of them.

His name was Silas.

Priscilla's betrayal had nearly destroyed her. Everything Asterin had thought that woman to be had ended up a lie. Half a *lifetime's* worth of lies. And worse still, Asterin had loved her. She really had. That was what you were supposed to do with mothers, wasn't it?

But at least Priscilla wasn't truly her mother, not by blood.

Elyssa *was*.

At long last, Quinlan tore himself away from the window and marched toward the doors, tugging Asterin along by the hand. "Let's go," he said.

It sounded like a command to himself more than anyone else.

As soon as they stepped into the corridor, Asterin almost crashed headfirst into a guard. Bright blue eyes blinked at her in surprise. "Ah, Your Royal Majesty! My apologies, I could have sworn—er, never mind. Hello, again."

"Carlsby!" Asterin greeted. *Again?* "Just the man I was looking for. Where is my mother?"

The young man chuckled nervously. "Same place that you left her, Your Majesty."

Asterin stared at him in perplexity and searched her memory for the last time she had seen Elyssa—right before she had left for Eradore. "You mean . . . the palace entrance?"

"Yes!" Carlsby exclaimed, his relief palpable. "You had me worried there for a moment, Your Majesty. With all due respect, of course. I hope I didn't overstep. Again."

Again with the *again*. "Are you quite well, Carlsby?" Asterin asked gently. "My mother isn't overworking you, is she?"

Carlsby laughed, a little shrilly. "Of course not! Anyway, I'll make sure to hurry down, too, since everyone is already leaving." With that, the soldier snapped into a bow and fled down the grand staircase.

"Since everyone is already leaving?" Rose echoed.

"No clue," Asterin muttered, the anxiety in her stomach rearing into full-blown panic. "We'd better hurry."

They broke into a run. As they flew down the stairs, Asterin craned her neck over the banister. Her eyes narrowed on the concourse floor far below, bustling with an unusual amount of guard activity. From what she could see, all of the soldiers were in various stages of donning armor.

Asterin skidded to a halt on the main floor. Rows and rows of soldiers were lined up and heading out of the main entrance. The guards that had managed to throw together an entire ensemble were hastening up the stairs to join them.

Some held ceremonial spears, some carried shields, and the rest bore the Axarian flag in one form or another—flags, banners, and standards of a snarling silver wolf against a field of crimson and black, two swords crossed behind it in an X.

"What in hell is going on?" Asterin growled. She stormed toward the landing above the concourse level and cornered a guard she didn't recognize. "You!" He was struggling to button his jacket while simultaneously juggling his shield. "Please explain the meaning of this."

"Oh, good!" the guard exclaimed. "Hold this for me for a minute, will you?" He passed the shield to her and finished buttoning his jacket.

Eadric swiped the shield from Asterin and flung it down the stairs, where its *clang, clang, clang* against the stone steps was lost beneath the cacophony of shouting and scraping metal and the heavy thud of boots.

The guard's cheeks colored cherry red with anger. "*What in*—" He cut himself off and actually took a moment to look at their faces—first at Eadric, and then Asterin. "I-Immortals." He bowed low enough for his nose to brush Asterin's shoes. "Your Majesty and C-Captain Covington, sir!"

"Apologize—" Eadric seethed.

Asterin put a hand on his arm. There wasn't time. She turned to the guard. "Tell us what's happening."

The guard frowned. "Pardon? Tell you . . . but—"

"Tell me as if I have no idea what is going on," Asterin interrupted. "As if I am someone else."

"It's part of an evaluation," Eadric added helpfully.

"Ah, yes, of course," replied the guard, his chest puffing. "Well, after you—er, rather, the Queen of Axaria returned a few hours ago, she called a citywide audience. From what I was told, she has some huge proclamation to make."

The world slowed.

"Where?" Asterin breathed.

"The Pavilion. Entertainment district."

"I see." Asterin gave the guard a placid smile. "Thank you for your time."

The guard saluted and dashed down the stairs into the sea of soldiers to retrieve his shield. As he was bending down, someone accidentally kneed him in the windpipe.

"Asterin?" Eadric prompted when she failed to speak. Rose and Quinlan joined them. They, too, were stunned into silence. "What in hell was that about?"

She closed her eyes and tipped her face to the ceiling. "I have no idea."

And then she summoned every ounce of strength within her and steeled herself for everything to come. Fury ignited in her chest, spreading faster than wildfire. "All right. Quinlan, get us to the Pavilion. Now."

Quinlan nodded firmly and held out his hands for another shadow jump. To Asterin's gratitude, Eadric didn't even complain.

Whoever the son of a bitch wearing her face was, prancing about her city and masquerading as the Queen of Axaria . . .

She was going to make them pay.

CHAPTER FIFTY-EIGHT

How fitting for the Pavilion to be my stage and Axaris my audience.

Luna paced the lobby of the concert hall, her emerald gown rustling softly with each step. Asterin had favored this gown for two reasons; firstly, it matched the shade of her eyes exactly, and secondly, because it had huge, deep pockets hidden in the skirts. Luna stuck her hands inside them now. Something crinkled in the right pocket, and when she paused to pull it out for investigation, she opened her fist to discover a half-eaten chocolate in her palm.

The smile rose to her face before she could even think to suppress it.

For a moment, she actually considered eating the rest of the chocolate—but in the end, she stuffed it back into the pocket and resumed her pacing, a habit she now understood why Asterin partook in so often. She took care to avoid the windows overlooking the Pavilion, except to steal a quick peek outside every now and then. Already, a few thousand people had flooded into the hexagonal marble plaza, crowding beneath the strange canopy twisting over it from edge to edge. It reminded her of a sea serpent's skeleton with the bones picked clean.

Dusk had fallen. Torches, affixed to the steel interior of the canopy and strewn along the sides of the surrounding theaters like scattered stars, flickered to life. Soon, the Pavilion would reach capacity, and only the Immortals knew how many people would pack themselves into the streets around it. She would make her address upon the makeshift stage that builders had erected at the top of the steps to the concert hall.

Asterin's mother stepped behind her and gave her shoulders a comforting squeeze. She kept her voice low, shooting a glance at what were apparently her own hand-picked guards. They lined the walls of the concert-hall lobby, motionless and fully armed. "Nervous?"

"A little," Luna admitted in Asterin's voice, with Asterin's smile. The less she talked, the better. While her powers allowed her to perfectly incarnate herself as Asterin, she still had to be cautious. She had stolen Asterin's face and voice and body—but not her memories. At least, not yet. One misstep, and Asterin's mother would *know*.

It had been so strange seeing Asterin's mother for the first time. Asterin had inherited so much from her—from the set of her shoulders right down to the length of her ebony hair. Luna didn't even know the woman's name, but she wondered how in ever-loving *hell* no one—including herself—had ever flat-out denied Priscilla and Asterin's relation to one another.

Asterin's mother stroked Luna's hair and sighed. "I still don't understand why you won't tell me what this big proclamation is all about."

Luna laughed, a laugh so perfectly *Asterin* that she almost confounded herself. "Trust me, if you knew, you would probably do everything within your power to stop me from walking onto that stage."

"How is that supposed to bring me comfort?" Elyssa demanded with a wry smile.

"It wasn't meant to."

A diminutive man with intensely snowy hair combed neatly away from his face descended the stairwell in a sharp suit and dark wool coat. The corners of his eyes crinkled with pleasure when he spotted Luna.

"Ah, it's Director Leval," said Asterin's mother quietly—much to Luna's relief. She'd never seen the man in her whole life. "I was worried he might lose his job after the whole chandelier debacle, but it turns out the city's adoration for him knows no bounds." She winked. "Or, more crucially, the sponsors' adoration."

"Your Majesty," greeted Director Leval with a nimble bow. "I take it that everything is running smoothly?"

"Flawlessly," Luna replied with a sweet smile. On the inside, she was grappling with a sudden, nauseating bout of nerves. *Stay calm*, she commanded herself. The consequence of the deception she was trying to pull off struck her in the gut. She had never even left the palace before embarking on the hunt for the demon just months before.

"I never got a chance to thank you, by the way," said Leval, oblivious to her turmoil. "For what you did."

What I did. Luna hid her frustration. Could he be any more vague? She only continued smiling, blinking twice for good measure.

"And for the hundreds of people you saved," Leval added.

Ah, much better. Luna bowed her head and imagined how Asterin would respond. The words came easily. "Absolutely no thanks is necessary, Director Leval. I value nothing higher than the well-being of my people and my kingdom."

Leval beamed, blindingly, and Luna knew it had been enough. In fact, he seemed so pleased to be simply conversing with her that she had the suspicion that she could have replied in gibberish and he would still be beaming. "You truly are the queen Axaria deserves."

You truly are the queen Axaria deserves.

Luna couldn't quite meet Leval's gaze. In that moment, it was hard to forget that she wasn't herself, or saying the words that she, Luna Evovich, would have thought to reply with. "You're too kind," she managed, and then tipped her chin toward the entrance of the hall. "Well, I'd better get ready."

"Of course, Your Majesty. An amplification charm has already been cast on the podium, so as long as you keep one hand in contact with it while speaking, you have nothing else to worry about." Leval shot her one last smile and gestured to the doors with a flourish. "The stage is all yours."

Asterin's mother nodded encouragingly at her. "Go on, dear. I'll be right behind you."

Luna took a deep breath and shook out her shoulders. Her hands were icy cold beneath the silk of her gloves. And disgustingly sweaty. She forced herself to put one foot in front of the other, marching toward the sea of people awaiting her out . . . *there.*

The guards on either side of the entryway saluted and pulled the doors open for her. The racket of no less than five thousand chattering citizens spilled into the air. Gradually, a hush swept over the hordes of people as they noticed Luna standing frozen in the doorway.

I am the Queen of Axaria, she told herself with all of the conviction she could muster.

But . . . there were *so many people staring at her.*

"Daughter?" whispered Asterin's mother behind her. "What's wrong?"

Panic leapt into Luna's throat. For so many years, she had been content to live out her life as the sweet, docile handmaiden of the Princess of Axaria. So many years, spent in Asterin's shadow, noticed by a scarce few. And the problem wasn't leaving that shadow.

It was facing what awaited her in the light.

Say, perhaps, five *thousand* spectators.

And, sure, she had managed to deceive Eoin, the most powerful entity in both realms, just fine—except, he had possessed something that she had very much desired. Somehow, her determination had drowned out her fear. Now, however, she had arrived before an overwhelming wall of doubt with no hope to break through.

The world spun.

She was going to faint.

Then, right before she lost herself in the sea of expectant faces, she found her anchor.

There stood Killian, directly in front of her about halfway down the crowd, staring her dead in the eye. By some miracle, that steady amber gaze stilled the pandemonium thrashing within her.

The anygné gave Luna a single nod.

It was enough to make her step out onto the stage and up to the podium.

Luna placed both palms flat on the smooth wood. The former Queen Regent took her place at Luna's right shoulder, about two paces away.

When she breathed in, it almost seemed like the entire crowd breathed with her.

"Beloved citizens of Axaris!" she declared. Her voice boomed clear and strong, loud enough to carry across the entire entertainment district and likely beyond thanks to the amplification charm.

A ripple passed over the crowd as the people lay their right hands across their chests to clasp their left shoulders in the Axarian salute. "Beloved Queen of Axaria!" they roared back, which Luna had *not* been expecting. It scared her nearly senseless, but as she gazed at them, a warm flame kindled to life within her chest.

Is this what being queen was supposed to feel like? To be adored? Treasured?

Luna straightened. "It is with my sincere gratitude that so many of you heeded the announcement of this proclamation on such short notice, and with great honor that I now stand here before you to make that proclamation."

She let her eyes travel across the enraptured masses. Waited for the tension to build.

"This world is the world we have always known," she confided in them. "But there is another."

Behind her, Asterin's mother drew in a sharp intake of breath. The people began to murmur amongst themselves.

Luna leaned into the podium, closer to the crowd, and lowered her voice. Like a magnetic force, the people leaned closer to listen, too. "There is another realm," she went on, "where beings from beyond your wildest imaginations are born and our Immortal ancestors—the gods and goddesses of magic—dwell."

She savored the silence, her absolute custody of their attention.

"You may wonder how I know such things. Well, you may remember the total eclipse that befell our world just days ago. During that time, I was visited by an Immortal and brought to this second realm. But not just any Immortal—King Eoin, the God of Shadow." She held up a hand when the air filled with exclamations of terror. "Before you make judgment, know that he brought no harm to me, nor did he bear any ill will of any kind. He merely made a proposal, which I will soon divulge. But first, beloved people of Axaria . . ."

She smiled.

"I must reveal to you the truth behind the forbidden tenth element."

CHAPTER FIFTY-NINE

S *he must reveal to us* what? Eoin exclaimed.

Quinlan wanted to stab himself. He could hear Eoin's thoughts like the god was talking right into his ear. Or shouting into his ear, as he was now.

Could you please keep your voice down? Quinlan thought back at him angrily. Was it possible to go deaf from a loud mind? He didn't even mind the god's endless, unexpectedly blithe stream of commentary; in fact, on occasion it made for some marvelous entertainment. For example, when that asshole of a guard got kneed in the windpipe.

Without missing a beat, Eoin had remarked, *That man may kneed a moment to catch his breath.*

Minutes ago, Quinlan had shadow jumped them onto the roof of the opera house, adjacent to the concert hall, just in time for the Asterin impostor to walk onstage. The roof had been Rose's suggestion. From there, she'd pointed out, they'd have a clear vantage point of the streets and alleys surrounding the Pavilion.

And they were *packed.*

With Impostor Asterin commanding all the attention, no one noticed the four of them watching the proclamation unfold from above, although Eadric took extra care to stay away from the roof's edge.

"We are all born with a fear of the dark and the things we cannot see,"

Impostor Asterin declared. "Too often we dread what we cannot comprehend and shun that which we do not understand. Much like the mysteries of what lies beyond the Mortal Realm and even, perhaps, the Immortal Realm, shadow magic will never be fully understood."

"That is literally you," Quinlan whispered with sick fascination to the Asterin crouched beside him. "They have your voice, too."

Impostor Asterin swept her hand across the Pavilion. "But like a sword, shadow magic is not inherently good or bad. It is simply *magic*, just like the other nine affinities gifted to us by our creators. And if anything, it is *more* magical than the other nine affinities put together—it has the ability to save those we love from the brink of death, to return memories forgotten, and to open doors to new universes we could never explore otherwise."

"They sound like they've had experience dealing with shadow magic," Rose observed.

Do you know who this could be? Quinlan wondered at Eoin, hoping he might somehow be able to sense Impostor Asterin's identity, but the god had gone silent. Worryingly silent.

"Queen Priscilla Montcroix spent a decade constructing an entire kingdom of lies around herself. Until our battle on Fairfest Eve mere months ago, I thought her to be my mother . . . when in reality, she was the mother of my closest friend—*sister*, really—Luna Evovich."

Asterin's fists trembled against the stone edge of the roof. "Who in hell is that?"

Rose bit her lip. "You don't think it could actually be . . ."

"No," Asterin snapped. "Absolutely not. She would never do such a thing. And she's still in Ibresis with King Jakob."

"How would you know that?" Rose said softly. "Did she write to you?"

Asterin went just as silent as Eoin.

"In fairness to Priscilla," Impostor Asterin continued, "she ruled the kingdom justly, but only to further her own malicious agenda. No one realized that she was wielding shadow magic until I exposed her on Fairfest Eve. You see, the tenth element itself is not evil by any nature. It only becomes so in the hands of wicked intent . . . but then, so does the power of any other element, albeit to a lesser degree."

What did Eoin think of all this? Quinlan gave the god another mental nudge, but still the god kept his silence.

"The only difference between shadow and the other elements is that no mortal is ever born with shadow magic running through their veins," Impostor Asterin insisted, "not because it is something nefarious, but because no mortal child would ever be able to endure power equivalent to an omnifinity. *My* omnifinance developed over many years, with new affinities manifesting gradually as I grew stronger."

Real Asterin stood up. Her face had gone pale. "Enough," she snarled.

The sudden movement caused a single face to swivel toward them. A petite girl with dark skin, dressed in a black cloak. The girl's eyes widened, which Quinlan thought to be due to the fact that there now seemed to be *two* Asterin Faelenharts, but then the real Asterin spotted her too and staggered back as if she had been stabbed.

"Lady Killian," she gasped.

Eadric whipped around. "Killian? From Orielle?"

"Who is Killian?" Quinlan asked.

"Hireling sent to hunt us down in Orielle. And an anygné. It was her along with Kane that killed Casper and Gino—"

"*Hold on*," Rose spat. "Did you just say *Kane?*"

Eadric looked like a deer caught in a trap.

Impostor Asterin's words filled the silence. "In conclusion, shadow magic has the potential to better our lives in incomprehensible ways . . . so long as it is in the right hands."

"Why didn't you say anything?" Rose grabbed Eadric by his coat lapels and dragged him close, her teeth bared. "*Answer me.*"

"It's not his fault," said Asterin quietly. "I should have told you, but I could never figure out the right time to do it."

"I could have," said Eadric, his guilt clear in his voice. "I *should* have. I'm sorry, Rose. I—"

Rose shoved him away. "Unbelievable. And to think that I thought you and I—"

Asterin glanced down at the crowds and cursed violently. "She's gone. Killian's gone."

"Don't be silly, I'm right here," a sultry voice purred at their backs. "Miss me?"

Without even turning around, Asterin blitzed her with a hellstorm of ice daggers. Killian backflipped into the air to avoid the worst of the onslaught and shifted to her demon form midfall. The tips of the daggers she couldn't evade pierced the surface of her skin, but were prevented from lodging deeper by the tiny barbs covering her entire body.

With a hollow smirk, she sauntered over to them. Delicately, she picked out the blades one by one and smashed them into the roof. Her high-heeled boots crunched over their shattered ruins.

Oh my, said Eoin, finally.

Despite her smirk, Killian's voice bore no trace of humor. "I'm calling in my favor, Queen Asterin."

Asterin blanched. "What?"

"A favor for a favor," said the anygné. She pointed at the ground. "This is all I ask for: you and all of your friends sit down, now, and watch Her Majesty's speech in silence until I say otherwise. None of you will move a single muscle—including the magical kind."

"That's two favors," Eadric gritted out.

Killian held up her fingers and ticked them off. "Opened a portal to another realm. Arranged an audience for you with King Eoin." She gave Eadric a pat on the head. "You're correct, Captain, that *is* indeed two favors."

No one moved.

Killian clicked her tongue at Asterin. "Well? Show me your *honor*, sweetheart, and sit."

Quinlan watched Asterin carefully. If she delivered the first strike, he would follow. They all would.

Asterin's shoulders trembled. "Why? Why here?" Then, mockingly, she added, "What's in it for you?"

Killian only grinned. "I didn't ask you back then. You don't get to ask me now. Here, I'll make it easier for you." The anygné gracefully seated herself and patted the space beside her. "Come, let's watch Her Majesty's show together."

"Don't give them that title," Asterin snapped, but she obeyed all the same, sinking cross-legged to the roof. The rest of them followed suit.

Killian raised one eyebrow in surprise. "Why not? It's true in a way you wouldn't know, little wolf, whether you like it or not." She tipped her chin toward the stage. "Now hush."

Impostor Asterin threw her arms to the sky and sang, "All King Eoin desires is your understanding! To no longer be feared or shunned, but merely accepted by a people he could never truly belong to. And . . . to allow shadow magic to thrive and flourish in the Mortal Realm."

To Quinlan's surprise, Eoin stirred in his mind. *Time after time I underestimate her*, the god mused in his ear, velvet soft. *And time and time again she proves me the fool.*

"What about the violent shadow entity that wrecked the concert hall and nearly killed hundreds of people?" yelled a woman standing a few feet away from the stage. Multiple shouts of assent and shaking fists followed. The guards lining the stage shifted forward, affinity stones at the ready, but Impostor Asterin raised her hand to hold them back.

"As I mentioned, shadow magic is not inherently good or bad. But every kingdom does have its monsters, and evil doings must always suffer punishment. Which is to say that, of course, just as with any other magic, regulations and laws will be put in place to prevent its misuse and protect the kingdom."

When it appeared that no one really seemed convinced, Impostor Asterin sighed and turned around to beckon Elyssa forward.

After a brief hesitation, Asterin's mother complied.

"Here," Impostor Asterin announced. "Take, for instance, my dear mother." Elyssa tilted her lips in an incredibly unconvincing smile. "She made a deal with King Eoin before I was even born."

Gasps of outrage swelled across the Pavilion.

Eadric reached for his affinity stone, but Killian flicked her wrist and a glowing blue blade darted into the air to press itself beneath Asterin's chin. "Don't even think about it," murmured the anygné. "I've been asked not to kill your queen, but don't test my patience. A deal is a deal."

Below, Elyssa shoved past Impostor Asterin and slammed her fist against the podium, the fury blazing across her features a perfect mirror to the real Asterin's current expression. "*Lies*," she snarled.

Impostor Asterin reeled back, her face crumpling. "Mother?"

But Elyssa didn't so much as waver at her plaintive plea. "Mother," she repeated with a snort. "I am not your mother. And I do not know who you are, but *you are not my daughter.*"

To Elyssa, Impostor Asterin, and the five people squatting on the roof high above, the declaration meant: *You are not my* true *daughter.*

Perhaps those were the exact words Elyssa should have said, though—because, to the thousands of unwitting citizens, it sounded like a denouncement.

"Also," Elyssa added, "his name is Director *Levain*, not Leval." And then, with a savage roar, the Queen Regent threw herself at Impostor Asterin and began strangling her to death.

Chaos erupted from every corner of the Pavilion. The people bellowed at the stage, cheering, cursing, calling for blood. Brawls quickly broke out among the crowd. Guards from inside the concert hall and all of the theaters bordering the Pavilion swarmed out into the open. Except, the Pavilion was so packed that their ranks dissolved and, alone, they were quickly engulfed by the frenzied hordes.

Onstage, Impostor Asterin struggled against Elyssa's ferocious choke hold, the fight slowly draining out of her body.

Real Asterin watched on with smug satisfaction on her lips.

Quinlan snuck a glance at Killian, expecting distress but finding nothing but lazy amusement. His blood ran cold. What game was she playing at?

Impostor Asterin's eyes rolled into the back of her head. Just as victory seemed irrefutable, a blond blur barreled through the concert-hall doors, right out onto the stage behind the grappling pair, a sword raised high above his head.

Quinlan squinted. Recognition jolted through him.

Orion.

The Guardian of Axaria let out a wolf's snarl . . . right before he cleaved his sword through Elyssa's chest.

CHAPTER SIXTY

"*NOOO!*" Asterin screamed from the rooftop. Her desolation shattered the skies, yet her cry was lost to the utter anarchy on the ground as fear spread rampant across the Pavilion like plague. Confusion rose thick in the air. Citizens turned to savages, fighting and clawing at those in front of them to get a better glimpse of the stage or those behind them to flee.

Impostor Asterin heard her, though. She looked up toward the roof in stunned shock, her shoulders heaving and splatters of crimson staining her cheek and the collar of her dress.

Though Orion hadn't seen Asterin's mother since a decade prior when they were still children, it took him less than a single glance at Elyssa's face to realize what he had done. He clapped his hand to his mouth in utter horror and fell to his knees at her side. His lips began moving furiously in an attempt to heal her.

Elyssa lay on her back, convulsing on the ground, suffocating on her own blood, one limp hand clutching the sword impaled through her body. Rivulets of crimson dribbled down her jaw. Harrowed emerald eyes searched the sky, desperately. *Hopelessly.* But as if an Immortal was answering a final prayer, her gaze somehow lifted to the roof and found Asterin—the real Asterin—for a fleeting, heartbreaking second of relief . . .

"Please," Asterin whispered. "*No.*"

And then she was gone.

Asterin clawed her nails down her face and let out a howl of rage. How had it happened so quickly? Magic was supposed to solve everything, even mortal wounds. *Especially* mortal wounds.

No. She shoved herself to her feet. She could still heal her mother. There was still time, there *had to be.*

Asterin hurled herself off the roof.

Multiple pairs of hands shackled onto her from behind, latching onto her wrists and ankles and waist and yanking her back before she could fall.

Rose gripped Asterin hard, devastation shining wet in her golden eyes. "It's too late, Asterin. I'm so sorry."

"*No*," Asterin sobbed as Quinlan pulled her into his arms. She buried her face into his chest. "*No, no, no, no*—"

Her head snapped up when Killian whistled, her expression grim. A signal to Impostor Asterin.

Onstage, shadows raced toward her outstretched arms, swirling around her body in a vortex as she began to shift. Bladed feathers shredded through her gown. Feathers of iridescent green and blue rippled down her arms, burgeoning into monstrously beautiful wings. From her brow flourished a helm—no, a *crown*, hewn from feathers and steel and blood.

Screams of terror and panic penetrated the air as the crowds struggled to flee the plaza, trampling over one another in the attempt to get as far away as possible from the stage and the demon upon it. It seemed like the screaming would never cease, each cry louder than the next.

When Orion saw the demon, a darkness passed over his face. Slowly, he withdrew the sword from Elyssa's corpse and eased to his feet. Asterin could see his hands shaking all the way from the roof as he crept behind its back, sword poised to kill—

The demon launched itself into the air and soared toward the roof. Killian was already on her feet, waiting. Asterin lunged for her, but there was Quinlan again, jerking her back, with Rose and Eadric further barring the space between them.

"Let go of me," Asterin screamed, her voice breaking as she thrashed against Quinlan's iron hold.

The demon didn't land long enough for Asterin to free herself. It did, however, glance back for the briefest moment, giving Asterin a perfect view of its features.

And it was wearing a new face.

The face that haunted her every dream. Her every nightmare. The face that belonged to the person she hadn't been able to save.

Her heart lurched to a standstill.

Her blood roared in her ears.

The world went very, very dark.

"*Luna?*" Asterin whispered.

Her old friend averted her eyes. "I'm sorry, Asterin. I really am."

With that, Luna opened her wings and shifted fully. A wicked beak sliced forth from between her eyes. Turquoise irises blinked ruby. Talons ripped through her silk slippers, extending past her ankles in hard knots of gold.

As Luna vaulted into the sky, Killian took a running leap into open air and latched onto those talons.

"Stop it!" Asterin shouted hoarsely. She summoned a handful of wet snow and flung it into Quinlan's face, causing him to recoil from her. It lacked elegance, perhaps, but it distracted him enough for his grip on her to loosen. She wrested herself free and threw her arms toward the heavens. "*Stop running away from me!*"

A violent shriek of wind knocked Luna sideways, followed by another that ripped fistfuls of feathers from her wings and sent both her and Killian tumbling. Before either of them had time to react, however, Asterin commanded a wave of water to slam into Luna from behind, drenching her from the tips of her wings down. The sharp *crunch* of frost crackled through the air, and in less than a heartbeat, Asterin had encased Luna's entire body in a husk of ice.

Luna careened through the sky. With her wings immobilized, Killian had no choice but to try and veer them back toward the roof.

They crashed down rather than landed. Killian grunted in pain as she twisted sideways, using her own body to soften Luna's landing.

Asterin stormed over to Luna, grabbed her by ice-stiff shoulders, and hauled her upright. "What have you done to yourself?" she demanded.

"Nothing I didn't desire," Luna replied simply.

"Desire?" Asterin growled. Luna winced as the ice crawled farther up along her neck. "This is what you *desired*? To dethrone me? To turn into a monster?"

"I had a choice between *this* or execution," Luna snapped back, "because my mother traded my life to a god before I was even *born*. What kind of choice is that?" She shook her head with a snort of derision. "Though knowing you, I'm sure you'd rather have had me accept death."

Asterin wanted to scream through her gritted teeth. "When will you realize that I never wished harm upon you at all? That I would have thrown myself in front of that damned arrow for you, or any other threat to your life? I would die an infinite number of times to save you, Luna. Even now."

The resentment in Luna's expression wavered for the briefest moment. "Even now?"

Asterin's throat tightened. It *hurt* how much she missed her friend. "Without question," she whispered. "Without hesitation."

Luna stared into her face, unnervingly silent.

No one dared move.

Finally, Luna's lips curled slightly. Except her smile didn't reach her eyes, not even close. "But see, that's the whole problem with you, Your Majesty. You would do that for almost anyone—maybe even, under the right circumstances, a complete stranger. That's just the kind of person you are. Selflessly brave . . ." Luna tilted her head back to look down her nose at Asterin. "And disgustingly indecisive."

Stunned, Asterin couldn't even summon a response.

But Luna wasn't done. "You're always the hero whenever the stakes are lowest, Asterin," she hissed. "Once you've made a choice, you know that there's no going back. Yet all you can find in yourself to do is regret." Revulsion blazed across her expression. "Regret is for the *weak*."

"Fine," Asterin said quietly. "Then holding lifelong grudges is for the weak, too. Only the strong know how to forgive."

Luna's smile returned, much wider now. "Oh, but I've forgiven you, Asterin. In fact, I should be *thanking* you . . . for teaching me the value of making a choice and rising from the aftermath, stronger than ever. So do yourself a favor, sweetheart. Turn your back. Leave me alone to become who I want to be, not who *you* want me to be, and I'll spare all of your lives."

With a deafening *crack*, the ice surrounding Luna splintered. Asterin threw her arms in front of her face as dozens of bladed feathers exploded forth in a shower of fractured ice.

"*Asterin!*" Quinlan yelled out as Luna shot straight up into the sky on newly liberated wings. He flung his arms out. Scorching heat bloomed around Asterin, melting the ice and even a few of the blades.

But something was horribly wrong.

Mouth agape, she lowered her hands from her face and stared upward. The flames . . .

The flames burned *black*.

Asterin cried out as the circle of black flames only surged higher. They licked at her, scorching her hair and shoulders. And they were closing in, *fast*.

"Put them out!" she heard Rose shout beyond the dull roar of the fire.

"I—I'm trying!" Quinlan yelled back, the panic clear in his voice.

Asterin called upon a deluge of water, but it passed *through* the flames. She sucked the oxygen out of the air, but the fire burned on. Ice did nothing to smother the inconceivable inferno, and wind only fanned it.

Nine elements at her beck and call, and she might as well have had none.

"It's spreading!" Eadric thundered. "Asterin, you have to get out of there!"

As if she hadn't thought of that herself.

The night sky overhead writhed and rippled from the heat. Every breath seared her lungs, and her head felt woozy from the fumes. She wobbled forward and collapsed onto her knees.

The roof quivered as a tremor rumbled through the building.

The bellow of arguing voices. *Need to get out of here. Need to stay.* They blurred together. Soon Asterin didn't hear anything at all.

Her eyelids fluttered shut.

So this was to be her funeral pyre.

Then, from high above, there came a *whoosh* of blessedly cool air. Asterin just barely managed to crack one eye open as great wings cut through the infernal flames.

A dark angel spiraled toward Asterin and snatched her up in talons of gold. Those wings shielded her from the heat as they burst through Quinlan's shadow fire and soared into the sky.

Over the city they glided, the districts strangely absent of their usual twinkling lights. Hazy blotches swarmed the buildings. Asterin blinked sluggishly and tried to clear her distorted vision. It didn't work. After a few more minutes of squinting, she had the sickening realization that her vision wasn't distorted at all.

But she still couldn't comprehend the scene unfolding below . . . because the blotches were flames, devouring her city.

And . . .

And Axaris was *burning*.

EPILOGUE

"Your Majesty."

Silence.

"Your Majesty. *Queen Asterin.* Can you hear me? Your Majesty?"

The incessant calls dragged her from the cradling arms of slumber. She floated to the surface and let herself bask in a moment of serenity before opening her eyes to . . .

More darkness.

She shot upright, her heart hammering in her throat, and immediately, featherlight hands brushed down her arms and rubbed soothing circles into her back.

"Easy, easy," murmured a familiar voice. "It's all right, Your Majesty, it's just me, Laurel. Hayley is here, too. And all of the others, but in separate cells."

"Laurel?" Asterin breathed. Everything came rushing back—her mother's death, Luna's betrayal, Axaris in shadow flames. "What's going on? Where are we?"

"In the dungeon beneath the palace," Hayley answered from Asterin's right.

"So it was true," Asterin whispered. "Nicole's letter. My mother arrested all of you."

"Ha!" exclaimed Jack's voice from somewhere to the left. "See? Nicole *did* get my letter!"

"Is that why you came back to Axaris?" echoed a new voice from afar. Asterin's mouth fell open. "*Silas? Is that you?*"

"Yes, Your Majesty."

The rush of relief made her head spin. "Nicole said you'd been executed!"

"We really thought so, too," another voice piped up—Alicia. "Until the Queen Regent arrested all of us and we discovered that she was keeping poor Old Silas crammed into a cell down here all along."

A tumult of emotions swirled through Asterin. Grief, of course, but also confusion. Anger. Before she could ask any questions about her mother, however, Laurel spoke up.

"Could Your Majesty provide us some light? Her Grace removed our affinity stones when she arrested us, so we've been stuck in the dark for a while."

Asterin summoned several dim orbs of light and sent them puttering off with a wave of her hand, distributing them to the other cells. Very gradually, she increased the brightness of the orbs, until a soft bluish glow immersed the entire dungeon.

As her surroundings came into focus, Asterin drifted to the bars of her cell to see the rest of her Elites. They looked haggard, but otherwise unharmed, much to her everlasting relief. With a start, Asterin realized that she was locked in the very cell her mother had occupied for a decade.

An entire decade, Asterin thought to herself with a shiver. *Alone, in the darkness.* While the dungeon was enchanted to provide all the necessities needed to keep its inhabitants alive for as long as possible . . . how had her mother emerged unscarred?

She couldn't have, she realized. *Scars don't have to be visible to leave their mark.*

Laurel came to her side tentatively after Asterin had spent a few minutes frozen and wordless by the cell bars. "Your Majesty?"

Asterin shook herself. "How long has it been?" she asked. "Where is everyone else?" Her eyes widened and she whirled on the Elite. "Orion. Where is he? What happened to him?"

"It's been three nights since the fire, Your Majesty," answered Laurel. "Although Orion faced no charges since his true intention was ultimately ruled to be in your defense, we believe he has sequestered himself in his father's home."

"So he's safe," Asterin mumbled.

Laurel nodded and went on. "With you incarcerated, Eadric appointed himself as Officiating General of Axaria. The Queen of Eradore is staying at the palace for a short while to aid him in handling royal matters. Prince Quinlan is missing."

"Ah." Asterin leaned one shoulder heavily against the bars. "I see."

"I imagine that Your Majesty might like to know what happened," the Elite murmured. "After . . . Orion . . . after he . . . your mother . . ."

Asterin's chest clenched, but she didn't fault him. Her mother was gone, and there was no way to bring her back to life. "He couldn't have known. It's like you said. He was just trying to defend me."

Laurel dipped her chin. "Well, afterward, according to Captain—er, General Covington, the winged demon returned to the roof and carried everyone to safety. She rescued you from the flames and brought you to the palace. Then she disappeared, and no one has heard from her or the hireling she was with ever since."

Asterin stared at the Elite in shock. *The winged demon.* "Luna . . . it was Luna. I thought . . ." She'd thought that her imagination had fabricated that part entirely—that it had simply been a fume-ridden hallucination, but she couldn't bring herself to say it aloud. "Luna came back to save me?" she whispered, her brow drawn. "Why?"

"Atonement?" Hayley guessed. "For your mother's death."

I'm sorry, Asterin. I really am.

Asterin rubbed her face. She had so many questions about her friend— her enemy, now?—but she motioned for Laurel to continue.

"The fire raged for hours before the guards realized it could only be doused by light affinities," said the Elite. "Even so, nothing but the sunrise itself proved terribly effective, and by then the blaze had incinerated half of the city."

The breath rushed out of Asterin's lungs. "*Half of the city?*"

"It was mostly the entertainment district," Hayley informed her. "Some of the manufacturing district, the fringes of the trade district, and a good deal of homes in the northern residential sector. General Covington ordered that the flames be pushed toward the mountain, which caused one of the palace wings to burn, but luckily dawn arrived just in time."

Asterin didn't care so much about the buildings. Magic could rebuild most structures. But so many people had flocked to the Pavilion for Luna's proclamation. Had they all managed to make it to safety in time? "What is the death toll?" she forced herself to ask, hoping that perhaps, by some miracle—

Hayley grimaced. "As of the last time General Covington came around to check on you, around eight hundred casualties, over two hundred deaths, and dozens of more citizens still unaccounted for."

The number punched Asterin in the gut. The tears welled up so fast that she almost forgot how to breathe. Head whirling, she had to steady herself against the wall. "A-almighty Immortals." She slid to the ground and put her head between her knees.

"The kingdom is extremely shaken," said Laurel, grimly. "Even though a few witnesses saw you on the roof—the real you, alongside the demon who stole your identity—and stepped forward to advocate on your behalf, General Covington thought it best to keep you here, with us and out of sight, until things calm down. For both the city's sake . . . and for yours."

Hayley scoffed. "Don't do Her Majesty the disservice of softening the truth, Laurel."

Asterin raised her face, brow furrowed. "What do you mean?"

Laurel fell silent, so Jack answered instead. "Luna did a very good job of impersonating you, Your Majesty. All of the people who are convinced it was you onstage—"

"Which happens to be nearly everyone," added Hayley.

"—also believe that you turned into a shadow demon, flew away, and set Axaris on fire. Word spreads fast, and now most of the kingdom is hostile to the idea of you walking free, let alone ruling Axaria."

At Asterin's expression, Laurel scrambled to reassure her. "Of course, you're still the Queen of Axaria, whether they like it or not."

"But General Covington worries that they may revolt if you return to the throne at this time," finished Silas, "regardless of who is to blame for the damage done and the lives lost. As of now, his hands are tied."

"How long until Eadric comes to release us, then?" Asterin said. "As long as it takes for the people to forget about this disaster? Which, incidentally, might be *never?*"

Somewhere, high above, there came an eerie *creak* followed by the clang of metal. Then, two pairs of feet descended down the stone stairwell—heavy bootsteps belonging to the first, and a hushed tread as soft as snowfall to the second.

"General Covington himself might not be able to release us," Laurel whispered. "But *they* can."

Asterin's pulse raced as two figures came into view. The first figure turned out to be a very fidgety and nervous Carlsby, dressed in his full black uniform of mourning. The other figure wore a brown hide cloak dappled with tawny gold speckles. Slender wrists bearing circlets of shimmering gold peeked out from underneath the cloak's heavy pleats.

Carlsby bowed deeply and whispered, "Hello, Your Majesty."

"There's no need to whisper, Carlsby, we're the only ones here," said Asterin with a half-hearted smile. "It's good to see you, though. How have you been?"

"Awful," the young soldier admitted. "But very glad to be of assistance. I couldn't stand myself otherwise, what with helping to arrest the Elites and all." He glanced toward the mysterious stranger beside him and bowed again. To them, he said, "She's all yours, Your Majesty."

Hands raised to lift away the hood concealing the stranger's face. "At last we meet again, Queen Asterin." Her voice resonated through the dungeon, a rich, husky alto. Sleek black braids parted leftward fell from one shoulder all the way to her waist. In the light of the orbs, her sage green eyes glowed like twin fireflies.

Surprise rippled through Asterin. "Queen Valeria?"

The ruler of Volterra approached her. "You never responded to my multiple urgent letters." She arched one perfect eyebrow. "And then your Guardian boy flew through our gateway with another mortal and a demon . . . the one that I hear sabotaged your crown and obliterated your reputation."

Asterin wasn't sure how to respond, nor did she know how to interpret Valeria's words. Were they meant to provoke her? She didn't know the Voltero queen particularly well, only ever interacting with her and her much younger brother, Prince Viyo, at occasional royal gatherings. They had never shared a friendship like Asterin did with Princess Rowena of Galanz, or Valeria did with Prince Sol of Morova, but they did share a mutual respect for one another—or, at least, Asterin hoped so, since one could never truly know with royals.

Valeria pulled out a familiar key from the folds of her cloak. It was identical to the one that Lord Conrye had given Asterin to free her mother. The other queen caught her staring. "Lady Siore paid me a visit," she explained. Lady Siore—the Goddess of Earth and Protector of the House of the Stag. *So Conrye isn't the only god meddling with mortals*, Asterin thought to herself. "She brought me this key, and a message by way of request—to grant you and your Elites asylum in my kingdom."

"Grant us asylum?" Asterin repeated in bewilderment.

"Yes." Valeria inserted the key into the lock and gave it a twist. No bolt clicked, but the door swung open on its own. The Voltero shot her an impish smile. "But only should you manage to escape this inescapable dungeon deep below your palace and flee to Volterra."

As Asterin walked right out of her cell with Laurel and Hayley at her heels, she couldn't help but smile at the sly glint in the other queen's eyes. Yet she couldn't help but wonder, too. "Valeria . . . why did you come all this way yourself? Why not send an ambassador here on your behalf?"

Valeria moved onto the other cells, releasing the remaining Elites one by one. "Queen Valeria is currently recovering in her royal chambers from a grisly illness," she replied firmly, pulling her hood up to shroud her features in darkness once more. She strode for the stairs. "And anyway, I wished to see exactly what we're up against with my own eyes."

"And what are we up against, exactly?" Asterin asked as the Elites fell into formation behind her.

The Queen of Volterra turned halfway up the third step, caressing the rugged stone banister as if it were carved from gold. "Oh, just the rise of the true wicked, a war to end all wars, and the eternal demise of this world as we know it." A grim smile rose to her lips. "Care to join? Otherwise, I suppose you could all just lock yourselves back into your cells if you'd like."

They all stared at her in stunned silence.

Finally, Asterin shrugged helplessly.

"To Volterra it is."

ACKNOWLEDGMENTS

I typed the final word of the first draft of this book just before midnight on my eighteenth birthday (after gorging myself on cake all day, of course). I remember sitting back and staring at the screen and thinking, *Huh. Looks like I just wrote another book, somehow.* Truth be told, though, writing and editing the sequel to *Shadow Frost* was a pretty daunting task—and I am so incredibly indebted to the people who supported me during the process. First I'd like to thank my editor, Marco Palmieri, for grounding me whenever my writing started torpedoing off into the unknown, and also my agent, Richard Curtis, for your constant reassurances and responsiveness. To my team at Blackstone, *thank you so much* for enduring me and my emails full of questions (looking at you, Megan, Mandy, Lauren, and Courtney). Josh, Josie, Jeff, and so many others, thank you for taking a chance on my debut and this trilogy. To have had the privilege of attending so many book events for *Shadow Frost* and meeting my readers has been an experience I'll never be able to thank you for enough. To Bryan and Jesse—you are my audiobook champions. And, of course, a humongous thank you to Kathryn G. English, who designed yet another jaw-dropping cover for the second book of this series.

Speaking of champions, I have to thank the authors who gave me the strength and confidence to take a big leap of faith in my writing career. Holly Black, Victoria Schwab, Nic Stone, Tochi Onyebuchi,

Stephanie Garber, Shelby Mahurin, Ryan La Sala, Rin Chupeco, and Angie Thomas . . . you are my queens. Thank you for all your wisdom, hugs, late-night counsel texts and phone calls, and cream puff dates. And of course, thank you to my big sisters, Natasha Ngan and Amélie Wen Zhao, for your much-appreciated encouragement and optimism. Also, thank you to Leigh Bardugo for the endless inspiration. I can't tell you how blessed I feel to be surrounded by such a loving and supportive author family.

I owe so much to all of my readers, but I want to say an extra-special thank you to those of you I've had the pleasure of connecting with personally, whether in person at signings or on social media. I keep every letter, DM and comment about *Shadow Frost* and/or how it has affected your writing journey very close to my heart, and it's been such a joy getting to know so many of you over the last year and a half. If you are a young aspiring author, know that you have my full support no matter what stage of the process you're at—publishing ain't easy (especially as a teenager), but apparently I've managed it twice now, so don't think for one second that you can't, too.

My everlasting gratitude to my crew: Emma, for always devouring whatever I write and baking the most delicious cookies for *me* to devour; Amy, for the *dank* daily memes; Jona, for always being no more than a Snapchat away and a queen in general; and Zhen, for all of your love and enthusiasm and energy and tea-spilling seshes over lunch. Also, huge shout-out to Madison for beta-reading/bingeing *God Storm* at the actual speed of sound. Your comments always make me cackle. Please never stop. And of course, Kevin, for basically everything. Love you.

And to Miron—friends may come and go, but I would be lost without you. Even though we go to different schools now, cities apart, you've always been my rock. Your ambition, hard work, and drive are endlessly inspiring, and once you've surpassed the stars and achieved the greatness you and I both know you're destined for, I hope I can be there for you just like you've been there for me (even if I don't quite understand what you're explaining to me most of the time. Sorry, lol. I swear I'm trying). You've helped push me toward becoming the person and author I wish to one day be, so this one's for you, bae.

And as usual, thank you to my super-talented dad for illustrating the stunning map of the Mortal Realm at the beginning of the book for this trilogy, and for always knowing how to bring a smile to my face when I need it most. And thank you to my mum for tolerating my BS and teen-age angst for nineteen years. All of my love to you both.

GUIDE TO GOD STORM

SPELLS

Avslorah aveau — to summon water

Avslorah fiere — to summon fire

Haelein — to heal

Helt Avsloradovion — (non-self) to all summon

Skjyolde — to shield

Náxos — to strike

Reyunir — to unify

Lumi — to flare

Ovrire — to open

Explosa — to erupt

Astyndos — to blast

Ovdekken — to expose

Volumnus — to radiate

Peneretrae — to penetrate

Holte — to cease

Zäär — to force shift

Iræs — to revert

THE COUNCIL OF IMMORTALS

Lady Siore (See-**or**-ay), Goddess of Earth

Lord Tidus (**Tie**-duhs), God of Water

Lady Fena (**Fee**-nuh), Goddess of Fire

Lord Conrye (**Con**-rye), God of Ice

Lady Reyva (**Ray**-vuh), Goddess of Wind

Lady Audra (**Aw**-druh), Goddess of Sky

Lady Ilma (**Ill**-muh), Goddess of Air

Lord Ulrik (**Ool**-rick), God of Light

Lord Pavon (**Pah**-von), God of Illusion

King Eoin (**Ay**-oh-in), God of Shadow

BLOODLINE

House of the Stag

House of the Serpent

House of the Fox

House of the Wolf

House of the Stallion

House of the Falcon

House of the Viper

House of the Lynx

House of the Peacock

None

THE ROYAL ELITE GUARD

Captain Eadric Covington (26)

Hayley Zalis (28)

Nicole Dwyer (26)

Laurel Kuru (25)

Alicia Lormont (15)

Silas Atherton (30)

Jack Lintz (26)